Patrick Colter, a young law clerk, looks to the past to solve a murder and find his role in life, while his wife, Shelley, rejects traditions keeping women in their place, and joins the movement for women's equality and the vote.

"We wait no longer – the third novel has arrived! Once again, Jan has given us historical events woven in with the lives of her engaging characters. It will certainly be enjoyed by all who read of the historical places and enduring people, who worked hard to make Montana Territory a better place in which to live."

—Margie Peterson,
Editor and Oral Historian

"Jan Elpel's passion for the land and its people is richly evident in her writing. The history of the era and the natural geography is artfully displayed throughout the story and lives of her characters. Her descriptions of the landscapes and nature invite the readers to see and feel it for themselves. Heirloom China rests on solid and enthusiastic foundations."

—Theresa Nichols Schuster,
author of *We Are the Warriors*

"In Heirloom China, Jan Elpel's third novel in a Montana trilogy, she writes with the same precision and graceful strokes that distinguish her drawings and paintings. Realistic characters build their lives in early Butte amid city shops, vivid landscapes, political discourses, and unsolved murder. From wedding gowns to meeting halls, historical details abound, providing insights into the times while expanding the story's charm."

—Anne Hepburn Ore
Historic mining town resident
and former bookseller

HEIRLOOM CHINA

JAN ELPEL

Silver Sage Studio & Press, LLC

Heirloom China

Publisher's Cataloging-in-Publication Data
Elpel, Jan 1937–

Heirloom China / By (Author), Jan Elpel

    ISBN: 978-1-892784-45-2 $16.00 Pbk. (alk. paper)
    1. Historical Fiction. 2. Montana Territory. 3. Women's
    Suffrage. 4. Butte Copper Mining. 5. Montana State-
    hood
    I. Elpel, Jan. II. Title.

Silver Sage Studio & Press, LLC

Published by
HOPS Press, LLC
12 Quartz Street
Pony, MT 59747-0697
www.hopspress.com

Acknowledgments

Heirloom China, the third novel in a trilogy, bridges the transition from the earliest gold diggings in Madison County, Montana Territory, to the silver and copper mining days in Butte in the late 1870s. The stories unraveled from pages of history painstakingly preserved in archives, newspapers, books and diaries. I am especially indebted to Ellen Crain, director of Butte-Silver Bow Archives in Butte, Montana, for the time she has generously contributed toward my historical research. And to Linda Griffith who secured my illustrations on the book covers with her sense of design and digital ingenuity.

My gratitude to the many editors and reviewers who have made me a better writer, and in the process, a more discerning person. My appreciation for my daughter, Jeanne Elpel, who has shared my journey into historical fiction; Margie Peterson, editor for meticulous care in proofreading; Rachel Phillips, historian and author whose knowledge of history far transcends mine; Anne Ore, for her perceptions that make me reach to attain a higher level; Theresa Schuster, author and editor, who also brings the past to life in her books; Judy Shafter and LK Willis for insightful reviews, as well as many others whose books, writing, and role models made this work possible.

Heirloom China, Berrigan's Ride and **Healers of Big Butte** became realities only because of the expertise, generosity, and time commitment of my publisher, Thomas J. Elpel, at HOPS Press, LLC, which features his many books, articles, videos, and blogs.

In all my novels I take responsibility for relating attitudes, cultures and events as I understand them from history, and as I lived them as a descendent of pioneer families. Thank you to my readers for all the support and encouragement which continues to inspire me. JE

1

DOUBLE WEDDING

A shadow crossed Antonio's face. Patrick grinned. He had called the ranch hand's bluff. The *TN* stockmen sat on their horses high above Deer Lodge Valley waiting for cattle to show up below. At mid-day the air was still; only last year's dried yucca pods chattered on the foothills. At last, Antonio let out a long pent-up breath.

"Maybe I will." His attention shifted to the Pintler's glistening, snow-capped peaks across miles of grassland. "Problem is, the woman is already hitched. Her husband went missing in the war. She's afraid he come back and find her."

Now Patrick understood Antonio's dilemma. Nothing new. Patrick was aware Danielle Hartman had offered this excuse to every suitor for the past ten years. A game she plays, a fictitious husband, or was it genuine fear?

"If he hasn't turned up in ten, no, fourteen years since he was last heard from, he doesn't deserve to have her back," Patrick growled. He wished he had access to the inner recesses of the foreman's mind, the man no one really knew whose pauses punctuated their conversation. Miss Hartman's tiresome excuses had hurt a lot of good men. Patrick did not want to see it happen to Antonio.

"You marry her and change her name," Patrick blurted, "then, by damn, if he's alive, he'll never find her."

"Maybe I will," Antonio said again after an interval, but without any more conviction than if he'd agreed to sweep out the bunkhouse.

"Are we going to sit here all day? Or can you find a pack of smokes to while away the time?" The dapple gray stallion's feet shuffled on the shale. Patrick shifted in the saddle to quiet the mount. "This horse is rarin' to go, same as me. When a man's getting married, it isn't easy to dally around." A silly grin swept his face as he accepted the usual cigarillo from Antonio. Patrick's smooth features glowed with the exuberance of mid-twenties youth and charm of a longtime eligible bachelor who had just claimed the woman of his dreams.

"You be one lucky man." Antonio offered a light.

"Lucky as hell. You ought to seriously consider doing the same." He risked sounding too familiar, taunting or pushing the wrangler more than he ought.

Antonio looked up, deep dark eyes questioning whether the jest was in fun, or if there might be a deeper meaning.

"The whole town has heard about your courtship of Miss Hartman."

A blush tinged Antonio's ears beneath his vaquero hat, betraying his embarrassment at being the butt of gossip, though his silence was not unusual.

"We could have a double wedding," Patrick urged, wincing that he might be talking out of place, babbling without consulting Shelley. After all he didn't know his betrothed so well that he could make assumptions, or grand-hand her wedding off to someone else and ruin her day.

"Seems my tongue runs on without my brain in charge. Fine thing for a man who wants to be a lawyer!" Patrick filed that warning away for future reference. "Well, time will tell." But soon impatience got the best of him.

"I wonder if Judge Kirschenbaum officiates in Butte. There's Fr. Remiquis de Rychers for the Catholics. Who is there for non-

Catholics? The Nortons aren't Catholic, and I'm not a real good one. Oops, excuse me. You might be."

"Whoa, man. You gittin' way ahead of me."

"I beg your pardon, Antonio. Being a twin, I'm accustomed to doing things together." Patrick needed to think about that one. *I can't even entertain the notion of my own wedding,* he mused. *I thought I had overcome those twin habits. Now where is this wild talk taking me—Shelley and me?*

Still they lingered on their horses, Patrick's lanky frame astride an imported stud he borrowed from his fraternal twin, Jackson. The Irish Connemara's proud bearing and gentle disposition had more than earned his keep and reputation over the past few years in Montana Territory. Not to mention that myths sprouted like faerie stories about his exploits—he had practically risen from the dead after a severe weed poisoning. He had outrun a Sioux warrior with a semi-conscious woman clinging to his back, and he had sired a filly that might beat him in looks.

Antonio straddled a dun mustang from the Tarynton ranch working string. The men had all day to wait for the herd to come their way. A meadowlark warbled its cheery six-note song from a nearby chokecherry bush. Deer Lodge Valley lay like a Persian carpet with bright spears of wet prairie grass and blue-greens of sagebrush interwoven with patches of pale gray snow. Hints of distinctive silver lupine leaves and larkspur's dark purple flowers drew the herdsmen's attention. Both plants were toxic to stock at certain times of year.

"Mac sent me to see the livestock don't drink bad water from mining tailings or graze poisonous weeds."

"You likely heard this stud went plumb loco on poisonous plants." Patrick stroked the Connemara's wide smooth withers. "He came close to being shot when he was half crazed."

"Mrs. Tarynton brought him back from havin' fits and throwin' himself. She has the gift." Antonio appraised the dapple gray's rounded hindquarters, stout neck and handsome head that bore scars from his seizures. The thick gray mane and tail set off the stud like a champion. "Mr. Huckins done well bringin' that horse from Ireland."

"And Jackson fared extremely well getting the stud from Mac as a wedding present!"

The cattle rounded a foothill and came into view toward the southeast. Well-bred Herefords with characteristic white faces and collars stood out among rangy Texas longhorns that Nelson Story had introduced to Montana ranchers. Mixed in the herd were a few old Jersey milk cows, stock bought from down-and-out homesteaders. Antonio headed his mustang off the ridge with Patrick following, and turned the herd to graze its way back. Afterward the riders found a clear stream sheltered by cottonwoods and dismounted to eat cold biscuits and ham that Julianna, the ranch cook, had prepared for them, along with large squares of applesauce cake.

Patrick rode with Antonio more frequently these days for the chance to examine the quality of the water that flowed from Butte mines toward the Clark Fork River. The water often showed a churlish red, orange and yellow signifying heavy metals that eventually settled into a green scum around the edges. He figured the water and sludge were probably as much or more toxic than the weeds. Bad water and bad relations with the miners were more than enough reasons for Mac Tarynton to quit the ranch his pioneer father had amassed on once prime land in the 1850s.

"I been thinkin' about what you said," Antonio ventured around a mouthful of applesauce cake.

Patrick wondered which part of what he said had made an impression. He had dared him, challenged him, almost bet he didn't have the nerve to propose to Miss Danielle Hartman. Her reputation as a recluse had whetted more than one man's appetite for the tall, quiet woman until it became clear she preferred her goats over their advances.

"I shouldn't have been so outspoken, my friend. If being in

love makes me shoot my mouth like a lad in knickers, I'll have a helluva time being married." But he couldn't erase the smile on his face as his eyes roved over puffy flat-bottomed clouds shaped like sailing ships, reminding him of fleets easing into Dorchester Bay seeking his hometown of Boston and its renowned harbor.

"I came back from Boston last year before I had much of an aim in life— before I met a woman who gave me purpose. I worked as a legal clerk for a law firm there and found I had a knack for it. My chances with Miss Charlotte Norton improved considerably once I had a job," he chuckled.

"You'll be settled afore I will," Antonio said. "Mac will be movin' the stock off the ranch. He is innerested in land between the Beaverhead and Big Hole rivers east of Hogsback Ridge."

Patrick waited. They still had all day, the rest of it anyway. Jackson had already told him that Antonio's courtship of Miss Hartman had coincided with his scouting for Mac's property, bringing him into proximity with the widely known but un-claimed war widow of Norwegian Creek, located near the de-funct mining town of Sterling. That kind of news spreads with a life of its own, especially among the women. If Antonio got mar-ried it would be one helluva celebration, him being close to forty, handsome as the devil, and a secret fantasy of darn near every single woman in the county, maybe some married ones, too.

"Maybe I will." Antonio continued the conversation as if it hadn't lapsed since early morning. "I'm thinking of gettin' my own place near the Jefferson River. Maybe further down towards the Headwaters."

Patrick knew then that Antonio was cutting loose of the ranch that had been his home and livelihood for decades. That he must have been churning over the notion of marriage when he got his own place, a place remarkably close to where Danielle Hartman lived with her sister's family on South Willow Creek.

"A man's got to make up his mind about things." Patrick knew he was talking about himself.

"This is the story I'll tell for the rest of my life. Now where is Patrick when I need him?" Shelley smoothed the yellowed tulle of her mother's wedding dress. "I have never been so scared." The cracked mirror in Butte's Masonic Lodge wash room failed to reply. Her mother and the guests were already seated in the hall.

"Neva, hurry, hurry. It's time to go."

Neva shimmied into her cotton drawers under the white satin dress that hid her limp. "I have a fairytale dress," she cooed, patting the billowing folds.

Nowhere was there a more dazzling smile than on her six-year-old face. Shelley, as Neva called her big sister Charlotte, grasped the child's hand and steered her out the door into the arms of their father. John Norton smiled in approval of both daughters, yet his face remained tight, nervous. Only the soft crinkle in his eyes registered with Shelley, likely reflecting back to his own marriage; Winifred wearing this dress, her features plain but unlined, his full of youthfulness and hope. Twenty-two years later, his rough hand escorted their daughter down the aisle in the slow halting steps of the bridal procession, enunci-ated by the squeaking tones of an ancient organ. The procession suited Neva's uneven gait as she dragged her paralyzed left leg behind her firm, strong leg.

Any irregularities of the flower girl's advance were lost upon the viewers. Their eyes followed the second couple in the pro-cession, Danielle Hartman on Mac Tarynton's arm. An elegantly embroidered lace veil trailed from her crown nearly to the floor. A slim foot thrust from beneath a plain gown gathered lightly at her waist. Mac, the beanpole rancher who had no children of his own, had proudly stood in as father for his wranglers and now for Danielle. Shelley had not met her before today—the wedding had been arranged by the grooms, Patrick and Antonio, on a slow day herding cows in Deer Lodge Valley. This was the story Shelley would tell.

Antonio, decked in new black pants and a western shirt tucked behind a silver buckle and belt, shied from the stares with an uncertain smile. Even without his hat his firm wide features attracted women, young and old. For Danielle, his thick black hair cut long on his neck and mustache trimmed short at the jaw had evidently been enough. Danielle's story was as unlikely as Shelley's— the woman had shed her long years of widowhood for a cowboy courtship and a double wedding.

How did this happen? Shelley wondered. She found herself sharing her day with a total stranger, a woman from the other side of the Continental Divide, solely because Antonio and Patrick were friends of the Taryntons. The organ music faded and the escorted brides halted side by side at a makeshift altar. Neva Norton turned to the nearest chair by her parents. Patrick Colter moved next to Shelley, tucking her clammy hand in his big warm palm. Antonio pivoted from the lineup of best men to Danielle's side, his new boots elevating him to a few inches shy of his bride's height. Mac Tarynton stepped aside with a grin as wide open as the country they lived in.

Judge Kirschenbaum intoned the service in words that might have been Gaelic or Chinese for all Shelley knew—the charges and responses lost in the stone walls of the Lodge. Her trembling frame threatened to crumble except for Patrick's steady presence at her side. Marry me? You want to marry me? she had asked when he proposed a few months ago. They would marry "when I get settled in my new job," he had said. He is marrying me, she breathed, as if disbelief had lurked beneath until she sneaked a glance at his strong, youthful profile. The judge announced "you may kiss the bride," as if the brides were singular. Afraid to disgrace her husband and her parents, as well as herself, Shelley suppressed an urge to fling herself into Patrick's arms, unsure what to feel. When Patrick's lips pressed hers a sidelong glimpse told her Danielle ducked Antonio's short peck, her cheeks flaming with embarrassment. Antonio held her at a distance like a porcelain vase.

Mac's laugh would have been heard down the street. He roared as the guests came to their feet, their applause drowning the Judge's benediction. Wranglers stampeded to congratulate Antonio—apparently the late-in-life catch of all time. Jackson Colter shouldered his way past Shelley's folks, nearly upsetting Neva who had stepped on her hem and lost her balance. He claimed Patrick for his own, a twin brother hug far more intimate, deeper, than Shelley had witnessed between men. Or that she had yet to experience with her new husband.

"I wish I'd been here when you got hitched," Patrick said, extricating himself from Jackson's serious backslapping. "I didn't know it would be this good."

"Gets better," Jackson said.

Judge Kirschenbaum motioned the organist to shake the rafters, sounding the exit. Antonio, beaming broadly, escorted Danielle Hartman Delgado up the aisle with Patrick and Shelley following, an order determined earlier by the flip of a buffalo head nickel. The overly enthusiastic crowd squeezed the wedding party with hoots and hollers.

"I'll make up for the kiss later," Patrick promised, a promise heard only by Shelley in the last thundering refrains of the processional while a nervous giggle threatened to surface. Patrick frowned as if wondering about this woman he had married. She turned away, exhaling a mixture of joy and pain, reining in an outburst with contrite thoughts, what will he think, what will everyone think?

In the crush outside, Jackson and the rowdy crew surrounded Patrick and Antonio, again separating the grooms from their brides. Mac edged in to confer with Patrick about gathering the wedding party for the reception at his ranch. Neva hobbled from one tall person to the next, searching until she found Shelley. In turn, Shelley scanned the crowd for Patrick, for her parents, for someone to take charge of Neva.

You are marrying both of us, Shelley had warned Patrick the day he proposed. She made sure he did not go into this strange arrangement blindly. No one could say he was sold a lame horse, so to speak, least of all Patrick who recognized Shelley and Neva's connection. He accepted the child. Yet Shelley's mood still plummeted.

Just this once couldn't someone take care of her? And where is Patrick? The brides and Neva remained stranded on the steps outside the Lodge, looking over the crowd for the men. Shelley's nerves rattled her composure. She justified her irritation with Neva, a rare occurrence prompted by this awkward event at her wedding.

"Neva, be a big girl, don't suck your thumb."

At last Danielle turned to Shelley, her veil now draped low over her shoulders like a shawl. "I hope we did not intrude on your wedding—that I—we did not spoil your special day." Her long slim fingertips kneaded the tulle, her gaze shy and withdrawn; both women clearly overcome by a sense of abandonment. A mountain breeze carried more than a hint of spirits from the cluster of cowboys below.

"Or intruding upon yours, Miss Hartman, or—Mrs. Delgado," Shelley replied between clenched teeth. The ensuing silence, their sense of estrangement, left a void Shelley imagined would tint their future relationship.

"We're not exactly sisters-in-law nor relatives. Since the men are friends I suppose we'll become acquainted with each other."

"I—I never expected to marry," Danielle confessed, her voice low and uncertain. "I find this all hard to believe."

"Do you like my dress?" Neva tugged Shelley's hand, pulling her closer to Danielle.

"You look like a princess," Danielle said.

"I am a princess," Neva smiled, showing a missing front tooth.

"I never expected to marry either," Shelley admitted, second-guessing what now felt like a lonely decision.

"I was shaking at the altar with Antonio. He is so kind and considerate, but I am still shaking."

"You looked more composed than I felt." Shelley wrapped her arms around Neva's shoulders, consoling herself rather than her little sister who remained entranced in a faerie tale. This was Shelley's first disclosure to anyone other than Patrick regarding her once-curtailed expectations. And her first chance to talk personally with the aloof and formerly distant Miss Danielle Hartman.

"I married once, a long time ago." The memory flittered across Danielle's face with a trace of sadness. "But it is time to look ahead, not to the past. Will you be living in Butte?"

"Yes. I could never take Neva far from Mother and Father. I will always be right here for you, won't I Neva?"

"Yes, you promised."

Traces of irony and resentment that formed an undercurrent of Shelley's words apparently went unnoticed by Danielle or Neva—they held the moment, each in their own way. For Shelley, the men's congregation in the street and their boisterous laughter set off a slow burn. The husbands were nowhere to be seen. The brides and Neva had little choice but to wait.

Neva twirled and fidgeted. Danielle fussed with her veil, cleared her throat, and murmured softly to herself. Passing strangers offered perfunctory congratulations to the brides. The Masonic Lodge had nearly emptied and someone blew out the long tapers.

At last, Antonio drove up in Mac's carriage bearing Mr. and Mrs. Norton. Shelley's parents scooped up Neva before she had a chance to cling to Shelley. Antonio stepped out to assist Danielle into the carriage beside him, and half the wedding party whirled away toward the Tarynton ranch for the reception. Following the carriage, a buggy driven by Duggan, Mac's diminutive Irish handyman, arrived with Patrick to pick up Shelley.

"I'm sorry, Shelley. Jackson and Nettie wouldn't let us go uncelebrated. They rented and decorated this horse and buggy for us. I had to drive off while they were still decorating it like a Maypole."

Garlands of pine boughs tied with ribbons circled the buggy, and sprigs of yellow bells and shooting stars decorated the horse's bridle and harness. Duggan sat proudly on a thick cushion in the driver's seat, his top hat and tails grand for the occasion. Duggan swung the buggy behind Jackson who rode his dapple gray Connemara stallion, also festooned with ribbons in its flowing mane and tail.

Patrick and Shelley's wedding parade attracted onlookers, yet Patrick had to coax his bride to sit by him in the plush, wraparound seat. Her new husband's six-foot frame seemed to loom over her, though she was nearly as tall. Shelley twisted her handkerchief in her lap until Patrick retrieved her hand, an effort not altogether readily accepted by his bride. Patrick loosened his cravat, searching her eyes for clues to this unusual chilliness. Shelley refrained from a nervous outburst, not the giggle she felt earlier, but the irritation. Both remained tense while Duggan drove the married couple across the mining town of Butte and up the hill to Mac and Carrie's mountain ranch west of town.

"About Danielle—"

"Let's talk about us from now on. This is about you and me, Shelley." Patrick's eyes misted, saying more than the words, and expressing feelings Shelley had been drawn to when they had walked the hills of Butte the past six months. His heavily muscled thigh pressed hers, his wide shoulders offered a shelter to take charge of her fears, her life. He kissed her hand.

Shelley sniffed and dabbed her eyes He had included that other woman at her wedding. He had left her alone with her. He thought he could kiss it all away now.

"Shelley, my love—"

"Did we have to—"

"The wedding snowballed beyond my expectations,"

"Where were you? We—I stood there with that woman—"

"You are understandably upset, but please know it will be just us from now on, Shelley."

"And Neva?"

"And Neva."

Patrick's firm reply left her drained, unable to mount a resistance. She had fallen in love with Patrick, though it seemed odd, Patrick marrying her and accepting Neva—Neva the crippled child that Shelley knew would dictate their lives in many ways, rather than the other way around. Neva faced a limited outlook in life, a fact Shelley assumed would also limit her life.

"You know I never expected to marry." Shelley's voice barely broke a whisper. Patrick gathered her in his arms, banishing his reserve, her caution, their sense of being strangers caught up in the wraparound seat. Happy-sad shudders shook her shoulders. He kissed her hair, smoothed the tears from her cheeks.

Shelley's heart leapt with every good intentioned gesture that finally overwhelmed her peevishness and grudges.

The wedding reception at the old *TN* ranch broke all records for a Montana Territorial celebration. Prior to Mac and Carrie's move from Butte to the upper Beaverhead Valley, the couple threw open their doors for a dusk to dawn party.

"Antonio, we're going formal today." Mac heartily welcomed his foreman and Danielle on the wide front porch.

"I dunno, man. The wedding be formal 'nuff for this cowpuncher."

Antonio walked through the front door of the ranch house for one of the few times in his many years of working for Mac Tarynton. He repeatedly reached for his worn hat to hide his discomfort, but the hat and his beat-up riding boots remained in the bunkhouse. Instead, he gripped Danielle's elbow, sensing she needed comforting as much as he did.

All these years Antonio and the crew occupied the bunkhouse behind the two-story frame ranch house that Mac built when he married Carrie. Mac's father, pioneer and founder of the *TN* ranch, constructed the original log cabin which became the bunkhouse that housed the crew and mess hall. Everyone had entered the ranch house through the kitchen door.

"Oh, what a beautiful home you have," Danielle breathed.

"We're happy to have you two here before we move. We will be leaving the mountain and settling down the other side of the Highlands." Mac's wince betrayed a world of hurt beneath the celebration today.

"Thank you for inviting us. I seldom ventured from my sister's farm. I enjoyed taking care of their goats." Her uneasy smile affirmed she would need to have her own place, and her goats.

Patrick and Shelley emerged from the dozens of guests milling about the yard, and followed Antonio and Danielle inside.

"Did I hear something about goats?" Patrick nudged Antonio. "You're making big plans for a farm as well as cattle ranch?"

"I figured hitchin' up with Danielle meant we'd have chickens and milkin' goats." He flashed a grin at Patrick who winked, having endured ribbing about having a ready-made family.

The spring wedding had been arranged on such short notice that Danielle and her sister, Genevieve, had little time to sew a bride's trousseau. Antonio's wife may have entered the union with few linens and towels, but he had purchased 200 head of cows in anticipation of marriage and setting up his own ranch.

The couples discussed their plans while circling among well-wishers. Carrie, the ranch cook Julianna, and Jackson's wife Nettie prepared a feast fit for appetites of men, yet garnered approving nods from the women. Dashes of paprika and splashes of fresh green watercress spiced deep-dish casseroles. Swirls of frosting smothered Julianna's thick cinnamon rolls. Nettie's crisp oatmeal lace cookies spread over heirloom platters. An enormous basket of white plum blossoms scented the room over and above the aroma of freshly baked bread.

Outdoors, wranglers turned beef ribs in a pit oven, the smell of savory roast luring guests to Carrie's landscaped side yard. Long tables were set for dinner under trees the Taryntons' had nurtured in the high, often harsh environment behind Big Butte, the knob that gave Butte its name. A small apple and plum orchard peaked its bloom for the occasion.

Antonio sensed the day's joys and sorrows were bittersweet. He felt his boss' pain in leaving the family ranch, this celebration doubling as a going away party. The Taryntons would start over and build up a new ranching operation on prime acreage fifty miles west of Butte. Antonio and Mac had discussed the myriad details of trailing 2,000 head of cow-calf pairs long miles over the Continental Divide. He had been a sounding board for Mac's tentative plans, as well as one who bore his boss' explosive temper about the mining that drove him off his father's land.

"Hell. I feel sorry for Mac. And for Carrie," Antonio said to Jackson. "He's a good man. He couldn't a done any better for me, nor for the wedding."

Mac broke in to gather everyone outside. Hatless, he stood on the porch, balancing awkwardly on his good leg, the other having incurred an injury when Mac rescued his horses stolen by the Sioux. He raised a toast, the breeze ruffling his curly, rusty-brown hair.

"This celebration today gives me the rare pleasure of welcoming all of you to the *TN* ranch. I count the presence of my crew, including Antonio, friends like Patrick, and all you neighbors and Butte folks as bestowing the highest honor a man can have. Thank you all for celebrating the newlyweds with Carrie and me.

"Antonio, you've been more than a wrangler to me. You've been a trusted foreman and more recently a bodyguard." Mac's voice choked. "How can a man express gratitude for that?" He glanced away to rein in a surge of emotion. The assassination of Kent Berrigan last year hung over his every decision. He could have been targeted as well. With an effort he continued.

"You've taken us all by surprise. We discover your noble origins as Don Antonio Delgado from a fine family in Nevada Territory at this fateful time of your marriage. Well, we couldn't have been more fortunate in having you on the ranch. You have my blessing and heartfelt gratitude for your unwavering service all these years. Carrie and I wish you and Mrs. Delgado all the blessings that come with marriage." He paused and handed his surprised foreman a livestock title.

"May this registered Shorthorn bull be worthy, and help you establish your ranching operation among the finest in the country. May he also represent a symbol of procreation for your future," he added with a grin as Pete, his wrangler, ran a dark red, two-year-old bull into the corral adjacent to the yard. The crowd turned at the whooping and hollering that was little different than that of a *TN* cattle drive, except that Mac and Antonio were afoot and filling their glasses.

The levity carried over to Mac's blessing of Patrick and Shelley's marriage, making light of Patrick's new affiliation with one of Butte's legal offices, established as a branch of the notable Bosworths' law firm in Boston.

"You've come a step up on us, son. It takes a good man to enter the law and justice profession. By God, I wish you well. Carrie and I extend our love to you and the new Mrs. Colter."

Only those closest to Mac knew he had once told Patrick "you're a better man than me," to take a stand on Butte's issues and hard cases. The assassination they associated with conflict between ranchers and miners over clean water still smoldered in Montana Territory. It had never been proven that the dispute was the motivation, however, the killer had not been found.

Antonio and Patrick knew that Mac Tarynton, spokesman for the ranchers, continued to be spooked by the unsolved case. Not one to let fear drive him off the ranch, he was forced off when creeks became toxic from mineral-laden runoff from the mines that threatened his livestock. The men exchanged handshakes, their grips long and heartfelt, anchoring the celebration in the depth of shared Western experience and understanding.

By the time Jackson toasted his twin brother, Patrick, and

his wife, Shelley, his speech reverted to the heavy County Galway brogue of the Colter twins' parents, and became lost in the rowdy gathering.

Shelley Norton Colter's reactions appeared tentative at best, her smile set and tense. Patrick tipped up her chin, a boyish earnestness in his hazel-brown eyes while a question flickered across his brow.

"Shelley, we both had time to think about this. You are more settled and wiser than I am, I think. I want you to want it as much as I do."

"Oh, I do. It's not that. It's just that I feel swept away."

Patrick laughed. "Yes, these wranglers have a herding instinct. I guess I'm one of them by nature."

Shelley's heart leapt with his good intentioned humor that finally overwhelmed her peevishness and grudges.

2
HAYWIRE

The unexpected luxury of honeymooning in a suite at Butte's finest, the Continental Hotel, lifted Shelley's mood. Patrick hosted his bride to novelties and companionship not found in her combined role as big sister and mother she'd had with Neva. Delightful days of the first week passed all too soon. Only when Patrick announced a short business trip did she again question his penchant for making plans without consulting her, and worse, leaving her alone.

"Patrick, please, surely you would not leave me so soon—after we were married. I am afraid, Patrick, I am sorry." She spun away toward the bed in the hotel's so-called suite.

Patrick stared in blank amazement at her radical take on what he considered business as usual, if that could be true halfway through their honeymoon. He had glimpsed Shelley's anxiety at the wedding. Yet he had courted few females in the ten years that he and Jackson had been prospecting. This was a new experience for him.

"I don't know what to do when you're upset." Patrick stumbled over the words. This was not like the Shelley he knew and loved. "What is happening to us?" He held back from the temptation to grasp her elbows, turn her to face him and hold her in his arms. But he had a feeling this was about more than his new position as a legal assistant in Lucas Bosworth's firm, and the uncertainties of law in the lawless Territories.

17

"How–how are we going to get along?" he floundered. "This trip seemed like a modest request, only for three days. I promised your father I would take good care of you—and Neva also. I have to work to provide for us. We will soon have our own place, Shelley. I want you to be like you were, free and happy. I think you are stronger than I am. I do not understand your fear."

Patrick sank onto the end of the bed as if clinging to the four-poster. Shelley leaned against the headboard and gathered pillows in her lap, creating a defensive barrier.

The suite in Butte's recently renovated hotel rose three floors from Park Street into the thin mile-high atmosphere of the Rocky Mountains. Its pioneer furniture dressed up in Old Country decor had delighted the bride and groom a week ago. An alcove housed a miniature bar. A small sitting room with horse-hair stuffed chairs completed the "suite."

The Boston law firm of Bosworth & Son had reserved the suite for two weeks for the newlyweds. Patrick had accepted with gratitude. He could not have taken his new wife to his room in the Tavern with its water-spotted ceiling and drunken miners carousing below. Nor to Shelley's home where she shared a bed with little Neva. Or to the Colter brothers' cabin now occupied by Jackson, his wife and infant son.

For lack of a means to solve their first falling out, the couple sat in stony silence amid reminders of the wedding. Patrick's clothes were heaped over a chair next to a box containing a negligee, an unused gift Shelley had dubiously accepted from her acquaintance, Miss Irmgarde Meyer. The clothing stated, in a sense, the first seven days of matrimony ended here like this.

Patrick slipped his watch from the wool vest beneath his dress coat, his eyes holding the desperate gaze of his wife. "I have made arrangements for you to stay with Jackson and Nettie and the baby while I am away. Neva may also stay with them if she wishes. They would like to have you, Shelley, before they move to Mac Tarynton's ranch next week."

Shelley lunged forward into his arms. Her night warmth and flowing blonde hair enveloped his neatly pressed clothing, her head buried on his chest.

"I'm sorry, Shelley. Truly, I am."

"I wonder that you have not considered me."

"Shelley, we are married. That means something to me."

She grasped his lapels and shook him. "Then do not go."

Patrick loosened her fingers and set her back from him. "Is this about my investigation into the murder? It occurred awhile ago—it is a cold case now."

A cry, rendered more like a howl, escaped Shelley's throat.

"You are afraid for me."

Her cheeks flushed red over a pallor he had not seen on her before. *She is afraid, terrified and terribly angry.*

"Shelley, my love, I have not seen you like this before. Must we have this scene?"

"This 'scene' you deplore is the only way I can get you to listen to me."

The Kent Berrigan assassination loomed over them, between them, swamping them in unknowns neither could identify. Patrick sidestepped the issue—at his own peril—Shelley would not let this go.

"I am sorry but I need this job. Surely you understand."

One look told him she was not reassured. "Get dressed. You will feel better when you are at work."

"I will stay with my parents, not with your twin and his family." She spit out "twin" as if to hurt him.

Patrick paused as if struck. He momentarily sensed she was leaving him. He did not like the way this was going.

"Certainly. I understand how you see us as twins getting in the way of my being with you. But now I have to go to work early today. We will discuss this when I return. I will only be away for three days." He slipped his new Homburg on, adjusting it forward on his wide brow. The hat had been a leap of faith that the legal profession would promote him one step above that of legal clerk.

Patrick walked out on Charlotte "Shelley" Norton Colter after only one week of marriage. Shelley would walk the few blocks to Parker's Mercantile and her position as a file clerk. At noon when her mother took the afternoon shift Shelley would go to her parent'a home to care for Neva.

Patrick caught himself cracking his knuckles on his way to the law office. Unexpectedly he and his marriage faced their first test when he was starting his position as a novice associate in the new Territorial law firm of Lucas Bosworth.

"You are better qualified than doing this grunt work," Lucas said, when Patrick arrived.

Lucas was two years older than Patrick but looked younger. He had the advantage of having grown up in his father's Boston firm. "I would like to see you study the law, get professional training. That is not my idea, it is my father's. But right now we need your insight as a longtime resident of the Territory. You understand it the way we outsiders do not. We need to address litigation regarding the stream pollution that is driving ranchers like Mac Tarynton out of the county. You are familiar with both ranching and mining issues.

"Candidates are reluctant to come forward since the assassination of Commissioner Kent Berrigan a year ago. We need to reopen the case, find the assassins, and make sure that people feel safe to run for public office. How are Territorial affairs to be managed when a struggle continues for balanced representation?"

"Territorial affairs will be managed by those in power—by biased representation." Patrick hung his new Homburg and coat on the rack. "Citizens in good standing in Butte and the vicinity are generally invested in the mines, not public service or politics. Mr. Tarynton put his life on the line trying to gain a voice for landowners. He may have become a target for his efforts."

Patrick felt he had said enough. Maybe too much. Reopening the assassination case gave him chills. And he was walking right into it with Lucas, an Easterner. Lucas might not gauge the West as a more seasoned attorney might, Judge Kirschenbaum, for instance. Patrick pushed the sense of caution to the back of his mind and braced for the stack of work on his desk before he left for Deer Lodge later in the day.

"Why do you make such a prediction? You must have inside information that I alluded to."

"If I had I would have struck it rich myself instead of spending years of backbreaking prospecting. No, this is not hearsay, either. My wife's father, a geologist, found copper in remarkable, no—in inestimable quantities, in Butte mines. He was discharged from his contract for not finding comparable silver leads. Silver has doubled the population of this town from five hundred to a thousand or so in the past year. Bill Farlin's Travona mine may have more than a limited run."

"You have likely heard of Marcus Daly, the man who bought the Alice silver mine. A whole town is springing up around that mine. He calls it Walkerville after the Walker brothers he bought the mine from in Utah. I suspect Daly will have an outsize influence on the Commission and everything else in the Territory."

"I may be a greenhorn from the East, but I have heard of Mr. Daly. I met him in this office a few minutes ago, as a matter of fact." Lucas allowed himself a sly grin, sat back in his pivotal chair, and fished a cigar from his vest pocket.

Patrick's paper shuffling stopped in mid-air.

Lucas chuckled. "That is why we are going to need the best damn lawyers in the country. He sounded me out about coming in with them, suggesting without saying so, that I close my firm and work with the Anaconda Company."

"I wish I could contribute to your making a go of this firm, sir." Patrick cut in.

Lucas' train of thought continued. "My guess is that Marcus Daly is a man of some experience who quickly grasps the potential in minerals here. Another opportunist, William Clark, a Deer Lodge bank president, already bought out owners of mines who fell on hard times. I imagine he is well-capitalized for investments, or he has a means of raising it. It behooves all of us to take note. Mr. Daly certainly is."

Patrick ducked his head and applied himself to the work at hand without attempting to further the firms' hopes or expound on matters regarding the cold case. Lucas was already formidably insightful about current events in Butte, which made Patrick wonder how secure his new position as a insider in the Territory was. But Lucas could speculate all he wanted about deviltry to come. It might be fascinating to an outsider; to an ex-miner it was more of the same old bull. He unconsciously patted his wallet. Flat as usual. Being newly married he was wary about taking risks. He had lost more to investor greed than he cared to remember, first on Norwegian Creek in Hot Spring District, then here in Butte when the placer gold ran out. He and Jackson had sold claims cheap that were now minting money for hardrock miners.

Patrick grimaced. He and Jackson had been gold prospectors, not hardrock miners for a reason. Blasting and separating minerals from quartz took money and mills, capital the twins figured they would never have. Instead, they had gone on payroll and down in the mines until last year, when Patrick determined that underground life was not for him. Jackson later hired on at Mac Tarynton's ranch crew.

"Daly caught on soon enough that I could not or would not accommodate him," Lucas admitted. "He left in a huff, advising me that our firm may be able to handle something less challenging than corporate cases. He probably figured I was too young and citified to know beans."

Patrick threw his head back and laughed. Something was cemented between the two men at that moment, a mutual feeling that they would be learning to dodge pitfalls, parry when they had the chance, and above all, press on when they needed to do so.

That afternoon Patrick took the stagecoach on his first independent legal business trip to the county seat of Deer Lodge forty miles northwest of Butte. The stage rattled past mining towns of Silver Bow and Rocker and down the valley, where he and Antonio had herded cattle away from poisonous weeds and streams contaminated by mine runoff. He recalled that they had wistfully, or jokingly, talked about their hopes of getting married. That wish had come full circle.

I am back here married but not joking at the moment.

He shuffled his long legs in the cramped coach and checked to see if the drunken sheepherder on the seat opposite him was asleep. The grizzled old fellow who probably had a bath in town now reeked of booze. He would soon be getting off, or likely tumble off into the wagon of his employer in the vicinity of Warm Springs. Patrick yearned for more time alone to sort things out.

Images of their innocence, his and Shelley's, over the past months sprang before his eyes, erasing the view of the flat meadows bisected by the stage road and Clark Fork River. Their tentative disclosures during courting now sounded in his ears, tuning out the snores of the sheepherder.

"I--I never thought of myself having much of a future, of belonging to someone else, except Neva," Shelley had said.

"Listen to me. As a twin, I have worked hard to become independent, to be my own self, even as recently as a year and a half ago. We, Jackson and I, were like one. I thought that was love. Finally, I fought to break it with every bit of strength and will power I possessed. Love like that is too binding to breathe."

"Would you break away from me?"

Patrick now realized her fears may be grounded in his own words, and how difficult the commitment to marriage had been for her. How fearful she was of losing him, just as she feared loss of Neva. Saying yes had been much harder for her than he was aware of at the time.

He remembered grasping for straws and asking, "What does love mean to you?"

She had immediately responded, "That I have to give up something."

Reflections brought back their most intimate moments, as well as the current uneasiness with its implications. Patrick fought off guilt about his impatience with her at the hotel, lost in recalling every word, nuance, moment of their first parting. He never expected her to be dependent and certainly not a fiery wife.

He knew that as a native Westerner, she has weathered more challenges than many women her age, but if this three day trip unsettled her, future travel related to his position would be a problem—he had experienced her temper beneath all that blonde hair. Certainly, the farfetched notion that he study law at Harvard was off the charts unless Shelley would go east. A chuckle rumbled from his belly, erupting aloud in the stage-coach.

I scarcely persuaded the woman to leave her parents' home in Butte. And that was only by basically adopting her sister. Now I want to take her to Boston! The city would never be the same again. Her pacing would chisel a path along the Charles River.

Shelley's vitality that first attracted him and soon won him over now revealed additional traits. That realization brought him back to the present and the complexity of marriage.

I married the two of them, Shelley and Neva. I will do my best by them. Is that what love means? If it is teamwork, I understand that. That comes natural to me. Jackson and I worked it out most of our lives.

The swiftly trotting four-horse team and stagecoach stirred up clouds of dust that stuck in Patrick's nostrils and stung his eyes. He slapped his hat against his knee to beat out the dirt, and yanked the heavy curtains wide open to let a stiff wind take the dust in one window and out the other. The sweet scent of clover in bloom, crushed by their passing wheels, refreshed the interior of the overly warm coach. He exhaled and refocused, the purpose of this trip becoming more pressing.

The cold case he was investigating was the assassination of Kent Berrigan, Montana Territorial Commissioner. With the support of cattlemen, Berrigan had been expected to take a stand against mill owners and miners who allowed discarded ore to oxidize and leech into streams. No one knew for certain if the gunman's motive was related to that conflict, Patrick recalled. Hired thugs usually do not understand the issues or get worked up about them. They just want the payoff in gold. Kent Berrigan had seldom stepped on anyone's toes, but he would have by addressing Butte's mine tailings issue on behalf of the ranchers.

Patrick batted his hat again on his knee, the swipe a symbol of anger and hurt that he harbored over the past year.

Helluva loss to all of us. I would like to thank him for encouraging me to study and aim higher. He deserved better, to live and set an example for serving in the public interest. Hindsight proves to be a dubious consolation. I need foresight to investigate the cold case; how far am I willing to go to solve it?

Kent Berrigan had been a close neighbor on Norwegian Creek in Hot Spring District, and a closer friend after Kent's common-law wife, Miss Marion Patton, left him. It may have been a casual relationship on her part, but Kent's grief for her meant he had made a lifetime commitment. Patrick felt his chest swelling with affection for his former neighbors. He tried to shake the memories, not wanting to invite sorrows back into his newlywed life. But the spell threatened to hang over him. Mr. Berrigan served many years as Justice of the Peace in Madison County. There were plenty of folks with might and power, but few with the moral integrity Berrigan possessed.

Patrick forced himself to relax in the corner of the stagecoach, mulling over events of the morning. He was caught unaware and hurtled from his seat when a sharp report slammed the coach to the side of the road. He dove for cover, catching the sheepherder, dislodged from his corner, in mid air. The two tumbled amid flapping curtains and curses. The driver hauled on the spooked team that still lunged, causing the Concord coach undercarriage to lurch and howl in protest.

"We done got a broken axle." The driver issued a stream of profanity and unhooked the team. Patrick parked the suddenly half-sober herder back on the lopsided seat and got out, his legs still shaking.

"Warning rumbles and cracks like that down three or four levels in the mines could scare a man half to death," Patrick breathed, "only to find it was an over or under loaded ore car wobbling off the rails."

He did not reveal his reaction had been to take cover from what might have been a sniper's shot, the very real notion that the man who downed Kent Berrigan may be lying in wait for him.

"My nerves are strung out. It's not all about being married. It's about being involved in this case," he muttered to himself. He dusted his trousers and wiped his brow. Though Patrick had been in Boston at the time of the assassination, the murder was fresh in his mind.

"I am not sure I can handle this investigation," a fear heard only by the sweet clover and brisk wind off the Pintlers while they waited for the next stagecoach to come by.

3

SHELLEY

After Patrick left the honeymoon suite at the Continental Hotel for the law office, Shelley confronted her first day alone as Mrs. Colter. The hand painted porcelain pitcher rested in its fluted bowl on a carved oak dresser. Double layers of Italian lace draped over clerestory windows where early morning sun filtered above a sloping roof on the second story. The shattered pieces of their parting littered the hotel suite more than the disarray of honeymoon clothing around her. She sank onto the bed, the buoyant confidence of a few weeks ago now eluding her.

"I wonder if he married me knowing he would work on dangerous cases."

Shelley let her hairbrush drop on the dresser and splashed cold water over her face. She checked the ornate mahogany-framed mirror to see if tell-tale traces of her crying remained. The plain cotton dress she put on to clerk at Parker's Mercantile appeared cheap, even frowsy, after the wedding and honeymoon gowns she had worn the past week. Straightening her shoulders, she took a last look at the suite that now felt inhospitable.

Sunlight sent wavy patterns across the rumpled iron bedstead with its enormous down pillows askew. The maid will take care of that, Shelley conceded, still feeling unaccustomed to receiving services rather than providing them. She could leave a tray bearing a floral-printed Colonial coffee pot, dirty cups and saucers. How different their late night coffee together had been—lounging, talking, fantasizing about their future. It all sounded wonderful and exciting, including the day she would no longer work at Parker's. Instead, she had looked forward to a home of their own and raising a family. The last heirloom Blue Willow teacup of a set her mother had cherished became hers as a wedding gift. One she hoped to pass on to another generation.

"But enough of that." She whisked her hairbrush into a top drawer of the oak vanity, closed the doors of the free-standing wardrobe, and left the suite without a final glance. Already dreading the walk across the lobby, Shelley forced her long legs down the hall past the communal toilets to the stairway with its two landings that led to the lobby. She swallowed hard when a prim housekeeper nodded a brief "Mrs. Colter," and passed on, jangling her keys.

She was gracious when I was with Patrick, Shelley realized, and when Mac Tarynton sent over a few bottles of bourbon, whiskey and rum for "the boys" who had nightcaps with Patrick a few times in the past week.

A tapestry-like carpet cushioned the inlaid marble floor of the lobby, an unlikely extravagance in wild Montana Territory. Under the soaring ceiling and hanging chandeliers, even the massive leather captains chairs appeared small. Tiny drop crystals on the chandeliers reflected rainbow colors from a few kerosene-lit sconces on the walls, yet despite the frontier opulence it smelled of cigar smoke, whiskey and miners' sweat.

Shelley gripped her shawl and snugged the ties of her bonnet as if to hide a plain merchant's clerk before crossing the lobby. Other than new brides the only women who frequented the hotel were those with the trappings of Dr. Adelaide Owens in her trim two-piece suits, or Mrs. Baumbier, the mayor's wife, stylish in a fake bustle, or an occasional politician's wife on a western campaign tour.

However, Butte did not warrant many distinguished visitors. Its ascendance a decade ago had become a downward trajectory after the Silver Bow gold rush. The Continental Hotel was an artifact of better days, but one promising enough that the building had been refurbished, another story added, and the dust of decline swept out with incoming investments in silver. John Norton, Shelley's father, had been lured from the silver mines of Nevada for that very reason, to read the mineral-laden underground geology and locate veins of silver in what was expected to be substantial quantities. The discoveries were heartening at first, and just as quickly exploited. The coterie of investors who owned the Continental Hotel benefited both as mine owners and hotel concessionaires.

The trappings of the lobby felt daunting to Shelley. She thought about Patrick's proud entrance with a wife on his arm a week ago. Without his presence she wanted to escape to her cubbyhole in the Mercantile, a building braced into the hillside, clinging to the steep inclines of Butte. Her anxious glance roamed the spacious and fortunately unoccupied lobby, as if saying goodbye to her first experience among the acculturated, when a bulletin posted in the window caught her attention.

Statehood for Montana!
Meeting tonight after supper
Summit Boarding House

Patrick might be interested, she thought, her mood brightening before remembering he would be away for three days. Outside she bolted free of what had become the oppressive atmosphere of the hotel and hastened to the Mercantile. Miss Irmgarde Meyer lingered at a similar sign posted in the store window.

"Yes, I saw the notice at the hotel, but I do not have time to visit right now," Shelley said.

"Did you wear the negligee I gave you for your wedding night?" Irmgarde, a street woman, was dressed in her trademark red stockings and blue high heels.

"I appreciate your intention, Gertie, but I did not need it." Shelley used the familiar name, their friendship personal though less than openly social.

Irmgarde read the look well enough to know what she meant. Shelley tried to push on past, but Irmgarde persisted "You might need it. There are times when couples have their differences and —"

"Gertie, I do not need it or your advice right now, and I am late for work." Shelley sped into the seclusion of the file room at the rear of the store with Gertie's remark "couples have differences" ringing in her ears. If Gertie only knew how quickly that came about. If my mother and father had their differences, I never noticed, or seldom did.

"They probably didn't their first week," she groaned, threatening to slip into her previous upset state of mind in which it was impossible to concentrate. Mother had not wanted to move from Nevada to Montana Territory, yet she had gathered Neva and me and the family belongings, including Neva's porcelain-faced dolls and her mother's carefully wrapped Blue Willow tea set, most of which did not survive jostling in the wagon bed.

The stacks of shipping labels in front of Shelley blurred. Receipts in need of filing escaped her fingers and fluttered over the edge of her desk. Flustered, she saw dates on receipts fall out of order and sales slips jumble together from both the Mercantile and Apothecary shop. The owner, Mr. H.S. Parker, came in to find her on hands and knees behind the desk.

"It is nice to have you back with us, Mrs. Colter. Congratulations. You have a fine husband. Is there something missing since you were here last week?" His mutton chop sideburns fidgeted around a suppressed grin when he peered over the desk, finding not for the first time his employee disorganizing the office rather than the other way around.

Shelley struggled to file the array of records, distracted by the humiliation she would feel asking her mother if she could come home after only one week of marriage. When her mother came to work at noon, Shelley blurted, "Patrick is away on business for three days. May I stay with you and father and Neva? Just while he is gone?"

Winnie Norton quickly replaced a look of alarm with a warm welcome. "Neva will be happy. She misses you. We all do."

"I will slip out after supper for a meeting on statehood. Patrick may want to be informed about it." Shelley did not know if she was reassuring herself or escaping from inquiries her parents might make. At least she would not be spending time envisioning something happening to Patrick. Or regretting romantic fantasies of what she expected her marriage to be.

"Patrick is obligated to travel occasionally," she added, attempting to sound casual. The reality that his commitments could take him away from her and the fact that she may have to continue clerking became a jarring awakening.

Lanterns flickered along Granite Street while the rough edges of Butte softened with the darkening evening. Music and laughter, both coarse and offensive, blasted from open doors of saloons that Shelley widely skirted on her way uptown. She found the meeting at the Summit Boarding House, a ramshackle frame building smelling of cinnamon-laced apple pie and unwashed clothing. She edged into a dark corner of the room. Benches and chairs were already occupied, the floor space crammed nearly to capacity. Irmgarde Meyer fluttered a handkerchief at her from the opposite side of the room. The District girls were there enforce, distinguished by lustrous hair held in playful disorder by wide combs, all flaunting a bit of lace or veil but lacking proper bonnets as head coverings. Shelley stood on tiptoes to view women she recognized as members of the Women's Christian Temperance Society seated primly on chairs in the front row. Dark capes disguised their identities. A few dignitaries unfurled flags of the Territory and United States behind a table facing the crowd.

"Jeff Davis, hoy!" shouted someone standing in the doorway. Benches skidded sideways when folks rose to condemn the Rebel. Laughter, cheers and jeers rose from here and there.

"It seems President Hayes has left work for us," the presiding gentleman remarked, attempting to be heard above the hijacked meeting.

"This could get rough," the man next to Shelley observed, "Some people are like the wild cattle herds the cowboys run through Butte. They stay ornery for a lifetime."

Shelley nodded and sheltered herself further into the shadows. She noticed Irmgarde nudging her associates about something likely known only to themselves.

"I dunno about this here statehood," another man said, "but I'm willing to listen. Some of us might benefit where we're not makin' a livin' now."

True, many laborers in Butte were not earning enough to prospect further West or go back home to the Midwest or East Coast. Shelley sensed that statehood could be a good thing.

History of the transient Territorial capital of Montana took up a better part of the first speech. Bannack claimed it first in 1864 and held it for a year before Virginia City's population and new gold wealth literally stole it. Virginia City's fight to retain it set off a bitter ten-year battle with Helena, whose remarkably durable Last Chance Gulch finally won the honor, but not without the capital city earning a reputation for corruption and polarization. Bitter political in-fighting aroused by the competition for state capital did not bode well for a unified campaign for statehood.

"The location for state capital has already stirred up a hornet's nest," the speaker said. "Pride and money oughtn't buy it for one place or another, including bids by Anaconda or Deer Lodge. But let us focus on the future of the Territory and benefits that come with statehood."

A man near Shelley nudged those next to him and spoke above the crowd. "We need to first deal with the crash of '73 and scarcity of flour. Nobody's innerested in lookin' ahead when they can't afford to buy a sack 'a flour."

Murmurs of agreement circulated, raising the tension. Shelley cast about for a pathway out of the corner. She wondered what she was doing uptown at night without Patrick. At the least, she wished she had come earlier and found a seat among the women.

The following speaker was candid, confident and well-informed. "Statehood in the West began with Nevada in 1864," he said. "I am not running for anything so you needn't worry that I am sharpening my own axe. I am a businessman from Kansas, not a native of your fine Territory, but I am here to tell you that Kansas needs Montana beef—"

"Awwww," the miners turned thumbs down at the idea. "Silver, silver, silver," a few chanted.

"We need that, too, in the form of United States minted silver dollars. Now consider how statehood might help line your pockets and help folks in the Territory. We will gain representation for miners and cattlemen alike."

Wranglers shuffled in knots here and there and stamped their boots in approval.

"No outlawin' whiskey," came from a cluster of hecklers, evidently consisting of saloon keepers, bartenders and miners. Shelley immediately recognized they had stakes in maintaining the present situation of minimal governance.

"Folks, this is about Statehood. The kind of state you get depends upon the kind of citizens you elect to represent your interests. I suspect you would like to vote for local—"

Again, rabble-rousing punctuated remarks pertaining to the night's subject.

"Let the man talk. We need roads that don't jar your teeth out and railroads to send livestock to market. Statehood will bring us benefits the Territory hasn't even thought about."

However, the notion of a potential ban on alcohol sent most of the bystanders scrambling out the door. Only a few old-timers, a drunk too inebriated to stand, and the women remained.

"Citizens with vision support statehood to benefit enterprises of all kinds, including mining," the speaker continued. "The open country between the States and California has been tamed by the transcontinental railroad. That means Montana Territory is not that remote anymore. Folks, you might feel cut off by the Continental Divide here in Summit Valley, but you'll see the Utah and Northern Railway coming around the bend in the not too distant future. It will offer opportunities for Montana to grow and become a major exporter of minerals and beef."

He riffled a stack of papers and wrapped up his talk early since the audience had dwindled. "Think about it, about the push for statehood. We need to join up or be left behind other states."

Shelley escaped along with the remaining crowd and drifted through conversations along the street, some for and some against. Glad for their preoccupation, she felt safe enough in the half-lit backstreets to race up the hill to Walkerville. Once in bed with Neva she felt as if she had never left home.

Two days later Patrick returned from his business trip to Deer Lodge. They sat in the dining room of the Continental Hotel enjoying what would be the last few days of their stay in the hotel.

"You seem to be happy about having spent time with your parents," Patrick observed. Excitement from her first venture into political issues permeated Shelley's story of the statehood meeting.

"It's not like you to get involved, is it?" Patrick asked, dipping a doughnut into his coffee. Shelley's sudden silence made him stiffen and lean back. The coffee and doughnut cooled untouched. He realized his tone had been critical of her initiative.

"Everything is going haywire, Shelley. This is not what I had dreamed for us. Hell, I don't know what I figured after we got married." Spinning his new Homburg between his thumbs appeared to be a safer bet than facing her.

"I am sorry I walked out on you a few days ago. You must have been very frightened to get angry. That is not like me. I should have stayed and comforted you. I truly beg your forgiveness, Shelley."

"Patrick, teach me to drive the buggy. When we leave the hotel we will move into your cabin with your brother and his family. It is far out from town, so how could I become involved in anything? If I can drive Old Tornado, I can take Neva home and get back and forth to work while you are away on business trips."

"Are you becoming accustomed to the idea that I will be traveling for the law firm?"

"This is the best way I can think of right now. I was not raised in the country, though Butte and Silver City, Nevada, hardly qualify as cities. I could walk the distance out to your place, but as you know, Neva could not."

"Lucas doesn't know a blessed thing about marriage, sending me off in the middle of our first two weeks together," Patrick fumed, allowing her immediate problem-solving to pass over his head. He vividly recalled his fright when the stagecoach axle cracked like a rifle shot. Wary of elements in Butte since the assassination, he remained on edge since he had picked up the case. Shellcy likely sensed how he felt. He chose to keep the incident to himself.

"I rode a horse once in Nevada. My best friend, Trudy, had a blue roan that all the kids in town learned to ride. Missy was her name. She had big soft eyes, kind of blue, too. She was a quiet older mare. I led her to the chopping block so I could jump on bareback. Before I gathered the reins Missy galloped to the barn. I screamed at Trudy and pulled on Missy's reins and shrieked for my mother, but the horse wouldn't stop. She ran right through the barn door. The only trouble was that the top half of the Dutch door was closed."

Patrick's attention shifted back to the moment. His mouth flew open, unclear how to respond.

"The scar is here," Shelley said, separating the heavy blonde hair on top of her head.

"Oh, god, Shelley, this is why I hitched my life to yours. You make me laugh or, I'll admit, extremely uneasy. Your experience riding makes me cautious about teaching you to drive a horse and buggy."

"I need to be able to drive."

"Your scar tells me fateful events are just over the horizon. I'm guessing our marriage may be one of waiting for them to happen."

Shelley suppressed a giggle. Patrick was on her side this time.

"I want to fold you in my arms and keep you safe for all time, Shelley. Somehow we will handle your fears about the nature of my work." He paused then resumed their earlier interrupted conversation. "However, I have trouble thinking of you involved in political gatherings."

"It is not like me to think of myself being married either. Or walking to an evening meeting alone, Patrick. I attended it on your behalf. It appears that many people will benefit by statehood. I found the ideas very stimulating. You need to think ahead, for us and for the good of the Territory. Yes, I am involved in more ways than I ever imagined!"

Her trilling laughter stirred nearby diners to stare.

Patrick tossed his hat aside. "That is more like you." He reached across the table for her hand. "I need you, Shelley. I missed you terribly on the trip. I do not want to go without you anymore. They are paying me to be the eyes and ears here in Butte, but apparently you are already assuming that role if I have to travel."

Butte squatted on wide, ragged, dirt streets that masqueraded as a daily World's Fair when its immigrant proletariats poured to and from work in the mines. Proud Cornish miners from the southwest coast of England commanded respect for their meat and potato pasties first, and their expertise and experience in hardrock mining second. They carried over-sized tin lunch pails with the hearty pasties to work, and on the way home filled the pails to sloshing with beer at a pub. Miners from Serbia and Croatia often wore articles of colorfully embroidered native costumes. Miners from Italy took a ribbing left and right, and never failed to deliver punches if it came to that, and it often did. The Irish paraded baggy trousers, bowlers, flat caps and battered fedoras, quick to sing a refrain of the Isles, quick to raise a temper, quick to hustle a job.

Shouts in every language mingled with curses of jerk-line mule team freighters struggling against the wave of humanity on the streets. Dust choked the air round the clock. Butte never shut down, nor did the bricklayers, carpenters, and Guildsmen who constructed a "city" almost overnight. Mine whistles told the time; there was no time and nothing but time to make a living or make a killing, depending upon the whim of fate or the luck 'a the Irish. If Butte was the World's Fair, Parker's Mercantile and Apothecary was the center of it.

"What did you think of the meeting last night?" Irmgarde asked while sucking on her favorite saltwater taffy. She usually came into the Mercantile for her treat around noon, and caught Shelley before she left to care for Neva. Shelley was one of the few women in town who would speak to her. The scarcity of women meant that the friendship was mutual if not puzzling to themselves and any observer.

"The drive for statehood is a conspiracy to get rid of us," she confided, before Shelley answered.

"What makes you hold such a view, Gertie?"

"The state would pass strict laws and endless regulations. I left the States for a reason, Shelley. You are fortunate to exist outside all the political conniving that goes on. I hope your husband does not work for statehood in that new job of his."

"What can I say? I hardly know what he is doing. You must be worried about this."

"If we get statehood and women get the vote, they would shut down men's liberties in a minute."

"What do you mean, women get the vote? I did not hear anything about
    that."

"Did you notice the women in black who crusade for abstinence? They will support statehood if they get women's right to vote with it."

"Are they from around here?"

"Some are, some aren't. They represent the organization of the Good Templars. Their message advocates total abstinence."

"I thought my husband might be interested in statehood," Shelley said.

"There is not much in it one way or the other for me personally. Evidently a good many others felt the same way or outright opposed it, judging by the number that walked out."

"We left, too, if statehood means coming under an abstinence amendment proposed by temperance advocates for the United States Constitution."

"I have heard of the Women's Christian Temperance Society, but I am not aware that the women have much influence over the affairs of men. Or the affairs of government." Both had an immediate personal connection for Shelley and her marriage. Let well enough alone, she told herself. Gertie was still storming about her personal experience.

"My family left Germany because of Minister President Bismarck with his divisive *Kulturekampf* and the fact he constantly bullied neighboring countries. Fear of engaging in war on three sides of us, with France, Italy and Russia, kept people alarmed. We left when it became intolerable. This wool shawl is my peasant garb from Hamburg." Gertie secured it tightly under her chin.

"I came over on the boat wearing this shawl. To tell you the truth, I expected something different when I came to America. I expected women would be better off here, but I find myself caught up in the poor, overworked lower class, lowest of the low."

"Oh, Gertie, please do not talk like that. You deserve a chance for a better life, and meeting someone nice. Something will come along—"

"There are too many of us and too little hope for miracles. But I do not want to look like some of the older girls in a few years."

"Shush, I will keep my eyes and ears open for you. Now I have to finish filing receipts."

In the light of day, lines of strain marked circles under Gertie's brown eyes and curled down the corners of her mouth. Shelley dwelled a moment on what it must be like for a young immigrant about twenty-years-old, her own age, and losing hope. Shelley's emigration from Nevada Territory had been unsettling enough. Her father's subsequent dismissal as a geologist had put the family in financial straits. Winifred Norton and Charlotte, as Shelley was known to those outside the family with the exception of Gertie, were grateful for employment at the Mercantile. The family was getting by but could not afford to move back to Nevada. Now with Shelley married it was doubtful her parents would ever return.

"Someone came along for me and changed my life," mused Shelley on her brisk walk home to Walkerville. "That is what I wish will soon happen for Gertie." Yet their discussion had prompted questions that she wanted to ask Patrick.

4

AMBITIONS

Three days on the trip to Deer Lodge had given Patrick Colter time to reflect on forces that moved with lightning speed in his life. He returned to Butte with high hopes for himself and his marriage, yet with limited findings related to the cold case. Striding uptown, Patrick marveled at the western branch of the Bosworth law firm located in the new Silver Bow Building on Park Street. The office in the building constructed of locally made brick represented far more than an outpost in the Territory's young legal system.

"This Boston lad has seen the whites of the dragon's eyes and come back to tell of it," he mused. "A subsistence placer miner living on sow belly, a poor country school teacher, a short-term hardrock miner now tapped for legal assistant could only be credited to the luck 'a the Irish."

He brushed past newsboys competing for sales on the corner of Park and Montana streets, their lilting cries, "Temperance Advocates Invade Butte," every bit as Irish as his origins.

His heels sounded hollow on the hardwood floor of the central hallway when he followed the scent of expensive cigar smoke into Lucas' office.

"Are we ready for bear?"

Surprised, Patrick grinned. "You are talking like a native born Territorial trapper." He turned his pockets inside out. "I'm sorry to come back empty handed. The folks in Deer Lodge don't get about much. We hear more local grapevine gossip, news, lies, and dang near everything on a street corner in Butte than those cattlemen ever knew."

"Precisely. That is why you are useful to our firm's Boston office. Those on the East Coast must determine their moves in the West from 2,000 miles away. With our office here and my father's firm there, we have the potential to become a formidable force in the Territory, if not in the county. Mr. Daly sounded me out on somewhat the same strategy. He is keeping an eye on Samuel Hauser and A. J. Davis, a Missourian and a Yankee. They bought the Lexington silver mine, sold with all its machinery to Davis. Apparently it is a phenomenal mine. Time will tell, but with all the mining competition, Daly is amassing his own fleet of attorneys."

"On my trip I met another formidable force, the Deer Lodge banker, Mr. William Clark, whom you mentioned earlier. He boasted of having been a mule-freighter who supplied Bannack with eggs and tobacco from Salt Lake City. He called it a humanitarian service for those on Grasshopper Creek right after the gold discovery in '63 and '64. His stories are about pulling himself up by his bootstraps, while most everyone knows he is raking in foreclosures and abandoned mining claims for Deer Lodge National Bank. I suspect he will eventually gain title to most of the mines through his investments on the side."

"Humanitarian? I already have a stack of litigation against his bank from mine owners. And miners who work his claims often charge they are taken advantage of. He also leveraged his power in Butte by buying up four of the major mining claims as far back as 1872."

"I heard he also has a raft of attorneys, Lucas. The Territory will soon have as many lawyers as it has miners."

"As well as bankers and those who aspire to be politicians."

"'*Is milis da' o'l each is searbh da' ioc e'*. It is sweet to drink but bitter to pay for it, my 'dere' mother' always said. They'll have their day, then what?"

Patrick loosened his cravat and sank into the chair behind his desk. The second-hand office furnishings hardly did justice to the Silver Bow Building. Desks, shelves and chairs had seen hard use in the back rooms of O'Farrell's Saloon where Lucas had hastily acquired them from the proprietor. Worn legs scratched the floor when Patrick scooted forward.

"We are starting on the bottom rung, this old chair and me," he said.

"I saw your wife at the statehood meeting. Civic-minded, is she?"

Patrick's head came up. "Not that I know of. Couldn't say she has been in the past. She mentioned going to the meeting on my behalf."

"There is sure to be a next one. If not here, then in Helena. You might consider attending."

A lapse in the conversation meant each man assessed what the possibility of statehood meant. For Patrick, it was personal and prompted an immediate reaction. It meant his wife might get involved and compromise his new career, entangling them with unsavory causes of which he would not approve. Evidently the meeting had attracted activists like fleas.

But Lucas continued to mull the prospects. "Embracing statehood will happen here as it did in twenty-some other states. It is a matter of time. This firm became fully aware of Montana Territory's stalled movement toward statehood before I came west. In the firm's opinion, bringing the Territory into the Union as a state presents an encouraging sign for trade, transportation, communications, and good governance. Of course, we will see many of those improvements occurring as soon as the Union Pacific tunnels its way through the Continental Divide.

All Patrick could immediately foresee was that expansion in the Territory or proposed State would mean more travel for him, and if the last trip were any indication, Shelley would be badly shaken by his occupation. It appeared doubtful he could talk reasonably with her about it, and it was premature to disclose sudden, unresolved marital affairs to his new employer. Patrick's hand unconsciously swept what felt like cobwebs from behind his brow. He saw himself caught between the exhilarating opportunities on the legal front in Butte and what appeared to be constrictions on his participation imposed by his recent marriage. That left one person whom he felt he could confide in, the judge who read them their vows. He might give a listen.

A few weeks later Patrick followed up his resolve to seek counsel regarding his own affairs. Judge Kirschenbaum peered over his spectacles at Patrick Worthington Colter, who felt every bit a newly married young man with a sappy grin on his face. The judge had agreed to meet him at the Continental Hotel for coffee. Patrick wanted to let him know he had accepted the legal assistant position in a local branch of an Eastern firm. He already had some misgivings about doing so.

"You are easing into the legal profession, you say? Lawyers and doctors we have aplenty and what are they are doing? Prospecting or speculating like everyone else, not lawyering or doctoring a'tall. There's Doc George Beal to prove it," the judge growled from beneath a thick white beard that failed to hide his kindly appraisal of Patrick Colter.

Everyone knew of Dr. Beal who bought up a majority of the gold mining assets of German Gulch, built a mercantile catering primarily to the Chinese, and never got around to opening a medical clinic. Instead, he opened an assay business, became mayor of Butte, and invested in the Centennial Supper Club with its superb dining catering to well-heeled comers such as William Clark and Marcus Daly.

"And there's Sid Edgerton, District Court judge. He sold his claims on Norwegian and Rattlesnake Creeks in Madison County ten years ago. I hear hardrock miners there took out as much gold as miners had done in Alder Gulch."

"Yes, sir. I had a claim on Norwegian Creek at the time, but I am done with mining." Lost in personal uncertainties, Patrick tried to overlook the judge's frown, likely for his failure to express a "Your Honor" that the judge had come to expect from more circumspect petitioners.

"If you proceed to eventually read the law, then we shall be fortunate to have an attorney with a solid reputation, one whose livelihood is not dependent upon the collusions of the mining industry."

"I may have more ambition than is warranted for my experience. But I am not beholding to any miners, politicians, or even the law firm since I just started there." Patrick tried to steady his voice. Despite his enthusiasm for bringing law and justice to Montana Territory, the assassination of Kent Berrigan was never far from his mind. It clouded his best intentions in the struggling and scattered environs of Butte, pretentiously called 'Butte City' until recently. He had made this appointment with Judge Kirschenbaum to explore the advisability of having joined the Bosworth law firm, about risks it might pose, and threats real or perceived he'd have to live with. He had already encountered one unpleasant reality—the suggestion of a rifle shot when the stagecoach broke an axle had made him dodge for his life. Doubts about plunging in now assumed an outsize role since he had married Shelley Norton.

"I am aware I would essentially be setting myself up for rancor, if not worse, in an arena where I am already investigating the cold case of the Commissioner who was shot. I needed to talk with you about the risks—I would never want to expose my wife and her sister to threats. My wife already fears for my safety since I began working on the case. These domestic concerns have become a major obstacle to my commitment to the law. But lurking in the back of my mind is the belief that I have some aptitude for it." He heard himself talking himself into the position, rather than out of it.

"The miner's courts are rough affairs, son. The law of the land generally ends up in their hands."

"Right you are, sir—Your Honor. That is part of what disturbs me about my decision," Patrick said, failing to listen to the small voice that told him not to cross the judge, at least not this soon at the outset of what might become a professional relationship. He paused to scratch his head, trying to appear older and wiser than his twenty-nine years. The Continental Hotel was the same place Patrick had brainstormed with Lucas Bosworth, Esq., several months earlier about the opportunity to bring the Bosworth firm to Deer Lodge County, Montana Territory. Today he wanted to hear Judge Kirschenbaums' wisdom gained from years on the bench—if he could control currents of his excitement, fear, and impatience that threatened to disrupt their meeting.

"May I offer you a cigar, sir?" Patrick hastened to add, tapping a fat yellow-ochre one from a vest pocket case. "You will likely not have had the pleasure of this distinctive tobacco grown in Georgia, in fact, on the family estate of Commissioner Kent Berrigan. He was a former neighbor of mine whom I held in highest esteem."

Judge Kirschenbaum's stern hazel eyes sharply assessed Patrick, as if determining whether this young fellow was out for blood, vengeance, or perhaps vigilante action. If so, he might sympathize, especially if the deceased was a friend, but clearly he did not want to hear it; he could not hear it for ethical reasons.

"I see. I see," he said at last. "The town has moved on after the assassination. Folks of all persuasions would strenuously object to reminders of it. Besides, it is risky to ride roughshod into entrenched affairs in Butte," he said. "Especially the unsavory ones."

Butte was generally awash with cash and whiskey; attitudes and reputations were quickly emerging that posed a threat to the good-intended and uninitiated. The judge's frown deepened. He took a long time lighting up and savoring the sweet, beneficent taste unfurling in light drafts over his tongue. Patrick pretended to relish his own cigar.

"And these Bosworths who set you up?"

"A venerable Boston firm, upstanding in all respects, and cautious about underwriting new ventures. I worked as a law clerk for Mr. Reuben Bosworth, Lucas' father, when I spent some time in Boston last year. The elder Bosworth, Lucas' grandfather, has retired, leaving Reuben as head of the East Coast office. Lucas is more adventurous, or I might say less traditional. He traveled here to personally assess opportunities for expansion of their offices in the West. I advised him that the Territories were attracting industries, settlers, the railroad, and even a drive for statehood."

Patrick's voice trailed off, though he hoped he had presented his case to the judge in a reasonably persuasive manner. It felt like a dry run. *Why am I doing this? I will not be presenting evidence or a case before him or any other judge—that is Lucas' job.*

Judge Kirschenbaum studied the cigar in his fingertips and listened, a life-long pattern of weighing petitions that drove Patrick to explode.

"Hell, clerking for the law is not like reading the law. I will never be the face you see in court." But as a clincher, he went on.

"I told Lucas Bosworth, and I can reveal to you, sir—Your Honor—that I have sound information about the future of Butte—in copper. It is well worth considering what that means in terms of cases and income for the legal profession." He stifled a grin. "As you are aware, I now have a ready-made family to support."

Patrick paused as if reading tea leaves in his coffee cup, leaves that his father-in-law, Mr. John Norton, had already divined for him. He momentarily forgot the judge, the amorphous concept of justice, the thrill of working on a case. Only Shelley Norton Colter filled all the aching, longing, loving recesses of his long lean body. The laughter in her voice filled his being to over-flowing. His need to support her and her disabled sister, Neva, prompted him to lay his ambitions naked in front of so august an individual as Judge H.D. Kirschenbaum. And then only to seek his blessing, while it was becoming clear to him that his major decision had already been made, perhaps solidly determined long before he walked in the door of the Continental Hotel.

"Perhaps. Perhaps." The judge had lived long enough to see the best of men come and go, their highest aspirations often evaporated into the thin air of the Rocky Mountains, but he edged forward, intent upon the purposefulness portrayed by Patrick Colter. "I will hear you out."

"The Bosworth firm expects me to provide local information and connections until they become established. Believe me, I was offered more by a coalition of jerks and cheats to do that very thing for their interests. In fact, an offer by these undesirable organized elements gave me the idea of continuing the work I had done last year for Bosworth & Son in Boston, only doing it here. Thankfully, my proposal to the firm was accepted after Lucas toured Butte and made a penetrating assessment. The elder Mr. Bosworth naturally heard of the brazen conflicts between the mining giants, Clark and Daly, and about the assassination, as well as the coming confrontation between cattlemen and mine owners over toxic water affecting ranchers' livestock. Lucas may be young, but he figured there was more than enough work here for a substantial staff in a western branch of the Bosworth firm."

Judge Kirschenbaum slowly heaved his portly body out of the chair, bracing

himself with a hairy fist on the table linen and the other on a stout walking stick.

"My rheumatics is acting up, always does in the mornings. Surely compromises the knees when one needs them the most. Be glad you are young, son."

Patrick half-rose from his chair, half waiting for the judge's wisdom, yet pursuing arguments for his own case. "I am thrilled with the opportunity the Bosworths have given me. I suppose the real reason I am telling you is my unease about my wife's fears for my safety. Mr. Bosworth has already advised me of the need to travel to Helena, Bannack, and Virginia City. My wife took it extremely hard when I went to Deer Lodge a few days ago. That limits one's travels and curtails one's effectiveness in a position like mine."

Judge Kirschenbaum tossed the stub of his cigar in a spittoon near the door.

"You are right about the stockpile of cases on the dock and more about to be unloaded on an unsuspecting population. The contamination of water by the mines is one of the innumerable urgent cases. You cannot put a plug in the mining works. There is too much money on both sides. But I cannot tell you what to do about legal affairs in Butte or elsewhere, son, nor about your wife's fears. It was a privilege for me to marry you two—that kind of thing does an old man's heart good."

"Thank you, sir. I am most grateful for your patience in hearing my story. Shelley and I appreciate you more than you know."

"I recall that when I was your age, I had a flaming desire to read the law."

"My flaming desire, if I let myself recognize it, is to learn enough in Butte to qualify me for Harvard Law School."

"Then it is as good as done," the judge said, beaming broadly. "I cannot meet with you anymore, you understand, now that you have declared your position with the firm."

"Of course. I understand. Perhaps we will meet in court one day." Patrick returned a wide smile, not that of determined legal clerk, but one of a glowing husband whose dreams just became a little more real.

"You might consider Georgetown University. You will find it is brand new and attracting attention among the elite."

The gruff advice came over the judge's shoulder while he haltingly made his way out. Patrick laughed and let the judge have the last word.

When the noon whistle sounded at the mines, Shelley rushed out the door of Parker's Mercantile to go home and care for Neva, freeing her mother to take Shelley's place in the store. The shared position worked well for their unique childcare situation. Neva implored her parents and Shelley to allow her to attend school, but they discouraged any prospects of her doing so. Schools were rough and tumble collections of first to eighth graders, many street-hardened newsboys. Neva was small for her age and defenseless if she encountered rowdy situations or the lads teased her for limping. The bleak outlook for a bright little girl dampened Shelley's mood. She foresaw a lifetime of care for her sister by her parents and herself, and certainly few if any of Neva's dreams coming true.

Irmgarde Meyer met Shelley at the corner of Park and Main. They fell into familiar long strides, their skirts whisk-whisking over churned up gravel, their chatter catching up on things large and small on the climb up to Walkerville.

"Tell me more of what you expected when you came to America, Gertie?"

Irmgarde's low, hollow laugh might have emanated from her father or grandfather in Germany. The 'I've been there' laugh of the disenchanted sounded incongruent from one so young. But her eyebrows knitted when she revisited early days before and after Ellis Island.

"I expected problems with English, but we had heard German folks already here would help our family. That was true in New York for the short time we were crowded in tenements with poor immigrants like ourselves. Fortunately, my father had means to move us to a farm in the Midwest. But for me, it was soon more of northern Germany with endless fields to till, plant and harvest. The same hard work and cold, although without the oppression. Father urged me to marry a fine German fellow who farmed a plot of land next to ours. But I tell you, Shelley, everything about me rejected it. I was not cut out to be a peasant. I left.

"*Glaubst du, dass ich dazu kam?* How did I come to this? Would you have guessed I come from good stock? I wonder if I will ever find a way to better myself."

The women walked on, the silence heavy between them. Shelley covered her blushes about Gertie's indirect reference to the brothels. Her own association with the well-known 'woman of the line' was considered socially unacceptable, a fact each countered by way of various subterfuges.

Their path led past the Alice mine perched on Butte's "rainbow hill," a designation earned by rich veins of minerals from black manganese-silver galena to those of peacock-colored copper, and others of gold ore anchored in quartz. These minerals were often markedly bound with molybdenum and zinc. Men hoisted a new headframe next to the Alice pit, already a landmark silver discovery site. An array of new smelter stacks below attested to energetic efforts to separate silver from other minerals and reap the windfall from the Alice, Lexington, Travona, and other silver mines.

A noon sun tried to penetrate the smelter smoke with sporadic rays, but the high altitude atmosphere lay close and strangled with the 24-hour billows from the mining operations. Shelley was well aware, from her father's assessment, of the astounding quantities of copper in the hill, yet there was no demand for it and little interest in separating it from other minerals. Equipment to do so did not exist in Butte.

Gertie's earlier 'if ever' statement that triggered Shelley's thoughts of her father's predicament did not leave much to say. He was very bitter about losing his contract.

Irmgarde tried to stifle an angry outburst, yet she betrayed her own bitterness. "This mineral or that to stake one's life on. This farm or that to break one's back on. Women demanding reforms, Russian peasants uprising to depose the Imperialists.

The legacy of War Between the States reinstituting oppression of former slaves. Women's right to vote denied. The German people bleeding to death over taxes for dueling powers of Church and State—*ahhh!*

"Shelley, I left Ohio under the spell of riches, *oro y plata*, gold and silver, yet found how little power a woman has on her own in this country, as in my *Heimat*, my homeland. I have joined hordes of women, unsettled, hungry, and helpless." Her scorching tone underscored a final "some marry, others take in laundry, and not a few take their own lives. I do not want to be any one of them."

"I—I don't know what to say. You have endured life far beyond my limited experience," Shelley sighed, having heard bits of Gertie's story before. Persuasive to be sure and drawing on her sympathy as well. Women lacked opportunities, not only the disabled among them, a topic Shelley and her mother endlessly debated. What would become of Neva or many women in Butte who became widows of men lost in the mines? Even a train ticket back home failed to be a resource; the railroad had not yet come to Butte.

A whiff of saltwater taffy that Gertie relished with concentration almost made Shelley laugh, despite the desperation behind her words. Irmgarde was not through bemoaning her disillusionment.

"I may not be highly educated, but I did not exactly fall off the turnip wagon." Irmgarde's voice sounded defensive, as if Shelley had not taken her seriously. "Even I can see that women, except for the well-to-do in this country, are about as bad off as they are in the Old Country."

A few days later Patrick and Shelley moved to the Colter cabin located east of Butte near Bison Creek. The brothers had claimed the property after leaving Norwegian Creek in Madison County where they had "sold out for nothing" and left seeking better prospects in what was then called Big Butte. Prospectors there rose and fell with equal rapidity, until the town revived as Silver Bow and later Butte City. Hardrock miners replaced prospectors who had sought their dreams in Butcher Town and Buffalo, Town, and Dublin Gulches, as well as in Silver Bow Creek until the placer gold was worked out. Silver mining required stamp mills, smelters, and shafts deep underground, remaking the above and below ground contours of the city. Butte came alive with new activity, elbow-to-elbow on the streets, and uptown lanterns flickered around the clock.

The Boston law firm of Bosworth & Son's generous wedding gift of two weeks in the honeymoon suite of the Continental Hotel might as well have been a sojourn in South America, according to Shelley Norton Colter, when she described the radical shift in her life to Gertie a few days later.

"We will have to talk fast. This may be our last walk. Patrick and I are moving out of town," Shelley said, when they met at noon out of sight of gossip mongers in town. She picked up their previous conversation as if it had never stopped. "I never had ambitions of my own other than care for little Neva, the dearest thing in my life."

She caught herself. "Next to Patrick. I am not sure what Patrick expects of me or what I expect of myself."

"You'll have a home of your own. That is not to be sneezed at, let me tell you."

"I'm sorry, Gertie, I am too involved in my own affairs to think of others. You sound so—"

"Envious? Yes, in a way. Begrudging? Yes and no. But you will not find me heating hot irons for my old man's shirts. Not in a long shot." With low, throaty laughter, she imitated downing a highball and cleaning her fingernails.

"I do not give a fiddling fig about gardening or shucking peas. Nor scrubbing long johns on a washboard and depriving the Chinese of their work." Nearly skipping in her blue high-heeled shoes and red stockings, Gertie chattered on and on with fresh denunciations of the homemaker's obligations until Shelley caught her arm.

"Wait. We can still meet. I will be a few miles out of Butte, but I do not want to lose you, Gertie. I see Patrick coming with the buggy." She waved goodbye. "I will find a way to take leave of the washboard."

Irmgarde stepped behind a building on a side street before Patrick stopped at the curb.

"Introduce me to your friend. May I offer her a ride?"

"Miss Meyer is very independent." Shelley took a hand up, adding, "We must pick up Neva on the way. Mother is going to work. Neva wants to visit our new home at the cabin."

Patrick's momentary hesitation registered with Shelley, but she did not withdraw the request. He turned his bay buggy horse with the plodding feet, Old Tornado, toward Walkerville to pick up a wildly excited six-year-old.

"Is Cousin Tucker there? And Aunt Nettie and Uncle Jackson? Are they going to stay with us? And the big horse and mule? Are they there, Uncle Patrick?"

Patrick laughed. "I am an uncle twice already it seems, to both you and Tucker. I admit sister-in-law seems as confusing to me as brother–in-law does to you. You are Aunt Neva to nephew, Tucker, however, you may consider him your cousin. I'll take 'Uncle.' I think that sounds just fine, Neva."

"Wait until she calls you Papa," Shelley whispered. Patrick shrugged as if one more surprise would hardly faze him.

Patrick and Jackson had built a sturdy, two-room cabin that they occupied for half a dozen years while they mined in Butte. After Patrick returned to Boston, Jackson met and married Nettie and they lived in the cabin. In a timely fashion it reverted to Patrick when Jackson and family moved to Mac Tarynton's new *TN* ranch on the Beaverhead River.

"I envisioned carrying my bride over the threshold," Patrick admitted after lifting Neva from the carriage and gently setting her down on her strong leg, immediately liberating her to explore the cabin.

In a stolen moment of privacy, Patrick firmly pinned Shelley to the carriage. "I love you, Shelley, your sunshiny hair, your eyes, the way you care for Neva. You make me the happiest man in the world. And even more so now that you are flustered and embarrassed that your little sister will see me kissing you."

The words were lost in a long breath-taking kiss that kept her from saying he was the best husband in the…before Patrick added, "I am proud to take you to our first home."

He lifted her despite Shelley's athletic frame and teetered over the threshold with her in time to hear Neva ask, "Where is Tucker's bed?"

"Tucker has a cradle, darling. They took his baby bed with them." Shelley anticipated the next question and eyed Patrick, who attempted to remove his coat and feel at home. There was nowhere for Neva.

"We will fix that right up," he said, pulling his work boots from the corner where he had stored his belongings. "You and I will go out to the woodpile and make another bed, just your size. How about that?"

He pulled on an old pair of pants and work boots while Neva explored the small cellar cooled by last winter's Blacktail Creek ice. Shelley found that Jackson had left a slab of pork for their supper. She made the standard fare of pork, potatoes and gravy on the old woodstove. Flat irons for ironing stared back at her from the edge of the stovetop, nudging her with Gertie's observations and disdain of a homemaker role. She stirred the gravy and wondered what she would be missing.

5
A THREAT

Spring of 1877 slid into a summer of blasting heat, followed by lightning storms dancing among the peaks of the Continental Divide. Only stagecoach lines and ox and mule freighters linked Butte to the outside world while it simmered in the high altitude. Small frame homes hugged the steep hillsides of uptown Butte in close proximity to the mines, allowing only tiny backyards for clotheslines and coops, where roosters crowed and hens cackled incessantly. Men straggled uphill or down on jagged dirt streets to the mines, only to find the heat much worse underground. Women washed and hung clothes which dried almost instantly if not purely in the acrid air. A few carriages with handsome teams transported business people smartly about town, and occasional buggies criss-crossed the sloping streets. Saddle horses were few and generally unneeded in the close confines of uptown or in Summit Valley. Other than the milkman who was as regular as the mine whistle, and several trash carts, citizens of Butte walked. Patrick, on the other hand, drove Old Tornado hitched to his much-used buggy from the cabin to Butte each day. He left Shelley at the Mercantile and Neva at Norton's home if she had been staying at the cabin. Old Tornado enjoyed the luxury of a livery stable until time to take the family home.

On his way to the Bosworth office Patrick brushed past a roughneck on the street in front of the Montana Territorial Bank.

"Are you one 'a the Tarynton bunch?"

Patrick shouldered the man who tried to step in front of him.

I said, "Are you one 'a the Tarynton bunch?"

"I heard you. What's it to you?"

"Were you with that bunch of ranchers runnin' that Southerner, Berrigan, for Commissioner against the miners?"

"You can stop right there." Patrick barely refrained from swinging a punch. "Say, what is it you're after?"

"Give you folks a message, that's all. That you're gettin' mixed up in other folks' affairs."

"Yeah, and it might be interesting to know who is giving this message." The man sounded surprisingly like Berrigan with his deep Georgia drawl, a confusing message in itself to Patrick.

"I will give you a message," Patrick said. "You are too late. The ranchers you are referring to have moved away. Is there anything else I can do for you?" He straightened and squared his shoulders to face the hostility.

The fellow spat and strode on ahead, his shoulders hunched, head down. "Their presence ain't appreciated around here. Neither is yours."

Without a pause Patrick hurried to fall in step with him. "Let's see now, who am I talking to? Who sent you?" Patrick's voice became conciliatory, even wheedling. His intuitive sense of danger cautioned him to hold his temper.

"Be careful whose side yer on, mister, if yer pokin' into that business about Berrigan."

Patrick kept pace with the message bearer who cleared his jaw of chew alongside the boardwalk.

"Are you representing the miners or is this personal?"

The man did an about face and left. Patrick stared at the retreating figure a moment, attempting to burn the image into his mind. Of medium build with a scruffy beard down his shirt-front. Hell, three quarters of the men in town were bearded, and even more stooped with injury or fatigue. Still, he recalled the man when he entered the law office.

Lucas had his hat and coat on. "Good morning. You are here in time to keep the office open and us in business another day while I go to the Continental for coffee. It is not good for a man to live alone and boil his own coffee, but no one has come along to change that." He glanced at Patrick and halted.

"My reputation seems to have run ahead of me. A scoundrel on the street just threatened me."

"Mr. Colter, what kind of history do you have in this town that you have not disclosed to the firm?"

"None or very little that every other miner doesn't have. Besides, I spent a good part of last year in Boston. I do not know what to make of it."

The two men stood, hats on, arrested by a negative presence they could not put a finger on. Finally Lucas signaled for Patrick to sit while he took a seat at his own desk with every bit of formality of an older, experienced attorney, a chip off his father, Patrick noted.

"The thug figured I was one of the Tarynton bunch. Said he had a message for me—for them. That their presence is not appreciated around here. I told him he was too late."

"Then what is the meaning of this confrontation? You look as though you were alarmed by the encounter."

Fortunately, Lucas was observant enough of the human condition and bold enough to pry—and listen. Characteristics of a good attorney. Patrick filed that thought.

"There is more. He said be careful about prying into the Berrigan case. I am wary, that's all. Getting married makes me think about these things a little more. My wife is fearful about me looking into the assassination. After all, the dead man, Mr. Berrigan, ran for Commissioner based on the issue of mining companies contaminating streams that ranchers depended upon." Patrick's eyes shone with a haunted look.

"Naturally I was on the side of the rancher that my brother works for. I often rode with Antonio, Mac Tarynton's right hand man. It was his job to keep cattle away from the highly mineral-ized water. I had seen enough run-off into pristine streams that caused red, yellow and green scum to make me take sides. Trap-pers claimed the fur-bearing animals died or left when streams became unlivable. That water was certainly not good for live-stock."

Lucas fingered his chin, likely absorbing the implicit mes-sage as well as the explicit. Patrick shuffled out of his coat without getting up from his desk. Several folders in front of him looked urgent, but his mind was far from clear enough for paper work.

"The man on the street said 'be careful who you side with if you're looking into the Berrigan case.' I call that a threat."

Lucas appeared startled as if events looming from the past suddenly became current rather than part of the history or lore of the silver mining town.

"I may be jumping the gun," he said at last. "My father has proposed something I ought to reveal to you. He runs this firm from Boston. I am the 'and Son' part here to keep abreast of mat-ters. It appears that this threat may upset our carefully laid plans for you to be our onsite authority for local affairs. How would you like to get out of Butte for the time being?" He toyed with his watch chain and observed Patrick, his brown eyes somber, speculating.

Patrick was not sure if Lucas would proceed to reveal his father's ideas or hold his hand for awhile.

"You seem to be taking the threat more seriously than I do. I sure as hell was not involved with Mac Tarynton and the ranchers in question, other than riding herd with Antonio a few times. Somebody may have seen us. As for Kent Berrigan, he was mighty good to me when we both lived on Norwegian Creek in the Tobacco Root Mountains. It was a huge misfortune that he became mixed up in the dirty political conflict regarding acid water run-off.

"Jackson and I worked for Mr. Berrigan some on his claim until he quit to build a nice home by the Jefferson River. He let me use his cabin while I taught school for a year in Sterling. I think he saw something in me that no one except my folks had seen. The folks never understood their two sons taking up mining."

Through this monologue Lucas tapped his fingers on a pile of folders and crossed his legs only to uncross them the other direction.

Patrick hurried on, buying time for what may lie ahead. "Mr. Berrigan supplied me with classics to study for teaching, but he also helped me aim for something higher. He was a learned man himself. I cannot believe the cruelty of shooting down a man like that." Patrick's eyes misted, his hands shook in his lap.

"I have made up my mind," Lucas said. "I—we, my father and I, want to send you to Harvard for a year or two. You may resume legal work in the Boston office, of course. We want you to come into the law offices with us."

Patrick gulped. Voices on the street intruded via the slightly open window, a breeze gently moved the heavy drapes. The back of his hand rose to wipe under his nose. He smelled Shelley's lavender soap on his wrist. The judge had prophesied, "It is as good as done." An involuntary glance confirmed the door was closed behind him.

"This is between the two of us, Lucas."

Patrick's thoughts raced ahead, running defense against the very thing he had wanted for a long time—to pull himself out of the mining business for good, to pursue the law which he found interesting and challenging. Attending Harvard was highest among those things.

"I had been wondering for quite a few years what I wanted to do with my life," he said, color flushing back into his cheeks.

The two men sat with the proposition burning like a lively fire in front of them. "Your generous proposal might solve the immediate threat," Patrick ventured, "but you and anyone else taking a stand on mining issues or the cold case may be threatened as well. That is the way it is here in the Territories. With the influx of money and miners I expect greater conflicts to come to a head."

"As a law firm we are not personally associated with the deceased and never will be. That is in our favor. And Marcus Daly has brought enough business into town for us to hire two more attorneys in the meantime. The cases we take on will be determined by prospects that arise from the relationships we choose from now on."

That may be naïve, Patrick thought, but he let it go. "My parents are currently in Ireland caring for my mother's parents, but they made considerable money available for an early inheritance for Jackson and me. Jackson bought property on the Beaverhead next to the Taryntons with his share. Mine could be invested in a few years of study at Harvard to make something of myself." His uneasy laugh failed to brush off the tension. Lucas stood up, the straight creases of his pin-stripe pants adding to his professional stature.

"Would you consider the offer? Do you want to do it?"

"Yes, I do."

The 'I do' felt like an echo of a life-changing vow he had made just a few months ago. He knew he would never be sorry for either commitment.

"I –I will have to talk with my wife, of course. This is not going to go down well, I imagine." He reminded himself how he had rushed into the double wedding without her consent. She had not seemed so carefree since. She may have found the huge social event daunting, though he guessed she resented sharing her special day.

"I would not dally around too long about it. The thug is still out there on the street," Lucas warned, and put his hat on to leave. Patrick sat in the office. The words bounced back to him off the walls, obscured his vision, pounded in his ears, and tore his heart in two. He wanted Shelley and he wanted to study the law at Harvard. Either way, he would pay dearly for it if he chose one over the other.

Weeks went by without incident. Patrick stewed over the offer, astounded that Lucas' firm had opened such an opportunity in his life. Each day he cleared his desk of routine legal papers and reserved plenty of time for Shelley. At last, he felt obligated to make a decision, one way or the other.

"I need to visit Antonio," he told Shelley. "I wish it was as easy as it used to be when he lived on the Tarynton home ranch here. But work is slow in the office so I can take off for three or four days."

"Patrick, take me. I will see if I can get days off, too. It would be wonderful! I have only been a few miles out to German Gulch with my father. And I have never been over the Continental Divide. I think it would be exciting for Neva—"

Patrick allowed himself a laugh, but it came out more like stewed prunes. "You two are as inseparable as twins, and I know a thing or two about twins. Never doubt that I accepted both of you when we married. But I thought you were not that comfortable with Antonio's wife, Danielle."

"She is so beautiful and distant she frightens me a little. We only met at our double wedding and reception. You and Jackson and Antonio were off celebrating—maybe if she and I became acquainted."

Yes, Patrick thought. I am going to pay for every decision I make that does not sit well with Shelley.

"I admit I was too quick to suggest we get married at the same time. It was because Antonio, the Taryntons, and I are mutual friends. I am sorry. You really should have made the plans, not me."

"I want you to plan, to take care of us, that's not it. I worry about disappointing Neva if I leave her. I have never left her. She does not know life without me. When she came to your cabin she intended to stay. Being together is as natural as breathing for Neva and me."

Shelley crossed her arms and paced the short distance of the cabin interior. "I wonder if that is the way it is between you and your twin, Jackson. Is this trip actually about Jackson?"

Patrick's jaw dropped, his eyes cast about for a way out.

"No, this trip is not about Jackson. I had not planned to see him. He and Taryntons live west of the Tobacco Roots up on the Beaverhead River. Antonio bought a place on the other side of mountains. They are linked by a series of stage stops, but it is some distance in between."

Shelley studied him as if assessing what just happened, how they misunderstood each other so easily, how they both came to the marriage with a close attachment to another person which inevitably posed a difficulty. Her lips trembled. "I will not ask you why you are going if you tell me what you need."

"I need you, Shelley, with all my heart and soul I need you foremost in my life. I do not want my travels to come between us. I will not go if you do not want me to." He let the words lie, allowing Shelley to heal the breach if possible. He had not said he would take her.

"I will stay with Neva. Mr. Parker probably would not want me to be away that long anyway."

Patrick scooped her into his arms, his chest heaving a long sigh of relief. Shelley's embrace told him that she needed him, too.

The memorial service celebrated on an open hillside for Kent Berrigan nearly a year ago was fresh on Patrick's mind as he set off for the South Willow Creek area in Madison County where Berrigan had homesteaded. The somber reflection drew parallels to Patrick's present situation. Dark forces lurked ahead, both the unsolved assassination, and the recent bizarre threat targeting him on the street in Butte. Berrigan had emerged from serving as a relatively unknown Justice of the Peace to become a public figure supporting causes unpopular with the increasingly powerful mining companies. Patrick's turnabout from an ordinary miner to his association with a new and already disputed law firm would likely set him on a similar course.

Driven by a single question, he now sought to ask Antonio what he knew about the murder of Kent Berrigan. Prior inconclusive investigations did not include interviewing a cowhand witness who, on Mac Tarynton's orders, began a search for the assassin within minutes after shots were fired. Patrick intended to sound Antonio out about leads, hunches.

It was difficult to imagine young Lucas pursuing such a risky case. He appeared to be a friendly neighborhood attorney who cared about the people of his adopted town of Butte. Mine operations had proliferated due to unlimited mineral resources in the last few years and owners were apparently heedless of side effects of their mines and mills. Rising corporate enterprises had substantial legal teams to defend themselves from ranchers or any other challenger. Other than empathizing with those closest to Kent Berrigan, and responding with the natural curiosity of an attorney to a cold case, Patrick was not clear why Lucas Bosworth's firm reopened the case of the downed Commissioner. Lucas didn't appear to be the type to want to make a name for himself.

Patrick's trip to see Antonio took him along the well worn Continental Divide ridge trail in a generally easterly direction. Turmoil in his mind made him unconsciously push the horse hard through Lime Kiln, a landmark near the gold camp of Highland City. The strikingly opposite decisions he was facing made his head swirl—stay and continue work for the firm at some risk since Shelley was tied to her sister, whose fragile condition limited her activities. Or leave Shelley for a time to pursue an opportunity of a lifetime. When the horse threw a shoe and required a rest, he stopped at the Cedar Ridge stage stop overnight.

The next day Patrick rose early for the long haul along the Jefferson River to Antonio's new property northwest of Willow Creek. Urged on by the message he sensed represented bitter opposition by unknown elements of Butte to an investigation of the Berrigan case, Patrick felt answers could not come fast enough.

"I do not know what the thug meant, but it is a good thing Shelley did not come," he murmured, thoughts lost in the wind that never stopped blowing down the valley.

Summer days brought out sweat on the horse and Patrick's Irish temper. Swearing to not let threats rob him or Shelley of their married life, he fumed, "The cold case isn't just a case, it is personal to me. I may have influenced Lucas to reopen it by my eagerness to see it solved. Because of that I stumbled into some kind of plot."

By evening Patrick had exhausted his anger and himself. He stabled his horse at a half-constructed barn at Antonio's place. Stacks of fresh-cut juniper fence posts were piled around the yard. The small frame house still had a few boarded up windows. The couple lived in two rooms that were finished and furnished. Danielle ran into the yard waving a handkerchief to greet him, her eyes alight at sight of a previous neighbor from Norwegian Creek.

"Greetings! It is so nice to see you again, Mr. Colter. We do not have many visitors and even fewer that we know." Danielle sounded more like her sister, the always hospitable Genevieve Sayles rather than the aloof Danielle he had known.

Patrick extended his hand to shake hers, their first contact since the double wedding. He felt stiff and uneasy remembering Shelley's account of the women's pseudo-politeness in contrast to the boisterous get-together of the men. Here was Danielle, her classic features browned, her black hair uncovered and shining; so far removed from her former austere self in drab clothing and nun-like white cap tied under her chin.

"It looks like married life agrees with you, Mrs. Delgado. Or is it the farm and the goats?" he grinned.

Danielle laughed a little self-consciously, though Patrick saw her as a strong and confident woman.

"Antonio will be here shortly. He is fencing. Come, I will show you around. We have more projects started than we will finish by winter, but the basic shelters are in place. We will be warm and cozy in the cabin." She blushed at the cozy part. Clearly, intimacy was still foreign to her. Patrick had heard her first husband, a crusader of sorts, had strict ideals that took him to war from which he never returned. She led him to the goat pen first, pointing out her prized ram, Duff. The herd grey and white goats provided much of the family food and income.

"His building puts mine and Jackson's to shame," Patrick confessed, seeing the horse barn and corrals. "These hand-hewn logs and lumber show artistry and skill. He is a proud man to have his own place. And you."

Danielle flashed a wide smile that Patrick had not seen before either. She appeared to be an altogether charming, aristocratic woman that fate had landed in the dry hills and prairies of Montana Territory. He marveled at the change, and worried, too, how Shelley might be drifting in the opposite direction, perhaps withdrawing into herself.

At that moment, Danielle said, "I do hope your wife is well. It was a pleasure to make her acquaintance."

Caught in the ambiguity of talking about his wife with his good friend's wife, and unsure about how well Shelley was doing, he managed to mumble a few reassuring words, certain Danielle had not failed to notice his hesitation. He reckoned it would all come out sometime, and wished Antonio would hurry. Supper warming on the kitchen stove smelled delicious. Antonio rushed to the house at last light of day when he saw they had company.

Patrick gripped the wrangler's hand. "Antonio, you have a nice spread here. You and Danielle are certainly thriving."

"And you? How did you get away from Mrs. Colter to ride over here?"

Patrick winced. "It was not easy. You would never guess the attachment she has to that little sister of hers. I almost had to bring both of them."

Antonio glanced questioningly at Patrick but left the subject for later. He motioned for him to sit for supper. Usually distant and silent, this time Antonio carried the conversation, reveling in telling Patrick about helping the Tarynton's move. "We run two thousand cows with calves up Blacktail crik canyon, and follered the Jefferson till it branched off into the Beaverhead River. Then we cut out my two hundred cows that I bought from Mac and I trailed 'em down here.

"I ain't been my own boss for a good many years. To tell you the truth, I rested easier at night being a hired hand for Mac," he added, his serious face crinkling into a broad smile.

"I am happy you and Mrs. Delgado have established your own place." Patrick hoped she'd never heard that he had advised Antonio to marry her and change her name in case the missing husband survived the war. It was the right thing, he figured, for two people who had been living for someone else's prosperity under circumstances not of their own making. They needed lives of their own.

After homemade gooseberry pie, Antonio put his elbows on the table and leaned forward. Danielle retired with her sewing to a rocker by the fire.

"What's driving you so hard to come all the way over here? You kin talk with both 'a us. We don't have secrets. At least I don't want to." Antonio's eyes softened when he looked toward Danielle, knowing she would agree.

"You know better than anybody how I jumped in the law business. I had an idea I could change things, maybe bring a little justice to the Territory." Patrick chewed his thumbnail. "I have had to take a second look at what is driving me. Maybe I miscalculated, or it is likely that any business in Butte sets one party against the other."

Patrick did not want to repeat what Antonio already knew, that a lot of resentment remained about the probe into acid wastewater from the mines. He scratched behind his ear, unsure whether to blurt out the rest, especially with Danielle close by. He dare not let word get back to Shelley.

"A Dr. Hough from Missouri came to Butte. He had an eye for public health and reported that conditions in town contributed to the constant outbreak of sickness. I have it on good authority that William Clark and associates effectively terminated inquiries into public health in Butte after Hough's report."

Antonio nodded.

"You and me, we know mine tailings leave creeks downstream toxic. I suspected at the outset that a coalition of mine owners rose up to scare out livestock owners. I could be dead wrong about that." His eyes bored into Antonio's.

"I had a strange encounter recently. I was threatened by someone's henchman on the street in Butte. There you have it. I should not burden you with this, but I have cause to open old questions about who was behind Berrigan's death."

No one spoke. Antonio's reaction was slow to come, and measured when it did. His fingers fiddled with the silverware or stirred his coffee.

"Antonio, what do you know about Kent Berrigan? And Danielle, you may have known him better than either of us." Patrick was surprised to hear a sharp intake of breath, see her eyes cloud, the memory as painful to her as it was to him.

"I am working on the assassination case of a year ago. One of the reasons Mac Tarynton moved was that it was getting too hot for him to feel safe in Butte. And he feared for the safety of his wife and crew, including you, Antonio."

"Specially me, I 'spect. Mac sent me out to hunt down the assassin that day. The rest of the crew guarded Mac then and every day and night afterwards. Me, I kept an eye out." Antonio dropped his head in a kind of reverence he held for those he worked for and held in high esteem.

"I asked questions. 'Probly too many questions. Didn't get any leads. None. I asked till near midnight that same day. There ain't been a word from anybody that I know or heard tell of that's talk'n. It's a damn shame. Mr. Berrigan was a fine man. Mac and Carrie, they ain't got over the shock yet."

Danielle sidled up to Antonio and he slipped a worn hand over hers. He had courted her when she lived near Berrigan's former home. There had been rumors about Danielle, as well as every single woman in the country, in connection with the handsome gentleman, Kent Berrigan. Now Danielle's story came out.

"I—we—became acquainted. He was terribly distressed when his wife left—rather his companion, Miss Marion Patton. My situation had been, shall we say, unresolved for seven years whether my husband was dead or alive. At that time, eight or ten years ago, there were a number of conflicts around Sterling between Federals and Rebels. One Southern miner had been shot, and the murder remained unsolved. But Mr. Berrigan had few if any enemies, even though he was from Georgia. As Justice of the Peace, he was known to be even handed. All I can tell you is that he was not the type to get involved with another woman, as some speculated."

Patrick cut in. "I am sorry to bring this up anew and involve you folks. Lucas Bosworth, my boss, may be young and naive to wade into something over his head, especially when he first opens a law office in Butte. There's a lawless element in the Territory. Hell, I am wading into this like a damn chicken at a Sunday picnic. But, I want answers and justice as well as anyone else." Patrick reached for his hat and bedroll.

"You'll not be campin' out. I'll throw a mattress by the fire and you be set for the night. I'll think on this till tomorrow," Antonio said. Danielle had already moved to the bedroom.

"This is bigger than we are," Patrick admitted once she closed the door. "Mineral investors like those we were up against in Sterling throw their money around like poker players, except

Butte attracts much bigger players. They hire lawyers by the dozens to protect their interests, none of which includes going after a dead man's killer, you can bet your boots on that."

"You got a lot ridin' on this. I wish I could help you an' Mrs. Colter an' the girl."

"Everything worthwhile in my life. My family and career ambitions are riding on it, my friend."

"Mac moved far 'nuff away he's out of it. He won't make the mistake of runnin' for the Commission or any other office. I'm outta it, too. It's a shame what happened to Mr. Berrigan, but how about gittin' out of it yourself?"

Patrick shook hands with Antonio in recognition of his well-intended advice, an understanding evident between the two, while Patrick privately queried whether he wanted to get out of it or not.

Antonio joined Danielle in the bedroom. Patrick knew he had plumbed the extent of what Antonio knew about the assassination. He settled his bedroll on the mattress and lay awake again assessing his options: refusing the case but staying in Butte amid potential risks, continuing the investigation with all due caution for the safety of his family, or accepting the Bosworths' offer to study law in the East, effectively removing himself from the case and unforeseen risks in Butte.

But hell, I'm a married man. I can't be thinking about myself. If I accept the offer, Shelley will choose to stay with the child in Butte. Leaving her may be risking my marriage.

6
CURTAINS

Leaving his friends' home with advice but without answers, Patrick plunged his horse back into the outer world. Late at night the Colter cabin's small windows lit by candles appeared like a beacon. His wife, and likely Neva, would be waiting. At the sound of hoof beats, Shelley threw open the door and stood framed in her nightgown. Blonde hair flowing over her shoulders created a soft aura against the light behind her.

Patrick's inner storm that had consumed the miles on the return trip dissipated. Within moments Patrick gathered Shelley in his arms, her rejoicing sobs melding into muffled words. A stiff night breeze nudged them back to the present. Shelley retreated to set out a late supper, a bowl of stew and warmed up biscuits, while Patrick fed and stabled his weary horse.

"The old man who raises mules down the valley gave Neva a bird book. The *Audubon Book of Birds* is almost as big as she is. She loves it and will not be parted from it, so she stayed with our folks the last few days."

"That old timer? What is he doing with a book like that? And why is he giving it to Neva?"

"He said it was his mother's and that she would want it to go to the little one who gamely got around on one good leg.'"

Patrick sighed, relieved that if it was the biggest event that occurred while he was away for three days, he was a lucky man indeed. And especially so if Shelley's quiet confession meant they would have these next days alone.

Patrick held off any revelations about his trip or any portents of change. For the first time in their new home he claimed the Colter twins' cabin fully in his own right for his wife. Shelley's hand-stitched blue and yellow print curtains on the windows indicated she claimed it, too. Several thick, bright quilts covered the beds, replacing worn wool blankets from Patrick's bachelor days. A handful of wildflowers tucked in Shelley's china tea cup decorated the wooden table.

"The cabin feels welcoming, Shelley. You've made it nice and homey." It made the decision he had reached even harder to tell Shelley.

Shelley beamed. "Oh, I have not yet told you everything."

Patrick raised an eyebrow. "Is there more?"

Shelley could no longer contain her news. "I drove the buggy. I wanted to surprise you. Father taught me. Honest, I did not wreck it. Please, don't look so alarmed."

"I was not aware your father drove. I never saw him on or around a horse."

"Are you not pleased, Patrick? You seem on edge about something. Father said I was a natural. We practiced up the road toward Bison Creek where miners and woodcutters were at work. I even trotted Old Tornado a little and nearly bounced off the driver's seat, but Father caught hold of my skirt."

"Enough. My god, Shelley, I cannot leave you for a minute. What will you be up to next," he laughed, knowing Old Tornado, despite his name, would do his best without a driver and still get the buggy safely back to the barn.

"No, we never had horses but father came from a farm in Ohio as a young lad. You would be surprised at his experience in many areas."

"And yours as well. I am pleasantly surprised—this time." Patrick had an increasing sense of unease about telling her he had decided to go East, to try it out for a year then determine if he wanted to continue for another year. He had not often found

Shelley in this happy mood since they had been married. He wanted to prolong it, at least for overnight.

Who am I fooling? I am afraid to tell her, the Shelley that I love. I do not want to hurt her. Or lose her tonight, tomorrow, or ever.

"Let's see you drive Old Tornado tomorrow after I get a good rest."

If Shelley had more stories to tell, she saved them and blew out the candles.

The next morning she had already given Old Tornado a pan of oats before Patrick got up. "I want to follow Silver Bow Creek south to Blacktail Creek where the forest comes down the canyon," she said. "I will pack a picnic if you hitch up the wild animal."

Patrick chuckled at Shelley's shift from anger for missing a trip to renewed energy on the home front, and that with a sense of humor. She spread one of the quilts over the buggy seat and tucked a basket under it. They followed the contours of the stream for a couple miles in silence, a rarity with Shelley concentrating on steering the beast who knew a road when he saw one. Patrick took the opportunity to lean back and reflect—the threat, Lucas's proposal, the frantic ride to interview Antonio. Shelley drove at a gentle pace, as alert and excited as Neva had been when she took the reins on their first trip to the cabin. Patrick's dark head fell on his chest. He dozed off and on the rest of the way.

The air cleared as they crossed Summit Valley, some distance from the smelters. Cattails lined a small stream where blackbirds trilled, sang, and squawked like a concert tune-up of uncertain instruments. Bright male Western bluebirds flitted among lower foothills, their color accented by an occasional brilliant yellow oriole. Shelley stopped the buggy in a grove of scrub pines and boulders where a patch of dry grass invited them into the shade.

"I notice different birds since Neva is so enthralled with the bird book. I had better learn about them or she will pass me up. Now is that a raven or a crow scolding in the pines?"

"A camp robber."

"Neva might say a blue jay or a stellar jay. I do not know which is which. She says they warn forest animals about intruders."

Patrick listened as he stiffly rolled himself off the buggy onto the inviting quilt spread on the ground. He stretched, his arms under his head. Shelley offered him the canteen.

"The water is good at your—our cabin. I still have a hard time thinking of as it as ours. I –I truly never expected to marry. I am so fortunate to have you, Patrick. The luckiest woman in all the Territory."

What was meant as an endearment fell like a blow. Patrick's need to reveal his decision, and the reasoning behind it, was getting harder by the minute. He held Shelley a long time on the quilt, the picnic forgotten. Old Tornado, never one to pass up a morsel of feed, grazed nearby. Clouds shifted in patterns replicating the formations of the Rockies, hugging its peaks and eventually shutting out the sun. The couple ate and packed up. Patrick did not broach the subject of leaving to study at Harvard, a subject that would throw a wicked kink into a special day. That night they enjoyed the cabin all to themselves, a far more cherished honeymoon than they experienced in the unfamiliar suite at the famed Continental Hotel in the rough-cut town of Butte.

Patrick presented himself as usual at the Bosworth offices. His outward composure hid a tortured soul. The Berrigan case had got under his skin. It called despite the positive course his life had taken. Marriage and acceptance in the law firm should have been enough.

Patrick fished out cigarette makings, crossed his long legs and leaned back. "During those days of privation on Norwegian

Creek, Jackson and I smoked Durham tobacco, with an occasional good cigar from the Berrigan family estate in Georgia. I was one of those lads who tries a lot of things before he decides what to do with himself. I was fortunate to have Mr. Berrigan's counsel on numerous occasions."

Lucas settled in to listen, foregoing a roll-your-own smoke.

"Jackson and I are opposites despite being fraternal twins. He dug into anything in front of him like a badger on a brand new adventure. Everyone laughed at me for teaching school for a meager but steady paycheck. If there is a badger in me, I better dig in now that I have family responsibilities." Talking out loud, even in jest, began to confirm the decision he had made over the past week.

"Antonio, the wrangler I visited, did not add much to what we know about the assassination of Mr. Berrigan. I was better acquainted with the former Commissioner than either he or Mrs. Delgado, but Antonio was on the tail of the assassin within moments of the rifle blast. Of course, there must have been terrible confusion when teams spooked, wagons crashed together, and bystanders scrambled and screamed. Antonio questioned people till midnight. He knew the cattlemen on the streets, the cowboys and wranglers and such, but not the miners or the camp-following crowd. Nobody knew anything and the rest weren't talking," he said.

"His wife, Danielle, bravely related her story." Patrick flashed back, noting she had blushed to the roots of her hair. "Mr. Berrigan had been a good neighbor of her sister and sister's husband when she came West. He and his huge horse, Big Ben, assisted rounding up stock and hauling as needed. Berrigan's wife, or rather a young woman from California, lived with him but left suddenly after some months. All the neighbors, including Danielle and myself, were shocked. Outwardly Berrigan and Miss Patton seemed very much in love. Danielle stated that Mr. Berrigan had been devastated. She believed that he never recovered."

Harvard, slipping the notion in between Neva's chatter about the bird in the book that ate a snake, or the snake that ate the bird; she would have to turn the pages and find out for sure. Shelley had refilled Neva's cup of hot cocoa and left her own oatmeal untouched.

"This is too sudden, Patrick."

Patrick had not been reassuring, nor particularly forthcoming. Only after Neva went outside did he add, "I am sorry to stun you with the news."

"Stunned? How could you even think of leaving us? You know how I feel about your traveling. Going back East alone? Patrick, that is an affront to me and Neva and all it means for our marriage."

Patrick had not yet encountered Shelley's measured fury. An outburst, yes, but this cutting condemnation was unexpected. He gulped down further explanations.

"We must discuss this further, but right now I have to go to the office. There could be telegraphs from the Boston firm regarding arrangements. Truly, I hoped you would want me to become an attorney. I have found something I want to do, for both of us for the future, Shelley." It all sounded a little thin to Shelley, as if he had not thought through what it would mean to her. He had kept it a secret until today. Why?

They had loaded the buggy in silence. Patrick dropped Neva at the Norton home then took Shelley to the store for her morning shift. She avoided his usual hug and peck on the cheek. Now sitting on the stone wall, drained and too confused to think of organizing files, she faced a future alone, her marriage abruptly severed by distance, by unknowns that dimmed her vision yet fired her imagination. Away for a year to try Harvard Law School? What about Neva and me?

"Are you coming in?" Mr. Parker rattled his keys. "I left the heater well banked overnight to take the chill off this morning. This can be a dark, dank old place if it is not properly heated, even in summer. You are looking pale, Mrs. Colter. Is anything wrong?" Mr. Parker's gaze lingered a moment while he struggled to find the right key.

Shelley mumbled something and fled to the cubby hole that was the accounting office. She went through the usual routine. Light the kerosene lantern. Hang it overhead on a hook. Sharpen a pencil. Sweep mouse droppings from overnight. She fought her way through the next several hours in a trance. Only when Gertie appeared in her latest get-up, a girlish pink pinafore with a huge ruffled hemline did Shelley become conscious of the present. Gertie rummaged deep into a red and white stripped candy bag for flavor of the day, and inspected a blue saltwater taffy only to exchange it for a pink one that matched her outfit.

"Have you seen a ghost?"

"Gertie, come in here." Shelley scrambled to clear a chair behind the door. A shoebox of nuts and bolts spilled over on top of a case of ammunition. "Oh god, I will accidentally blow up this place someday with me in it. Sit down, sit down."

Gertie flounced into the seat, carelessly displaying her red stockings in broad daylight.

"Patrick is leaving me."

"No. Fickle men."

"No, I don't mean like that. He is going East to study for a year, but I suspect it will be two. I have been married for three months, now I will be an old maid. I am afraid he is not telling me everything. Is it about Neva? Me? I am terrified, Gertie. He first went off to Deer Lodge on business during our honeymoon, then recently hurried away for three days to see Antonio and Danielle. Lately he has been so preoccupied I just knew something was up. Have you heard anything?"

"If there was anything worth hearing I would have heard it, and if it was something bad you would be the first to know." Gertie fluffed up her skirts to scratch her leg. "I have ways of finding out. Any man in Butte would spill everything he knew if he were approached the right way."

Her assuredness grated on Shelley. "How would you know about my husband if I don't?" Tears crowded out a further retort. Gertie licked the sweet treat in unaccustomed deep thought.

"Antonio was foreman for the Taryntons. Your husband was terribly close to the Taryntons—"

"I know Antonio and Patrick were close friends with the Taryntons,"

Shelley snapped. "That is why we had the double wedding that no one consulted me about."

After a long pause, Gertie continued. "Danielle was a single woman rumored to favor Kent Berrigan, the Commissioner—"

"Stop, Gertie. He is dead and Danielle is married. How could you even begin to link them. It—it is sacrilegious."

"Do you want to hear this or not?" Gertie took her time selecting another treat. "Your husband is a lawyer—"

"Not yet. He will be. He must attend Harvard University and that is the whole problem."

"But he rushed off to secretly talk with Antonio."

"Gertie, that is unkind of you. You are hurting me today of all days when I have never been so upset in my whole life. I feel like my marriage is no longer a marriage but a storybook tale I imagined all along. In short, a nightmare. You may go now."

"I will go, but I am trying to tell you—Antonio came to the District the night of the murder."

Shelley's already stricken face became deathly white. Her hands fell helplessly into her lap.

"Not for the girls. He asked me like he asked every other girl if we knew anyone who would have a reason to shoot Mr. Berrigan."

Shelley was unaware when Gertie left or how long it was until Mr. Parker came in.

"The nuts and bolts, Mrs. Colter. We need to complete the inventory. I came in to get that case of rifle ammunition for a customer."

Shelley's arm raised of its own accord then fell under its weight. Mr. Parker paused. "Did I see Miss Meyer leave here? I am afraid she has distracted you. I will not have women from the bordello becoming nuisances in my store."

"No, please, Mr. Parker. In her own way, she can be strangely helpful. I will inventory the case of rifle shells."

Mr. Parker escaped from the unfathomable world of women, absently stroking his graying sideburns. The rest of the morning slid by while Shelley gathered and sorted myriads of nuts and bolts into separate small boxes. The trudge uphill to Walkerville at noon felt like a reprieve. Neva would keep her occupied the remainder of the day.

———————

The meandering cow path streets of Butte meant little to Patrick when he left Old Tornado and the buggy at a livery some distance from downtown. He used the precious time alone to clear his mind during his walk to the Bosworth firm. Shelley's curtains, her happy homemaker side and Neva's engrossment in studying the bird book told him one thing. Their lives had gone on after the double wedding; why not his?

At the office he had barely taken off his coat before Lucas spoke.

"I telegraphed my father regarding our discussion. I admit he was concerned about the palpable threat that has emerged on the heels of our inquiries into the Berrigan case. In fact, he encouraged you to remove yourself with all urgency from the vicinity. I took it upon myself to contact the University."

Patrick fumbled his way to his desk like a snow blind horse.

"I assume you have discussed this with your wife."

"Yes. I wish I could say the matter is resolved. At the moment we have yet to come to an understanding." This was as lawyerly language as he could muster concerning his personal affairs, given that Shelley had blown his arguments to pieces.

"I did not reveal to her that I had been threatened by a shady tramp on the street. That would have frightened her terribly. I merely stated the truth, that I wanted to attend Harvard to become qualified in the field of law."

"Between you and me, we will proceed on the premise that you need to go for your own safety. I hope that when the dust settles you will find this realizes one of your dreams, as well as that of your parents. Perhaps your wife will accept your decision in time."

For a youthful man dressed like an outsider and speaking in a wavy baritone, Lucas could be remarkably astute, a good thing, Patrick conceded, since I exposed marital distress between my wife and I. But I basically trust him and his omnipotent father located two thousand miles away.

"I sense more than a bit of the urgency myself. I will clear this up at home. My wife and I have yet to become adept as a team in double harness. I certainly do not want to do something I will be sorry for later."

Patrick wanted to flee, to pick up Shelley at her parents' home and try again to talk this through. He paced the hallways of the Silver Bow Building until his mind cleared, and he could focus on the work at his desk. Lucas was out when he left late in the day to collect his family in the buggy.

"I had a bad dream," Neva complained, climbing into Patrick's lap and rubbing her eyes with the back of her fist. He shot a glance at Shelley to see if she thought the same thing he did, that they had alarmed the child who now had night terrors. But she could not have known. He had not openly brought up the subject until this morning.

"You can tell me," he said. "When did you have a bad dream?"

"The bad dream came last night and it comes sometimes on other nights." She scrubbed harder on her eyes, making them red and blurry. She appeared to be either very tired or trying to erase the dreams. "A big thing like a ball of yarn spins through the window and hangs in the air right over my bed. I don't like it because the yarn comes unraveled, and I have to wind it back on again."

"That sounds like a very hard job. Do you get it wound up again?"

"I try and I try but it keeps coming undone." Neva ducked her head into Patrick's arms, her tiny body heaving with sobs. The effect of his decision became clearer for him immediately.

Shelley's nod meant she thought the same thing. They must prevent any kind of relapse for Neva. Infantile paralysis was a terrifying disease that struck the most vulnerable randomly and without warning. Neva had been very sick when she was stricken. The doctor had cautioned her family to keep her quiet as much as possible. She was a frail child.

After supper when they were sure Neva was sound asleep, Patrick and Shelley held each other as if the unraveling dream had forced a reconciliation of sorts.

"Shelley, none of us can live with the undercurrents of strain that we have tried to contain yet Neva has sensed," Patrick whispered. "I will go to Harvard University for one year. I will come home after the next spring session. We can lock up the cabin—"

He felt Shelley squirming to get out of his arms, thrusting him away when he tried to hold her close.

"I understand it will be hardest for you, dearest, but you and Neva will be safe with your parents just like you always were. I will not worry if you are both there."

Patrick faltered. The one-sided conversation was not going to reach a comfort level for either of them before he left. "I will be back before you know it," he added, words lost in her hair. He never asked, and therefore never knew Shelley's deepest feelings.

7
FATEFUL CHANGES

Patrick Colter's mind leapt far ahead of the fifteen mile an hour stagecoach, trying to imagine what Boston held for him. Lucas originally assumed he was a Butte native, but he had grown up in one of the teeming Irish immigrant sections of Boston. He recalled the smell of fish when he and Jackson worked alongside their father on a fishing boat. The twins' parents were strict Old Country Catholics and descendants of generations of Galway citizens who would not let the twins run wild with the ragamuffins in the narrow streets. Their modest Boston flat was now managed by Patrick's uncle while Patrick's parents were in Ireland caring for Mrs. Colter's aged parents.

There had been little time to make advance arrangements after Patrick made the difficult decision to go East, a forced choice that flew in the face of his recent marriage and commitment to care for little Neva. The jouncing stagecoach matched his turbulent thoughts. He would take a chance on renting the flat if his Uncle had not made other arrangements for it.

Next he must visit R. C. Bosworth & Son's firm to ascertain for himself that the financial support offered and accepted was in order. The firm's sponsorship, along with an earlier advance on his inheritance, would ease his financial worries. He had left considerable personal funds at Shelley's disposal. She had flared up, cutting him with a remark about the double wedding and her being single within three months. His provisions for her now felt like a token gesture of spousal responsibility.

83

His pleas for understanding had gone unheard: "I wish this were otherwise, Shelley, you have no idea how pained I am to leave you and Neva. Yet, I—I—am doing this for both of us."

She had not made it easy. He did not care to remember their leave-taking. In fact, Patrick wondered what she might do in retaliation, not that he thought Shelley would purposely want to hurt him, but she was strong minded. There was the matter of her getting involved in the statehood meetings, and also driving the horse and buggy when he was away. That was Shelley. He could not imagine what his wife would do next, bless her. She was not far removed from her sister, Neva, who exercised big ideas—Neva had begged a newsboy in the neighborhood to let her sell papers and get half the pay. She had squawked "*Butte Miner*" on the street corner until she was hoarse. Winifred found her and carried her home.

Patrick shifted from the new and admittedly perplexing relationships with the females he had left behind to dealing with his immediate plans. He would try to minimize grants from the Bosworth's in case a future partnership with Lucas failed to work out. He would continue his legal clerk position at the firm while he studied the law. He looked forward to eventually reading the law like Judge Kirschenbaum who had kindly remarked it had once been his burning desire, also.

The financial details churning in his head served to distract Patrick from images of Shelley and Neva, their wide blue eyes staring and scared when the stagecoach pulled away from them in Butte. Shelley held Neva high in her arms to wave until he could see them no longer; Shelley's own waving was confined to brief hand gestures around the child, her lips blowing a kiss.

"She is a strong woman. Stronger than I am in many ways," he mused, reflecting that her initial flare-up, rightly called restrained fury, had become a stoic acceptance. Finally, it was a brave send-off, for whose benefit he was unsure; Neva's, his, or her own. Thoughts blurred one into another like a collage, intertwining the recent newlyweds merged too soon into a family, then lost by an untimely separation.

I guess I always expected to marry. She faced life as a spinster caring for Neva. I doubt I would have given my life like that. I may have been protective of Jackson—he was ten minutes younger, ha! For now, Shelley will go on as before, though obviously crushed at the moment. I unexpectedly went down a new trail, not of husband, breadwinner nor comfort to my wife. I am going away as if I were still a single man. What I am doing to her, to us by choosing to study at Harvard?

Patrick heaved a sigh and slouched in the corner of the rattling stagecoach while it sliced through the Elkhorn Mountains toward Montana City, and then on to Prickly Pear stage stop near Helena, with its next stop at the Sieben ranch. After a change of horses and barely time for passengers to have supper, the coach barreled on into the night, a vast, starlit cocoon sheltering a ribbon of the Mullan Road leading to Fort Benton on the Upper Missouri. Passengers dozed beneath buffalo robes, a familiar experience to Patrick who had crisscrossed Montana Territory to and from Boston. Ranch owners hosted stage stops before and after Birdtail Divide, a geologic feature well-known to fur traders long before the Mullan Road was constructed.

Montana Territory had it all and the country knew it; Patrick knew it and envisioned his future back here in service to the justice system that underlay the wild and reckless capitalism in its glory and opportunism. Investors and their proponents basically owned the Territorial Legislature. Adequate representation for the citizenry was sorely needed. Statehood was a distant notion. The mining industry fought both sides of that issue, some for recognition and stature, notwithstanding the regulations that would come with it. Opponents undermined lofty goals, opting for the shady side of wheeling and dealing without much oversight. Patrick had already seen close at hand the unjust escape the law. Not to mention those still fighting the Civil War, both openly and subversively.

Miles past while Patrick was lost in his conjectures until he saw Square Butte, a towering flat-topped formation rising out of the plateau, a landmark defining eastern Montana Territory. Here the Sun River cut a winding swath through prairie grasslands. Sun River Crossing offered a speck of shade for a short break under tall cottonwoods along the river's cool green banks. Merchants benefited from traveler, rancher and Indian trade in the small town that provided a sturdy schoolhouse and other amenities to remote communities out of Fort Benton.

The Fort served as head of navigation up the Missouri River, not too distant from the Canadian border. The Missouri, channeled between steep earthen banks, became known as "the vast muddy river that would put weak coffee to shame by its color," according to flat boatman, Fred Bond, who plied those waters.

The stagecoach left passengers on the levee where Patrick boarded a departing steam-driven riverboat. Flowing with a low current this late in summer, the riverboat trip offered a gentle hiatus, half-way between one question mark in his life and another in Boston. What would happen to his newly-minted marriage? What would come of the threats that maybe he had taken too seriously and let them drive him away?

"I am trying to determine how to further my education in law while managing a family," he said to a passenger, when asked where he was going. "I find myself pulled both ways at times, which makes me question my choices." It was true, and disturbing.

Patrick disembarked at St. Louis, Missouri, and boarded a train for Boston, carrying him ever further from Shelley's bright, hand-sewn blue and yellow curtains and the homey feel in the cabin. Slicing his recent marriage into halves was the price he paid to one day "read the law." That much, and only that, was clear.

———————

The dog days of August drove even the hardiest women in-doors, yet Shelley clamored about the rocks and brush north of Butte in a desperate search for solitude. She had not seen Gertie since their last spat—and preferred not to.

She took alternate paths to and from the Norton home, skirting uptown by climbing the steep incline of Excelsior Street, passing not far beneath the Big Butte knob, circling back and forth to the Mercantile and home to Walkerville. Only on empty backstreets could she cry unobserved. Rutted roads and blades of wispy bunchgrass received teardrops she dared not shed in front of Neva or her parents. Moving back to her parent's home proved a bitter pill after establishing herself in the Colter cabin, a mercilessly too short a time to experience the joys and tedium of one's own home. The hot irons she used to press her husband's white shirts there had prompted a wry smile. Even they would be a welcome sight.

She found a lone juniper up Dublin Gulch that held her broken dreams, flashes of anger, and loads of humiliation in confidentiality. To Shelley, the now infamous double wedding dimmed with each passing day since Patrick's departure. Stumps of trees hewn for homes and mine timbers formed a landscape as bleak as her outlook. Today she lifted the dusty hem of her skirt to wipe her eyes, leaving dark stains on her cheeks when she left the Gulch and slipped behind the desk in the rear of the Mercantile.

"I need not ask. 'Parting is such sweet sorrow,' a line from Shakespeare's Juliet. So romantic." Gertie appeared for her usual sweet tooth treat.

"I feel as though I had one of Neva's bad dreams. A prince kissed me and I turned into a frog," Shelley grumbled.

Gertie laughed her low, companionable chuckle. "That is not the way the story ends. Go shopping. It makes a girl feel better."

"Gertie, that is not comforting. Are you suggesting I brush off my husband, my wedding, my first new home with a new hat? I never cared about shopping anyway." Shelley fluttered her fingers in goodbye to Gertie and delved into masses of shipping bills in front of her, a blessing to have an overload of work to keep her occupied. Freighters had delivered fourteen bales of miners' clothing, one hundred hickory-handled, double-sided pick axes, and a thousand or so miscellaneous items that needed to be inventoried.

Cleaning up the accounts several days later Shelley spotted a catalog at the bottom of the last crate. She left it on top of a pile for Mr. Parker, but not before flipping through the pages of women's fashions.

Shelley exchanged shifts with her mother, whose weary features appeared even longer and more strained than when Shelley left that morning for work at the Mercantile. Clearly, her daughter's upended marriage had taken a toll. Shelley felt she was to blame for hardships and worries inflicted upon her. On the contrary, John Norton's eyes brightened with the prospects of having a son-in-law "in the professions." Two years of concentrated law school were little to sacrifice for a lifetime of rewards earned by a professional status, he often said. Shelley did not reveal that Patrick agreed to a short course of study to pacify her.

Mr. Norton admitted his own status had been tarnished by mine owners terminating his mineral contracts due to sheer ignorance. His studies at the School of Mines in Colorado were generally considered the hottest reference a man could have west of the Mississippi, even west of the White House. Suppertime at the Nortons' was seldom without his treatise on the United States' demand for gold and silver, bedrock of its economy. And that he, John Norton, held a degree in geology and mineral analysis, ready to explore the nation's vast natural resources. As it was, John Norton watched it all with a tired but persistent interest from the sidelines.

"We may be scraping by now," John told Winnie and Shelley, "but there will come a day when Mr. Daly or another investor will acknowledge I was right about the wealth of copper beneath Butte. Surely rewards will follow when electricity extends beyond the street lights of Paris. You women may well hold your heads high. There will be better days for Neva, too."

"Don't worry, Papa. Patrick will help us out. I know he will," Shelley said, aware that her marriage had noticeably given him a spurt of his former vigor. He fixed sagging doors on their weathered frame house and constructed a shelter for firewood outside. At last he began wandering uptown again, conversing with miners, speculators, and hangers-on alike. The bounce in his step spoke volumes of encouragement to those in the household.

"Statehood is on everyone's lips," he reported at supper one night. "The *Butte Miner* reminds us that Nevada became a state in '64, thirteen years ago. Idaho and Utah have stonewalled it so far. Adequate representation beyond the biased Montana Territorial Legislature is sorely needed. State government would provide schools, maybe even one Neva could attend."

"A school for me, Papa?"

"Yes, love. You need to learn to read your Audubon Birds book." When she scampered off to find her book, he continued his monologue.

"Patrick would appreciate an adequate justice system. And statehood would likely bring leadership that would address the need for roads, bridges, and care of the poor. I don't know who would oppose those improvements over what we now have in the Territory."

His comments were largely lost in one cup of coffee after another, his audience often inattentive when he counted his chickens before they hatched. What was different this time was that he seemed to believe the rumors and speculation regarding statehood. He sensed a change was coming and became energized by it. Shelley hoped vindication for his unappreciated expertise would soon follow.

"I hope you are right, Papa," Shelley kissed the top of his head. "I have to read to Neva before she goes to bed."

The Audubon book felt real while the remainder of her life seemed as far removed as the mythical statehood and wheels of government that would do this or that. Shelley placed the giant book over her lap and Neva bent her head over the pages, her finger running over the meticulously painted illustrations. Neva described details she found with infinitely more comprehension than Shelley had at the moment.

By the end of the first week after Patrick's departure, Shelley felt the empty spaces closing in on her life. Patrick had been the one who told her she was beautiful and sunshiny, and that she enlivened his life.

I was soon spoiled on compliments, soon married and even sooner marooned in a mining camp while he sashayed off to Harvard. Shelley idly thumbed the pages of the fashion catalog she had found in Mr. Parker's last shipment. I almost wish Gertie would drop by the Mercantile. I regret being so harsh. She is often too forward, but I shouldn't have let it get to me.

A drawing of a tall, thin model in the fashion pages caught Shelley's eye. The model's impossibly tiny sixteen-inch waist set off a full bust and wide shoulders. She wore a high-crowned felt hat and a wool coat with covered buttons down the front. It looked trim and very smart over a dress of soft wool with a flared hemline. Shelley visualized it in blue, though the drawing was black on the pulpy white of the catalog pages.

The image stayed with her. Not the ridiculous waist, but the sense of elegance. The outfit appeared to flow with the graceful pose of the model. She imagined the woman striding purposefully toward an important public event. At church the next day her frayed cotton dress felt depressingly dowdy. By Monday she had decided to order the ensemble, complete with the extraordinarily dressy hat, one likely never seen in Butte and certainly one Shelley had never dreamed of. She added high-top, kid leather shoes with sturdy walking heels to the order, bypassing the fashionable pencil-shaped heels that signaled Gertie, not her.

Patrick had left money for her keep, funds to be drawn on his accounts "so I don't have to worry about my dear wife," he had said.

Shelley wrapped her plain winter coat closely around her and walked down Main and Park streets to and from the store. She kept the coat on inside as well, too embarrassed to reveal her old dresses to which she and everyone else in Butte had grown accustomed. Gertie failed to show up and neither did the order until six weeks later. A teamster braved easterly storms whipping from North Dakota to haul the last of the freight from a steamer docked at Fort Benton. From now on through winter the river would revert to being part of the formidable wilderness inhabiting the vast eastern portion of Montana Territory, along with bison, snow-white jackrabbits, and pronghorn antelope. Commerce would continue further south at the mouth of the Yellowstone, weather permitting.

The closing of Montana Territory's only port linked to the East mattered little to Shelley after she received her sizeable parcel from Dubuque, Iowa. Alone in the office, she almost felt Gertie's smug stare at her for shopping—and Gertie's shock at Shelley's uninhibited selections. Embarrassed again and feeling foolish, Shelley was unable to open the twine-tied box. She shoved it and the chair it rested upon behind the door.

Safely at home in her room away from prying eyes of her parents, Shelley let Neva open the carton as if it were Christmas. Inside, a high round hatbox nestled among yards and yards of kitten-soft material of the blue skirt of the dress. Fishing deeper, Neva nearly fell into the box, until she scrambled out with the pair of shoes that smelled of fine new leather.

"Oh, help me put these on."

Salvaging the kid leather from Neva's fist, Shelley suggested, "Let's see what else is in the box." Beginning to wonder if the long wool coat was missing, she rustled packing paper to find a large, flat package bearing the elegant calligraphy of Priscilla's

Fine Women's Wear. She set it on her lap and glanced up in time to see the hat box upturned and its contents sitting on Neva's head. Neva giggled when the hat slipped down to her eyebrows. Its firm rounded crown rose to a jaunty slant, accented by a variable width brim that sloped gently to the right. The headband, decorated with a single embroidered rose, was tied securely with loops of silvery ribbon.

"Neva, what are you doing? What am I doing—ordering for myself and not for you!" Shelley tumbled over on the floor, laughing amid tears. "You look ever so much better than I will in that silly hat."

"I want one like this," Neva announced, with no indication she would give up the one currently perched on her head.

"Come, let's open this big package. You will be surprised. It has buttons like huge gumdrops all the way down the front." Shelley managed to corral what could only be described as an uptown *chapeau* in the hat box until she could try it on later. "Let's remove the wrappings from the coat."

Shelley slipped it over her old dress before Neva trailed it over the dusty floor. The hand mirror on her dresser revealed only a portion of the coat at a time, but the overall effect from what Shelley could see was far beyond what she had expected—almost humiliatingly elegant. Padded shoulders enhanced her already athletic frame, the waist was ample for comfort, and the length perfect to accommodate her long stride. She turned aside, wiping her eyes and nose on several hankies with trembling hands.

"We had better go show Papa and Mama. What do you think, Neva?" Parading the garb would be easier amid Neva's antics. Explaining the extravagance was altogether another matter. She had settled the shipping bill with Mr. Parker as calmly as if she frequently shopped in Dubuque. His indulgent smile told her he approved of the purchase, though he witnessed only the outer parcel. He typically maintained a trace of formality despite

Butte's utter lack of it. As proprietor, he dressed in a gentleman's tweed coat, heavy wool vest, and matching trousers. Since Shelley was sequestered in the rear of the store, she rarely witnessed Mr. Parker's reactions to the few well-dressed ladies in town, nor to women of the line in their outlandish wear.

"Charlotte, honey, did Patrick send something?" Winnie glanced up from her cross stitching, then looked again. Her skin, aged by Nevada's intense heat, had made her appear older than her years, but the flickering light from candle lanterns brought out a sparkle in her eyes. The royal blue of the coat gleamed as well. Shelley slowly turned, the coat draping softly in the back.

"Papa, do you like it?" Shelley held her breath, feeling like a school girl, like the Shelley of a few months ago when Patrick knelt and said he wanted to marry her. John Norton's lips crinkled at the corners. It seemed like forever before he found the words.

"You are a credit to your husband."

Shelley flew to him and threw her arms around his neck. The tears came unbidden, not unnatural for a bride left behind.

"Shopping, are we?" Gertie's quick steps caught up with Shelley near the Mercantile.

"Oh, Gertie, where have you been? I wanted to show you ever so long. Do you like it? I have become quite accustomed to gussying up by now."

"*Sie sagen nicht!* You don't say. Your husband will not recognize you."

"That concerns me a little," Shelley laughed. "Get your walking shoes and meet me after work up Main past Daly's store so we can talk."

Work had ceased to be about filing dreadful shipping bills and inventorying countless identical men's long johns. The hours in the mousy office at the rear of the store were incidental to Shelley's blossoming personal and civic life.

"Gertie, let's take the long way behind Dublin Town and Meaderville and up the hill. I have so much to tell you. You know the statehood meeting we went to? That was first in a series that I have attended. Aside from the pros and cons of statehood, I discover what is happening in Butte and the whole country. I am so excited."

"The whole country, eh? I hear about efforts to promote abstinence from alcohol without leaving the, uh, house."

Shelley shook Gertie's arm. "Be serious."

"I am serious."

"Then let me tell you. I have no one to talk with except Miss Owens about current affairs. I have missed you, Gertie."

"You discuss things with Dr. Adelaide Owens, the midwife?"

"Yes. She is a highly educated woman's doctor. She objects strenuously that the medical profession tries to keep women physicians in their place. Miss Owens has the unenviable position of being considered second to Doctor Gallagher and her practice as only midwifery."

"Keeping women 'in their place' means America maintains an unacknowledged class system." Gertie's voice rose with an edge. "Yet it blatantly exists between men and women, the races, the poor, and a hierarchy of immigrants. Believe me, I know the difference between Fifth Avenue, New York, and Mercury Street, Montana Territory."

Shelley's limited knowledge of the wider world provided no argument against Gertie's assertions. She took up Miss Owens cause instead.

"Miss Owens prefers to rule her own roost with her Women's Clinic across the hall from Dr. Gallagher. I have had the good fortune to become acquainted with her."

"The girls see Dr. Gallagher when they have to. He is better'n no doctor at all, which was true when Butte was little more than a camp."

"Gertie, my understanding is that Miss Owens attended a Women's Medical College in Pennsylvania and received training equivalent to men, yet in residency at a hospital, male physicians refused to give her the respect men physicians receive. She is very bitter about it."

"So why are you so involved in women's causes? You go to work and earn your pay. Do you have higher aspirations now that you hobnob with Miss Owens, M.D.? I am not sure that women have many choices these days."

"Honestly, I would not be able to answer that, but you said you did not expect your life to –to—be like it is. I did not expect mine to change either until Patrick came along. Now that he is bettering himself I ought to do the same. I couldn't bear to think he might be disappointed with me when he comes home."

"What a difference a two months make. New husband and domestic responsibilities already on the shelf." Gertie's candid, and often insightful, comments again touched a nerve.

"Gertie, it's not that. I am so lonely without Patrick. I can cry my eyes out or fill my time going to meetings where something interesting is going on."

Gertie examined her painted fingernails and pursed her mouth. "What is interesting to you certainly is not interesting to me. Does it not seem amusing that a few ladies would try to get men off liquor in a mining town? It would destroy a lot of businesses in the country. Can you imagine Butte's sheriff and deputies enforcing temperance bans on alcohol. They would be all over the place with lanterns and billy clubs busting up stills and stockpiles while buying and selling bootleg themselves."

"That is not what I am talking about, Gertie. Just as absurd is the notion that if women gained the vote and achieved power out of the home it would make them masculine and men feminine."

"Do you believe that?"

"No, but I think men do. I heard men speak up at the meetings. Some sound terrified of women getting the vote."

"I doubt it will happen. Why worry about it?" Gertie had a way of dismissing inconvenient ideas.

"All the same, Miss Owens has been good to me. I think she is lonely, too. People seldom take kindly to her. She is a rather daunting presence and has very strong opinions."

"And that makes her masculine."

"That's not true. Why do you argue with me? Women like Miss Owens deserve the vote. She and other suffragettes will get us that much closer to it." Shelley sensed her voice had taken on a firm quality, perhaps reflecting Gertie's, or likely nudging her naïve, giggly self to move aside.

"So you have joined up with the liberals already?"

"Gertie, quit. You can be—be insensitive."

"I did not ask for a crusade, nor do I care to join one."

Shelley's strides matched her assertions until she outpaced her companion. "I am sorry. I truly do not understand why this is important to me. I guess for now it keeps my mind occupied."

For once Gertie did not reply. Shelley bit her lip and weakly waved when she turned toward the Norton home in Walkerville. Gertie continued her walk and contemplation up to the pinnacle fondly called Big Butte.

———

Shelley barely had time to shift from the uncomfortable exchange with Gertie before Neva ran limping and screaming out to meet her.

"Shelley, I want to go to the cabin and see Old Tornado. He is lonely and I left my dolls there."

"Whoa, pardner. Do you have a bee in your bonnet today? Let me make us a little dinner and we will talk about it. What did Mother say?"

"She said to ask you, and I am asking you, and I have ever so many more questions."

"Then we will have a very busy afternoon. Why are these newspapers all over the floor?"

"I am going to be a paper girl. See, I am folding Papa's old papers." Neva plunked herself on the floor to fold and tie facsimiles of artful *Butte Miner* bundles.

"Practicing is a good way for you to learn to tie your shoes, but I'm not sure you are ready to be a newsgirl. Paper boys get up in the middle of the night to go out on the street."

"Old Tornado will take me and my news bag." Neva left off speculating on transportation logistics to concentrate on the task before her.

Shelley laughed. Clearly Neva also needs something to occupy her mind. She must be lonely and missing Patrick—maybe as much or more than I.

"You had fun driving Old Tornado with Uncle Patrick. I miss the old horse, too, but he is safely far away at Mr. Delgado's ranch for the winter."

And I miss my always absent husband, a frequent silent postscript to Shelley's comments, but she dodged a trip down that futile avenue by firing up the cookstove. Soon the aroma of rosemary and thyme let her know the leftover venison stew was hot. She spooned two dishes full and buttered several warm biscuits, distracted by how to resolve her relationship with Miss Irmgarde Meyer.

Gertie makes me think, though she has become argumentative—or is it me? It is strangely satisfying to have her back in my life—Gertie of the hundred and one costumes; today a pair of men's overalls hidden beneath a floor-length dust coat, tomorrow likely a becoming yellow shawl over her curled hair. My mail order fashions are hopefully less conspicuous, Shelley chuckled.

Shelley's new outfit had opened a door to the world outside the Mercantile and the dreary routine she had fallen into since Patrick left. To her surprise, Miss Owens had been drawn to her fashionable appearance and invited her to a meeting.

Shelley had experienced a similar disbelief when Patrick proposed. "Marry me"? The words formed a reflecting pool: her image seen one way by herself, another by Patrick. She wondered what Miss Owens saw in her. Had she seen her as higher class, a new recruit for meetings, or perhaps a lonely woman not unlike herself?

The conjectures had become tiresome. Shelley knew deep down that she was Shelley, not someone else's preconceived notion of what a woman is or should be. She had not asked for much in life, nor did she have much to exploit. Miss Owens' personal story of being well qualified yet ostracized made a lasting impression on her.

The woman has spunk and she is articulate. Women I have known seldom talk about their situations in life, Shelley mused. Except Gertie. She talks about everything with a certain irony, her life honed by unsavory experiences. But I'm sure Gertie will rise above her circumstances. Perhaps we both seek "bettering our lives," the reason we find common ground, the reason we need each other.

Neva left her neatly packed paper bag and again pleaded her case while they ate stew. "I want to go to school, and I want to be a paper girl. My friend Jessica goes to school every day 'cept when she is sick. Papa says school would be too hard for me because I cannot walk, but I can walk. See." Neva gave her everyday version of a modified crab walk, one leg pulling the other after it. She beamed as if the problem were solved and broke into a lopsided trot around the table. In moments she collapsed out of breath.

Shelley scooped her up and sat down in the rocking chair. "Once upon a time—"

"There was a beautiful paper girl who flew over the town and dropped newspapers on people's houses, and she flew over the paper boys and dropped rain on their heads." Neva ended with a chorus of giggles, her hands cupped around her mouth to cover her glee.

She knows her limitations, Shelley reminded herself, and she is better at dealing with them in the faerie stories. Still, she shook her head. She and her mother and father were not the only ones concerned about Neva's future. Miss Owens had taken a particular interest in "your little girl with infantile paralysis."

"Oh, Miss Owens, she is not my daughter, though some people mistakenly think she is. She is my sister, one who came later in life to our parents. As a baby she became exceptionally attached to me. That attachment became even greater after her illness. My husband has practically adopted her since Neva often lives with us, or did until he went back East."

Since that day on the street Shelley had frequent discussions with Miss Owens about the difficulties facing Neva and other youngsters who were crippled. Their conversations were hardly limited to physical hardships, however. Miss Owens spoke of the poverty she witnessed daily in Butte, and the fact that amid such riches in minerals, most women and children fared badly. She expressed concern about the condition of every person's lungs above or below ground in town, and particularly of those less able.

"The air is dense with smoke spewed from heap roast smelters, burning piles of timber and ore right in the open. Sulphur from smoke rivals industries in Pittsburg," she often said. "I came from Philadelphia, but I find that Summit Valley shields the air from cleansing winds. The mix of smoke and chemicals is hazardous to respiratory systems of any age." However, she remained in Butte, providing services in her Women's Clinic and walking her little dog after hours.

For Shelley, it was easier to acknowledge insurmountable barriers to a decent life, such as the vast consumption of alcohol and poisonous air, than to accept that an insidious disease would attack and maim a small child. She could not bear to think of Neva being teased at school, or being called "a cripple" all her life.

Setting Neva gently down on her feet, Shelley said, "Sugar plum, you can draw pictures while I write to Uncle Patrick."

"I want to write a letter, too."

"You want to do a lot of things, Neva. I wonder if all these came true at once, what would you do?"

"They will never come true. I wait and wait and they don't come true. Maybe I will write the ABC's." She perked up and ran for a piece of broken slate and dab of chalk to demonstrate her proficiency.

"Neva, I believe you will write letters to your family and friends someday. That is a lovely alphabet to G. Let's go to N for Neva." The two blonde heads bent over the slate, the handwriting magically appearing and disappearing under a rag until the letters stood at attention in a zigzag row around its contours. The handwriting kept Neva busy until naptime.

With a few moments to herself, Shelley's handwriting flowed over pages and pages of happenings with Neva. Her news from home to Patrick reveling in homespun stories did not mention Gertie or Miss Owens or her fashionable outfit.

8
RESCUE

In the summer of 1878, a steady flow of travelers passed through a stage station at one of Granville Stuart's ranches on the Big Hole River, midway between Dillon and Twin Bridges. Seasonal traders came there to offer cookware, needles, horse medicine, and heavy boots that travelers and locals would only find in distant general stores. However, Mac Tarynton and Jackson Colter pushed on through the trading post towards Iron Rod and Silver Star, where saloons attracted miners from the Green Campbell and Broadway mines. After a brief rest for their horses, the riders hurried on to meet Antonio Delgado at the Cedar Ridge stage stop who had ridden from the other direction.

"We don't know for sure that Shelley and Neva are in immediate danger," Jackson had insisted when the men discussed plans to rescue Patrick's family. "Maybe it's more in my mind than in reality." But his intuition nagged him—he was a twin and he had a sixth sense about anything associated with Patrick. He knew Patrick had been involved in the investigation of the Berrigan case. And any risk threatening Patrick's family gave him chills.

That sense of urgency allowed the riders only a brief holdover at Highland City to feed and rest their horses. The men gathered at the boarding house for a supper of potato soup with ham and fresh baked bread then rode on into the night. Slivers of moonlight between layers of heavy clouds and dense pines lit their way over the Continental Divide and across the valley to the Colter cabin that lay dark and deserted under the night sky. Stark shadows of corral poles divided the empty corral into geometric shapes. Old Tornado and Patrick's saddle horse were long gone, pastured at Antonio's place out of Willow Creek.

Patrick's clothes still hung in the wardrobe, Shelley's quilting pieces lay in a basket and Neva's dolls were tucked in her bed. The men lit candles, trimmed the wick in the kerosene lantern, and swiped dust from the table and stove tops.

"Looks like the place is waitin' for the family to come back." Jackson's voice wavered, his grim remark signaling that may not happen soon. Mac sipped a cup of cocoa and Antonio stepped out for a smoke, all too exhausted for small talk. Three bedrolls hit the floor out of respect for the newly married couple's four-poster bed that had not seen occupants for months.

"It's been bothering me that if Lucas takes on high risk cases after Patrick was threatened, the low life who threatened him might try something else."

The other men had picked up on the urgency, the absolute horror of the assassination still fresh a year later. Any threat was a wakeup call to get the hell out of there. Mac had done that; he got the message and moved to Madison County. Antonio, homesteading a good seventy miles east of the new Tarynton ranch, had heard that Mac and Jackson were going to Butte for a few days. Anytime his former boss and benefactor, Mac Tarynton, went to Butte, Antonio felt obliged to cover him. Wild horses—even a new wife, couldn't have made it any other way.

Jackson had ram-rodded the rescue party since he felt the same way about his twin's family. "I appreciate you men comin' with me, more than you know. Antonio, how was your wife about the idea of Shelley and Neva living with you folks for awhile?"

"She say she be worried sick I'd come to harm in Butte. But having a little girl around the place would be nice. Maybe a bit of a challenge since the child is not real strong, she said."

Jackson suspected Antonio wasn't disclosing everything, but apparently Danielle did not question him, or his part in the scheme.

"A lot of water's gone under the bridge among the three of us," Jackson recalled. His mind kept unwinding until near dawn. He and Patrick had come to Butte in '74 with high ambitions for prospecting after Norwegian Creek and Sterling placer claims dried up. Silver Bow, rich in placer gold around Rocker west of town and in German Gulch to the south, were also short-lived. That left the twins a choice of hardrock mining below ground or cutting logs for mine timbers and firewood on the East Ridge. Jackson proved to be least squeamish about dropping underground into the often 90 to 100 degree temperatures of dusty tunnels extending every which way. He had to smile at the contrasts. Patrick could cut wood all day and still sit on a barstool in the Hound and Hare Pub with Danish woodcutters for half the night.

Jackson turned over, "Threats make a man stir crazy."

Lucas Bosworth in the Butte law office had been keeping the firm's headquarters in Boston apprised of happenings in Butte. Therefore, his father, Reuben, had his finger on the pulse of affairs in Montana Territory. Patrick was employed by Reuben, who often consulted with Patrick about relevant issues in the West.

Recent Butte news had signaled alarms for Jackson, Mac and Antonio. An upcoming regional Commissioners meeting would deal primarily with three pressing issues: the startling influx of workers attracted to jobs in the flourishing silver mines and prospective copper mines; the conflicts between investors in the largest cattle operations that usurped prime grazing land in the Elkhorns and smaller ranchers who were being edged out; and the issue linked to the assassination a year ago, the acidic red, yellow and green oxidized minerals in creek water had become unfit for human or animal consumption around Butte.

"It's a powder keg," Jackson moaned and sat up. As a miner he well knew the connotations of that term. Folks on both sides of every issue felt above the law. It was no secret Daly, Clark and others had attorneys and well-lobbied legislators to protect their interests. The Territory was ripe for the plucking, and Butte was the largest plum hanging from the tree.

"Despite Patrick's faith in justice, there ain't much here to speak of," Jackson swore and slipped outside. He wandered over to the horse corral that he and Patrick had built. The moon, slanting from western skies, cast long shadows over the empty space where the Connemara stallion had recovered from severe weed poisoning or unknown cause to become a sought after stud, a money-maker for Jackson, Nettie and little Tucker Colter. Jackson propped his arms on the top corral pole, half asleep until Antonio came out.

"I thought we had it made, Patrick and me. Out of here and married with good women and kids to take care of. You with Danielle and your own ranch. I don't want to throw it all to hell by getting' mixed up in Butte's affairs again."

Antonio shuffled and blew steam through cold lips in the chilly September dawn. True to his nature, he kept his thoughts inside. They were riding to town to pick up Charlotte and Neva. If Patrick's family was in danger, that was all he needed to know. A sharp breeze from the west swiped his hat from his brow. He separated it from tumbleweeds jammed against the unused fences. Jackson turned back to the house to brew coffee, his steps as heavy as his heart.

Antonio whistled for the horses in the pasture and tied them up for an early departure. Mac was the last to rouse, growling that his bad leg made him a one-legged banty rooster, unable to get up off the floor.

"Souvenir of the Sioux never lets me forget." The shot to his left thigh during an Indian raid of his livestock left him with a limp and difficulty inserting that leg into a pant leg. The task took stamina that the other men didn't care to observe, only a shared nod between them that Mac could still out man and out ride both of them put together.

Mac had insisted that he come when he heard the scheme to sneak Jackson's family out of Butte. "We're in this together, men. I haven't changed my mind about the devils who likely shot Berrigan for speaking out. What goes on behind the scenes in town scares the hell out of me."

"I best telegraph Patrick before we uproot his wife and child," Jackson cautioned, when they neared the Bosworth office. "I wonder if I been hasty barnstormin' into town on a rescue mission. I'd feel like a darn fool if we ain't needed."

He knew Lucas' father Reuben was a proud and possessive father who looked out for Lucas, albeit at a distance. He evidently felt the same about Patrick, his legal assistant, and his family that was left behind.

They soon arrived at the imposing Silver Bow Building housing the law office only to find it cordoned off and a sentry on watch. Jackson and Mac drew up their horses in the street. Antonio flanked Mac, his pistol in hand.

"Who are ye lookin' for?" A thick brogue challenged the newcomers. "It's all over now. Yes siree, there was a shootin' last night. Not the first one in Butte, begorra, nor the last. Ye're lookin' for that lawyer lad, ye gotta go to Doc Gallagher's. I'd take ye, but I'm on guard."

The men were gone before the words rolled off the sentry's tongue. Jackson warned, "I'll go on alone. Now you two git outta sight or I ain't leavin' you."

Mac pulled his horse into a blacksmith shop that was opening for the day as if his horse needed new shoes. Antonio slipped behind the shop and tied up his mount. He took off on foot.

Jackson galloped up the empty streets and bounded out of the saddle in front of the building he knew so well, the one housing Dr. Isaac Gallagher's clinic. He had called on Doc more than once after Mac had been shot. He swung through the unlocked front door and entered the dark lobby. Lights in the clinic meant Lucas was likely inside, dead or alive. Jackson braced for the worst and followed Dr. Gallagher's voice into a well-lit operating room.

The doctor hovered over a long thin form on the examination table. Not much was moving from either party, but Jackson could see the sheet rising and falling. He felt his own blood leap in his otherwise exhausted body—thank God he's alive, and thank you, Lord, it's not Patrick. With that thought he sank against the wall, his hands trembling, his vision misted with tears.

"You looking for Lucas Bosworth? We haven't had anybody come in to claim the victim. He's been here since about ten o'clock last night."

"My brother Patrick worked for him."

"It's a good thing someone found him or he would have bled to death. A street woman came straight to me. Said a man was shot dead by the Montana Territorial Bank building. I got the sheriff and a couple guys to haul him in here. He was darn near gone, but young as he is, he will likely recover."

Dr. Gallagher wiped his brow on the arm of his white coat. "Two bullets, one high that exited just under the shoulder blades. Another low that tore up a hip but missed the vitals. The woman said shots came from a wagon."

Candles burned down as first light filtered through the office curtains. Lucas' breathing smoothed into a steady, though wracked rhythm. Jackson's stomach turned with the smell of ether in the room. Relieved when Doc motioned him out, he said, "Mac, Antonio, and my brother Patrick need to know. Hell, where do I start to notify family?"

"Sheriff Ford likely found information in the Bosworth office as to whereabouts of family. I suppose he has telegraphed them by now."

"I'll send a telegraph to Patrick. It'd be a shock to him to hear from anyone else. I'll let him know we're taking his family out of town." Jackson almost revealed that Patrick had been a target of a threat earlier, that he suddenly left town for fear of his life, but for some reason he kept that to himself. Time enough for whys and wherefores later.

"Thanks, Doc. You've been awful good to my friends and now to Patrick's. We'll do right by you for gettin' you up in the middle of the night so often," he grinned. Dr. Gallagher waved him away.

Miners made their way on and off work all over Butte when shift whistles reverberated against mountain sides. Ore cars, loaded overnight, rattled down the road through town to smelters on the flats, or west to Rocker by the nearly abandoned Silver Bow City. The normal hustle reduced but did not erase Jackson's sense of unease. He walked his horse, keeping it between him and any cluster of unknown wagons or teamsters. He met up with Antonio and Mac at a coffee house near the blacksmith shop.

"He'll live."

Mac ground his teeth around a toothpick. He was deathly pale and looked as though he hadn't eaten for days. "We better order up some hash browns and bacon. Double orders," Jackson told the waiter.

Antonio wasn't volunteering any conversation. They stirred their coffee while Jackson relayed what he knew about Lucas' condition. Not wanting to conjure up any motives or speculate about a shooter, they talked a bit about the expansion of Butte since they had moved away. The headframe of the Alice had a string of lights and bells all the way to the top, powered by steam engines used in the mine. The Lexington and Anaconda headframes silhouetted toward the east were familiar, but a host of new stacks indicated a swarm of mines clustered on The Hill, clearly a response to the rising value of copper.

They were halfway through their hash browns before Antonio sat back and told Jackson they better *vamoose* right after breakfast. "They told me in every saloon in town the same story. Butte won't slow down to look for shooters of do-gooders like a city lawyer, *bien sabe*."

Jackson jerked a glance at Mac. Saw him shudder. The murder of Kent Berrigan was on everyone's mind. "Who—?"

"I didn't git names but most folks suspect Lucas Bosworth got in the way of somebody with money."

"Hell, this won't even be investigated. I doubt the Berrigan case ever did either," Mac sighed.

Jackson didn't want to burden the older man with any more troubles—that Lucas had opened the cold case and Patrick had been assigned to it. Also, that Patrick had a personal interest, maybe an obsession, in securing justice after Berrigan's death.

"Let's git," he said.

It was barely daylight. Mac and Antonio headed back to the cabin to grease Patrick's old buggy wheels. Jackson galloped uphill to Walkerville to round up two unsuspecting passengers for the sixty-mile trip to Willow Creek.

Doc Gallagher caught a few winks in the clinic before his patient stirred. He pulled the window curtains aside to get a better look. Lucas was still alive. Doc exhaled a mix of relief and fatigue. Straps lashed the young man down while he came around after suffering two close-up high-powered rifle wounds, shots not intended to leave a victim alive. Early intervention and a tough constitution despite a slim frame likely brought Lucas through the night. Immobility served to stop the blood flow. The question now was how to move him from the rock-hard exam table yet maintain the little progress they had made.

"We need a few stout men, but Lucas' friends are high-tailing it out of town if they know what's good for them," he said to Miss Owens. "We will have to do the job, if you will kindly give me a hand."

Miss Owens had come in early to her clinic. The sheriff would be along in his own time. Doc and Adelaide slid Lucas to a firm cot on one side of the exam table that could be moved later. Doc stepped outside and signaled a newsboy to get some breakfast for him, and a bowl of soup for the patient. The child's allegiance to the newspaper boss man shifted immediately. Doc amply rewarded the boys for running errands, as well as treating their medical emergencies at one time or another free of charge.

By eight o'clock Lucas' eyes opened. He stared steadily at the carved, tin paneled ceiling. Doc leaned close to hear anything intelligible from his lips. "East side gangs—rough up," then some names that sounded like gang members'—"take out pigeons—run like harbor rats." Jackson Colter had mentioned the Boston Bosworths, so the rambling intermittent stream of consciousness likely related to flashbacks and gang fights there.

Dr. Gallagher went about seeing patients in the front room of the clinic until noon. As expected the friends did not return, but a telegraph arrived from Reuben Bosworth, Esq.

"Coming next train."

Eastern railroads extended to Salt Lake City, but would not reach Butte for four more years. Lucas' father could board a stagecoach in Salt Lake for Butte, subject to weather and availability. He would arrive in two weeks at best, a challenge Dr. Gallagher did not fail to note, considering the scourges of infection, blood loss, and other complications his patient may suffer. However, Doc snoozed in his chair over dinner hour before opening his doors again in the afternoon.

Miss Owens was the first to come in. "When you get a moment, Doctor," she said, then went across the hall to her suite of offices.

Doc Gallagher trailed her over there. "What is more pressing than the miner's lung sitting in my waiting room? Rest in decent surroundings would be a blessing for the poor guy. From Wales, I'd guess. Likely sick as a dog before he even arrived in Butte."

Miss Owens' usual studied deference to the respected physician dissolved in her eagerness to talk. "How is the nice young man from Boston? I have been on edge, but I have not seen the hearse wagon drive up."

"It is one of God's wonders that it hasn't. What do you know of the case?" Doc knew she would not have called him over for a tea party. Never had, likely never would. She was a hard woman once she felt slighted, though Doc swore he had nothing to do with attitudes in Philadelphia that put down women physicians.

"Mr. Lucas Bosworth had the misfortune, or rather made the mistake, of investigating the Kent Berrigan assassination. Evidently he nearly paid for it with his life," she said.

"You have this on good authority?"

"Yes. No. From a report, let's say, from a reliable source."

"The District woman with the red stockings?"

She nodded, adding, "You get around fast, Doctor, er, I mean news gets around fast."

"The woman, Miss Meyer, found the victim last night and rushed to get me. He owes her a big debt of gratitude if you ask me."

"What I know is that she is friends with Mrs. Patrick Colter. To make the story short, and Miss Irmgarde can talk a leg off, Lucas Bosworth sent Mr. Patrick Colter away to Harvard. His wife thinks they feared retaliation for reopening the assassination case."

"Maybe Lucas ought to have taken his own advice. He is young and a newcomer to Butte. This town doesn't like upstarts, especially those instigating investigations linked to local citizens.

"He may be naive, Doctor, but he has courage and the decency to seek justice," Miss Owens persisted. "A good many citizens held the Commissioner, Kent Berrigan, in high regard."

"Well, I better go and save Lucas Bosworth for another day. His father is on the way here from Boston. Anything else?"

"Miss Irmgarde intended to alert Patrick's wife and her family about the incident. They will be terribly alarmed and just sick about Lucas being shot. I agree with her that they may be in danger."

"I suspect she has already been evacuated. Jackson Colter had a head of steam up when he left my office last night. No doubt those twins have some kind of sixth sense about each other."

"I am awfully glad to hear it, Doctor. I have become very fond of Mrs. Colter. She is a remarkably brave and intelligent woman. You may be aware she has basically dedicated her life to care for her sister, the little one crippled by paralysis. I wonder what will happen to the child in the midst of all of this."

"You have a most sympathetic side, Miss Owens. I am happy to make its acquaintance. Good day." Doc hurried back across the hall and put his closed sign in the front window before he went in to check Lucas and examine the miner with black lung.

Jackson sent his horse to the cabin with Mac and Antonio who galloped back to fetch Patrick's buggy. He walked up Main Street to Walkerville and found Shelley and Neva already packed and waiting at the front door of the Norton home. A huge lump rose in his throat when he held Patrick's family in his arms, shielding the tears he felt like shedding. John Norton, stooped and worn, hung back, appearing helpless in the face of unknowns.

Neva spoke first. "Gertie told us to leave. She ran all the way up here to tell us."

"Gertie? Oh, Miss Irmgarde has been here already? She's a saint. We will have the buggy here in no time. I will take you away."

"May I drive?" Neva's expectant face broke the tension.

"I'll drive you like the wind, sweetie. Now tie on your bonnet for a real buggy ride."

Shelley had not said a word. She shoved Jackson inside the house, ostensibly to talk with Papa, but Jackson realized she was watching his back while she glanced down the road for the buggy, their ticket to safety.

Helluva way to tear up this family, but through an exchange of telegraphs, Patrick had given his blessing to remove the family from Butte.

"Patrick will come as soon as he can get here," he assured the wide-eyed group, and patted Neva on the back. "Doc says Mr. Bosworth will recover. It's a sad day in Butte when good citizens on the right side of the law get shot."

He wished he hadn't said the last part in front of Neva when Shelley flashed him a warning. His knees almost sagged as they had when he saw Lucas near death on the operating table. Too much was riding on this rescue to mess up. *This was for Patrick. And our families.*

The buggy rattling up the road brought everyone to the window. A sturdy man in a miner's fedora and dirt-stained coat drove an unruly horse to a halt in front of the frame house. Jackson had to laugh. It was Antonio wearing Patrick's old mining garb and driving Jackson's saddle horse.

"All aboard, folks, afore my horse decides he doesn't like pullin' a buggy." Jackson smiled at Neva who had her thumb in her mouth and clung to Shelley. The child did not look reassured. Shelley had yet to say a word.

"I made Mac swear he'd stay put in the cabin while I was gone," Antonio said. "He'll be ready by the time we git back."

Jackson did, indeed, drive like the wind back to the cabin. The horse steadied somewhat with the weight of four people and a trunk in the buggy.

Cleared land was spotty among the reaches of greasewood, sage and rabbit brush claiming the rambling foothills above the Jefferson River northwest of Willow Creek. In 1867, a U.S. survey established a meridian line starting at Willow Creek for measuring sections and homestead allotments of 160 acres, and town lots. Prior to the survey, all Federal lands claimed or homesteaded were occupied by "squatters" for lack of official property boundaries. Afterward, land was quickly settled in rich, arable river bottoms east and west of the Headwaters of the Missouri.

Antonio claimed land that extended north from the Jefferson River to limestone cliffs abutting Milligan Canyon that opened to dry foothills over the ridge. He soon expanded his ranch by buying out settlers who moved on to the Willamette Valley in Oregon Territory or to the Yakima Valley in the Northwest. The view from his place framed the river in endless stands of cottonwoods. Great horned owls' haunting "whoo-whoo" drifted from dead branches. Whitetail deer slipped in and out of the shadows at dawn and dusk, their tails bobbing like white flags at the first hint of alarm.

The Delgado place made a splash of newly peeled logs and fresh-cut lumber where Antonio built a new cabin and rambling corrals. After their lightning-fast rescue Shelley wandered around Antonio and Danielle's home appearing shell shocked. She slid into a melancholy, becoming more detached each day, seemingly unaware that days had passed or that Danielle had taken over Neva's care, with the help of her baby goats. Shelley rarely ate or visited. Her cotton dress hung loosely over her gaunt frame, her unwashed hair slipped from its pins in tangles along her neckline. Day and night she walked the foothills above the ranch. A cascade of stars encircled three mountain ranges, the Bridgers, Gallatins and Tobacco Roots. The Big Dipper hung low above the horizon, while the bright North Star tripped across the sky with the Little Dipper.

"Do you think they woulda' been better off staying with Jackson, Nettie and their son?" Antonio asked Danielle one morning when Shelley failed to appear for breakfast. "I wonder if we made the right decision to bring 'em here."

"Nettie surely has her hands full with little Tucker and farm chores. I doubt she could manage Neva, not that Neva is a chore, but their house is less finished than ours." The plan had evolved among the men that the Delgados keep Shelley and Neva for an undetermined length of time. Their parents elected to stay in Butte since John Norton had secured a position as geologist with one of the mines.

Danielle's complacency with a houseful of unplanned guests surprised Antonio, given her former distant character. The double wedding had resolved many things, foremost that Patrick had urged him to overcome the war widow's fear of marrying again. From there, they took it slowly, always aware they were in their thirties, not impulsive youngsters. So far it appeared to Antonio that his marriage had worked out better than Patrick's.

"I worried myself half to death when you went to rescue them. I understand how she feels being abandoned. I keep telling her time will go by and he will be back."

"You have the wisdom of grandmothers and the patience of *Madre Maria*," Antonio told her. "I'm lucky as hell to have you, Danielle. You women carry on as best you can and I'll stay out of it." The compliment was about as high as they came from the wrangler.

Days were getting shorter as summer neared the autumn equinox. Early dark evenings and later dawns meant long nights for mischief if any arose. Antonio had not told Danielle he had rigged the disguise of a miner in order to safely escort Jackson, Shelley and Neva out of Butte.

9
INTRIGUE

Isaac Gallagher kept his patient in the clinic for several weeks until danger of relapse and infection had lessened. Doc had come to respect Lucas Bosworth for his physical tenacity and idealism. The man had resilience to make a comeback after a direct hit with two rifle slugs. Spilling a good portion of his blood on Butte's street said a lot more for him than Sheriff Bill Ford's entire tenure could claim for cleaning up Butte. Doc's practice limited his exposure to fissures in the silver boomtown to that of patching up the living and pronouncing the dead. Notably, the dead included Mr. Kent Berrigan, last year's newly elected member of the Regional Territorial Commission. He knew the unsolved murder rankled the attorney. Bosworth's intervention likely led to the attempt on his life. Sheriff Ford had not been overly keen on investigating this latest violence either, judging from the single brief interview he'd had with Lucas.

Doc wrapped Lucas' right arm across his body, immobilizing the shoulder to protect the wound. Lucas could put weight on his right leg and balance with the help of a cane. The shattered portion of his hipbone meant he would never walk normally again, but with time he could get around. Judge Kirschenbaum made it his duty to regularly stop by the clinic to share a nightcap with the patient.

"You are biasing yourself in the eyes of the citizens, aren't you?" Lucas warned, "This town talks, you know."

115

"And the citizens can rightly go to hell with their yammering. There isn't a one of them above the law. I dole out justice without a second thought." The judge appropriated Doc's chair as usual and commenced to fill the room with smoke.

Lucas chuckled. "I appreciate your visiting more than I can express." He lifted his glass. "It takes my mind and the edge off the pain and makes time go faster. Weather permitting, my father ought to arrive soon. He sent a telegram from Kansas City. We do not have a plan yet about the law office."

The judge's chest heaved with the weight of his body and the years. "I saw a good deal as a young attorney myself, and it is only by luck and by the grace of God I have been privileged to live out my days on the bench. I cannot advise you, son. My sense of the brew out there is that Daly and Clark are fighting for the same orbit and only one can win, not that they would stoop to murder, mind you. But they are moving pieces around as if Butte were a chessboard. Sacrifices large and small mean very little to either of them."

"It sounds as though our law office ought to exercise due caution if we reopen. I am concerned that people will have forgotten it if we don't resume taking cases fairly soon."

"It's folks like Doc and Miss Owens and you who build decent communities, but you are paying for your efforts. I hope it doesn't cost you a leg."

Lucas grimaced. Any slight movement sent stabs of pain through his system.

The judge continued. "There is fortune enough in the hell holes of the mines for half the country to live well, but the capitalists duke it out for themselves." He pulled out a handkerchief and wiped bits of tobacco leaf from his moist lips.

"I expect to run into the devil's dilemma whether I open the office or close it up and skedaddle out of here," Lucas concluded. He reached for his wounded leg with one hand and winced with the effort it took to heft it into a more comfortable position. "The skedaddling will have to wait," he grinned.

Judge Kirschenbaum shifted in the chair and grappled beneath it for his cane. "As far as maintaining legal or medical businesses go, you may have noticed that Doc Gallagher treats ninety percent of his patients for free or darn near free. And I see welfare cases that would make the granite on the Divide cry."

There didn't seem to be anything more to say. His shuffling footsteps followed the steady tapping out the door and down the street. Judge Kirschenbaum left a mood in the clinic that reflected his heavy breathing and prophetic outlook.

In 1869, transportation binding eastern states with remote territories in the West underwent rapid transformation with the connection of the Union Pacific and Central railroads at Promontory, Utah. Motivation to extend rails from St. Louis, Missouri, likely had more to do with subduing Native tribes and fighting Mexican border wars than the humanitarian needs of the citizenry. The U.S. military constructed the Mullan road for expansionist purposes, and the days of tedious, time consuming travel by covered wagons gradually came to an end.

Unfortunately, Butte had yet to gain a Mullan Road, or a Utah and Northern rail line, largely due to its inaccessibility in the uppermost reaches of the Rocky Mountain range. However, a determined and well-heeled traveler could make good time by catching stagecoaches into Butte. Reuben Bosworth, Esq. begged, borrowed or bought the fastest means of travel to reach his wounded son.

He sweat out his alternating rage, impatience and downright fear while he covered the distance from Boston to Butte. The Territory sounded as if it had gone berserk since respectable men, innocent of all wrong-doing, were shot down on the streets. In Butte he went to the clinic before registering at the Continental Hotel, hoping to arouse someone, anyone, to inform him about Lucas.

He hammered on the door with his fist. "Bosworth here."

Halting footsteps made their way to the door. Lucas unlocked it. His father stood tall and erect for a man of sixty, powerful even in the glimmer of the street corner lantern. Lucas' nightshirt whipped above his knees by a stiff breeze coming through the open door.

Reuben saw at once that his son had no free hand to shake, nor arms free for hugging. Lucas balanced carefully on a cane, the other arm strapped down.

"You are on your feet, son. I am proud of you." All the relief, grief and love he felt shaped the words he could say, and stopped up words he could not express. He leaned against the door and wiped tears on his coat sleeve.

Lucas two-stepped back to the Army cot that had been his bed in the clinic since he had graduated from intensive care. He motioned to Doc's chair, vacated so recently by Judge Kirschenbaum.

"If you could light the candle over there." Lucas eased himself down on the edge of the cot and drew a blanket over his bare legs, his voice weak, as if opening the door had cost him his breath and an elevated heartbeat.

Rueben noticed how white Lucas' legs were beneath his nightshirt. He feared blood loss had set his son's health back indefinitely.

"I am thankful you are here, Father. You cannot know how I have longed to see you." Lucas caught a few breaths. "I have had good care. Dr. Gallagher received his medical training in Philadelphia. And Judge Kirschenbaum pays a nightly visit to cheer me up. Bless him. I have good friends here." He did not mention the woman from the District who saved his life. That would come later.

Traveling two thousand miles across country had allowed Reuben Bosworth plenty of time to decide upon the best course of action for his son and the Bosworth law office in Montana Territory.

"You have done well, son, and I will be forever grateful for Doctor Gallagher's competence." He paused. It seemed untimely to burst out with his plans, but he could hardly contain himself. "Thank God you appear to be recovering, Lucas. Your mother is on the edge of a breakdown. I will telegraph her first thing in the morning."

Lucas' deep, soulful sigh betrayed a sense of guilt for having been shot. Reuben's rage surfaced, despite the late night, his fatigue, and Lucas' delicate condition.

"This violence is senseless, Lucas, you know that. Butte does not deserve professional legal services from the East. I plan to take you home to Boston for recuperation. This town has proven to be untamable." Reuben's fury drained—he knew he had upset his son.

Lucas swayed, from both the judge's nightcap and a strenuous effort to attend to his father's scathing words. Lurching back and forth on the cot, Lucas caught himself and laid down before his father reached his side.

"Lucas, son. I am being hasty. Forget what I said and get well. Your mother and I, we only want the best for you. That may mean sending you by hospital ship, if necessary, back to Boston."

Lucas' wan smile was answer enough.

Reuben knew immediately that plan was ridiculous. Butte was about as far inland as one could get from a hospital ship. Reuben Bosworth's mind went blank. All the weary miles and worry had drawn his fine features into a lengthy, haggard appearance.

"I am sorry, Papa." Lucas unconsciously reverted to the childhood name. He slumped further under the blankets, unable to hold his father's gaze.

Doc ambled into the room holding a candle in front of his nightshirt. He peered from one man to the other. "You look very much alike."

Before the attempted murder, Lucas had been tall and slim with wide shoulders and a determined jaw like Reuben's. Their light eyes were deep set and serious. It was the attitude that marked the similarity of father and son, chins slightly raised, confident, thoughtful miens indicating character.

Doc nodded to Mr. Bosworth and immediately grasped the impasse. Mr. Bosworth was in shock. No wonder. His son had barely survived the ambush.

"It's time you folks get some sleep. You will have plenty of time to chat in the morning. I will ring for Paddy to walk you to your hotel." Without waiting for a reply, Doc went to the door and jingled a small silver bell.

Reuben followed, whispering hoarsely, "Frankly, the horrors of this town terrify me. Just being here makes me feel like someone's target. I realize now that Lucas was not safe here, regardless how highly he praised Butte and the Territory."

Edging closer to Dr. Gallagher's ear, he said, "If my son gets out of your clinic, the next shot could be fatal."

Dr. Gallagher clutched Reuben's elbow and waved over the night watchman.

"Walk this gentleman to the Continental Hotel, will you?"

Doc slipped Paddy enough for a pint, assuring his guest's safe arrival.

––––––––––––

The Boston law office appeared to be formally abandoned by the founding family when the senior Bosworth left in haste to attend his wounded son in Montana Territory. A few years prior, the passing of Reuben's father seemed like cleaving the firm in half, until Lucas completed his studies at Harvard and shouldered the partnership with his father, R.C. Bosworth. The two of them parceled out an overload of cases to cooperative firms. Eventually, Patrick Colter from Montana Territory showed up to handle the clerical work, thus freeing both attorneys of time-consuming tasks to focus on legal matters. Patrick knew he had demonstrated more enthusiasm than aptitude at first, but Reuben recognized his own youthful zeal in the Boston native and gave him every advantage to learn the legal business.

To Patrick, a more than sufficient number of years wielding a pick-axe on solid quartz had done wonders to sharpen his appetite for anything but more of the same. It was not the mines that had lured him back to the Territory after a previous year's so called sabbatical in the East. Patrick could not have articulated exactly what had called him back West. The Bosworths openly speculated that it was a matter of twins being unlikely to separate. Patrick knew it was something deeper.

It had been Lucas' and Reuben's belief in him, as well Patrick's inspired notion that the firm would do well in Butte that had brought him and Lucas together again. Of course, the aftermath of the Berrigan assassination blew up in their faces. His sudden decision to attend Harvard solved some problems while creating others he dared not address. However, he realized his present tenure in the firm had a more committed, permanent feel to it. Therefore, the shocking news from Montana Territory threw both his intentions and his dedication to someday read the law out the window.

Patrick's reaction was instantaneous—gather his few belongings, close his parents' apartment, and follow Mr. Bosworth post haste back to Montana Territory. By way of a flock of telegraphs, he gained assurance from Jackson that Antonio and Danielle would look after Shelley and Neva.

"Thank God Lucas survived," he told Reuben. "Jackson and my friends made sure my wife and child are safe."

Patrick did not say that any other man might have died from the rifle wounds. Or that his own escape from Butte had not lessened the threat—it had come back tenfold to pose danger to his loved ones.

I was a fool to leave them, he fumed, while he made arrangements to travel.

———————

Time passed with deadening slowness for Shelley stranded at Antonio's ranch outside the small cow town of Willow Creek. She waited for Patrick's return, not even counting days, weeks or months. His earlier, frequent letters had come weeks after posting. She replayed parts over and over in an effort to hold on to him, to converse with him in her mind.

Shelley, my love,

I never expected that Boston, home of my youth, would feel so lonely. I wonder about my choosing to attend Harvard when it separates us from the comfort and joy of our newly married lives.

My dearest Shelley,

I await your letters with impatience. The postal service is impossibly slow cross country. I trust this finds you and Neva well and at peace in the protection of your parents in Walkerville. Perhaps someday we will look back and be thankful that the Bosworths' generosity and faith in us advanced our opportunities.

My Wife, My Love,

Once again I sit with pen in hand to express my sense of loss without your always vibrant and loving presence by my side. Please know that law school fully absorbs my time when I am not at the Bosworths' office. Studies require reading endless case law at the library. Wish you were here,

Your Always loving,
Patrick

Now that he was traveling homeward she heard nothing at all. She wrote to her parents in Butte informing them of Patrick's expected arrival at the Headwaters. The Headwaters, forks of three rivers, earned national fame as the rendezvous site by Lewis and Clark's 1804 – 1806 Expedition. Winnie Norton replied that they would meet the couple there, *"in light of unsettling affairs in town. We have a surprise for Neva. Papa has good news, and I have news about a woman who comes into the Mercantile nearly every day."*

In the meantime, Shelley walked through woods bordering the Jefferson River that were interspersed with swampy sloughs teeming with crawdads. Swarms of mosquitoes often chased her upland, where she found a copse of aspens sheltering a tiny spring in one of the draws on Antonio's property. Spritely water bubbled from a stream hidden far inside a cave in crevices of the limestone cliffs. Bits of watercress gained footing in water warmed enough by the earth to withstand year-round temperatures.

This spring alone was reason enough for Antonio to choose this piece of land, Shelley thought. It has the purest water she had ever seen, not that mining camps she had lived in were a remotely fair comparison. Wild strawberry plants nestled in soft grass along a rivulet that tumbled over broken shale, forming a miniature waterfall. Aspen leaves rustled like crisp paper above her head. A flat lichen-covered outcropping among junipers offered a private nook where she hid her heartache; even the sun barely found her bent over her lap, head in her hands. She had cried buckets of tears for Patrick, for her marriage, and for Neva since she had been rescued and moved into Danielle's home. This time she cried for herself.

"I wish Gertie were here—." The words surprised Shelley. They often argued. Gertie made stinging remarks. But they talked. They debated the cry for bans on alcohol, current fashions, and why women's lives were so bad. When she thought about the ease with which they could talk and argue, Shelley railed against her discomfort living with the woman who had robbed her of her wedding day, for Neva who was robbed of her beloved "uncle" whom she called Papa, and for her own sense of abandonment.

Reflections became exaggerated and unreal, as if she poured her heart into water pools and the images dissembled by their own volition, returning to her magnified and regrettable. Shelley's bitterness tasted vile even in her own mouth. In her mind, only Gertie remained true.

Gertie of the outrageous clothes. Gertie of the District. The stocky imp with the saltwater taffy who gave her unsolicited opinion about everything. Gertie who saved a man shot down in the streets. Shelley raised her face and howled much like the coyotes above the cliffs, the sound lost in nature's many voices. It could have been Patrick—she sensed that was what he had feared, they all feared, the very reason he left.

I don't remember exactly what they told me, but I think they spared me because of Patrick. Poor Lucas. So brave to take on a murder case, so young to be wounded, perhaps disabled for life like Neva.

At last Shelley could vent no more. "Who knew such cruelty would reach so far into our lives?" The curious stares of antelope followed her back to Antonio and Danielle's place.

"Never have I been so careless about Neva," she admitted to Danielle. "I am sorry, but I have often not thought of her at all. I do not know what has happened to me—this is a strange experience. I feel as though I am not really here at times."

"You have had a terrible shock, Mrs. Colter. It is quite understandable." Danielle paused. "I am also afraid for my husband."

Shelley looked up at the tall dark woman whose deep, reserved eyes and angular features always intimidated her—Danielle at their double wedding, so regal and beautiful, the gasps of the crowd when she and Antonio made such a handsome couple leaving the church. Shelley saw herself, awkwardly present at the ceremony and tear-stained now, but she instantly understood. Danielle is afraid for her husband, too. She noticed Danielle's softer look now, almost pleading.

"Please, I am Shelley to my friends and family." The words came out without her thinking. She suddenly felt ready to turn a page, to come into a fold of Patrick's making, one she had strenuously resisted from the beginning. Decisions had been made for her and Neva. She did not remember being consulted about leaving her parents' home, or living under the roof of the one woman who frightened her—and to be truthful, of whom she felt resentful. Plans had fallen into place out of necessity, but they seldom felt like her plans. She had foreseen an endless year ahead as being a mere appendix to the Delgados who might be anticipating their own family, and she begrudged every moment of it. And Neva. What of her?

"I did not want to come stay with you," Shelley admitted. Danielle leaned forward to catch the small voice. "I was afraid we would be in the way and intrude upon your lives." Previous hurts and resentments failed to emerge with her confession. Shelley momentarily wondered why.

Danielle laughed with relief. "Oh, my. Well, I am pleased with the arrangement. Neva brings so much joy to our lives. We live too far from Jackson and Nettie, or Mac and Carrie Tarynton, to see them very often. Believe me, you are welcome here. Please call me Danielle."

"Thank you, Mrs.—er—Danielle. You are much stronger than I. And much more clever. Did I see Neva wearing a pair of trousers with knee pads that you made?"

Danielle laughed a husky chuckle as she whisked flour, butter and eggs in a bowl for scones. "The ground is awfully rough here. Neva fell over stones, tripped on weeds, and became off-balance when chickens were underfoot. I thought her legs needed protection. She seems to be thriving on the farm, though I have to be sure only the baby goats are out with her.

This was news to Shelley. She sat blinking, wondering where she had been while Neva was "thriving." She rushed outdoors to the animal pens. The child, so pale and fragile in Walkerville, was feeding the baby goats. They had a fully engrossing conversation underway, something about a tea party answered by little bleats and blats. Shelley tiptoed back into the house.

"The padded knees are perfect. She has never had so much freedom to do what she likes."

Shelley automatically picked up the gallon churn to turn cream into butter, and continued their stories of earlier. "I think Antonio was afraid, also. He was disguised in Patrick's old miner's hat and coat when he picked us up in Butte."

Danielle stopped stirring.

"He said he snooped around quite a bit after the murder and feared someone might recognize him," Shelley hastened to add, suddenly aware that Antonio had evidently shielded his wife from the incident. "I am sorry to alarm you. You see, it was a wise move on his part and he brought all of us safely back here."

"He never talked about the murder of Mr. Berrigan, but I understand from Jackson, that Antonio possibly saved Mr. Tarynton's life. He rushed him away from the shooting, and guarded him until they were some distance from Butte."

Weariness crept over Danielle's face. She turned toward the window and view of the winding river, its streak of silver between stands of dense woods. Clusters of settlers' cattle grazed among deer in the meadows below the greasewood covered hills.

"I had hoped to leave conflict behind when I moved west," she continued. "You may be aware my first husband was lost in the war. So this violence near at hand chills me. Nothing, I mean nothing, can happen to this husband. I could not bear it."

Shelley set the churn aside and took Danielle in her arms. The woman shook with a fragility Shelley had only known in Neva. However, Danielle soon collected herself and wiped her eyes on the hem of her apron. "He assures me our whereabouts are unknown. We were not a party to the controversy over Butte's toxic mine tailings. I wonder that your husband waded into such a volatile matter."

Now it was Shelley's turn to feel threatened. Or defensive or fearful. She wasn't sure what to feel. Was Patrick naïve and taking undue risks at the expense of his family? Why couldn't Patrick drop the hot poker? She shook her head, releasing a long breath that came from the bottom of her shoes. "I am exhausted with it. That is all I know."

Gradually the fact that Patrick and Mr. Bosworth were on their way to Montana Territory turned Shelley's thoughts to her husband's imminent arrival.

Both men would travel to Salt Lake City and take separate stagecoaches north, Mr. Bosworth to Butte and Patrick to the Headwaters where he and Antonio would meet him. Again, plans were made and soon to be executed without consulting her. Shelley felt a familiar connection to Miss Owens' unchosen fate and the larger, stronger forces of the men's world.

"I would prefer meeting my husband with you, if you do not mind." She spoke softly, aware that Miss Owens would have been more assertive. "Patrick knows I have never been a patient person," she laughed, shelving the term 'docile.' Antonio's good intentions deserved better than a rebellion from his houseguest.

A few days later while Neva napped after a romp with the goats, Danielle motioned Shelley to the table for tea and a slice of hot pumpkin bread. The industrious woman seldom relaxed, Shelley noticed, so this was a change.

"I rarely have someone to talk with," Danielle began. "I am worried already that Patrick will take you away. Antonio is a fine man, more than I ever dreamed for, but it is not the same as women's talk. I miss my sister, Genevieve. I lived with them when their baby, Peter Sands, was born and for the last seven years. Since we moved here Antonio works outside all the time, hurrying to prepare the place for winter. Of course when it's cold he will install a water tap inside, I hope."

Danielle's rambling speech revealed personal history, dreams, and especially a lonely side that Shelley was surprised to discover. The striking, self-contained woman had never appeared to be in need of anything.

"I am happy for you and Antonio. You have been a godsend for Neva and me. What would we have done without you? I was out of my mind and you cared for both of us." Shelley swallowed hard and went on. "I do appreciate becoming better acquainted.

Fate and a couple enterprising men threw us together. We may be like sisters-in-law after all!"

They laughed and finished the pumpkin bread to the last slice. Fortunately, Danielle baked enough for a work crew. Several loaves remained for supper.

———

Patrick Colter spent the tedious miles going north by rail and stagecoach to meet his family at the Missouri Headwaters by rehashing precipitating events. His thoughts scattered among shreds of news he'd heard about Lucas' condition, reassurances about his family's safety, and his own sense of guilt about exposing his loved ones to danger in the first place. Reason enough to leave the East for good.

For the past year Lucas had kept him informed by telegraph and letters to Boston. Each week Patrick had fished for more detail regarding the welfare of his wife and Neva, knowing he left them stunned and unhappy with his decision to attend Harvard. Yet the attempt on Lucas' life confirmed his suspicions that elements related to the Berrigan assassination were real, a reality he had second-guessed a thousand times.

He also questioned the safety of residents in the East for different reasons. Tensions had been rising, pushing Congress for and against the vote for Negroes. Reconstruction inflamed both North and South in the wake of the War Between the States. Telegraphs flew between New York, Boston and Philadelphia aligning supporters, pro and con, for "rights of all citizens."

Patrick sighed, relieved to be on the sidelines of political issues. As a legal assistant, his work shifted from former litigation concerning mining interests in the Territories to Eastern cases involving contracts and a wide range of disputes from deep sea fishing, housing, and assorted immigrant problems on the Coast.

As his travels neared home it brought other more critical considerations to mind, namely his strained relationship with his wife. Uncertainty soared as he contemplated a reunion—facing a welcome or her anger or temper. He inventoried his misgivings about the interruption of his legal work and Harvard studies. Yet the interminable miles of travel were well-spent once he spied Neva standing on the carriage seat waving her little shawl over her head. Her beaming greeting revealed she had lost two front teeth. Jackson tightly held the child, while Shelley burst from the greeting party and ran ahead to meet her husband.

"Shelley, dearest, I thought I would never get here. Are you all right?" He buried his face in her hair and held her like never before, sobs welling against each other's chests. He turned to receive Winifred's brave smile and John's hearty handshake, finding himself at a loss for words with his new family's welcome. Winifred soon spread a blanket and set out a picnic. Patrick held Neva. Small talk hardly sufficed to fill long gaps created by Patrick's absence—or curtail his earlier apprehension about their reunion.

"Neva, I have a surprise for you!" Winifred slipped her a package containing a colorful picture storybook.

"I can read this. I know I can," Neva declared, tracing words with her finger.

"We have good news," Winifred said. "John has a new contract lined up to locate veins of copper for a major new mining company."

"That is good news. Congratulations, sir." Patrick heartily grasped his father-in-law's hand, suppressed energy more easily translated between the men than he with Shelley.

"I am so happy for you," Shelley said, and kissed his cheek. "You deserved it all along." She moved aside to sit by Winifred.

"Tell me, Mother, you have news of Irmgarde?"

"She asks about you, Shelley, every time she finds me at the store. The poor soul is lonely, I think. She said something about finding Mr. Lucas Bosworth bleeding on the street that night."

"I heard about that, but I do not know what really happened."

Shelley abruptly tossed her freshly baked oatmeal cookie back in the tin after only one bite.

The family tried to relax but an undercurrent of haste prompted them to cut short the visit. Any further news about Miss Irmgarde Meyer was lost in Patrick's determination to make things right.

"I am coming home for good."

"No, you ain't, Patrick," Jackson cut in. "Right now you're comin' to my place. Nettie is expecting us. There's time enough for plannin' later."

Jackson's sharp look clearly disputed Patrick's decision to quit Harvard, but his twin would have his reasons. He'd say so in time.

"What about Antonio and Danielle? I thought you and Neva lived with them." Patrick turned to Shelley.

"We did. We came directly from there. If you only knew—." Her voice broke. Unable to briefly summarize their transformative stay, she turned to Neva. "Get in the carriage. We are going to see Tucker."

Patrick offered a hand to Shelley to board and followed her inside. Neva immediately wrapped her arms around his neck. "Papa," she cried, forgetting she had previously called him "Uncle" Patrick. Patrick lifted her into his lap. The family felt complete. He would work on his relationship with Shelley later. They waved goodbye to John and Winifred Norton who headed back to Butte. Jackson turned the team around for the two-day trip to the Beaverhead, while the family became reacquainted.

"I have a goat." Neva had a backlog of news a mile long. "Her name is Cookie." Her tinkling laugh made everyone smile. By the time Patrick heard all the entertaining stories, they arrived at a stage stop near Point of Rocks, where they spent the night. Later that evening Patrick met Jackson on a juniper-studded slope under a clear black sky above the Tobacco Root Mountains. Patrick wanted an explanation for Jackson's earlier emphatic rebuke, and

Jackson was eager to share his thoughts—away from Shelley and Neva.

"You've gone far in law school, Patrick. We're proud of you. You deserve to finish. That's all. We all want the best for you, and it ain't here in the Territory. This is fine for me and Nettie, and Antonio and Danielle. It's the way we want it. More than we ever asked for and we're grateful. But you, and Shelley too, need more. She's come a long ways—you'll be surprised." He flashed a wicked twin grin. "She hasn't been idle since you left."

Patrick figured he'd have a helluva surprise coming.

"I rode into town to see Lucas despite the risks, but I had to see how he's doin', and check out a few things. He had been stonewallin' mine owners about joining their legal teams. That left him with the cases brought by citizens and ranchers. Ranchers are spittin' mad about acid water runoff. It's not hard to see which side Lucas would take despite the known risks."

Jackson drew a breath. Patrick knew his twin was stalling for time, delaying telling him something.

"Naturally, newspapers headlined the Berrigan murder again, connecting it, right or wrong, with the ranchers' demands to clean up the runoff. It appears to have turned back on Lucas." Jackson searched Patrick's face. "There's naïve and there's foolish. Then there's courage. Take your pick. It could have been you shot, Patrick."

"How is he?"

"Alive, but not good."

The men kicked around small stones, listening to them clatter as they tumbled downhill. Patrick felt a chill beneath the fresh dry air under his collar, smelled the night settle around the sage and rabbit brush. But Shelley was forefront in his mind.

"Shelley has been dragged through all this. I know she is strong, as purely a solid western woman as I have ever seen, but neither she nor I bargained for these tragedies." An image of Eastern women whose tight corsets constrained their lives were a notable contrast. "Then there's Neva with sun-browned arms and shining eyes, and new strength in her legs. She's walking better, isn't she, Jackson?"

"Yeah, the scamp gets around pretty good. I'd say Antonio and Danielle's farm has done wonders for her."

"There you have it. I am convinced that I need to stay here in the Territory—and hope it soon becomes a decent state with some damn stiff laws. There is nowhere else I want to be." Patrick turned to go, but Jackson gripped his arm.

"Mr. Bosworth is evacuating Lucas and closing the office. Let it go, Patrick. It's too risky to even think of returning to Butte. Please, for all of us, go back and finish studyin' law, then decide."

Patrick halted, too tired to dispute Jackson's reasoning, but he had come too far to change plans right now.

"You'll figure out somethin' if you wait 'till things change here. Silver ore won't last at the rate mines are plunderin' it every day. We been there when minerals run out. Ranchin' will come back and statehood will happen. You'll have a better chance in a few years' time."

"Yeah, we've both experienced the difference between wide open spaces and a harbor built on salt water marshes, despite all that Harvard has to offer. I'll sleep on it."

By morning Neva claimed "Uncle Papa" Patrick and told more stories about the farm animals, Cookie being foremost among kids, and six other milking goats with Duff, the shaggy ram.

"The mama pig had nine babies but she laid on one so there are eight. There are too many cows to count. Uncle Antonio lets me take care of Old Tornado. He catches wild horses."

"The child has the gift of gab like her sister," Patrick joked to Jackson and Shelley.

Patrick indulged Neva's stories, but found himself more absorbed by Shelley's maneuvers to maintain distance from him. For a talker she was silent as Old Chief Mountain, a profile of granite dominating the west side of the Madison Range.

"Are you all right, my love?" He wanted to hear how she got along with Danielle, how the two newlywed brides shared the same house. A difficult situation he would not have consigned her to, but she had not disclosed a word, except "If you only knew—," alluding to something she had not yet disclosed. He was afraid to ask again.

After hours of wearying travel in the wagon, she took Patrick's arm, what was left of it after Neva went to sleep in his lap. "I am not letting you go again, Patrick."

"And I am not leaving you again. You do not have to worry. I more than learned a lesson this time. Scared the hell out of me, truth be told. I could not get back here fast enough. A man's got to stick with his family."

"Do you want to finish at Harvard University?"

"No, I have made up my mind that we need to remain together as a family."

"You have found work you are passionate about, Patrick. You believe in it, in law and justice. You cannot step away from your convictions."

"What makes you think—?" The woman was uncanny, a mind reader.

"We are going with you to Boston, Neva and I. We can use the money you gave me. I only bought a few things, dresses and such." She giggled, the girlish Shelley that Patrick had fallen in love with. "I spent the money I earned at the Mercantile for everything else."

"Shelley, I have not seen you for more than twenty-four hours and you have next year planned. Sure takes a load off a man." He and Jackson chuckled.

"Nettie's the same. Let a woman have time on her hands and she seizes the world. Nettie worked in a bakery, you know. Now she's making wedding cakes. They sell for more than I earn in a whole season. We'll soon be buyin' out the Taryntons."

The twins' amusement at the notions of emancipation of

their wives left them bantering pro and con before they fell silent. The team hiked right along to cover the trip up the Jefferson Valley and across the expansive land and foothills along the Beaverhead River.

Patrick dozed until they reached Jackson's ranch, located next to the Taryntons where Jackson still worked as a cowhand. The mood of the group lifted and Neva wriggled with unbounded energy.

"Jackson, I think you and Shelley are in cahoots about something you're not telling me."

Shelley's low, runaway giggle only invited intrigue. Jackson laughed.

Nettie ran out with apron flapping from the half-finished cabin to greet them. Tucker toddled along to claim Neva's hand. She seemed to understand his babble perfectly.

Jackson hauled Patrick's trunk inside the door, placing it next to a trunk, packed, latched and ready to go. The small, dark interior of Jackson and Nettie's kitchen erupted with Shelley's laughter. Jackson had spirited Patrick and Shelley's belongings away from their cabin on Bison Creek in Butte at Shelley's instigation. She meant business about going to Boston with him.

This time Patrick was too overcome to speak.

"Can we take Old Tornado?"

"Neva, your sister is about as determined as Old Tornado, and a darn sight more hard-headed."

10
LUCAS' DECISION

Lucas Bosworth, Esq., equated the passage of time with his healing. He had lost a week strapped down on the operating table in Doc Gallagher's clinic because his gunshot wounds were so extensive and his recovery questionable. Another week passed through a haze of pain and morphine when Doc allowed limited movement. A milestone of sorts occurred when Doc and Miss Owens shifted his now lightweight body onto a gurney and rolled it into the patient exam room, a graduation of sorts from intensive care. Lucas followed the subsequent lapse of days and nights by light through the windows and Judge Kirschenbaum's visits. He exerted himself as much as a paucity of breath and an iron will would allow. Eventually he dwelled upon the shooting and pulling up stakes in the Territory. These times of feeling that none of his earlier dreams mattered generally coincided with setbacks and a melancholy that Judge's Irish whiskey failed to erase.

"I have too much time to think about being crippled for life," Lucas finally confided to Doc.

"You could have been dead," Doc growled, but he left a pot of St. John's Wort tea on a side table before he went to see his next patient.

Lucas nodded and decided to buck up. By the time Reuben Bosworth had stormed into Butte and spilled his fury at it and the lawless Territory, Lucas was up, using a cane, and resolved to state his wishes.

"I plan to stay, Father. You needn't worry about finding an inland hospital ship to take me home." Lucas slowly eased himself onto a straight-backed chair in the dining room of the Continental Hotel. The trip from the clinic to the hotel was his first attempt to walk down the street since he had been cut down by bullets. He knew he had to demonstrate sufficient healing for his father to accept his announcement.

The decision caught Reuben Bosworth by surprise. "I cannot imagine that Doctor Gallagher would clear you to do any such thing. As your father, I would never allow you to risk your recovery, indeed risk your life in Butte again."

Lucas chuckled. "Doc discharged me from inpatient medical care, but my apartment is upstairs on a poorly lit street. He was more concerned about my living situation than my injury. I agreed to room and board in the clinic for no other reason than that Doc fussed over me like a mother hen. He fetched soup, sent out my laundry and read me bedtime stories—you may have a hefty bill to settle with him."

"This notion of staying is not advisable if the villains are still at large. Do they have any leads? You seem remarkably comfortable for one who has been ambushed in the dead of night." Reuben tended to grind out his sense of irony as if sharpening an axe.

"Ambushed, yes, but it was similar to the ambush of Kent Berrigan, the Commissioner who was gunned down a year ago. A gunman hidden in a freight wagon fired shots. The horses bolted and the varmint escaped in the excitement."

"I sure as hell will not set you up for that to happen again." Reuben's fist struck the table, his frowns a measure of attempts to gather disparate pieces of a puzzle while their coffee became tepid.

"Father, we have a lead this time. Did I tell you or did Doc tell you about the woman who found me? I surely could not have seen or heard anything myself, but she did. She saw the night trash man's wagon speeding from the scene. His horses plunged out of control. The watchman, Paddy, later dragged the trash man into Sheriff Ford's office. He was drunk but he swore on a stack of Bibles he did not know a man was hidden in his wagon. All he heard was a man yell, 'One for Jeff Davis, hoy!'"

"That does not impress me as being much of a clue. In Boston it is a rallying cry for every kind of devilment."

"The Seceches in Butte get a little liquor in them and toast the former President of the Confederacy, but it is only talk as far as I know." Lucas began to fade—tired, out of breath and taxed by the day's exertion.

On the contrary, Reuben Bosworth's voice rose. His checked fear and rage had simmered for weeks since he had received the telegram that his son was near death in Montana Territory. He had not rested a moment of the trip west until he saw Lucas with his own eyes.

"What is the sheriff doing about this? He should have the criminal in custody by now, as well as whomever was behind the plot. Someone has to be backing this kind of activity, especially when it is serial murder or attempted murder. Law enforcement should be all over this, but Butte appears to protect its inside jobs, if this is any indication. That chills me to the bone, Lucas."

"If I knew more I would tell you. I only know that I collapsed on the stone walkway." Lucas rubbed a lingering sore spot hidden beneath his thick hair. "Miss Irmgarde Meyer covered me with her shawl and ran for Doc and the night watchman. She and Paddy apparently waited with me until Doc came." He paused to draw a breath, painstakingly adjusting himself in the chair.

"I had not been informed of this until later when Doc told me, but I assume these must be the same cowards who shot Commissioner then blended in with the crowd. What is different this time is that the trash man and Miss Meyer both linked the suspect to a Rebel."

Reuben scowled and dismissed the connection. "The Lost Cause has been over for twelve years. What is this, a throwback?

A group of malcontents and deserters who do not accept that the war is over?"

Lucas braced himself to get up and leave the hotel. Reuben realized that the conversation with his son had hit a dead end.

"I will hire a hack to take you back to the clinic. We will talk later."

That evening Lucas was somewhat revived after a long rest and a ritual nightcap with Judge Kirschenbaum. While the judge poured, Lucas grinned and asked him if he knew anything about St. John's Wort tea. The remark earned one of the Judge's trademark "harrumphs."

Lucas' father dropped by after the Judge's visit to apologize for upsetting Lucas with his remarks at the hotel.

"Rebels are not unknown in the Territory, Father. We have a much larger population of Southerners than Northerners here. Try counting the local Dixie saloons. The problem is that efforts by Southern Democrats to gain seats of power are vigorously opposed by Northerners, generally investors and mine owners. Mr. Berrigan, who came from Georgia, had been recruited to fill a seat on the Territorial Commission because he was sympathetic to the ranchers, clearly a dicey stand in a mining town."

"Go on."

"From what I hear the District women are wary of the Rebels who try to stir up sectional trouble. The women do not want to get on the wrong side of the conflict. I have come to the same conclusion." He stretched his good leg. "I promise, Father, I will be a lot smarter going forward."

"Ranchers, rebels, a drunk trash man, rumors and whispers among the low life. I do not see much of a case from what you are telling me."

For the first time in Lucas' memory, words failed Reuben Bosworth. His father looked like a deflated balloon, a pathetic sight for one so strong and entrenched in Old World gallantry, yet leveled by raw violence striking his family. Lucas hastened to change the subject and lift the mood—his father had seen only the sordid side of Butte on his first trip.

"I discovered Miss Irmgarde Meyer is a friend of Patrick's wife, the mayor's wife, and a physician, Miss Adelaide Owens. I understand Miss Owens has initiated a women's movement across the Territory that has quite a following. Miss Meyer's role is unclear considering her other affiliations. However, my sympathies would be with the suffragettes if the issue were not so divisive. I agree that women eventually need the vote to "create any lasting change," as they claim."

Reuben morosely followed Lucas' talk about a prostitute engaging in civic affairs with prominent citizens of the city. Patrick had not disclosed that his wife was an activist, and a controversial one at that. He had stated was that she was a remarkable woman. True, if one were to believe a newlywed husband.

"Excuse me, but I fail to comprehend how this tangle of women has anything to do with us."

"Trust me, Father, stranger things have happened in this town."

"All thanks to the street women, apparently." Reuben's snide comment made Lucas wince. His social preconceptions bent, Reuben raised an eyebrow signaling doubt. "Are you suggesting she has leadership abilities or a civic consciousness?"

"My only suggestion would be that if you feel like helping her—"

"I will not give money to a creature of the night."

"Miss Meyer is a friend of Patrick's wife, for better or worse. It seems the young women came together like lost sheep. There are few women in this remote town."

"If you imply this Miss Meyer has ambitions above and beyond life in a brothel, then I am willing to compensate her for saving your life. That is, if she has any intelligence to speak of."

Lucas overlooked the slights, given the unique opportunity to find out how far his solidly conventional Boston father was willing to bend to "compensate" for his son's life.

"Miss Meyer and Mrs. Colter have apparently expended considerable energy in an effort to improve conditions for women. I believe they have been influenced by Dr. Owens, who serves Butte through her Women's Clinic. Miss Owens strongly favors higher education for women and promoting women in the professions."

"Does this woman physician stop there, or is she a flag-waving fanatic?"

"I am sorry, Father. My experience with physicians in Butte extends to two bullet holes that brought me into Doc Gallagher's clinic."

"My experience with the Woman Movement is that they clamor for every cause under the sun in their efforts to upset traditional social systems."

Wearing thin, Lucas said, "I invite you to discuss these matters further with Miss Owens across the hall from Doc Gallagher." A short, painful cough cut him off.

Reuben Bosworth's scowl deepened while he struggled with the many unsavory concepts raised by his son. Thrumming his fingers on the table, he alternately glanced at Lucas and about the room, as if a palpable resolution other than paying a prostitute for saving his son's life would manifest itself.

His own course of reasoning finally led him to squarely face his son. "I find this a difficult personal decision, but evidently we have this, er, Miss Irmgarde Meyer to thank for your rescue in the dark of night."

"You might consider a scholarship to a Women's Academy if you feel like helping her."

Reuben brightened. "If she is interested and willing to get out of the gutter, of course."

Lucas let the matter lie.

His father abruptly turned inward, evidently searching his moral compass, ascertaining whether this sponsorship was one he dared countenance. At last his chest heaved with resignation.

"I would agree to help the whole damn District if they had saved you."

The moment held all their unspoken words.

———————

Reuben Bosworth's restlessness and discomfort soared over the next few days. Not one to sit down with Butte's favorite beverage, a Sean O'Farrell, to contemplate the West's blazing sunsets from the heights of the Continental Divide, he fired off telegrams to his firm in Boston day and night. In between, he stormed Sheriff Ford's office for details of the ambush, charging him with inaction after an assassination and an attempted murder, even suggesting that he and his henchmen were involved. If external foes were justifiably targets of his anger, Lucas knew his father's inner conflict was likely the driving force for his rage. In addition, he would wrestle deep within his soul before he would associate the Bosworth name with the sponsorship of a street woman. The proud aristocrat had not changed his tune very much when he met Lucas at the hotel at noon.

"I am determined to find out if there are any suspects in your case. Sheriff Ford has been less than forth-coming. If he knows something, he is not divulging it to me—an outsider and an attorney. Obviously, he is protecting his position for some reason, likely politically motivated. Yet weeks have passed and nothing has been done."

Lucas' ears had regularly burned with a variation of this theme. He had given it some thought.

"You may be helpful there, too, Father. The Territory needs a good shaking up from Washington, D.C. As you know, Federal appointments to Judicial District Courts in Montana Territory yield considerable authority. Yet their silence or absence regarding the assassination of a Territorial Commissioner is a glaring omission. They tend to their interests here fast enough regarding revenue. Distance is no excuse. You have found that the telegraph reduces the distance from Butte to the East Coast to minutes."

"Believe me, I will make sure the heads of agencies in government listen up or bear the consequences. However, Lucas, I am baffled by your stubbornness in staying here where, by your own admission, those in law and justice are derelict in their duties."

Lucas had tamped down a blast of outrage echoing his father's charges during his recovery—he had been too wounded, exertion too painful, to arouse his rampant desire for vengeance. But he expressly avoided revealing to his father, of all people, that he was personally committed to solving the case. Evading a direct response, Lucas kept his reasons, excuses, and defenses to himself. Reuben Bosworth was in no mood to tolerate his son's insubordination.

"That street woman has been a damn-sight more helpful than those in the whole Territory or Washington, D.C. Is that any way to run a country?"

Lucas' grinned, wincing in pain around suppressed laughter.

"Drink your coffee, Father. If you walk down to the Mercantile, you may chance to meet Miss Meyer."

Reuben, Esq. knew when the chips were down and his hand was called.

Lucas continued, trying to allay fears of potential danger that sent his father into paroxysms of fury. "I will get a room here at the Continental until I can find a ground-floor apartment near the police station."

The elder Bosworth's clean-shaven chin jutted forward; his scowl would have stripped a lesser man of his self-assurance. Poised in his chair, he tapped his walking stick on the floor, but delayed leaving the dining room until Lucas gathered enough strength to limp out the door. Reuben Bosworth followed, turning uptown to meet the courtesan.

Lucas felt so much better that he straightened his shoulders and left the hotel chuckling.

Lucas had no advance notice that Patrick would visit him in Butte a few days later. He heard a knock on his hotel room door at eight o'clock in the morning and found his father's legal assistant in wrangler's boots, hat and coat.

"Come in, my man. I hardly expected you to come to Butte when you beat it back here to see your family." Lucas managed a one-armed welcome around Patrick's shoulder.

"You forget. I am a twin. When I hook up with someone, I do it like a twin, the only way I know how to be with folks." Patrick's voice faltered. "It is good to see you, Lucas."

"Breakfast and coffee? We can go to the dining room. You must have ridden all night." He fished under the bed for his cane.

"I came in at first light when any shady characters would be sleeping off their drunk."

Patrick kept his hat on, a Stetson he had borrowed from a ranch hand at Taryntons' and sat facing the front door.

"I hear you plan to stay in Butte. Not much news goes unnoticed. That must mean you are on the mend."

"On the mend and restless. Getting a few holes bored in one's body sure clears the mind about what is important." Lucas paused, settling his wounded hip more comfortably. "It means a lot to me that you came, Patrick. I know you went into law for a higher calling. I did, too, in the beginning." Lucas' two years on Patrick were not that much, but under his father's influence, he had started in the profession at a young age and matured early.

"I lost a lot of idealism over time, got too busy and forgot it, or began to see the world as it is, not as I would like it to be."Lucas paused for a labored breath. "But I have had ample time to stew about it. My decision to stay was the simple reason that this is what I want to do. I believe in it, and I feel Butte is the right place for me. I have to tell you, prior to this latest ambush I wrote up a few contracts for your father-in-law. Now that makes this work worthwhile."

"The Nortons met us at the Headwaters with that news. They are extremely pleased and thankful."

"Mr. Norton is a brilliant geologist, and an unrecognized one until now. There are half a dozen mine operations muscling in, in addition to the Anaconda and Clark's Colorado Smelting Company. Several snapped up his services in a minute. He is in the gravy now, finding veins of minerals I can't even pronounce. He says molybdenum, copper, lead and zinc are everywhere you turn. Of course, there is little market for copper yet, but he anticipates a bonanza with the advent of electricity."

The recognition is well deserved. He has been discouraged for years, knowing the veins were packed with green gold."

"You picked an exceptional family, one to be proud of, Patrick. Charlotte is not only a stunning woman, I understand she cares for her little sister like a hen with one chick. You are the envy of more than one fella around town."

"And I went off and left her to criminals on the loose. Well, never again. Shelley was packed and ready to escort me back to Boston and my course of study. Her sister's health has improved enough that she is able to travel. We will start our marriage over on a better footing. Being separated, especially so soon after our wedding, has been a hardship for all of us."

"I understand. Father will be pleased. Say, you should have seen his face when I suggested he trot down to the Mercantile for a chance to meet Miss Irmgarde Meyer. I am sure he wondered first off 'what would Mother think?'" Lucas laughed. "He was indignant as hell, but he went."

"I am beginning to wonder about this Irmgarde myself, but more interested in what you have to say about the shootings. If it is about sectional strife, that is 180 degrees from our previous assumptions. Before you arrived in Butte to establish a law firm, we figured the ranchers' opposition to toxic mine waste was a threat to the mine investors. That is why Mr. Berrigan made a campaign issue of cleaning up the streams."

Lucas seemed to be in a mood for talking. "The silver boom has magnified that problem. Ranchers or not, the runoff is like an artist's palette, so full of cadmiums it would make anyone a believer. However, my guess is the ambushes were not related to mine operations. Current outcries indicate conflicts will become violent when workers ask for decent pay, and mine owners turn against unions. As for ranchers in Deer Lodge Valley, they are running their livestock further away from the effects of water pollution and smelters. They can't sell sick stock. Conrad Kohrs' spread extends to the Canadian border. But you did not come in to hear all that."

"I want to hear it, right after I hear what exactly is driving you to stay."

"I have to tell you, this movement toward statehood has caught my fancy." Lucas' clear eyes sparkled, a vision shining through where defeat had recently taken hold. "Think what it means to be on the legal side of maneuvers for and against establishing a state constitution, state judiciary, and legislature. I am excited, Patrick. These are interesting times—if one lives through them."

Patrick felt as though a detonating cap was set off too close to his head and affected his hearing, his sight, and his mind. Lucas could joke about damn near getting himself killed. Now his fancy is leading him to leap into another controversial arena before his wounds are scabbed over, before he has recovered enough to hobble a block without losing his breath.

"Father was adamantly clear that he would not allow you to regain your position in this office, Patrick. The war still simmers and feelings run deep. Old rivalries and grudges emerge unexpectedly, fueled by the saloons. For me, the question of statehood draws in a new cast of characters. I want to maintain our friendship, but you are free to determine where you want to practice."

Lucas' release of Patrick's prior commitment swept away Patrick's past world and a new one had not yet been revealed. He managed to say, "You will make a name for yourself here, Lucas."

Lucas laughed. "I am not in it for a name. Father said statehood sounds like a cat and dog fight to the bitter end. To me it is history in the making. I would honestly like to be a part of it. There are good people in Butte who feel the same way."

———————

Several months later Lucas Bosworth, Esq. opened his new office with less fanfare than it takes to open a can of beans. He hired four new attorneys who represented a cross section of Butte. They carried on anonymous lives, several with wives and children. Two Irish, one German, and a big Scot all blended so well into the immigrant town they could have been the butcher, baker and candlestick maker.

Lucas made sure his firm's legal work scrupulously respected privacy and disclosure ethics, as well as Territorial law. The Berrigan case remained an unattended sore spot. Lucas warned the new attorneys that the Jeff Davis enclave was suspect and remained at large. Members of the firm got the message. They would keep a low profile.

Reopening his law firm had drawn down Lucas' reserves, financially and physically. He also remained out of the public eye, which coincidently favored his slow recovery.

———————

After almost a year's separations, Patrick and Jackson Colter celebrated their reunion at Jackson's ranch by riding, setting a few corral posts, and talking far into the nights. Shelley good-naturedly, even charitably, shared her long absent husband with his twin, smugly knowing that her family would soon be well on its way East, according to her plans.

A few days later when they regrouped at last and sped on their way to a new adventure, she casually mentioned by way of one of her implausible stories, that she had maintained contact with Miss Adelaide Owens, M.D., and the mayor's wife, Mrs.

Baumbier, who were firmly committed to the rising women's movement. From her expectant pauses, Patrick assumed she expected him to remark about his "wife's involvement in causes" that he had disparaged when they were first married.

Patrick's awareness of the suffragettes parading the streets of Boston had given him a sense of their avowed dedication to the cause and a taste of their agitation. He dared not reopen discussion of Shelley's involvement. His marriage seemed strange and tenuous since their long separation. Shelley apparently took his silence as apathy, though he had no doubt that she resolved to continue her connection with Miss Owens, her mentor for the cause.

Neva related more convincing tales of the past year than her sister, which relieved Patrick of hearing other confessions Shelley might make. Happily overwhelmed about taking his family to Boston, Patrick would not find out until later that her trunk held her upgraded fashions.

———

By the fall of 1878, Butte exercised its muscle and expanding population to challenge Helena, Anaconda and Deer Lodge for prominence in the statehood movement, though no other city matched Butte's 24-hour-a-day exuberance. Saloons, mines and smelters never shut down. Rival immigrants encountered each other on the steep hillside streets. Daily knifings, fisticuffs, and mine accidents provided a sufficient number of patients that Dr. Gallagher hired a married couple, a nurse and a male intern which made the situation all the sweeter.

Reuben Bosworth had left a generous settlement for Lucas' emergency care, permitting Isaac Gallagher to snap up a larger clinic. Doc would catch a few winks while the couple treated whooping cough, chronic bronchitis from polluted air, measles and warts. They all labored over sad cases of diphtheria and scarlet fever, not to mention regularly occurring injuries inflicted by gambling run-ins, domestic altercations, drunkenness, and casualties of severe weather. The proverbial "many were saved and many were lost" defined the state of medical practice in Butte.

Miss Owens jumped at the chance to convert Doc's former clinic in the Silver Bow Building to an informal meeting room for the campaigns she championed. She was frequently the principle speaker to a disparate group of women, budding politicians, and often antagonistic men who turned out in fair weather or foul in support of or curiosity about statehood or women's suffrage. She was known for her stout figure encased in severe, dark dresses with starched collars and an inevitable black hat perched over upswept gray-streaked hair. A commanding voice further set her apart, giving her recognition that the M.D. after her name rarely did. The meetings also attracted stern temperance advocates and previous abolitionists who pushed their particular concerns. Woman's suffrage proponents claimed in well-rehearsed speeches that if given the vote, women would solve the social problems of alcoholism, wife-beating, unfair child custody, property rights, and education for women.

On the one hand, women loudly charged men with usurping power from over one-half of the country's citizens. On the other hand, they advocated women's nurturing qualities that would bring much needed softening to the affairs of men, and uphold the highest and most cherished values of the nation. Married women generally listened a time or two, but did not commit to the campaign for a variety of reasons. Married men felt that their vote represented their wives' views, therefore women's votes would be redundant. However, after the novelty of the issue wore off, most citizens of Butte returned to their homes and pubs.

"Adelaide, am I ill informed, or do you have an army of footmen trying to take away all the vices enjoyed by men?" Doc chided her when they passed on the street.

"You will not find me an anti-saloon crusader." Miss Owens patted a flask of *grappa* hidden in her coat. "Nor take anything away from men. I want to see that women get the same privileges and treatment under the law as men, that's all.

Strangely, many women are either too absorbed in home and child care, or too poor and uninformed to recognize their own bondage. Most of the advocates for women's rights filter in from the States."

Miss Owens' voice carried the grudges she endured. Dr. Isaac Gallagher, usually received payment for fees in gold dust, when and if he received fees at all. Miss Owens, M.D., frequently received a pail of eggs from her women patients, or a bundle of rutabagas grown in questionable circumstances among mine tailings and feral dogs.

"I agree that women here are almost as bad off as those in Appalachia. The money hauled out of the earth is not benefiting those it should, generally the workers who become your patients and mine. It's a crying shame. It is time this town grew up and created a decent welfare program for poor folks." Doc shook his head, premature gray hair protruding from beneath his bowler.

"I must inquire, Miss Owens, if you know the whereabouts of that street woman, Miss Meyer. She seems to have ceased checking on the progress of Lucas Bosworth. I wonder if she fears repercussions for her own life."

"I am not at liberty to discuss the personal affairs of women who may or may not be my patients or attend the gatherings. However, I can tell you that recruitment from the District has unfortunately failed to yield another social activist such as Irmgarde Meyer." Miss Owens clamped her lips and strode downtown, leaving Doc Gallagher puzzling over the mystery.

Yet gossip regarding the "brazen escape" of one of the District girls circulated around Butte in no time. So did Madam's attempt to tighten the privileges of those remaining. Only Miss Owens was privy to the senior Bosworth's offer to send Miss Meyer to an eastern Women's Academy for what he hoped would be "fruitful training."

Regarding her own fruitful training in a profession, Miss Owens found payment for her services with chickens, dead or alive, especially irritating. Aside from remuneration, her post-graduate experience from a prestigious eastern medical school had been generally demoralizing. As a result, on any particular evening, Miss Owens closed her Women's Clinic promptly at five o'clock and joined whatever movement showed life.

Her activism for statehood, surpassed only by a visceral fervor for the cause of women's equality, prompted her to advertise regular meetings of a Women's Book Club in the *Butte Miner*. The books members turned to time and again were dog-eared 1869 copies of *The Revolution*, a journal promoting woman suffrage that Miss Owens had secreted to the West. The journal comprised a recruitment arm of the National Woman Suffrage Association, founded by Elizabeth Cady Stanton and Susan B. Anthony for promotion of a Constitutional Amendment for universal suffrage.

Her fervor caught on with some.

"I want to divorce my husband," a woman announced at a meeting, "but I am afraid to lose my children and the small inheritance I received from my grandfather back in Iowa. Judge Kirschenbaum is sympathetic to helpless women like me, but legally his hands are tied."

Heads nodded in agreement around the circle of miners' wives who suffered at the hands of drunken husbands.

That evening after a Book Club meeting and the chance conversation she'd had with Dr. Gallagher, Adelaide took pen to paper and composed a moving argument outlining the need for a welfare program benefiting women and children, the sick and disabled. She scratched out "working poor" and inserted "those denied their rights and protections under the law."

Welfare for the working poor was wishful thinking—it had never materialized, and never would, as far as she could see, and Adelaide felt she had as much prescience as anyone. The welfare plea would add fodder to the arguments associated with causes now sheltered under the roof of her building. She sent a copy of the draft to Irmgarde, her suffragette associate in Boston who might assess the type of public assistance available from a more established and refined part of the country.

Boston, one of the oldest colonial settlements, certainly qualifies as being established. I would be interested in learning whether the city offers welfare programs other than church charities.

Adelaide fired off a similar letter to a medical associate in Philadelphia.

"I will turn over every stone to find a way to benefit women," Adelaide confided to Doc Gallagher the next time they met on the street.

Miss Owens made up for the loss of local interest in her causes by posting voluminous letters and pamphlets to Irmgarde, keeping her abreast of Butte's progress in the women's movement. In return, Irmgarde's letters, news clippings and reports more than made up for her effort. Adelaide felt she now had eyes and ears on the East coast, therefore on the pulse of the nation.

11
HEIRLOOM CHINA

Patrick Colter and his family arrived in Boston in time for Harvard University's first get-acquainted social of the fall school term. Patrick beamed from horizon to horizon presenting the tall blonde woman on his arm to one of his professors who greeted the guests.

"My wife, Mrs. Charlotte Norton Colter."

"I am pleased to welcome you, Mrs. Colter. You and your husband have the healthy glow of true Westerners."

Patrick's high-altitude tan from Montana Territory was set off by a stiff white clerical collar and slim black tie. Shelley extended her fingertips encased in long white gloves that bared a bronzed arm below the full sleeves of her gown. A nod of her head with upswept hairdo and classy hat spoke more than words—to her it meant "insecurity," to Patrick "nervousness," to the professor was anyone's guess. She desperately sought her repertoire of responses to his greeting and found none.

She had sensed Patrick stiffen when they encountered the professor. When her husband suddenly became overly formal, Shelley took the cue, but having been raised in Nevada's mining camps, a silver spoon in her mouth did little to bestow any particular social graces. Aware that her western twang might sound offensive to the professor's ears amid English accents and the drawl of a remarkable number of Southerners, she remained silent. Patrick was not the only law student from west of the Mississippi, yet one of a few. She realized he adopted a hint of his Boston Irish brogue again as naturally as breathing the salt air.

The tense moment of greeting the professor passed graciously as the well-oiled gears of the University moved guests, newcomers, and their hosts through the halls, and referred them to tours of various specialty schools and residential buildings. The School of Law was located on the main campus of Harvard, the original site of the nation's oldest institution of higher learning, established for men in Cambridge in 1636 by John Harvard, a minister. He donated his personal library to the University. Radcliffe College for Women stood across from Harvard on the Cambridge campus. Its graduates received Harvard degrees.

The antiquity of the University gave Shelley a sense of the Pilgrims who founded it. A sense of being on a pilgrimage herself prompted her nervous giggle, hidden behind her hand. She encountered several wives as overwhelmed as she was before Patrick briskly separated her for a private excursion to the chapel and a glimpse of Harvard Yard. The Yard, an open grassy area, lent an inviting feeling to an inner courtyard surrounded by Georgian three-and four-story brick halls of learning.

"Oh, it is beautiful. I love the serenity," Shelley whispered, captured in a sense of reverence created by the surroundings a world away from Butte.

"Let me show you more. Come see my favorite vantage point along the bank of the Charles River."

The world was aflame with autumn's colors. Old hardwoods formed a canopy of red and orange. The sharp scent of resin from mature maples and sycamores laced the air as their leaves crunched underfoot like bright confetti. Delicate birch branches caught the daring slanted peak of Shelley's high-crowned hat. The soft silk and wool blend of her navy blue gown swished suggestively against Patrick's leg, echoing the lap of waves below in the river. His arm embraced her waist. They stood a long time enveloped in the distinctly humid enclosure, united in time and place.

"I will never forget this," Shelley said, turning into his arms. "Reflections of the trees and red brick buildings are wavering with the ducks' passage."

"We must go to the ocean, dearest. I want to show you everything I enjoyed growing up here."

"I can smell the ocean. I can almost feel it heaving against the coast—immense compared to our small lives."

"I cannot dispute that. It has been good for me to be near it again, though I was never adept at sailing or fishing the open seas. I was not the son my father might have desired, neither of us were. They could understand our going West with the huge migration of Irish, but they never came to terms with us wanting to stay. They have since frequently returned to the Isles where our grandparents are aging.

He paused when a flock of geese thrashed their wings to lift off the river. "These wild fowl do not begin to replace those in Montana Territory, nor do they outshine you." The last was muffled in her ear.

"Careful, Patrick. You will muss my hair."

"We better join the crowd for tea and crumpets. I intend to escape afterward with the most beautiful woman there."

Shelley threw him a quick, surprised glance and squeezed his hand. "That is lovely of you to say so, sweetheart."

"Shelley, I have to say I am stunned by how fashionable you have become. Had Mr. Parker encouraged you while I was away?"

Shelley's long low laugh turned heads of passersby. "I am a married woman. Is it not fitting that I dress for my husband?" She laughed again, and tweaked his cheek.

Patrick smiled, disbelief at her stylish fashions still lingering in his soft, brown eyes. "Once I am working, I shall have to rise to the occasion. Right now I will have a heavy load of coursework as well as work for Lucas' father. I intend to spend a tremendous amount of time reading case law at the library. The more I accomplish, the quicker we will be able to go home."

"I felt a little guilty for splurging on this outfit, Patrick. Was it all right for me to do so when you struggle to make ends meet? I could have selected something less extravagant yet suitable for attending meetings with Miss Owens."

"I fail to recall from your letters that you regularly attended meetings, though you mentioned several times that such occurred in Butte. Did I miss something?"

Caught in more of a disclosure than she intended, Shelley stammered that Miss Owens attempted to help poor women and children of Butte. The omission in her letters had been by choice.

"You are aware, Patrick, that a great deal of the miners' earnings are left in the pubs. And the brothels."

Shelley sensed the conversation had taken a wrong turn when Patrick became distant and distracted. She knew proper women did not refer to brothels directly, nor did proper wives associate themselves with street causes, but that would have to come up later.

A petite woman caught Patrick's eye as she moved across the room to greet them in a whirl of rustling satin and lace, her girdled waist accented with a corsage of fresh violets. Before Patrick fully transitioned from brothels and causes, she had taken his arm and propelled him aside.

"You have been away, Mr. Colter. I wonder that you left so suddenly. Surely there must have been extraordinary circumstances for you to abandon Professor Quincy's ethics class. It was our privilege to also have him speak at our Women's Assembly." Words flooded a space silenced by her proprietary manner. Patrick tugged his arm still firmly in her grasp and turned toward Shelley who stood wide-eyed and aloof a few steps behind Patrick and the woman.

"I suppose you will be able to retake the course in due time."

"Excuse me," Patrick interrupted, "I—I—uh—"

"Yes, of course. We are at a social event. We shall converse later."

"Shelley—Miss Hamilton," Patrick managed to stammer. "Shelley, I would like you to meet Miss Violet Hamilton. Miss Hamilton, I am pleased to present my wife, Mrs. Charlotte Norton Colter."

"Welcome to Harvard, my dear. Your gown is remarkably fashionable." With a hesitation, imperceptible to anyone other than Shelley, Violet dropped Patrick's arm to face Shelley. "You are also from the Territories, I presume. What do you think of our fine University? This must all be quite new to you."

Shelley shot a look at Patrick, a plea for help. "I hardly know what to say, Miss Hammer. Yes, it is all quite foreign to an outsider."

"Miss Hamilton is a law student herself. From Tennessee I believe. We were all outsiders a year ago when we began our studies here. Excuse me, Miss, we really must be going."

"So nice to meet you, I am sure." Miss Hamilton curtsied, a deep and exaggerated exit.

"To meet you, also," Shelley chimed.

Patrick reclaimed his wife and marched on, considerably pale and quiet. Shelley matched his steps, her high, button-up shoes markedly loud on the marble floors.

"Who was that woman?" Shelley glared, even before they fully alighted from the carriage that transferred them from the University to the Colter apartment on the outskirts of Cambridge. Patrick had hired the carriage for Harvard's social occasion to treat Shelley to a romantic night out and a celebration of their move to the East Coast. It was rare that they dressed formally since their wedding, and he had intended to make the evening special and show her off.

"Shush, let me unlock the door and stoke up the fire. It is so late that the house probably cooled off. This damp air is chillier than a full-blown blizzard at home. You will be glad to have purchased warm winter wear that will serve you well in the East."

The longtime Colter family residence in a three-story brick building in a crowded section of town had aged with sea moisture, soot, and history into a dusty gray like other apartment buildings Shelley had seen in Boston.

"We are fortunate to live here while my parents are in Ireland. The complete furnishings are a blessing, even the small heaters, though they're not as efficient as pot-bellied stoves in the Territory."

Patrick's babbling had not addressed Shelley's question. They slipped inside. His uncle's daughter had come in for the evening to care for Neva, freeing the Colter's to attend the Harvard social. Shelley checked to see that Neva was asleep in her tiny bedroom, originally a pantry off the kitchen. A small front room with dining area and kitchenette served as living room and parlour. The main bedroom featured gleaming white pillows stacked against a curved iron bedstead, neat doilies on the dressing stand and a large mahogany wardrobe. Shelley had asked if his mother made the doilies, but Patrick admitted he paid little attention to those things earlier in life. Like other assorted knick-knacks, an empty gilded cage, and a leather-bound steamer trunk in the corner, the objects were just there, always had been.

Flames leapt from a single stick of wood behind the isinglass window in a small heater in the bedroom. A copper kettle of hot water sputtered on the stovetop.

"I'll make hot cocoa." Patrick shuffled from cupboard to table gathering cups, saucers, and spoons.

Shelley removed the royal blue coat, a part of her ensemble that Miss Violet Hamilton had not seen, since it had been at the coat check. She shook the folds so it would dry from the damp night air, and draped it over the wardrobe door. Twisting, she reached behind her back to unhook the long row of tiny fasteners on the dress, allowing it to fall at her feet, then loosened the girdle's similar hooks, leaving her in a chemise and leaving Patrick out of the rare pleasure he had of undressing his wife.

A nightgown covered her head to toe before she slipped out of pantaloons and kid-leather shoes she had purchased especially for events in Boston, principally those she would be privileged to attend at Harvard. Shelley crawled into bed and lay back against the bank of pillows. Patrick sat fully clothed on the side of the bed and faced her. The old clock from his youth stuttered on the wall. A hand-crocheted rug near the bed had the worn, welcoming look of a family relic.

"Shelley, what is happening to us? I—we—this strangeness—"

"You did not answer my question."

"The woman is Miss Violet Hamilton. She is a law student like myself. I am sorry she has upset you, or are you displeased with me?"

"Patrick, she did not know you were married. You are married! Any woman deaf, dumb and blind would know that. She took hold of your arm in a terribly familiar manner. She was possessive, as if you belonged to her."

"Shelley—"

"And then, ignored me as if I were merely a potted plant."

"You have this all wrong."

"That woman practically ran off with you right in front of me."

"Shelley, listen to me. You are making too much of this. She was only welcoming us. It is her way, rather outgoing, a Southern hostess type."

"North, South, East or West, she has the manners of a feral dog."

"True, she may not have known you were coming. I had not seen her at the library for some time because I left hastily to travel back to Butte."

"So you meet in the library. And where else? I am afraid I allowed you to be here alone in the clutches of a she-wolf."

"Shelley, what are you saying? This has been my home. I have met a few people."

"So you were not alone? But you expected me to stay behind all alone."

"I never expected that you would attend meetings with God knows who about politics and saloons and women's strident causes in Butte. I never suspected a wife of mine would go about the streets behind my back."

Patrick's eyes flashed while he yanked the high, stiff collar from his shirtfront and tossed it on the dressing table. He similarly discarded his coat and vest. His cheeks tinged with red from the cold chill of Shelley's accusation; he turned to find she had disappeared beneath the pillows that heaved with her sobs.

Taking a moment to collect himself, Patrick gathered wildly churning responses meant to lash out, and stomped down the untruths that threatened to spill from his lips. For some reason an image of Kent Berrigan crossed his mind. As true a gentleman as Patrick had ever known, a mentor when he, Patrick, needed direction. Mr. Berrigan was a man in charge of himself, if not entirely of his own life.

Concentrating on the calmness and maturity Mr. Berrigan had possessed, Patrick's fear and fury began to dissipate. He hung his clothes and snuffed out the candle lantern. Remnants of the fire flickered, casting a warm glow over the colorful rugs. Patrick slid into bed and carefully slipped an arm over the curve of Shelley back. He moved closer to her unresisting form until they were sheltered in a cove beneath the pillows. When her sobs became soft whimpers, his own pent-up breathing came in short bursts until his heart stopped racing.

We are safe at home. I swear I will never hurt her again.

———————

The next morning before Patrick had an opportunity to make amends, a piece of his mother's English bone china flew past his head, smashing against the far wall under the cuckoo-clock that had long ago lost its bird.

"You don't think I would forget in one night that you have been spending time with that floosey. I trusted you, Patrick," Shelley seethed through her teeth.

"Listen to me, Shelley—"

"I trusted you would remember we are married. We had little time together, but I know what marriage means. How could you have forgotten so soon, Patrick? My heart is broken. What am I to do now? Go home and let her get her hands on you?"

A saucer followed the salad plate she had already snatched from the china cabinet and thrown. "What about your letters to me? Am I to believe what you wrote?"

Patrick ducked. "My God, let's not do this to each other. We have so much to look forward to."

"You do but there is nothing for me without you. How could I have been more humiliated?" With a glance toward Neva's closed door, she dashed a floral serving bowl on the floor at Patrick's feet.

He side-stepped the crash, his brow furrowed with alarm and questions. The Colter flat fell silent. Only the shuffling of other early risers in the apartments formed a backdrop to the impasse.

Shelley stared at the shattered china bowl, its shards rocking back and forth in lifeless rainbow pieces. "It was chipped anyway."

Her hands suddenly went limp. A gilt-edged teapot dangled by its handle from her fingers. An image of her own mother's Blue Willow china took her back to her childhood in Nevada. Her shoulders slumped; she turned her face away and fell into her world of sentimental memories far from the flat.

The Blue Willow china was all we had that was beautiful in our home, a poor mining family shack. I escaped by walking under the painted willow trees and over the bridge into a magical world far from my dreary one. I cried for days when all but one piece, a teacup, were broken in the move to Montana Territory—including the teapot with its cracked lid and broken spout. I shed the tears my mother would never allow herself to cry. Oh, how we all quietly suffered the loss, even father because he knew how much Winnie loved the china. Much joy faded from our lives at that moment, at least in mine. I always wanted to give my mother another set.

Shelley bit her lip and straightened, not having voiced a word, and turned to meet Patrick's stunned gaze. His coat and books lay within reach, but he had made no effort to leave; a sad, puzzled look spread over his face, his lips parted yet no words were forthcoming.

Shelley appeared equally stunned at the sight of shattered remnants that had skittered across the floor.

"I am sorry, Patrick. I once wished for a complete set of china with my whole heart. China means marriage and a home to me." Her voice rolled over withheld sobs, betraying her sense of loss—her short married life in Montana Territory had taken a sharp detour before she acquired either home or china.

"Forgive me. Your mother's one joy may have been this heirloom china she brought over on the boat. She may have valued them as much as my mother and I loved our Blue Willow china when I was growing up." Shelley steadied herself against the wall opposite Patrick.

Patrick stood transfixed, the drama unfolding before him revealed a startling side of Shelley, as if he had encountered a lioness yet witnessed the tender fantasies of a child.

"This is not about the china. Or my mother's attachment to it. You will not believe this right now, Shelley, but I am sorry for offending you. You are my only love, the only woman I have ever loved. I would give my soul to right things between us, and so it *'tis,*" he said reverting to an Irish end statement.

Shelley awkwardly placed the teapot on the table, careful to set it safely back from the edge. Still immersed in the destruction, she murmured, "The dishes may have been her only comfort when she came here. She did not speak the language, and found herself surrounded by everything new—much of it dreadful—worse than she feared."

Trembling, she knew the monologue was about herself. She sensed the magic had gone from her marriage as surely as broken pieces lay all over the dining room. Was this reckless fury related to her earlier disillusionment, that Patrick would not be there for her? Too confused to make sense of her actions, delayed overnight by sheer will, she reached for the broom.

Gradually, she felt the anger draining from her body. She hid looming tears from Patrick just as she had from Danielle. Attempting a stiff upper lip, she announced, "I will see to it that Neva benefits from our stay in Boston."

She swept the broken dishes into the trash bin.

Patrick gathered his coat and books and left for classes, but dragging his feet as if first needing to reconcile differences with his wife.

The gentle click of the door behind him immediately closed Shelley's world—Boston now felt stifling. She longed to run away to the sheltered stream above Danielle's cabin, where the music of a tiny spring had consoled her; to walk and talk in the hills of Butte with Gertie; to drown her sorrows on her father's shoulder. Anywhere but here where the insistent harbor fog lived like a regular tenant among the dank interiors of flats crowded into acres of apartment buildings.

Her mood plunged. Every moment she imagined Patrick meeting that woman in the library. Or taking her to his favorite spot along the Charles River where he had taken Shelley. But Neva peeped from her room, her warm, tousled-haired-self in a flannel nightgown ready for breakfast and a new day. While Shelley prepared porridge, Neva whirled around the apartment like one of the little goats she had tended at Danielle's home. Unable to endure the tension any longer, Shelley took her outside, scouring the streets for interesting places to entertain her. They walked along the river, despite the stabs of pain Shelley suffered. But the outing aired their minds and exercised Neva's leg. Neva had always been there to give Shelley's life purpose. Now the child represented a life raft, holding the family together as surely as small boats lay tied and anchored at the icy river's edge.

Time faded through Shelley's mind for many dreary weeks, until she happened to recall a conversation at the Harvard social with a parent who mentioned the convenience of a nearby church Mission School for childcare.

"Neva, we are going on an adventure."

"I want to go to the river and feed the ducks."

"You wanted to go to school when we lived with Mother."

"We left the school with her."

"We might find another one if we look hard enough."

"We will look really hard. I want to walk there by myself."

"Well, I will walk with you." Shelley bundled Neva for the adventure.

They found the Mission School bordering a dense immigrant ghetto, mossy-brown tenements stretching in every direction among narrow, alley-like streets inhabited by riff-raff, pickpockets, and fishmongers. The school held classes in the church basement in two half-day sessions to accommodate the many families that needed child care.

"Where is the school house?"

Shelley startled, then laughed. "This is the school, Neva." Words defied a simple explanation. Neva held an image of a one-room, log cabin schoolhouse, an image now challenged by an amorphous swarm of ethnic humanity crammed into rooms surrounded by the church's stone and mortar foundation. Older lads in knickers and knee socks shouldered past pint-sized students. Small children clung to hands of mothers, fathers or grandparents, both young and old appearing too overwhelmed to deal with one more transition in their lives. A few well-dressed adults stood to one side, conveying they were a world apart from the ragged and hungry masses. Shelley moved toward that side, unconsciously identifying with parents associated with Harvard or Cambridge. She glanced at Neva.

"I can go to my very own school?" Neva clung to Shelley's hand with a shy but undaunted half-smile. She had seen few other children in the Territorial camps, many of whom became the tough, streetwise newsboys widely known in Butte. Neva would have been unable to hold her own in the rough silver town school. Here, Shelley had similar doubts.

"How is a crippled child to cope in this melée?" Shelley whispered to a woman about her age.

"Children find commonality among themselves. They become assimilated regardless of their differences. You will be amazed. Many of us assist with teaching here. The children are a breath of fresh air."

Shelley noticed that the adults were grossly outnumbered, and even they had trouble conversing with each other in a smattering of languages. Shelley wondered about the "amazing" part of the woman's testimony, but too much was at stake to back out now. Neva had been introduced to a school. Her tenacious soul would never, ever let that pass her by.

Before they left that day, Shelley had volunteered as a teacher's helper, thereby solving two problems at once. It helped pay for Neva's schooling, and it allowed her to oversee Neva's wish come true. Perhaps dedicating her time to the Mission school would push back thoughts of Patrick and the Southern belle, a certain Miss Violet Hamilton.

12

SHELLEY IN BOSTON

Dense, heavy clouds persisted along the shorelines of Dorchester Bay and the ocean while Shelley drifted through the short days of late fall. Temperatures felt colder to her because of the moist air, a contrast to the year-round dry atmosphere of the Rocky Mountains. The magic of the East Coast had lost its spell for her; she hugged herself in the blue wool coat and plodded to the Mission school and back with an excited seven-year-old school girl. Shelley and Patrick danced a reel of sorts, bypassing each other and mixing with others, most faceless strangers they encountered in their everyday lives. Their own lives had quickly become less about adventure and ambition than about pain and recriminations. She prepared meals when he came home late at night, ironed his shirts, a chore that now became tedious, and shopped street markets which seemed as dirty or dirtier than Butte's.

Eventually other events edged into Shelley's consciousness. Of multiple bulletins and news flyers advertising activities on the Harvard campus, one listed lectures and debates that were open to the public, reminding her of the meetings she enjoyed with Miss Adelaide Owens and Gertie. But Shelley usually found the topics boring or beyond her. Typical offerings included "The Fredrick Douglass Debates," "Maritime Laws During the Revolutionary War," or "Radical Reconstruction and Compromise."

More promising was a panel discussion of Sojourner Truth's 1870's speech that advocated land grants for blacks in the West, an idea Shelley endorsed, though Congress under President Rutherford Hayes had failed to act on the proposal.

Shelley frequently scanned the bulletins then ducked into empty hallways to avoid being seen. Embarrassed by her lack of a higher education and the refinements that come with an upper class culture, she dragged her feet home and wrapped her life around Neva and the Mission school, which limited her time to explore other avenues. Her commitment to assist teachers in the classrooms tended to grow, given the endless influx and turn-over of immigrants.

Neva refused to miss a single day with her newfound friends, though they spoke a dozen different languages. The blessing was that children communicated with other children in often intricate and unspoken ways. A sideways look offered an apple to a lunch partner. A pat on a soft pillow meant two could sit and take turns reading a story by the pictures. They knew which children hid pencils or biscuits or other children's mittens inside their coats, but they did not tattle. The half-day sessions flew by, and Shelley soon became assimilated along with the children.

"Mission school offers quite a change from my former life," she confided to one of the mothers. "Here I am part of the thrill and chaos and often grim side of Boston, a city I found over-whelming a few months ago."

Yet she still felt drawn to attend events at Harvard, another previously unfathomable notion. The campus offered a vigor not previously available to her, a thriving intellectual climate and a diversity of stimulating individuals, both an invitation to step up to challenges she had never imagined.

Miss Owens, M.D., had engaged Shelley in the currents of local, state and national issues. The women's movement inhabit-ed causes affecting all three levels of government at a profoundly intimate and urgent level. Shelley had not only attended meet-ings in Butte, Montana Territory, but she had made the cause her own. If, as Gertie said, women in the United States were often little better off than those in countries abroad from which whole families fled, then something was amiss in this country. The status of women was one glaring factor. Unfortunately, Shelley had thus far found herself so involved in a woman's traditional role that she had little time to join the movement in Boston.

A day finally came when Shelley took an opportunity to escape their drab apartment building to attend a public talk she had noticed on one of the bulletins. Patrick stayed home with Neva, both sniffling from a cold front blown in from the Maritime Provinces. She walked confidently across the Harvard campus between stolid buildings, feeling in the presence of history, if not entirely aware of what transpired there. At first, Patrick had delighted in introducing her to this memorial and that colonial edifice, but after awhile it all ran together in her mind. Alone she sensed generations who trod the walkways beneath her feet among centuries old hardwood trees. Trees that might have witnessed the birth of the colonies, onslaught of the Revolution, unfolding of independence, and more recently, the ghastly Civil War that attempted to preserve the foregoing.

New life surged in Shelley's body as invigorating as the snappy sea air off the Atlantic. Surely the lecture discussing Elizabeth Barrett Browning's modern poetry would be exciting as well. She visualized a cherished dividend—upon her return to Butte, she would be able to engage in a discussion of contemporary literature with Miss Owens.

She knew Miss Owens kept abreast of happenings in the East by an exchange of letters and news clippings, as well as by speakers visiting Butte. Educated women helped fill an intellectual and cultural void for her in the far West when they met for tea in Miss Owen's apartment. Mrs. Baumbier, the mayor's wife, frequently attended, making sure everyone knew that her father had been a preeminent professor at Cornell University. Whether Mrs. Baumbier had a higher education or relied on the proximity to higher learning was not entirely clear.

Shelley felt in a similar situation. Her father had distinguished himself at the School of Mines in Colorado in mineralogy, a subject completely foreign to Shelley's mind and aptitude. The accolades he had earned had been temporarily purged in the "silver city" of Butte, Montana Territory, however he had risen above the crowd to distinguish himself.

Shelley found her way to the Assembly Hall and entered a bit late, in time to see Miss Violet Hamilton rise to the podium. The woman apparently celebrated her name at every opportunity; a wide violet ribbon draped elegantly across the crown of her becoming hat, dropping seductively down her bodice. Shelley's easy stride halted in mid-air. She could turn at once and flee. No one would have noticed her, given the fascinating speaker with a voice as smooth as cream. Yet her inner struggle lasted only a moment. Shelley daringly strode down the aisle, even further than she intended. Further than politeness permitted, though Miss Hammer, as she privately called her, continued without interruption. Shelley was certain she had seen her, particularly since Shelley wore the same blue outfit she had worn to the social event where she met her nemesis.

"Miss Elizabeth Barrett Browning was a poet of extraordinary talent whose love poems may have been England's greatest export to their former colonies, next to English black tea."

Titters followed Miss Hamilton's remark.

"Her *Sonnets from the Portuguese* speak to women's long repression of their feelings and desires."

Shelley nearly choked, stifling the sound with the back of her glove.

"I would like to quote from Sonnet 21. '*Say thou dost love me, love me…*'"

The fiend. The lowlife creature. She is speaking of Patrick to hurt me, Shelley screamed inwardly, her scowl disavowing any connection to the woman.

Yet responding to the rapt attention of her audience, Miss Hamilton read a number of passages illustrating the modern thinking of such an unlikely herald for the advancement of womankind, a deathly ill woman who dared write of her inner-most feelings.

"You may know by her reputation that she has shaken up the worlds of men and women for completely opposite reasons. Her outspokenness was often considered "unfeminine" by men, implying a wantonness improper for women. Her advocacy of social justice infringed on matters dominated by men. However, many women found her epic poems expressed what they felt and were not allowed to say. The poems recognized their yearnings, their hurts, and the social limitations placed upon them in society. Miss Browning's openness continues to challenge women to represent the age. Women increasingly find her words inspiring, indeed a calling."

The remarks seemed to receive more of a thoughtful, non-committal silence than that of the bold love poem. Shelley's experience that few women heard the "calling" proved the difficulty of moving them to the cause, even though the women's movement would entirely benefit them.

"You are here today because Miss Browning's poetry speaks for many of us. The love sonnets hold and caress all our deepest desires."

Oh, God no, Shelley fairly screeched, grasping her throat. Your deepest desire for my husband, you weasel-mouthed predator.

"And she speaks to those of us who want to better the lives of women and children at home, and end their exploitation in the workplace. You are here today because in our own ways, we are each seeking to live more fully, personally and professionally. You may be aware we have no men in attendance today."

Murmurs swept across the hall. Miss Hammer had the women in the palm of her hand. Shelley could not have moved if the petite woman had lifted Patrick in triumph over her witty head. Shelley's fury simmered while she determined to listen, even if every single word stuck in her craw. If this is what she needed to better her life and Neva's, and possibly her mother's she would sit here and listen.

"As a result of Miss Browning's social justice poetry, significant legislation passed in Parliament limiting the hours children could work in the mines and factories."

The words blurred while Shelley absorbed less of the content than Miss Hammer's even, cultured voice. She held her breath in awe of the assured intellectual discussion and studied gestures of the woman's very feminine hands. Shelley involuntarily glanced at her own hands, and sighed. I can understand why Patrick was attracted to her—she is so—womanly. Shelley's lips worked, her pain held back. Miss Hammer is warm and educated.

Gathering her thoughts, she listened to Miss Hamilton conclude her remarks.

"It is interesting that this woman and many others have found a means of expressing their passions in literature despite the fact that women generally have no voice."

Shelley blankly looked on while the crowd of women sprang to their feet in affirmation.

"Our next speaker's platform will present a discussion of Nathanial Hawthorne's *Scarlet Letter*. I urge all of you to read the book beforehand. Thank you for your kind attention. I hope to see you in the library."

Cruel, you are a cruel, devious monster—Shelley felt Miss Hammer brazenly, purposely fired an arrow piercing her heart—"passions"—"library"— only she knew how to hurt Shelley in a crowd.

Woodenly, Shelley rose and followed the women from the Hall. Retracing her steps over the winding, leaf-covered paths, alternately crying and storming, she vowed never in a hundred years to venture to the same library where Patrick studied law with this vixen.

At the flat, Patrick bore into thick law books day and night. The pattern of disengagement generally left her to entertain

Neva so Shelley rarely had to deal with him. The fury and attendant insights she carried after the Assembly had nowhere to go. Loneliness shadowed her like a constant companion; yearnings went unfulfilled. Homesickness prevailed. Shelley often excused herself from Patrick and Neva, saying she did not feel well.

Left alone in her bedroom, Shelley reflected on what seemed like the distant past. Danielle has a steady husband and a home. What went wrong with our half of the double wedding? I feel strangled by the East, by the distance across the country—and by my own seething resentments.

However, a few days later, the vow forgotten and needing to get out of the flat, Shelley asked for directions to the Humanities Library, one of dozens of libraries in or near Harvard Yard. She required further assistance to locate volumes of Miss Browning's poetry and Hawthorne's *Scarlet Letter*. Once steered to the proper shelves, within moments she had selected an armload of books that she absolutely could not do without.

The adrenalin rush of delving into the world of literary treasures maintained Shelley for weeks, while Patrick's alleged betrayal continued to fester. At last Shelley resumed the cross examination as if she had never stopped. Patrick reacted as if he were on the stand devising his own defense.

"I—we—became friends over time."

"In the library. You told me."

Patrick searched for words.

"Did you bring her here?" Shelley fervently wanted Patrick to say no. She needed the Colter home to feel like her own.

"We studied together. I found Miss Hamilton to be an interesting student of both literature and the law. I assure you it was no more than that. She invited me to several social occasions. Over time she became quite possessive, as you witnessed. God forbid that should ever happen again."

Shelley crumpled, her shoulders slack. She felt the wound could not go deeper. She envisioned intimate hours, days, weeks, months may have passed with him enjoying her as being "interesting" in the library and on "social occasions."

And I was crying my eyes out at a hidden spring in the dry hills above the Jefferson River. Cold shouldering Danielle who upstaged me at my own wedding. Ignoring my sister until I'd forgotten her presence for months. All because of my grief and loss for you. This rift in our married life goes back to being separated too early.

Unsure whether the rift was repairable, Shelley spoke up, "I saw her again." Now that there was nothing to lose she abandoned caution.

Patrick sucked in his breath. "In the library?"

"No. In the lecture hall."

"Umm, what lecture was that?"

"Please, Patrick, I couldn't tell you what lecture, but I can tell you what she was wearing."

A giggle involuntarily escaped with Shelley's nervous explanation, upsetting her intention to strike at Patrick as deeply she had felt stricken.

"So silly of me—." She vividly recalled the dark maroon gown with bands of black velvet trimming the floor-length skirt.

"Now you sound more like the woman I married," Patrick smiled. "Please believe me, she never came here and there was never anything unseemly between us."

"For her, there was. She doesn't fish without bait."

It was Patrick's turn to laugh. "I am that much of a catch, eh?"

"Never mind. I would assume that I envy her as much as she envies me." Shelley's voice quavered, still eluding the control she desired to deliver a tongue lashing.

Patrick slipped on his coat to leave for the day, then turned back. "You envy her in what way?"

"She is confident and charming. It is no wonder she catches men's eyes. I found her lecture in the Assembly Hall full of women to be quite brilliant. I felt so—so common." This definitely was not going the way she intended.

"Charlotte Norton, I marvel at what goes on in your mysterious head. Or is this true for all women? By all reports I heard in Montana Territory, I am fortunate to have a beautiful, charming and, yes, highly intelligent wife with uncommon strength of character. I am the envy of Butte and certain dignitaries in Boston for whisking you away as my wife."

Shelley stared, mouth half open.

Adopting a phrase from his Dublin born mother, he began, "*'And this is what it was,'* though you may have difficulty believing me, I hold you and Neva dearest to my heart above everything. Everything, dearest. I would not betray you, and I did not betray our marriage."

Shelley sat down hard on the dressing table chair, relieved she had not exploded with accusations that their marriage was irreparable.

"*'And so it was,'* you and Neva would say," she added.

Patrick hovered over her to seal his agreement with a kiss, resounding enough to smother any objections before he left the apartment.

———————

A drizzly winter month crept past, punctuated by blasts of icy snow from the Arctic. Shelley rarely ventured forth except to circle past the Humanities Library for another armload of books on her way to pick up Neva at school. She purchased fresh bread, fish or poultry on their way home. Storms, the holidays, and whole weeks passed while Patrick labored under a heavy load of studies, as well as legal cases at the Bosworth firm. Shelley and Neva had their books. They read and read, one frigid day and evening after another, huddled next to a miniature fire in the less than adequate wood stove, wood being a limited commodity despite thickets of trees all over New England.

Neva's finger traced words she pronounced far beyond her class level. Shelley's copy of Chaucer's *Canterbury Tales* caught Patrick's eye. He grinned, closing their former distance with a shared commitment to learning.

Inner cities bursting with immigrant populations suffered dire winter deprivations, while established families lived quite well in fine mansions spread over Boston's hilltops and lining the waterfront of Dorchester Bay. An unrivaled aristocracy still reigned in the northern states, though that of the South had been roundly defeated. Waves of black emigrants continued to move north, freedom a mantra on everyone's tongue yet a reality for few—a concept that generally excluded black women who joined cadres of disenfranchised white women.

Years ago a new literature had arisen from the turmoil. Sojourner Truth's 1850s appeal for woman equality transcended issues of race, education and origin, and became an enduring rallying cry after the Civil War. Further impetus for social justice arose in 1873, when Boston's own Lucy Stone and a colleague, Julia Ward Howe, replicated tactics of the Boston Tea Party by organizing a protest against taxation without representation at Faneuil Hall. Miss Owens wrote to Shelley

I would have joined them but I was in medical school at the time.

Yet the North and South defied women's cries for equality and social reform. From her unique position between the Mission school in the ghettos and Harvard University, Shelley saw how entrenched aristocrats were in the Northeast. These same families donated to refugee relief at the Mission school, but failed to further legislation relieving those who required charity. She wrote much of what she witnessed to Miss Owens.

You would find resistance to the cause firmly established here. Our former ally, Frederick Douglass, has since opposed women's demand for the vote on the grounds it would hinder passage of Amendments guaranteeing full rights of citizenship to black men. In the name of expediency, he has forsaken his earlier commitment to enable all citizens to vote.

Finding herself soon mired in melancholy from such reading, Shelley sought contemporary women writers such as Louisa May Alcott, Jane Austen, the Brontë sisters, and Willa Cather. Shelley later wrote to Miss Owens.

It's not that I object to ironing my husband's white shirts. Truly, if I did not, some other poor woman would do it for a pittance, making both of us less than what we are. What I object to is the notion that we, as women, are "unfit" for public affairs.

Shelley lost herself so deeply in heavy themes, even in the newfound fiction treasures awaiting her at the library, that she was surprised one day when Patrick handed her a letter in a manila envelope.

"A letter from Irmgarde?" Shelley turned the letter over in her hands. It was stamped Butte, Montana Territory, and had evidently been in transit for some time. If there had been a date it was smudged. Patrick stood aside, curious but skeptical about correspondence from a woman in the District.

Shelley looked up at him. "This came to Mr. Bosworth's office? And he handed it to you? Did he say anything?"

"He asked me to deliver it to you. He appeared to be pleased. I cannot imagine why." Patrick turned toward his desk, always piled high with law books, reams of research, and legal papers that should have gone out yesterday.

Shelley slit open the double-wrapped envelope with a kitchen knife and read.

Heirloom China

Dear Shelley:

I hope that sending this letter to you in care of Mr. Bosworth is not entirely presumptuous.

In case you have not heard, the reason for his involvement is that I found his son, the attorney, shot and bleeding on the street and ran to get Dr. Gallagher. Mr. Bosworth credits me with saving his son's life. He extends entirely too much credit to be sure, since I chanced to come along at the right moment. However, Doc or Lucas may be behind this, too.

I must thank you for directing me to gatherings at Miss Owens' office, or I would not have been going home at that particular moment to find Mr. Bosworth's son. There is much more to the story but you know how I ramble. Your absence here has been a loss, as well as the times we walked in the hills and discussed many important issues, dare I say obstacles, which confront women. The more I learn about these obstacles, the more I understand about myself and my life.

Now for the surprise! Mr. Bosworth insisted that he reward me with the opportunity to attend a private Women's Academy in Boston. Naturally, I blurted out (my rashness is a major character flaw) that I knew you. Shame on me! This did not seem to come as news to him. I suspect Dr. Gallagher is behind that, also. My benefactor returned to the East and made all the arrangements. I slipped out before first light this morning and posted this letter, then left on the stage without (you may guess why) any goodbyes.

I do believe my life has made a turn for the better, and I may become a decent woman after all. Your friendship has helped me believe in myself. Just look what a little bit of kindness can do in the world. It has the most amazing rippling effects.

If you care to correspond once I am relocated, you may reach me through Mr. Bosworth's office, since he will kindly find a place for me to live when I arrive there. Just so you know, I am paying my personal expenses from my horde of Montana gold!

Irmgarde

Shelley's knees nearly buckled. She sank down into a chair with the two sheets of coarse paper dangling from her fingers. Butte seemed so long ago, its drama, its tragedies so acute that one must blank out those days to go on. She swallowed hard remembering. Patrick had been threatened. It may or may not have been serious, but it robbed me of my new husband. Rumors were that Lucas was dead, or mortally wounded. Antonio came in disguise and smuggled us out of town as if we were criminals.

The memories were so bleak and frightening she forced herself to see the other side of Butte. Funny that Gertie represented much of that. A childish joy in simple things, a bag of candy, colorful costumes, a girlish need to talk. Shelley shook the wrinkles out of the paper. She laughed. Gertie had signed with a flourish taking up half a page. The blue smudges at the bottom smelled like saltwater taffy. She must have been so nervous!

"Oh, I can't wait to see Gertie!" She handed the letter to Patrick who appeared completely baffled by this latest involvement of his wife.

He accepted the pages gingerly as if a certain ill repute might rub off on him. "You want me to read this? I am not comfortable doing that. Do you mind telling me? I have other business to attend to."

Shelley snatched the letter back and braced herself for a confession she had long known she would have to make to her husband.

Patrick securely replaced the cap on the ink well and set the pin in its holder. Neva had attended a neighbor's play school with a small friend. He leaned back and crossed his legs; his peripheral vision hovered over his workload. Beyond Shelley's head, his eyes unconsciously sought the china cabinet, a reminder of another volatile marital discussion. His left hand absently stroked his beard, as if gleaning a piece of wisdom that might absolve him of any wrong doing this time. After all, this business with the woman from Butte's infamous bordellos was Shelley's doings, not his.

"I cannot talk to you when you look at me like that."

"Uh, how am I looking?" Had his recent practice in cross-examination already taken root in his visage? He dared not alienate his wife while he strived to be a powerful if not ruthless prosecutor; at least that was a semblance of his professional goal.

"I am sorry, but I refuse to feel guilty about having a street woman for a best friend. Or for that matter, for buying nice clothes or attending teas or meetings about causes you despise, OR about—"

Shelley's outburst escalated until Patrick raised a palm for quiet, as he might have done with Neva.

"Just tell me if you care to divulge what is in the letter, and how you happen to have this—this unusual relationship. It seems to matter a great deal to you."

Shelley sat in stony silence.

Patrick knew as well as she did that the Mercury Street women spent their days and money mingling with the citizens on the streets of Butte, if not interacting with them on a more personal level. Their presence was tolerated, not respected. They were as much a part of the landscape as the pointy butte that gave the town its name, as commonly encountered as the miners coming off their shift, the freighters that jammed uptown streets, and the newsboys hawking competitive papers.

In Boston, he and Shelley never walked an hour off campus that they did not pass women of ill repute, often brushing elbows in the congestion. The rollicking, riotous harbor city was a seedy counterpart to New York City, both immigrant destinations where poverty, desperation, and exploitation were the sad reality. Respectable women were generally escorted by male figures out of Old World gallantry and New World precaution. Patrick tried to rationalize that his wife would not have compromised her reputation—or his, even when he was two thousand miles away. Or that she would have knowingly crossed his will.

His feet hit the floor. Shelley jumped.

"Other men's wives seem to do their husbands' bidding socially, and do not rock the boat politically. I distinctly remember "to love and obey" in certain vows that matter to me. If there is something I need to know, I am listening."

"There, that is what Miss Owens was talking about. I did not expect it of you to take such a stodgy, intolerable stand against me."

Patrick strode across the room and faced Shelley directly. "That is what that Miss Owens told you? I suppose this Miss Irmgarde Meyer is part of a conspiracy against men, too."

"If you could find it in yourself to respect me, that is what I want, Patrick." Shelley's breath came hard and fast, but she did not yield.

"Shelley, I beg your pardon. We were talking about the letter." He dropped his voice. "How did it come to this? Please, I cannot bear to see you upset." He added, his voice tapering off, "I want to understand."

She left the room, her bearing expressing more dignity than Patrick could find within himself at the moment.

"I think I lost the case," he muttered. He picked up the letter and sat down to read.

13
RISING STAR

Shelley fled to her roll-top desk, worn from passage aboard a ship a generation ago. She scrambled for paper and pen to write a message to Gertie, to be sent in care of Mr. Bosworth, with hopes he would be amenable to forwarding it. Her hand raced over the page.

"Once I answer her letter Mr. Bosworth will no longer be involved," she assured herself.

Could you meet me at the arched stone bridge on the Charles River tomorrow noon?

She posted the letter when she went to get Neva at school, an overcast day brightened by the merry child and the letter from Gertie.

The Charles River cut artful curves through Cambridge, feigning domesticity amid the relentless expansion of Boston's population, yet it maintained woods and waterfowl of the former wilderness. Tall dry grass slumped in clusters over the river's ice-crusted edges, casting long, waving reflections in the slow movement below where a few geese and ducks circled and squawked. Bare tree limbs created striking silhouettes against hovering dark clouds.

Shelley hastened her steps toward the bridge, her eagerness reminding her of meeting Gertie on the corner of Main and Park in Butte when Shelley got off work at the Mercantile. Those days seemed long ago but Shelley savored the memory of walking above the density of smelter smoke that tended to hang low over Summit Valley. She felt much younger then, carefree despite the vision of caring for Neva forever, a vision as familiar to her as her own skin.

Unexpectedly, it was Gertie's irreverence toward all things, her blunt, unsolicited advice, and most of all, her acerbic humor that had engaged Shelley. Today Shelley smiled, hummed, and drew the river's damp air into her lungs.

Am I being unfair to my husband in being true to myself? I seek the most implausible woman in the world—Gertie, who just parted overhanging branches. Gertie strode confidently to the center of the bridge in a pale beige two-piece suit, the skirt draping to her well-hidden ankles.

"Gertie! Bless you. Am I seeing things?"

"This is me reincarnated as a quite-a-bit-older student in the Women's Academy, and now a resident on the East Coast. Can you imagine?"

"I am so happy for you, Gertie. Excuse me, Miss Irmgarde. You don't know how I have missed you." Shelley's hand flew over her mouth to stifle cries. She threw her arms around Gertie for a close hug, hiding her tears. It was the first intimacy they ever shared, if they didn't count women's talk. At first Shelley felt speechless, a mystifying occurrence since her relationship with Gertie had always felt natural.

Gertie's frankness cut through the awkwardness. "It can't be that bad for you, married and all. And, 'Gertie' is fine, if we can be informal with one another."

"I have had no one to talk to," Shelley mumbled. "The law students' wives are so—so absorbed in their own lives. The women at Neva's Mission school mourn for their countries and struggle for a living. It seems I moved from one location where women barely survive to another. I avoided telling Patrick I was meeting you here today. He has become quite negative about my activities. I never expected that in Patrick. Let's walk. We may see some loons."

She knew she was delaying what she was bursting to say, what she needed to get off her chest. Gertie hiked up her trailing skirts to walk the winding dirt path along the river, revealing a glimpse of the trademark red stockings.

"Gertie, why are you wearing those? Didn't you say you would be a decent woman? Those—those—"

Gertie's laughter rang from the treetops. "Must I change all at once? Besides these are my only pair of stockings."

"I know what you mean. My clothes are dowdy except for the one new outfit I bought. In due time I may learn to sew a gown rather than washday cotton dresses and little outfits for Neva.

"Sew my clothes? It is doubtful I will change that much! We need to go shopping!"

They giggled and walked, talk flowing as easily as if their last conversation occurred yesterday. Shelley pried details of the ambush from a reluctant Gertie. "Mr. Bosworth must be so grateful to you. You saved his son's life." She discouraged Gertie from downplaying her role.

"And nearly got myself arrested. Doc called Sheriff Ford. Would you believe the sheriff interrogated me during an event like that? 'Why am I on the street again? Didn't I learn anything the last time I was picked up? Who would believe a whore? Did I have a grudge and shoot Mr. Bosworth? Didn't the poor jerk pay me enough?' God, Shelley, I left before he locked me up."

"Maybe he was in on it."

"That is all behind me. Mr. Bosworth said Lucas is determined to remain in Butte. You have to hand it to him. He has courage. Your husband was wise to leave."

"I have to tell you about my husband." Shelley's voice dropped. "He was seeing a woman before I came East." Shelley felt as though she dropped a hot ember.

"No! I hardly believe any man alone for months at a time would think of it."

"Gertie, be serious. He is a married man though we were married only a short time before he came here. Miss Violet Hammer is a charming young thing. She tried to make off with him in front of me."

"Better to know the enemy than not."

"And I saw her again lecturing in an assembly hall. She is studying law just like Patrick."

"What is it about this woman that fascinates you and your husband?"

Shelley glanced sideways at Gertie, decided she was serious, and considered the pointed question.

"Why do I give a tinker's damn about her? What's done is done. He swears it was nothing, but now I have to live with my— my anger, distrust, and envy."

"You talk like a disgruntled Butte miner."

Shelley shrugged, sensing emancipation of her language and anger if not her situation. "I think I envy Miss Hammer. Not her real name. I would like to be like her. Maybe Patrick would love me more if I were like her."

"You definitely need to go shopping! It makes a girl feel better about herself."

"Oh, leave off. Fashions get me only so far. Patrick was suspicious about your letter, about you contacting me. I could not speak civilly with him. I am sorry, but I may not be able to meet you on the up and up."

"Miss Owens would frown. She is the one who set us on a different path. Me, at least. She sees the larger picture for women. I, for one, am convinced she is right. We are all whores and victims if we remain powerless. Posters in Cambridge prominently advertise talks and events concerning the women's movement."

"Are you going to meetings or organizational teas?"

"Not yet, but I will. I have been so nervous among all the

people and hubbub, I ate two bags of candy the first week after I arrived. A leopard's spots are not changed overnight."

They laughed and turned back along the path, arm in arm.

Shelley hurried home alone, rehearsing the stories she would tell Patrick. *Gertie is a hero for saving Lucas. Gertie understands me more than you do. Gertie is my best friend and will remain so. Gertie has put her past life behind her. She said so.*

None seemed suitable for the confrontation ahead.

Shelley's sighs shifted her mood of gaiety to one of dread. She picked up Neva and walked a few doors down to a fish market for the day's catch. Neva skipped a few steps before righting her balance. Muscle tone in the paralyzed leg had improved and feeling had returned to part of her leg and foot.

"I have a new friend. He is smaller than me and he reads!" Neva exclaimed. "We read books at school. We should buy another book. I can read the pictures of the bird book. I already know the story in the picture book Mama gave me."

Her bounce always lifted Shelley's spirits. She made a note to provide more reading material for Neva. It was late when Patrick arrived home for supper, his face drawn and haggard, his body stooped with fatigue.

Neva had already fallen asleep. Gertie's letter lay open on his desk. "Shelley," he said, and took her in his arms.

Unexpectedly, Shelley shook with sobs instead of the apprehension she had carried home with her. The made-up stories about Gertie were forgotten. Her warmth pressed into his, both holding closely as if they sensed each other's unease. Patrick stroked her hair, loosened the pins, murmured in her ear, and kissed her brow, cheeks, and lips. Shelley saw mist in his eyes, the sad droop around the tired edges meant he'd had a hard day. *Is it my fault? Was it the letter?*

She burst with remorse. "I apologize, Patrick. I certainly did not intend to offend you about the letter—"

Her words were muffled in the tight fold of his arms. The letter could wait, but Shelley had to spill her guilt. "I met with Gertie today. We walked along the Charles River. I needed a friend—I am grateful she is here."

"So am I, if you are. Who is to say why this—this unusual turn of events is happening in our lives?" Patrick unfastened the long row of looped buttons on the back of her dress one by one.

As Shelley wheedled the knot undone of his cravat, she remembered the night she was angry and distanced from him. Shelley let him talk. Or not talk. A ray of contentment surfaced in place of what she feared was lost, the acceptance of her husband. They said little until early morning when the racket of awakening streets sounded in their apartment.

———————

A heavy snowstorm brought out boots, fur-trimmed hats and cozy muffs. Bookseller nooks jammed between artisan shops invited browsers to duck in out of the chill. Enticed into a major bookstore by patrons hovering over huge tables of books, Shelley craned her neck to view shelves laden with additional books from floor to distant ceilings.

Outside along the narrow sidewalk Shelley caught their rosy-cheeked reflections in the tiny panes of shop windows. Wind chimes above doorsteps composed endless small concerts for shoppers. Dozens and dozens of candle and stationery shops, no two alike, offered tall tallow tapers to stubby vigil lights and candle lanterns. Wildflower-pressed and embossed candles mingled with intricately engraved wax creations. The assortment dazzled the eye, sweet or spicy fragrances tickled the nose. Gertie fingered etched ivory stationery and cards, ornate with a blush of pink or blue on scalloped edges. "I wonder how they print these. They are so delicate. I think we lived in the Territory too long! You must see the latest in the hat shops."

They found an entire display window of fashionable headpieces, one with plumes and swaths of silk over a velveteen crown. A wide, sculpted brim showcased a pearl-studded band.

"Oh, I could wear that," Gertie said, fluffing her dangling curls.

"Imagine Miss Owens indulging in excesses of fashion. Which reminds me, the women in the residency hall asked me to inform them about the political climate in Montana Territory. It seems that Wyoming Territory granted women's suffrage years ago. I was not aware of its significance at the time. The prominence of the national women's movement is astonishing, Shelley, and here in Boston we are in the midst of it."

"You will be speaking?" The notion of public speaking was beyond Shelley's comprehension—except that she had seen, if not fully heard, Miss Violet Hamilton at the podium. "I dare not mention speeches or 'causes' to my husband. He fears I am not traditional enough as it is."

"Lyceum sponsored lectures occur regularly at the Women's Academy. Women gather for 'enlightening discussions', their words, not mine. I find this intellectual climate quite a hoot at times. Apparently, I am an oddity from the frontier, like Daniel Boone or Jim Bridger, a female scout required to report findings of uncharted lands. Never fear, I will not reveal that the Bosworths' sprung me from Butte's infamous District."

Ignoring Gertie's self-deprecation, Shelley said, "Well, this came about quite suddenly. I congratulate you. The woman I referred to, Miss Violet Hammer, could not have attained the position of public speaker any faster than you, and she had the advantage of coming from a prominent family."

Pamphlets stuck in Cambridge windows advertised poetry readings, lyceums by visiting dignitaries, Frances Willard's Women's Christian Temperance Union meetings, medical and law lectures, and a plethora of modest but enticing invitations to join various causes supported by women.

"You know, Gertie, I have not seen a single advertisement for a quilting bee," Shelley quipped.

Shelley threw herself into the Mission school routine, teaching several English classes to younger children and a separate assimilation class for their parents. The staff was nearly as fluid as the stream of students at all levels in the school. Individuals and families soon gained a level of competence and moved on to seek independence in their adopted country. Their languages contributed to a reverse assimilation—Neva requested a craic, thanks to her little Irish friends.

"*Dia duit*," she greeted her playmates, her voice a lilting copy of theirs.

Patrick occasionally found himself addressed as "*Da*," a charade of family relationships that accommodated Neva's concept.

"Neva, my little lassie, you have taken up with the Colter family's Irish side. My mother, your *gran*, would be right proud, aye, I think we need to honor you with a wee gift. One handed down in my family from distant relatives in the Emerald Isles across the ocean."

Patrick selected a key from behind a heavy oak cupboard and unlocked the dented steamer trunk with its frayed bindings. Neva leaned forward, nearly disappearing into the layers of pointed lace and cross-stitched fancy work. Patrick extricated her and a small wooden box etched with a Celtic knot. She climbed into his lap to better view the contents. Little fingers pricd and poked to raise the creaky lid.

"Ohhh!" A tinkle of rings and clasps and brooches mixed with the tap-tap of orange and green stones tumbling against each other. "Oh, my!"

Shelley gazed at the delighted pair, seeing a light sweep across Patrick's face that she had not seen before, the handiwork and jewelry apparently a connection with his mother. His lips trembled, eyes misted, until Neva's ambitious investigation threatened to spill the treasures. He pulled out a necklace of small round jasper stones. The length lifted slowly, elegantly from the tangle of jewelry, then snapped.

Neva threw her hands in her lap as if fearing she had broken it. Loose polished stones rolled over her dress to dance on the floor. She looked at Patrick in dismay.

"The string was old. This belonged to your grandmother's grandmother. These stones are jasper from Ireland. See if you can find them and I will find a strong fish line. You may string a new necklace just your size."

Neva was already scrambling after errant green and orange "beads," their shiny surfaces beckoning in the dark confines of the room. Shelley gave her a bowl for her collection and rescued the jewelry box before any more mishaps occurred. Patrick tucked a strand of line in the bowl for Neva, and encircled Shelley's waist with one arm, leading her into the bedroom. He carried the jewelry box with the other hand. They were seated on the bedside, as curious as Neva had been, and relishing a few moments to explore it at leisure.

Patrick hefted a slim silver Claddagh ring in his palm, a soft mysterious expression on his face. He slipped it on her left hand, its heart pointing toward her wrist, its silver crown and hand finely modeled in tiny relief.

"With this I thee wed."

"Ohhh—," swept by his tenderness, Shelley lost words to reply. Passion wilted her knees and collapsed her against his firm arms and chest. Patrick pulled her over on the down pillows, dislodging her hairpins and releasing her long blonde hair, muffling her snuffles in his vest.

"I want to marry you again, Shelley, just between us. We will celebrate a private wedding."

Shelley sensed Patrick held her as if she were "like porcelain," the way Antonio had embraced Danielle at their wedding.

"I was too young and eager to think it through the first time. I barged in where I shouldn't have to orchestrate the double wedding. Will you marry me?" he persisted.

"Patrick, dearest, I treasure this ring, and you. Yes, I will marry you. I do."

Shelley flushed. Despite the testimony of the broken pieces of heirloom china, she was able at last to let go of Miss Hamilton, knowing she nor any other woman would ever lay claim to Patrick's affections. His lips edged under her hair, his promises reaffirmed his intentions, his commitment, and his joy in marrying her again.

"My mother would be pleased. My ancestors, too."

For long moments neither could do or say more, not even for *snogging*— Patrick's long kisses. Nor could they express their love in a certain other language with Neva stringing beads in the other room.

––––––––––––

Weeks went by and gusty storms nipped the grasshopper weather vane on Faneuil Hall, sent gulls inland from the waterfront, scattered leaves along Congress Street, and rushed adults and children into the sheltering arms of Mission school. Neva proudly wore her jasper necklace beneath a *jumper*, a long wool sweater.

In addition to Mission school in its basement, the Protestant Church's commitment to service included feeding the hungry once a day at the annex next door. Queues extended far down the street and around the corner. Women huddled in heavy shawls, and pressed insufficiently clad youngsters to their hips and skirts. Men slouched in light coats in the cold.

"What are they waiting for?" Neva once asked when they passed the line.

"Their next meal. It is very sad. They are poor."

"Why are there so many poor children?"

"Maybe they came across the ocean and speak another language like so many of your little friends. And maybe they have not yet found work to make money so they can buy food."

Shelley felt her explanations failed to express the extent and magnitude of human deprivation they experienced every day at the Mission school. Neva's questions and her own sense of inadequacy in the face of such need raised many concerns about society and its responsibilities. Miss Adelaide Owens dealt with welfare problems in Butte, Montana Territory. Surely she would have a clear sense of the problem here, and its solutions, both of which were extremely fuzzy for Shelley caught in the midst of mass immigration.

The Board at the Mission school requested the teachers meet regarding the overwhelming needs of these individuals whose bodies, minds and souls the church attempted to serve. The few men in long black coats and clerical collars appeared to represent the Church hierarchy. But most of the teachers and other volunteers were Irish Catholics who reminded Shelley of the people in Butte—for both teachers and immigrants who showed up at the Mission school, the American dream had yet to be realized.

Entrepreneurs and miners in Butte found unfathomable opportunities given the wealth of minerals and the rapidly expanding population, yet misfortune, exploitation, and hardship often robbed them of their dreams. Shelley recognized the same eagerness to succeed in the immigrants of Boston. East Coast industries such as fishing, ship building and trading each relied on a multitude of workers, who unfortunately faced obstacles similar to workers in Butte. The prevalence of powerful capitalist corporations, low pay, pubs and saloons all too readily spelled the downfall of otherwise dedicated breadwinners.

Yet the Mission school teachers' meeting could hardly be expected to address these larger issues given the immediate needs. However, it attracted a surprising number of Cambridge's nearby residents, wealthy parishioners, and representatives of groups pleading for assistance. The tightly packed crowd held the night's chill at bay. Charlotte Norton Colter heard her name called as one of the teachers asked to describe everyday conditions at the school. She instantly rose to her feet, but her head held a vacuum.

"This is unexpected. I did not plan any remarks," she heard herself saying. "To tell you the truth, I have been so involved with small children that I lack an overall picture of the services the church provides."

She faltered, stalling to gather her presence of mind. The Board, all males clad formally in black, remained silent, waiting. After a momentary pause, she continued, "But I appreciate this opportunity to tell you about one child, my younger sister. She is seven years old, and she has attended Mission school for one year. In that brief time she has met children from all over the world, and communicated with them as children do. She has learned to read, and often asks unanswerable questions such as, 'Why are so many children poor?'

"Because classes are so crowded, the older children mentor and care for the youngest. My sister, a cripple, helps little ones read and takes responsibility to see that small, shy children get a fair share of food. My parents, my husband and I always accepted that my sister would be dependent upon us her whole life. Now we credit her learning and her potential to become a teacher to the stimulating environment of your Mission school."

She dropped back into her seat, a Quaker chair as upright as a human body could bear over an interminable board meeting. After she spoke the meeting room held an unusual tension, as if people were uncertain whether to applaud or get on with business. Scattered coughs and scuffling of chairs finally brought the Board Chairman to his feet.

"Perhaps we have posed unanswerable questions ourselves." A bearded man in a stiffly starched shirt, gray wool vest and coat, he steadied himself on the dais and cleared his throat. "It seems we have focused on the tide of humanity as forces to be reckoned with Christian charity rather than seeing the plight of each individual."

He glanced at the Board members seated on the dais, then added. "I am pleased to be informed of the successes of our program rather than its deficiencies. Thank you for your observations, Mrs. uh—Colter, yes." His finger found her name on the schedule.

A woman next to Shelley squeezed her hand, the warmth flooding Shelley's palms, cold from nervousness. Shelley's thin smile in return came from the sudden realization that she had worked her heart out for a year in the Mission school and to the Board she was a name on a list. She whispered an excuse and slipped out of the meeting hall at the earliest opportunity.

———————

"Patrick, I may have ruined your reputation by my ignorance," she blurted on entering the flat. "Why, oh why, do I talk without thinking? It is a character flaw that humiliates me in front of—"

"I thought you went to a school meeting. How could that get you into a questionable situation?" Patrick roused from dozing in the rocker before the fire with Neva curled on his lap.

Shelley motioned that he carry Neva to bed before they talked. She heated water for chamomile tea to settle her nerves and thaw the icy chills in her bones. She handed Patrick a steaming cup then stumbled over her words.

"I talked about Neva at the meeting, how she thrives and how she helps other children, and how we thought she would be dependent all her life, but now we think she might be a teacher someday—"

"Whoa. Wasn't the Board tackling the problem of excessive demands on its resources and space? I am not sure that fits—"

"Oh, I am sure it was inappropriate. The Chairman was very gracious—the others stared blankly at me. I feel so guilty about airing our personal concerns." Shelley swiped the back of her hand across her runny nose and rubbed away tears.

Patrick yawned and patted her on the back. "They have invited 'the huddled masses.' My guess is they can survive one child and a somewhat hysterical mother— mother figure," he corrected.

Shelley found him deep in sleep when she went to bed around midnight, the inner turmoil exacting a toll that cost her several days of illness and time away from the school.

Cambridge circulated numerous newspapers and daily news bulletins. The churches evangelized the down-and-outers through newsletters and journals. A few days later Shelley heard from another teacher that a paper, perhaps a daily, mentioned her name in connection with the Mission school.

"Oh, no!"

"It said they offer successful programs that include youth mentoring to help younger students."

Shelley found a copy of the daily to examine the article.

"The Mission school includes not only an astounding ethnic variation, but a range of social and economic differences. They often find churches offer a cushion until they can adapt to their new world. Children of political refugee families mingle with those from impoverished families displaced by famine or strife in their homelands. Youngsters readily absorb multiple languages in the relatively unstructured Mission programs. These exchanges are apparently richer in content and vocabulary than one would find in a single income or ethnic stratification.

"According to the Board and one of the teachers, Mrs. Patrick Colter, the Mission school shows remarkable progress in language and learning skills for children and youth who participate in the programs. Youth mentoring of the younger children is one of the mainstays of this type of education that benefits both the mentor, who may find a calling in teaching, and even the youngest children who come through the door temporarily.

"The Mission school is pleased to acknowledge that this blending of talents and diversity is a healthy first step for those who aspire to be new Americans."

"If 'remarkable progress' generates more donations, my hat is off to you," the teacher said to Shelley. "Perhaps the recognition will empty pockets all over Boston."

In her state of self-doubt, the teacher's comment and article that lauded the Mission school sounded insincere to Shelley. She brushed them off until huge boxes of new school supplies were delivered to the back door of the Mission. The head teacher asked her and her sister to distribute them.

Shelley and Neva subsequently handed out a fair share of prized pencils, tablets and readers to each of the younger students.

The venerable law firm of R. Bosworth & Son in Boston might have been just one more gray office front in a classic-style commercial building except for its longevity. Its plain block lettering in gold had become as common a sight as the trolley that looped through the historic district or the gulls that penetrated the city ahead of Bay winds. Several generations of Bosworths represented a name and reputation that Patrick had grown to respect. As august as it was, it seemed a steep climb to ever become a partner in the family's Western office located in Butte, Montana Territory.

Patrick Colter shrugged, the unspoken commentary muffled beneath his slicker. The old Boston he'd known as a vibrant port city seemed to shuffle along with the same exporting and importing, the typical stratified classes representing new and old wealth amid a heavy dose of weather, sanctimony and self-satisfaction. But Patrick had lived on the knife-edge of the frontier. He'd felt the blast of blizzard air in the mountains, 90 degree heat down in the mines, and experienced heady times of gold and silver discoveries. His present unease, he determined, related to something Boston and Butte held in common, a vast underground of criminal activity, much of it gangster-style anti-temperance conspiracies, as well as outright thuggery, thefts, and murders.

The reflections he carried into the Bosworth office that day were disquieting enough that the usual thrill of finding his niche on the premises failed to lift his spirits. Reuben Bosworth was away at a convention. Patrick's inbox held nothing more exciting than a stack of shipping contracts that relied on exacting skills required to keep shippers out of lawsuits. Language can cover a multitude of sins but omission of specific language would invite the devil's own wrath. He had learned the tediousness required to become an attorney.

"Looks like another windfall for legal assistants," he grinned to Howard, who served in a similar role. "And I need to prepare for debates this afternoon. Socratic teaching methods somehow survived their masochistic originator."

Howard laughed, rather guffawed in agreement. "I am thinking of going into mediation and let the combatants split hairs." From the cut of his coat and ruffles of his shirt it appeared he was already well established among Boston's elite.

"A bonnie idee. If I go back to the Territories, I doubt that debates or shipping contracts will save my skin in rough and tumble mining towns." There, the words had come out, expressing the deep reservations that Patrick had been mulling. His mind instantly sharpened, the parameters evident.

I may have to reconsider the course of action that I have chosen to advance myself.

14
IRMGARDE

A blitz of bulletins and handbills posted all over Boston declared women's rights were "issue of the day," making the cause a moral imperative that drew ordinary women from ironing boards and butter churns and lured aristocratic dames from teas and charities.

FULL SOVEREIGNTY
NOT BONDAGE

Shelley met Gertie at their favorite spot along the Charles River. True to Patrick's earlier prediction, they energetically wore a path while focused on recent news and gossip. Chief among these were the latest strategies of a growing number of suffragettes from coast to coast.

"They have become more radical, have you noticed?" Shelley asked.

"And they get themselves arrested."

Gertie's flat dismissal threatened to end the conversation. Red light districts were raided regularly and the women arrested as well, but Shelley dismissed the wayward thought and cautiously waded in. "On the surface it appears to be a strange way to achieve their goals."

"The courts are not helping. Not all citizens are yet privileged to have the vote, or have their 'natural rights' to vote. According to Mrs. Stanton's *Declaration of Sentiments*, men have been willing to allow women to lead 'abject' lives." Gertie's downcast eyes betrayed deeper feelings. She tipped her hat to hide beneath its broad-brim.

"Why should I become involved in protests against the government when my family made great sacrifices to come here? Believe me, we learned that citizen opposition to the *Kulturkampf* in Germany led to a sense of helplessness, or worse, death. I plead guilty for supporting the movement, but others can commit to marching for change, not me."

Even the ducks dropping feet first into the current and happily splashing water over themselves failed to lift the mood that the *Sentiments* had aroused. Gertie hiked her skirts above the tall grass, revealing her red stockings without embarrassment, and hastened back to the Academy saying something about attending a lyceum that afternoon.

Shelley retraced her steps, an uneasy concern dampening her spirits as well. Deep in thought that afternoon, she sliced scalloped potatoes into an antique ceramic dish in preparation for supper. Neva occupied most of the kitchen table with tiny glass beads, fashioning them into wildly colored necklaces for herself and her dolls.

Patrick came home early from the University and flung his coat over the back of a chair. He yanked at a stubborn knot in his cravat. "I have decided to terminate my studies here."

Shelley's knife hung in midair. If Patrick had said he would stop the incessant rain that kept them inside for the past fortnight, she could not have been more stunned. Her mind searched for clues. This was unlike Patrick. She studied his face in alarm. Surely he must have been considering this for some time without telling her. Quick to blame herself, Shelley thought he must have been unhappy or discouraged, and she had failed to notice or comfort him.

"A decision such as this is not made without foresight and planning," she said, resuming the meal preparation.

"These dress clothes make me feel like a stuffed form in a tailor's shop." Patrick's fingers flipped buttons open on his vest revealing a shirtfront soaked in sweat. His brow likewise gave evidence of exertion once he removed the tweed flat cap worn by students. "I shall be relieved to see Antonio and Jackson as soon as possible."

Neva shrank into her thin shoulders, her eyes fixed on stringing the next bead and the next. Shelley did not know what to make of his turnabout, but she knew Neva had never seen him so distraught. She saw her own immediate plans disrupted, her dreams dashed, and her future threatened. An image of Danielle, a serene and proper wife on a farm, caught her by surprise. It made her unspoken ambitions seem reckless and unwarranted.

As if reading her mind, Patrick talked of ranching. "I would prefer ranching on the Jefferson River near Antonio and Danielle. We could farm and raise horses. With Antonio's expertise we could build up a barn recognized for the quality and training of fine walkers, possibly from Kentucky or Tennessee. After all, my Colter ancestors of County Cork were known for their line of exceptional horses, including the Connemara like the stallion Jackson owns. We could see Jackson and Nettie and the baby anytime in Montana Territory."

"Is this sudden decision about Jackson?"

"Of course I want to see Jackson and his family. But you are asking, is it about being twins? No."

"You once said you tried to break ties with Jackson that felt too binding."

"I also told you I had enough love for both you and Jackson. And Neva, of course. You would like to play with your cousin Tucker, Neva. He must be a big boy by now. Almost two years old, I think."

Neva's wide eyes strained to measure his promises against Shelley's disbelief.

"This comes as quite a shock. I wonder if you have been considering this move for some time." Shelley was curious, too.

What precipitating event had been the catalyst? Or had Patrick been drinking?

"I have plowed through research, cases, and examinations for almost two years, and I still feel as inexperienced as a toad. I have enough sense to know that competence comes from taking on a workload and doing the job. I did that as a legal assistant. At the time I wanted to better myself. Now I have other considerations that make me question my enrollment here."

"A toad, Papa? No, not a toad."

Shelley knew Neva reverted to 'Papa' when the child was stressed.

"Maybe not a toad, chum. Maybe a do-nothing. I need to go to an ethics class, but this is not over."

A cheery afternoon of baking soda bread for St. Patrick's Day had magically changed for Shelley. She determinedly sewed woolen trousers for Neva for the changeable spring weather, and tried not to imagine the upheaval moving would entail. When Patrick came home, they ate supper with trifling conversations, most directed to Neva. Shelley formulated a few questions she would ask Patrick at bedtime.

Since the previous fall, Shelley had been engaged in a life independent of Patrick, and it shone brightly through a rush of unscripted storms in her personal and volunteer life, mocking the storms off the sea. Order had come to Mission school by way of a reprieve. Another church opened its basement for a similar program, thereby reducing the overcrowding. Both schools attracted credentialed teachers, including professors from the immigrant pool who contributed their knowledge and techniques, thereby enhancing the teaching standards. Naturally, they would move on when they found employment, but in the meantime Shelley was surrounded and influenced by an educated coterie at the once desperate school.

Incidental to volunteer teaching, Shelley's self-imposed educational pursuits had introduced her to the poetry of Alexander

Pushkin that criticized oppression by Romanoff Emperors. She had also been exposed to more information about Germany's *Kulturekampf*, which Gertie derided and found futile to contest. The suffering and uprisings of people at home and abroad led to a constant feeling of unrest that Shelley shared with Gertie and other women in Cambridge.

Reflecting on her full and satisfying experience in Boston, she cleaned the kitchen nook and gathered up Neva's beads. Above all, she enjoyed the lilting folk songs of Ireland that Neva sang in Gaelic while the other children learned English.

"Oh, dear heaven, pulling up roots would be very difficult—and it would be even more so for Neva to leave her school and little friends," Shelley whispered, when she and Patrick were behind their closed bedroom door.

"Are you going to fret over this, Shelley? I assumed you would be more than ready to return to the Territory."

"You do not understand. You brought me into your world as an awkward, gawking neophyte, and it has become my world, too. I don't know what it is exactly, but—but—"

Claiming her world on the East Coast felt like the first time she had claimed anything in her life. Shelley choked over the words, "I like what I am doing," with the realization she did not want to leave, that she had invested herself in the school and the women's movement in ways that were personally gratifying.

"It is true Neva is happy here, but I use her as an excuse to stay, when it is I who wants to stay."

Patrick's blank stare and wandering attention hardly encouraged her to explain. She mumbled, "I believe I am a better person for it. My father would agree. He would be proud that I teach and that I spoke up at the school."

She felt Patrick wince.

"Are you moving us away because of me? Because I dared speak in public?"

"Can you allow this to be about me, not about Jackson or you or Neva? For some time I have been questioning whether this is right for me, whether it is best for the future I want to carve out for us."

His grudging remark through gritted teeth sounded final. Shelley hung up his vest and white shirt and set his shoes under the bed, aware that she had furthered his dream to become an attorney—she had followed him to the East, ironed his shirts and picked up after him with the belief that is what he wanted.

Neither found words. The ancient trunk in the corner was as responsive as Patrick. Shelley wiped the ornate washbowl on the dressing table and kept her thoughts to herself. Why am I rambling? As head of family he makes the final decisions. Yet I will not deny that I am hurt and disappointed—neither of which are good for me or for Patrick.

Patrick said little all evening. He withdrew into himself, a protective barrier that Shelley dared not disturb. He left early the next morning, hardly touching his coffee, and barely brushing her lips in passing.

Shelley stacked the dirty breakfast dishes and hustled Neva out the door before gloom devoured them both. They hung dripping rainwear in the hallway at the Mission school and joined a circle of children reciting the Pledge of Allegiance, high thin voices obscuring the words with thick accents. Shelley arranged to leave Neva so she could "attend a meeting." Once free of the church grounds she sped across Cambridge to find Gertie who had likewise sounded unsettled during their last encounter.

Blue skies and early blossoming apple, cherry and plum trees transformed the usual gray atmosphere along the North Atlantic coast. Steps were lighter, a cheery "good day" here and there lifted the spirits, and sunshine penetrated narrow streets. The faded brick apartment building where the Colters lived escaped from winter a bit more worn, presenting a soft face among the shimmering green leaves of overhanging hardwoods.

Patrick said little about moving, grousing occasionally that he felt like Old Tornado plodding to work. He gathered his books early each day, kissed his family, and absent-mindedly left for one nameless class or another. The family fell back into moody routines. Left to herself, Shelley pursued the women's movement as the downtrodden poor, property-less divorcee, and uneducated girl children of most families gave urgency and purpose to her stay in the East.

Buoyed by momentum women like herself had created, Shelley dove into the subject one day when Patrick was home in the flat.

"I find it in my conscience to make an effort to advance the welfare of women and children, particularly because of my involvement in the Mission school. For all the church's charitable efforts, I believe this is best done by political means. If this requires many of us women to protest and lobby locally and in Washington, then I feel called—"

"Charlotte Norton." Patrick stood and practically shouted. He never called her Charlotte. Nor her maiden name, Norton. Even when she had thrown his mother's heirloom china at him he had cowered and ducked but not raised his voice. Shelley's eyes widened in shock.

"It is the way it is for a reason," Patrick began.

Shelley knew that nonsense would never succeed with her. She too raised her voice.

"The notion to join other women in social and political movements has become a part of me, part of my entire being over the past two years. Exposure to women's groups has confirmed my belief that the efforts of all citizens are required, particularly women, black or white, who have no representation. In the aftermath of the bloody and misnamed Civil War the time is ripe for women to step forward—"

"I will not hear such banality." Patrick cut her off from launching her first campaign speech. "I considered going into politics at one time. Perhaps I will reconsider it in the future. However, the reputation of an attorney or a politician should not be sullied or ridiculed because one's wife campaigns against the sorry condition of humankind."

Patrick drew a breath. "I will not have my wife become an ordinary trumpet for causes, you hear?"

Bracing her hands on the back of a dining chair and engaging on her terms, Shelley started to bark, 'But you admire Miss Hammer for becoming a lawyer and a public speaker and God knows what else.' She caught herself, the words unsaid. Opening that old wound might never allow it to heal again.

She said instead, "Elizabeth Cady Stanton raised the *Declaration of Rights of Women* into public awareness at the American Centennial two years ago. Suffrage is not going away just because men do not like it. Susan Anthony will see the campaign to its rightful end."

"You forgot or do not know that prior to the Exhibition, the *Minor Decision of 1875* found that citizenship meant membership in a nation and nothing more." Patrick ground home his point: "It left the decision regarding who could and could not vote to the various states. These distinguished women you mention are wasting their time working for a Constitutional Amendment."

Shelley felt the rebuke in her most vulnerable part, the lack of an advanced education. Her husband ruled by his superiority, as well as by the law and Scriptures and a culture of patriarchy. Mrs. Stanton's words spun in her mind: *"We suffer daily humiliation of spirit..."*

That humiliation stung, sinking deep in her heart, stifling tears that would, if allowed to flow, woefully undermine her new found assertiveness. More objectively, Shelley knew that foremost advocates for the "natural rights of women" met strenuous objection from both men and women, delaying if not killing what appeared to be an obvious and innocuous right.

I barely dare stand up to my husband, Shelley realized. How can I gain the fortitude to become a spokesperson for any cause whatsoever?

Garnering her inner resources, she stated, "If we return to Montana Territory we will find citizens supportive of gaining statehood, one cause you had tentatively supported. We would be going back to an entirely different experience."

This time Patrick appeared caught off guard by an unimpassioned purview of affairs he had been too distant and too busy to follow.

"Surely you know the rise of Marcus Daly and William Clark has precipitated a huge turmoil. The wealth and power centered in Butte is unprecedented in the Territory. *The New North-West* newspaper reports William Clark supports statehood for the Territory. Surely Montana Territory will not lag behind statehood of other states for long."

"How do you know this?" His voice sounded lame, impotent. "Is it from your association with that street woman?"

Shelley drew herself up to eye level with Patrick. "Miss Owens regularly posts letters and news articles to me. I am her eyes and ears on the East Coast." She tried not to triumph over her inside knowledge—that would not be fair to Patrick, who had buried himself in his books and Mr. Bosworth's cases for almost two years. Now he looked expectantly at her.

"Exactly what else do you think you know?"

"Statehood was an issue for Miss Owens because it presented an opportunity to write specifications for women's suffrage into a new state Constitution. It may seem strange and distant to you, Patrick, but there is a strong movement across the country for women's right to vote."

Without missing a beat, Shelley offered her own insights. "Miss Owens had personal experience and a grudge about the politics of men. She was equally trained at a Philadelphia medical school, yet discredited for being a woman. I find her situation fits with the sentiments I often hear in women's groups here at Harvard."

By now Patrick had his head in his hands, his fingers lacing and unlacing as if he could unlock some insight into the woman he married, much less the movement across the nation.

"At one time I had been charged to be the eyes and ears of Lucas Bosworth's office in Butte. Unfortunately, that role linked me to the investigation of the Berrigan murder. Now it appears you straddle the white horse of civic involvement."

"You are troubled by your dear wife. Let it lie for now and concentrate on your academic work." She reached over to smooth his hair but playfully ruffled it instead.

Patrick exhaled pent-up tension and pulled her into his lap, wrapped his arms around her and stroked her long hair. His kisses trailed over her neck, ears and cheek. Shelley yielded as if she had never taken a stance against the 'politics of men,' as if the progressive views she stated were not her ambitions after all. He relaxed and chided her.

"There may be two politicians in the family when we get settled on a farm. You will likely find women concerned with your little causes, while I elevate issues pertaining to justice in the Territory." He chafed her cheek with the stubble of his beard. "I wouldn't have it any other way, although it might take getting used to."

Shelley bolted to her feet, his references to a farm and "her little causes," reigniting her resentments. Still stinging from his earlier fury, she found what she could of her normal voice. "I am sure I can support you in your campaigns in an honorable fashion."

She heated a flat iron on the stove, her aspirations belittled and further from reach than ever. Left alone, Patrick went into their bedroom and slipped off his shoes, resting his feet on a stool near the heater. Soon uncomfortable with their separation, he followed Shelley into the dining room.

"I failed to anticipate that it would be so difficult for us to talk. If you must know, I fear you are exposing yourself, or us, by involvement in highly controversial issues. I once ventured to do that and put myself and my family at risk."

"Must one iron shirts and keep quiet?" Shelley found herself espousing the very attitude that Gertie expressed two years ago—but it sounded horribly rude, even to her ears.

Patrick blanched. "How does brother Jackson do it? He and Nettie seem to have a happy marriage and a cozy home."

Shelley stoutly ignored Patrick and the implication of his remarks.

"My marriage feels more like fireworks." Patrick smiled in spite of himself. "My mother had an Irish temper and slammed the dishes. As a matter of fact, that is how the china became chipped in the first place. More than once Father put on his cap and wool scarf to walk the streets of Boston half the night."

Not a flicker of interest crossed Shelley's face while she ironed Neva's school dress.

"'*Is ola anchearc nach scriobann di fe'in.* It is a bad hen that doesn't scratch for itself.' Mother often quoted maxims from her mother's side of the family. I am sure she would approve of your industry and disposition. Perhaps women's emancipation, as well."

Shelley persisted in ironing the entire basket of washing, all of his white shirts and even his socks without speaking. At a loss for dealing with Shelley in this mood, Patrick pulled himself and family maxims into the bedroom. He lay staring at the ceiling, not even pretending to be asleep when she came in and sat on the bed. The blaze in the heater died down, sputtering with the last wet wood.

"I want to explain that I changed my plans for reading the law and returning to the Bosworth law firm in Butte because of you and Neva."

Shelley wrapped herself in layers of nightwear and topped the cocoon with a nightcap.

He went on. "I want you to understand this is not about Jackson or me. I fear for—I fear exposing myself and my family to danger."

Shelley did not need to be reminded of the assassination and attempted murder in Butte. The events were too hurtful for either of them to revisit.

Breathing hard, Patrick tried once again. "I thought you would be happy about a change of plans. I need you, Shelley. I will find a way forward for us."

Shelley sensed his speech about justice and politics had paralleled her spiel. She recognized that he wanted to realize his ideals, yet he hid behind traditional taboos and the prerogatives of men. She had not failed to notice the lack of specific plans for his political or legal pursuits—or hers.

"If it takes a farm, we will move to a farm," she conceded. "Having a horse ranch would be realizing your youthful dream."

Each had voiced thwarted yearnings without the fanfare of deeply emotional connections. To her, his sounded like empty promises.

15
RELAPSE

Weeks slipped by with the Colter family in limbo while nature continued to burst forth in a carnival of color and fragrances. Cherry trees bearing giant pink pom poms swayed in the breeze. Willows along the Charles puffed their limbs with gray pussies, and the scent of rising tree sap permeated the Cambridge campus of the Women's Academy.

Shelley asked for Irmgarde Meyer at the women's residency house where Gertie lived. A student new to the front desk rummaged through name lists, dormitory rooms and schedules, unable to find such a person living there at this time.

Shelley gaped, rooted to the spot, and stammered, "I must have made a mistake. These resident halls look so much alike, but I am certain we met here before."

The student moved aside to help someone else. Shelley drifted outside to a bench. Young women dashed in and out, chattering like chipmunks, unaware of a stranger fighting back loneliness in their midst. Shelley's anxiety escalated, wondering whether Gertie had said anything unusual, whether she was all right.

Shelley fought the confusion and hurt of not knowing—not knowing either Patrick or Gertie had even thought of leaving Boston. Neither had consulted her beforehand. The shock waves kept coming. She blinked, kicked fallen leaves, and surveyed passersby for a familiar face. She failed to recognize anyone then or later when she wandered the downtown streets of Cambridge. Emptiness rang loudly in her ears.

A sudden damp wind off the Atlantic roughed up the coast and claimed the cities. Pink blossom petals spun through the air chased by fluff from the willows. Last year's dried maple and elm leaves took flight, their soggy skeletons soon plastered on windows and walls. An odorous whiff of seaweed, fish, and mud scum lay low across the land from the tidelands of Dorchester Bay. At last, tired and chilled, Shelley retraced her steps home.

"Gertie, what happened between us?" she moaned, until the bite of cold and surging anger brought clarity to her thoughts.

Am I to be treated like a coat rack? Miss Owens' emphasis on respect for women is caustic to relationships, mine included. Why do I hold on to anything for myself? It is not worth it. I can and will do whatever it takes for Neva and Patrick. That is enough.

The toll of crashing hopes eroded the joy Shelley found in the women's movement in Boston. That many women refused to join the effort made it seem counterproductive. The Woman's Suffrage group now felt shallow, if not self-defeated. The whole world outside her life felt cold, resistant to change. Shelley wished she had never known it. It led to disappointment and heartbreak. Resentment hardened her jaw, burned in her eyes and numbed her senses. She washed and dried dishes, soaked lentils for supper, and threw her dirty apron over a chair.

Patrick came and went, remarking absently, "I have a backlog of cases to complete at the law firm before we leave."

Shelley hid signs of her stress and disillusionment in order to support Patrick. "I would expect them to encourage you to stay with the firm and finish the coursework. They have been generous and encouraging from the beginning."

"I could not have asked for more. They have treated me like a son, yet I cannot see myself following in Lucas' footsteps."

"I understand. I'm sure they do also. Lucas paid dearly for his efforts."

Patrick bristled. "He chose to stay against reason and good advice."

Shelley noted he stated no other plans regarding dates of departure, as if only his affairs needed to be in order. He was too prickly for her to ask whether he would complete his studies for the term. He seemed to be terribly preoccupied. She vaguely wondered if it had to do with Miss Hammer.

Without knowing how long she would remain in Cambridge, Shelley gave indefinite notice to the Mission school and sheltered Neva from the uncertainty. The child was radiantly happy with her friends and books. These included a shabby *Atlas of the World* and a threadbare copy on rag paper of *Brer Rabbit*, in addition to her worn *Audubon Book of Birds*.

Shelley had generally allowed Neva, as a child, to struggle along in a halting gait with her right leg dragging the left. As she grew older her demand to walk and do things with the other children strengthened the limb and kept it mobile, allowing her to walk upright more easily. The nerves in her paralyzed leg had evidently partially revived.

Gradually, Shelley's mood softened as she reflected on their time in the East. The Humanities Library sprang to mind first, drawing her time and again to its stacks, opening history and cultures far beyond her former schooling. She became acquainted with historians, novelists and poets, ancient to contemporary philosophers and scientists, studied works on Tutankhamun's tomb, the Ottoman emperors, and the Greek god Ulysses. She read Henry James' recently published *Transatlantic Sketches* while biting her nails. In James Joyce she found "Seanachie," the Irish story tellers. "Their maxims live on in my marriage."

She reread her earlier favorite series, Jane Austen and Emily Bronte. The wildly passionate *Wuthering Heights* alternately challenged her views of enduring love and marriage while cementing it in the end.

No one can take these treasures and this knowledge away from me, she vowed. I have become a better person since my pursuit of studies, but Patrick refuses to change with the times. The women's movement taught me that passion for change upsets the order. Also, that the order should be upset. Well, that idea must have come from an unmarried activist.

The idea lent her the least bit of satisfaction.

With Shelley's tacit acceptance of his plans, Patrick's crustiness seemed to soften. They moved seamlessly through routines of the day, her humor gently prodding his seriousness as it had in the early days of their marriage, her stories of Mission school adventures legendary. Neva asked to "go on a ship to Cornwall with my friends to get pasties."

In the meantime, Shelley put the causes behind her, except for occasionally meeting with friends who had been equally involved in the advancement of women's issues. She printed a small card which she kept in her pocket, reminding her of the most compelling slogans.

THOSE WHO OBEY THE LAWS SHOULD HELP CHOOSE THE LAWS.
LAWS AFFECTING THE HOME AND CHILDREN ARE VOTED BY MEN.
OBJECTIONS TO WOMAN'S VOTE ARE BASED ON PREJUDICE, NOT REASON.
PUBLIC SPIRITED MOTHERS MAKE PUBLIC SPIRITED SONS (AND SISTERS)
JOIN US FOR THE COMMON GOOD.

"I am joined, regardless where I live," she told herself.

The least painful story she invented to explain their prospective return to the West was that her husband had completed his studies. Congratulations usually followed the disclosure, for her husband, of course. She found wives of law school students typically went unacknowledged for supporting their husbands through their ordeals. A few of the women expressed a desire to flee the congestion of the immigrant port for the frontier.

"Montana Territory is a frontier of immigrants," Shelley informed them, implying the West was rough and unsettled with a transient population. Several recognized Shelley's deep regret, the loss she felt in abandoning their mutual cause, if not the exhilaration of the University environment.

"I understand you met a remarkable physician who greatly influenced your views before you came East," observed Katerina Von Dorson, a student at Cambridge University. "Surely you will find that individual to be a comfort when you return."

"We will relocate to a farm some distance away from her medical practice in Butte." Shelley's tone elicited a picture of life becoming impossibly dull.

"A dream for many women who would like to live in Montana Territory," Katerina insisted.

"I was very uncomfortable living on a farm with Patrick's friends with whom we had a double wedding. When Patrick first entered Harvard, Neva and I were their guests for a time. Neva grew like a weed. But my husband—well, it's a long story."

"And you?" Katerina could be persistent, often forward, and occasionally insightful; in short a friend similar to Gertie.

Shelley stalled, trying to recall the woman she was then— the girl who counted girdles and cigars in the Mercantile, the maiden incredulous of a proposal who replied 'Marry me?,' the wife who shared her husband with his cowboy twin. Sadly, a woman robbed of her husband too soon after nuptials.

"And how about your sister?"

"Oh, she has always been with me and always will be."

"It seems your life is quite divided and appropriated by others."

"I never thought of it that way. I--I--only feel frustrated at times."

"You have not solicited my opinion, but if you permit me, I suggest you find a way to pursue your own studies to preserve your sanity."

Shelley started to laugh, a silly giggle she might have indulged in with Gertie, but caught herself. "How did you know? I have been on the verge of insanity since I married!"

Katerina nodded, her straight blonde hair swinging loosely with the movement. Whether she understood from experience or sympathy, Shelley couldn't guess.

"On the farm I will cook bacon and eggs for breakfast, milk the cow and clean the barn. For the remainder of the day I will have an immense number of chickens to pluck."

"You would be a traditional farm wife with no time to advance or apply what you have learned here. That leaves little energy for anything else."

They both laughed at the truth.

"I would be out of town and tied down. I would be unable to attend meetings. That would please my husband to no end." Shelley's hilarity turned grim. Katerina continued undeterred.

"Women in the West would surely benefit most by the cause, given what you just described. Our thinking has been liberated so why not their lives."

Why not? Shelley embraced the question that was more a statement, one she linked to Gertie's irreverent and generally unsolicited commentary. Katerina's bold, open manner was so like Gertie's that Shelley's voice caught.

"I had a friend who said the same thing, but I believe she has moved away."

"I have to attend a meeting," Katerina said, "but one more suggestion if I may. I believe you have experience of interest to other women if you would be willing to share it in the Assembly Hall."

"If they are as sympathetic listeners as you have been, I would tell the world. I am so grateful for your understanding. Since I am relatively uninvolved in the movement, I find the loneliness of our flat unbearable at times. Please know, though, that I am not now or ever will be a public speaker."

Shelley went home and made shepherd pie, reams of ideas rolling about in her mind. She must devise a future for herself if she was destined to live out her days on a farm—not a joke that she exaggerated to her friends, but an honest-to-God farm with pigs and piglets and roosters and hens.

Neva sat in the old rocker and turned the pages of an animal book as if she also patiently waited for the move.

Shifting to her present tentative situation, Shelley realized she must prepare remarks for an assembly of women if Katerina went to the trouble of arranging it. She explored the idea of talking about Miss Owens who had initiated discussions of women's issues, or the problem of little or no welfare for the poor, issues Butte and Boston had in common. She could read recent news articles and try to explain the truncated drive for statehood in Montana Territory. The so-called beating women were taking in the West on temperance and women's suffrage would not be a surprise to anyone, and none inspired more than a passing thought in Shelley's present mood. She served supper and lingered with Patrick until distraught feelings from this morning overflowed.

"I went to find Gertie—Miss Irmgarde—this morning and she is gone. She left the residency hall with no further address. I cannot understand it. She would tell me if she changed her plans. I worry that something happened to her."

"Something did happen to her." Patrick spoke in her ear.

"Oh, no. Not Gertie!"

"She got herself arrested."

Neva's eyes solemnly followed one then the other seated at the table. Neither 'parent' chose to speak. She chewed her lower lip with her few new upper front teeth. Her hands fidgeted in her lap.

"You may be excused," Shelley said.

When Neva disappeared into the bedroom, Patrick whispered. "She was picked up on the streets. Apparently old habits—." He evidently thought better of disparaging her in the face of Shelley's shock and dismay. "Mr. Bosworth, her benefactor at the Women's Academy, was notified. He was the only contact the Academy had for her. She was released from detention with a small fine and ordered to return to wherever she came from."

Humiliation swept over Shelley as if she shared Gertie's downfall. "Surely Mr. Bosworth must have felt betrayed and bitterly disappointed. The vision he held for Gertie to have a decent life evaporated in a stroke of human error." Her voice dropped. "I held that vision, too."

Patrick kept his own counsel—Shelley accepted the silence as recognition of the women's friendship.

Gertie's relapse made Shelley's own righteous yearnings for women appear even more futile. In a corresponding stroke Shelley lost any sense of her ability to change or influence society, either individually or as a whole. Her pressing need to find a role for herself in the immediate future felt dimmed if not completely thwarted.

Gertie's dismal choice felt like a condemnation of Shelley's personal aspirations; a wake-up slap telling her to stop trying to improve herself and settle for a respectable life as a farmer's wife. She sat as if numb, unable to admit or accept the news. After awhile she brushed a kiss on Patrick's forehead and went to bed.

―――――――――

No letters came from Gertie nor a follow-up from the Bosworth office. Shelley became hollow-eyed, her attempts to focus scattered until Patrick became worried.

"I am afraid the news regarding Miss Meyer has hit you hard, Shelley. I did not intend to shock you. And when I announced we would be moving back home it appears to have been equally if not more distressing to you. I assumed you would be in agreement, even delighted. It seems to have drained you. I wonder if you might be, uh, umm, with child."

The last captured Shelley's attention. She shook her head.

Patrick pulled a chair by her side. "Are you sure? It seems, after all this time, it could be a possibility." Patrick's eyes could be soft as an Irish hound's. He reached for her hand.

"No. I'm not." The words snapped from Shelley's lips. She had wanted a child earlier, a year ago. She was not aware of what had changed, but Patrick's assumptions felt like an insult and his prying uncalled for.

"I would tell you, would I not? Or have we become so distant from one another we seldom talk anymore? I wonder if I have become an appendix to your life?"

He failed to respond and Shelley could not go on.

"I am sorry, Patrick. I should not have said that. I am devastated that Gertie failed to stay with her academic program. She so wanted to lift herself from—to live a life of decency. It is not unknown for anyone to fail or change their minds or get discouraged, but I thought she was committed. I truly do not know what to make of it. Maybe she needed more support to keep going, though she was active in the women's group in the residence hall. Surely someone there would have further information. However, I did not see anyone I knew to ask about her."

"She knows where you are. Let's leave it at that. About what you are in my life, I want you to know the truth." He pressed her hand until white formed around the edges. "I decided to get out of law for the very reason I left so hastily from Butte. I am afraid of inviting violence into my family."

His voice choked and continued. "I never want to experience such fear as I did for you and Neva when I was threatened. That fear has never left me. Nor you, I suspect. Danielle told me how nervous and tearful you were when you were rescued from Butte and forced to live at their home for months. I have assisted with cases here in Boston as bad or worse than those in the Territory. There is a vast underground of gangs, gambling and corruption. The lawlessness is startling, even to veteran attorneys such as Mr. Bosworth."

He paused to see if she was listening. "Doubtless it is similar in the Territories. Butte has its rivals in terms of escalating conflict between emerging powers and the grassroots forces for temperance. I am trying to find a way forward for us, for you and Neva. Many of my ideas may lack merit, but farming and ranching is the best and safest I have at the moment." He released her hand as if he gave up trying to be the man he expected of himself.

The gauzy confusion that Shelley fought for the last few weeks began to clear. It was plain to see that Patrick chose to leave Harvard University for her. For Neva. In his mind he had not been estranged. It was my reaction, my sense of being shuffled like a deck of cards, she realized. This man reveals a deeper character than I've given him credit for. I sense I can trust him. Is that how men continue to patronize women, by superior power of character?

"Patrick, I am beginning to understand a little of how and why you made your decision." Shelley sorted priorities of needs in the family in rapid order: Patrick's, Neva's, and hers. In moments she found herself aligned with his.

"You are doing this for us."

"Yes." His sacrifice, if it was that, hung around his eyes, in the strain he had endured at work, and in making the decision to quit. The corners of his mouth turned down, a sad expression that aged his usually youthful features.

Shelley swept into his arms, as though they were united for the first time, that the wrenching circumstances had formed a new, more solid marriage, a common purpose. She told herself to never question him again, or maybe not on those things he most cared about. Women's uprisings against men failed to account for certain things in one's marriage.

16
ASSEMBLY

The move to the farm did not occur immediately—the move that would alienate Shelley from the women's movement. That involvement gave her purpose while Patrick floundered with decisions and what she considered half-baked plans. In the end, he was set on finishing the term, which left time for Shelley to adjust to the idea of leaving Boston. Late spring with its attendant warmth eased her soul and bathed the city in shiny greens of new oak and maple leaves.

Shelley kept familiar routines for Neva's sake and held on to the tenuous new relationship she had with Patrick. Neva had a birthday. She was eight. Five of her best friends came to the Colter flat for cake and ice cream that they churned in Patrick's grandparents' old ice cream maker. Laughter filled the rooms, lifted moods up and down the hallways among other residents, and proved a fulfillment of Neva's dream to be a normal child. Shelley beamed.

"I think you are ready to attend school by yourself now that you are eight," she told Neva after the party.

"I will walk with my friends," Neva announced. Shelley's eyes misted, *a girl after my own soul.* She had never expected to see this day, or see Neva gain such self-confidence.

Free from the Mission school, Shelley spent more time with her colleagues, much of it dedicated to the rapidly accelerating women's movement.

"*Self development is a higher duty,*" she said to Katerina Von Dorson, quoting one of Patrick's Irish proverbs. "Unfortunately, it seems my husband has the impression the advice pertains to men instead of all people, including women."

"It is evidence of the work we have cut out for us," Katerina replied. "Attitudes and behaviors are as deeply entrenched, but the Centennial Exhibition a few years ago led to progress. Women are allowed higher education and freedom to write and speak in public. Perhaps we will one day be accepted in the professions."

Shelley attended speeches at Faneuil Hall celebrating Julia Ward Howe's Women's Tea Party, a protest Howe organized six years earlier against taxation without representation. But Shelley usually avoided other gatherings and street protests advertised by the American Woman Suffrage Association based in New York.

"They only want attention. These tactics are unseemly. I forbid you from attending," Patrick had declared on a day when a woman had been knocked down by police and her flag ripped from her hands.

This time Shelley agreed. I absolutely cannot set myself up for arrest, damage Patrick's reputation, or interfere with caring for Neva.

Letters from Miss Owens in Butte informed Shelley that Lucy Stone's women's movement from Boston had campaigned throughout the West. They pushed women's need to vote for their interests in local school elections and other affairs, as well as those at the national level. Shelley applauded the news of their efforts alone. Patrick was absorbed in his academics, and Gertie had sadly disappeared.

Katerina, however, had not been idle on Shelley's behalf. Events moved faster than Shelley had anticipated. Shelley was stunned at first that Katerina had scheduled her to speak in Harvard's Assembly Hall, the same Hall where Miss Violet Hamilton had spoken movingly about Elizabeth Barrett Browning's poetry and its influence on contemporary attitudes.

But she rifled through letters from Miss Owens to prepare her speech, searching for both content and moral support. Miss Owens' keen intellect and devotion to the advancement of women had drawn Shelley into a sisterhood she wished to portray in her speech. Elizabeth Cady Stanton stressed that women need to "own their own souls." Unable to consult with Patrick about her presentation, and distraught that Gertie was not available to discuss it with her, Shelley found the day of her speech had arrived, and she had yet to form it clearly in her mind.

Katerina seated Shelley to her right on the Harvard Assembly Hall dais under the banner for Woman's Suffrage. Several other women were seated to Shelley's right. The chairwoman occupied the stage on the left, along with two dignitaries from Political Science Studies. Katrina was introduced first to deliver a brief survey of progress or lack of it to date in the national movement, and to assess support for suffrage at the University.

"Our appearance here today, as well as protests in Boston and New York represent the tenacity and courage of women who refuse to bow to the notion that women in public affairs is 're-pugnant.' Your University women's suffrage groups are actively involved in keeping the Women's Right to Vote Amendment in the forefront of our legislators."

Applause interrupted her remarks. The hall was about half full, many choosing to sit in the shadows of higher tiers in the back. Shelley recalled when she had thoughtlessly dashed into the center section in the middle of Miss Violet Hamilton's presentation. She had wanted to hurt her, the only means she had to strike back at the woman who had become Patrick's companion, if not more.

I was fresh off Danielle's goat farm in Montana Territory, a world away from Boston. I know now why Miss Hammer appealed to my husband. She was articulate, confident, dressed like

Laura Spelman Rockefeller, and had her bonnet set for Patrick. What man could resist, though I am not excusing him or her.

Shelley shifted her attention back to the audience in the Assembly. She was among women she knew fairly well from the women's movement, and felt relatively comfortable with them. Katerina had always been more than encouraging.

I would not be here if not for Katerina's intervention, she mused. She brought me into University women's circles—the very thought once intimidated me.

Yet Shelley gratefully accepted the lengthy remarks of previous speakers, giving her time to focus on her speech though her thoughts continually shifted as if a waterwheel washed ideas overhead into a pond and picked up new ones, only to cycle around until they were likewise emptied. Shelley twisted her handkerchief with rising tension until it came her turn to speak.

She rose, still unsure what she would say when Katrina presented her as "a speaker who gained her first experience in the women's movement in the West, Mrs. Charlotte Norton Colter, originally from Nevada and lately from Montana Territory."

"Many of you have been engaged in the Woman's Suffrage movement much longer than I have," Shelley began, fussing with the folds of her dress that did not want to hang properly. "I—I'm afraid I could only repeat information that most of you are aware of regarding any of the pressing issues confronting women these days. These include loss of property rights when women marry, exclusion of voting in public school elections, and powerlessness in civic affairs. As you are aware, women have no recourse to address spousal abuse or loss of custody in divorce cases."

The speech sounded dull, even to her ears. She realized that she would quickly lose her audience with lists and platitudes so she raced on. "Therefore, I have discarded ideas of general topics, and chosen a specific one. I want to describe a relevant case I am familiar with."

Patrick often spoke of "case law." "Cases" sounded professional, and she could rely on the little she had learned from his experience. This specific type of approach had been successful at the Mission school, and she hoped zeroing in on one person would suffice here. She straightened her wide shoulders, breathed a prayer and plunged on.

"This may appear to be an unlikely, even questionable subject, but the case concerns a woman of ill repute."

Rustling and coughing instantly became subdued, the audience fully attentive. Shelley hesitated only long enough to formulate the story without divulging names or localities that might lead to her subject's identification.

"This young woman was caught up in the westward migration when boomtowns attracted all kinds of people—miners, settlers, ranchers and investors, as well as women alone after the war, and immigrants seeking better lives elsewhere." Shelley felt her throat straining to speak, knowing she was expressing Gertie's yearnings.

"The allure of gold and silver in the West draws the best and worst elements of society. Most fail to find riches, hence they become the working poor, similar to those you find in the tenements of Boston. However, the frontier is harsh and unforgiving, a merciless region with few cultural amenities compared to what you have here. I cannot say for certain what drove this young woman into the streets, into prostitution, but it must have been desperation."

Shelley glanced down at her hands lying at ease on the podium. There were no notes, no written remarks. A few dignitaries shuffled their feet. The audience remained silent.

Nods, a few pursed lips, and a "let's wait and see where this goes" attitude prevailed among the listeners in the Hall.

"Women drawn to Montana Territory often arrive because they found their lives intolerable back home. It is well known that men in the West generally support independent women, and even encourage emigration of settlers to the Territories. These are women who suffered poverty or starvation in this country or abroad, those who had been trapped in marriages, those educated or not who are unable to get jobs except to take in washing, or those enslaved in red light districts elsewhere. Yet in the West, many of these women suffer similar conditions including widowhood with little opportunity to support themselves and therefore unable to escape their circumstances. These same women may be driven into unsavory trades that deviate from public acceptance."

The audience murmured uncomfortably.

"No one reached out except a woman physician who did accept this young woman and gave direction to her life. Over time, the doctor found this previously alienated person had dreams and ambitions like any other woman. Maybe more so because she was not dependent upon a husband to provide for her.

"As an underappreciated woman physician, the doctor was sensitive to women's degradation. Trained in a noted eastern medical school, the physician had a good understanding of women's issues that were endlessly debated without resolution in the halls of government or seats of the courts. She deplored the need for women to protest under threat of arrest to gain rights she knew, and we know, are the natural rights of citizens of the United States."

Among the scattered applause, Shelley heard a rustle of skirts a few rows down from the dais. She glanced over to see Miss Violet Hamilton quietly take a seat. She was followed by a gentleman Shelley had seen on campus—she could not immediately place him. She gathered her thoughts and continued.

"An opportunity arose for this young immigrant woman to attend an Academy for Women, which she did. I am pleased to tell you that she set herself on a higher path. For a time she was reformed with excellent prospects."

Shelley felt her eyes misting. She knew she must conclude with honesty, however difficult that would be, or Gertie's story would be lost and so would empathy for women whose fates hinged on desperation.

"But her life turned around. It is unknown what happened. Perhaps in the face of constant struggle, she relapsed into her old ways."

A few gasps escaped from the dignitaries behind Shelley. She noticed a few members in the audience dabbing their eyes with handkerchiefs. She wanted to wipe her own when a tear slid down her cheek onto her hands.

"Imagine how her life might have been different if women were given equal rights to education, acceptable employment and decent pay."

Shelley visualized her mother scrounging to pay bills, herself inventorying socks and gloves and cinnamon sticks for a few dimes per hour. An image of Gertie on the street corner heisting her skirt to reveal red stockings fired her indignation.

"This young woman is like any of us. You understand that this is why we are in the women's movement. We must gain equal rights and the vote. Only then will we be able to help each other and ourselves."

Shelley nodded to Katerina and took her seat. In an ensuing daze, Shelley barely heard the rest of the program or the sympathetic words accorded her afterwards. Miss "Hammer" waited her turn to shake hands with Shelley and confide, "I agree with you," and intuitively recognizing Shelley's personal loss, she added, "I'm sorry."

Shelley stared at the gentleman who led Miss Hamilton away. He was a law student, one of Patrick's associates as a legal clerk with Bosworth & Son.

"I may have seriously jeopardized my marriage with this bid for equality," Shelley whispered to Katerina on her way out. Katerina raised her eyebrows, and tilted her head questioningly. Shelley managed a grim smile.

On her way home from Harvard, Shelley breathed the sweet scent of wood smoke hanging low in the heavy ocean atmosphere over Boston. A "soft old day" they called it here. Walt Whitman's words spoke to her about the novelty of venturing near the Atlantic:

"The fishes that swim—the rocks—the motion of the waves— the ships with men in them. What strange miracles are these?"

And stranger still, that I, from the silver camps of Nevada and Montana Territory, discovered not gold or silver but endless treasures in the Humanities Library at Harvard University. Whitman, Shakespeare, William Jennings Bryant, and not to be overlooked, what feels like a personal encounter with the romantic poet, Mrs. Browning.

Braced by the edifying effect of her private pursuit of classical and contemporary literature, Shelley tightened her brown scarf and matching gloves and strode across the Cambridge campus, rehearsing her rebuttal to Patrick's anticipated condemnation.

Gertie became my best friend. She listened when no one else did. She is a human being, bright and fun to be with. She saved Lucas' life. Isn't that enough? I could not, or cannot condemn her, even when I learned about her life of pimps and police and being an outcast. That's why I care. I care so women everywhere can live and earn their keep in acceptable occupations, not only as washerwomen or scrubwomen or tramps.

The indignation and subsequent self-defense left her exhausted, her defenses weakened by the time she reached the flat. Patrick was not home and he remained out late for a meeting. Shelley's delayed rebuttal faded over time. But the following night at supper he mentioned over fried cod and hash browns that "one of us in public service is enough."

His level, controlled remark carried an edge that Neva readily picked up. She busied herself avoiding the conversation and the fish by nibbling on hardtack with her new front teeth.

After two days of suppressing her anxiety about Patrick's reaction, Shelley could not hold back. "I spoke to an assembly of mostly women. Miss Violet Hamilton was there. She applauded my concerns. Your gentleman friend and associate accompanied her. He no doubt informed you of the event. I went as a guest speaker and that is the extent of my public service."

Patrick's steady gaze over his teacup held hers. Shelley felt an aggravating pout about to purse her lips. "Perhaps I should continue in public service if you are leaving it."

"If, at one time, I entertained the notion of a political career, it seems I have already been eclipsed by my wife."

Shelley blushed and smiled. She had been this route with Patrick before—rational discussion with him failed to register if he was in one of his moods.

"A bit down in the mouth, aye?" she mocked.

"Shelley—"

"—or even a little jealous?"

Patrick's expression of an injured party competed with his husbandly duty to control his wife.

Shelley shrugged.

Patrick shifted his approach. "Of course you contributed greatly to the Mission school. I'm proud, Shelley. And my associate, Howard, was impressed with your presentation in the Assembly Hall. You would make a formidable politician."

Lost momentarily in reflection, Patrick added, "I considered becoming a politician at one time. Kent Berrigan, my mentor, made a huge impression on me. He stepped up as justice of the peace and commissioner when others failed to do so. I have mentioned before that he saw something in me that I hadn't. I'm not sure that I have yet found it. Perhaps I am jealous that your star is rising."

Neither spoke while they finished their meal. Shelley suddenly realized Neva had endured the conversation and witnessed the impasse, neither of which they had previously subjected her to, and that her sister had been so involved in it that she ate every bit of her fried codfish.

Shelley smiled. "Perhaps we will have another politician in the family someday," she said, indicating Neva.

Their one-sided conversation resumed later in their bedroom, the door tightly closed and voices subdued.

"I apologize for proposing that we go back to Montana Territory and live on a farm. That notion is unworthy of me and certainly of you."

"Patrick, the living proof that I will go where you go is that I am here in Boston."

"I know we both want to return to the Territory. You to be near your family, and I'll admit it, I want to have Jackson and his family in our lives."

"And sacrifice your professional training eking out a living on a farm?" Shelley whipped out her brush and began a nightly ritual of brushing her hair one hundred strokes.

Trudging through Shelley's blunt, emotionless minefields, he said, "I have been considering moving to Helena. The capital is an up and coming Territorial city. If, as you say, statehood is achievable in the near future, I would like to see it happen."

Seeing it as the plan *du jour*, Shelley failed to cheer or frown. Patrick went on as if half musing to himself.

"I would like to see order established in what has been a lawless Territory run by unscrupulous coalitions, criminals, and vigilantes rather than an understaffed judicial system. I may even run for the Legislature. My law studies and experience will further my career in politics. I assure you, I will not waste my hard-won training of the last two years." He stopped. "Forgive me for my dissertation—you may find the capital city stimulating."

Shelley didn't know if she had won or lost her dreams. His challenge to move to Helena dangled between them like a chilly draft in the room.

"I agree with the Woman's Suffrage in the respect that one must act at the highest levels to effect changes," Patrick continued. "Certainly granting civil rights to the Negro has taught us that the vote is the means to advance other causes."

"While it maintains men's superiority."

"Point well taken," Patrick said.

"I—I don't know what to say," Shelley stammered, dropping the hairbrush on the dressing table. Patrick's plans, his vision for the family, and his stepping into political life infringed upon her tentative steps into issues of public concern.

"Lack of your agreement or opposition undoes all my carefully scripted arguments. Law school provides little practicality in amicable resolution of matters of matrimony."

To Shelley, there it was all at once—Patrick sounded more like himself, the person who wanted to work for the common good as well as to honor her. The idealist who could not get his mentor, Mr. Kent Berrigan, out of his head.

"Patrick, don't forget that Mr. Berrigan sacrificed his life because he supported a cause." However encouraged Shelley was with prospects suddenly opening for them, the reminder of the murder was sobering.

Patrick again leveled a look at Shelley as if seeing the person behind the figure of his wife. "We would not be content if we let the past rule our lives would we, Shelley?"

She swallowed hard, a "yes" or "no" stopped before she uttered the wrong thing. His former assertion that "one of us in public life is enough" derailed her ambitions, but Patrick was feeling his way, and this time in consideration of her feelings.

17
OBSESSION

Summer months cloaked Boston's colonial legacy even more deeply in old traditions. Rowing crews plied the Charles River from early mornings tinged with golden sunlight over the Atlantic to late evenings scented with flowering undergrowth. Students flung open doors to musty halls on the Cambridge campuses and fled classrooms, many leaving Boston for their homes across the country. Patrick Colter felt the same liberating air. He removed his Homburg and draped his coat over his shoulder while walking from Harvard Law School back to his flat.

The family would soon gather their belongings once again, this time for the long journey back to Montana Territory. Strange, he thought, how it sounded to go "from the States to the Territory," as if his adopted land was somehow lesser of the two. Certainly many citizens of Boston, of the East as a whole, would concur. The Territories held the reputation of barbaric Indian massacres, road agents, Vigilante hangings, and an utter lack of culture. The latter observation, imposed by native Northeasterners' aristocratic airs, had gained the reputation of gospel.

"I wonder if I'm doing the right thing," Patrick confided to a classmate, who was walking in the same direction. "We will be leaving behind every advantage. I believe my wife has come to appreciate what the East has to offer. We have lived here nearly a year. In that time she and her sister have thrived beyond all expectations."

"I would go West if I were not apprenticed for life to my rich uncle for sending me to Harvard." The classmate grinned and saluted Patrick. "Good luck on the frontier." He joined a group of passing men and left Patrick to his musings.

The Colter family had little to pack and less to say goodbye to. The long anticipated leave-taking occurred without a wail or whimper. Patrick notified his uncle they were vacating the flat and turned the key over to the manager. They left on the next train out of Boston bound for St. Louis, Missouri.

Every moment became one of discovery for Neva. She kept up a constant chatter with her excited explorations, free in many ways from her former limitations. Patrick and Shelley relaxed in contented silence, until Shelley nudged Patrick.

"Remember when you asked me what love meant to me? I said 'that I have to give something up.' That seems to come true over and over again, good and bad."

"Are you sorry, Shelley?"

"A little. I find it difficult to let go of one thing to embrace another."

"You can embrace me," Patrick grinned, pulling her toward him.

"Not here."

"I went through the pain of letting go of a twin. Now I am letting go of the law at Harvard. The Bosworths are understandably disappointed, and I imagine Judge Kirschenbaum will be also, which makes me question myself. I am not sure how your father will take it."

"My father respects you as if you were his son, Patrick. You needn't worry. He will be impressed with whatever you choose to do. Your mother will think you married a harridan when she discovers I destroyed her English heirloom china."

Patrick's boisterous laugh filling the rail car was all Shelley needed to hear, a confirmation that he had done the right thing in leaving—he sounded like himself, young, free, and happy.

"And what would you choose to do, my dear, if you could choose?"

The question, the inclusion that Shelley had desired, but given up expecting, caught her by surprise.

"I—I tend to want to experience the whole world, but if given a choice, I would still choose you. And Neva."

Neva, a school girl of eight, had exerted her independence and exhausted herself in flurries of explorations. She returned to snuggle in the seat next to Shelley.

The Big Muddy, an endearing name for the Missouri River, was moderately low for the summer, the snowmelt having already run off, creating the infamous coffee hue of its waters. Patrick and Shelley boarded a steamer behind Neva, who tugged Shelley's hand and raced with her galloping limp onto the boat. The battered trunk that had crossed the Atlantic with the elder Colters contained Patrick's law books, Neva's beads and books, and Shelley's royal blue coat and wool dress.

Travel with Neva set the itinerary every day, namely keeping her from falling overboard. She and Patrick made maps of their trip from Boston to Butte, and colored in the distance they traveled each day until they arrived at Cow Island Crossing on the Missouri, well below Fort Benton. Tons of goods destined for Fort Benton and other points north were unloaded from steamers plying into the Crossing, typically the *Benton*, *Silver City* or *Big Horn*. From there the freight for Fort Benton, along with a year's supply of goods for the Canadian Mounted Police, were hauled from the Crossing by ox train the rest of the way to the Fort and on to Canada. Passengers continued north on smaller, steam-driven boats.

Fort Benton's trading post flags snapped in the winds off the prairies, a welcome sight in any weather to weary travelers. The small family disembarked on the levee, and snaked their way around towering piles of out-going cargo. The Fort of adobe blocks would have appeared a formation rising from the land and soil had it not been constructed with squared corners and turret, in contrast to the rounded foothills wandering into the distance beyond the steep, earthen slopes of the Missouri River.

"We're almost home," Shelley whispered to Neva, coaxing her to sleep in the stagecoach that propelled them through the night on the Mullan Road to Helena. From there, they changed coaches for the last leg to the Headwaters of the Missouri, where Antonio picked them up as he had done before. He and Patrick loaded the trunk in his buckboard and drove to Antonio's ranch near Willow Creek.

"Danielle will be glad to see you," Antonio said to Shelley.

"The welcome means a great deal to me," Shelley said. "You took Neva and me in when we most needed it. I fear I was moody much of the time."

"Patrick, you're just in time to round up cows with Jackson and me. He'll be over here tomorrow." Antonio grinned at Patrick, betraying a friendship that, among other things, had melded during a certain double wedding.

"I'll do that. Say, it's good to be back. Timing is perfect to see Jackson. I doubt I can go from sitting in a lecture hall to straddling a horse, though I'd sure like to try."

The Delgado's cabin had become a charming home with extra bedrooms, a floor-to-ceiling fireplace with a generous stone hearth, and water on tap from the spring in the foothills. The women left the men talking horses, elk hunting, and a rendezvous with Patrick's twin.

"Patrick is going off with Jackson already. I knew that when I married a twin," Shelley said.

Danielle laughed. "Antonio married me and my goats! Neva is out there right now. Cookie is a mature milking goat. I should watch her around the animals, but she appears to be strong and able to walk quite well."

"If my sister can handle the stream of immigrants in Boston's crammed tenement district and go to school by herself, I'm sure she will cope with a few goats."

"You must be so proud—and relieved."

"Going to Boston was a blessing for Neva, and for me. For Patrick, I'm not sure. He seems to be pulled so many ways, one to reunite with Jackson." She did not mention she suspected he was still obsessed with finding the assassin who killed Kent Berrigan.

Danielle was near term with her baby and Shelley was careful not to disturb her by bringing up the old tragedy. Antonio had been too close and too involved in both incidents when the shootings occurred in Butte. Danielle would be terrified if she thought he would risk himself and his family again.

"I'm not sure what brought us back from the East before Patrick completed his studies. His change of plans caught me by surprise. But then, he has always been that way since I've known him. He struggles to find direction."

"You seem to manage the changes very well." Danielle could hardly comment on Shelley's husband's behavior.

"Oh, I have to. He has never questioned Neva living with us." Shelley's open, candid look and expression reflected her Western roots. "Not outwardly anyway. I suspect that being a twin exerts more influence on him than I'm aware of. Accepting a sibling along for the ride is normal in his world. And Patrick set us up with a double wedding! Did Antonio ever say anything about that?"

"He is a very formal, quiet man. He wouldn't say, but I think he is happy about it." Danielle's face softened, strands of black hair bobbed loose from combs while she mixed biscuit dough. "I think we are closer since we are expecting a child. He worries, I'm sure, but I have had an easy time."

"I'm happy for you both. You seem so—so contented."

"Rather late in life for us, but—"

Antonio was over forty and Danielle older than her sister, Genevieve, who had a twelve-year-old son. "A child will be a blessing. We do feel blessed beyond our dreams. Rumors had it that Antonio had been as skitterish about women as his wild horses, and I hadn't expected to marry again."

"Certainly you had much to overcome after loss of your husband."

Shelley thought back to the day she and Danielle stood together as brides on the Masonic Hall steps. She and Danielle had only to fall into plans the men had made—falling into Patrick's plan had a familiar ring to it; hadn't they just moved from the East Coast because of similar planning on his part?

The women's conversation became a hazy backdrop to Shelley's sudden anxiety, her fingers twisting a strand of hair into a hopeless tangle. Danielle's complacency markedly contrasted with her sense of unease and impermanence. Have I been remiss in acquiescing to Patrick's every whim?

One doesn't move a family on a whim, for heaven's sake. She wanted to flee to the quiet spring in the foothills and sort out the craziness of their lives. Why hadn't he finished his studies? Why is it so hard for me to find a home near women I care about— Gertie? There it was. The unknown whereabouts of Gertie continued to drag her down.

———————

Twilight spread a special radiance over the squares of farmland along the Jefferson and topped the riverside cottonwoods with auras of coppery green. The men, whose every hour was generally filled with more than enough duties, hung around outside.

"Have you heard any more about those behind the attempt on Lucas' life?" Patrick had not wanted to broach the subject, yet it burst forth of its own volition—and from the pressure he had sustained to control it. Few long, tough days, weeks, and months in the East had been without similar questioning.

"Nobody's talkin' that I know of," Jackson said.

"I've been two thousand miles away for a long while, but I have a number of suspicions of my own." Patrick did not elaborate. The case had burned in his soul for the past two years. The twins exchanged glances, wondering whether to spare the wrangler further involvement. The decision was made in that instant to keep it to themselves.

"I'll pay Lucas a visit one of these days." Patrick doffed his hat, reset it on his head and fiddled with the brim, his voice shifting from its clipped Boston accent to a languid Western style. "I have a lot of catching up to do. Say, it's good to be back. I'll take the aroma of sagebrush over fishing docks any day."

The change of subject and tone wasn't lost on Antonio. "We can ride out tomorrow and search for a few lost cows. That way you can see the ranch. There's always more work than I can git done." Antonio signaled they go inside and prepare for the next day with a nightcap.

Rounding up a few lost cows in a million unfenced acres of limestone hills and juniper-filled draws challenged Patrick to tough out saddle sores he earned on the ride. From high above bench land that swept down into bottom meadows, he marked the bends of the Jefferson until it disappeared behind a cliff. The mouth of Milligan Canyon spilled a trickling "crik," the spring runoff having long ago poured into the Jefferson. Sturdy cottonwood groves traced the course of its mostly dry streambed to the river. Dots of settlements with small log cabins were scattered over the land.

Patrick found himself intrigued by whether Rebels inhabited that area. He wondered if he had to see them to satisfy this obsession with the murder. Obsession? Am I obsessed? He hadn't exactly named it before. Patrick hadn't given his involvement much credence beyond the threat it held for himself and his family, beyond the debt he felt towards his mentor. A debt that now appeared magnified.

The realization slammed his chest with a spurt of adrenalin. The bay mare picked up his fire, danced and tough-mouthed the bit, interrupting Patrick's attempt to attain perspective, to question why he needed to get involved again, why he needed closure. He held in the mare that would work cows all day, but couldn't stand still long enough for a man to think. Pondering what his next step would be, Patrick figured if he followed his immediate temptation, he'd ride down and confront any Rebels he could find and likely get himself killed. Then what?

The churning in his gut told him more plainly than words: this is an obsession. I took it all the way to Boston and back twice and never gave it up. I never once forgot it, not for a minute if the truth be known. A lump choked his throat. An image of Kent Berrigan, youthful, self-assured, a Southern gentleman for all time, arose as surely as if Berrigan sat on his horse, Big Ben, on the hilltop beside him.

Patrick felt his lips tremble, his nose threatened to drip. He remembered how Mr. Berrigan, as he called him then, gave him his own set of classics and encouraged him to study and develop the talent he had; he had made him feel intelligent and competent, attributes born out in subsequent work on legal cases and academics.

God, I cared for that man, the way he was good to me. I'd give anything to make it up to him. Damn cruel he was cut down in the prime of life. He essentially gave himself to public service, first as Justice of the Peace and then as Territorial Commissioner.

The inclination to be of service jogged Patrick's former aspirations, tugged a short cord of recognition, and sliced his soul.

"I don't know if my studies or ideals amount to anything if I'm back here chasing cows."

Patrick turned the horse toward the ranch. She fell into an easy lope, picking up a couple cows they found. The gentle rocking motion over clumps of sagebrush and white shale cradled Patrick's thoughts, at last setting them on a different tack. Did I transfer my twin attachment to Mr. Berrigan when Jackson and I went our own ways? A natural affiliation claimed my loyalty and inspired my venture into law—and sure as hell tore my heart with the loss.

"I miss him. I miss that kind of guidance," words uttered on the wind, the horse's ears barely flickering back at the sound of his rider's voice. "Maybe Jackson and I both found substitute fathers in this wild, remote land called Montana Territory."

Patrick found his wrath mellowing when he thought of his twin. Jackson had always seemed like a younger brother, though only minutes younger by birth. Jackson was carefree, spirited, indifferent to books and higher learning. Patrick guessed his twin would most likely ride for Mac Tarynton for the rest of his life. *Maybe Mac is to Jackson what Kent was to me.*

"But hell. I can't any more turn my back on Kent Berrigan than Jackson can on Mac Tarynton, even on Mac's worst day when he feels targeted."

Jackson had wrangled for Mac when the Tarynton's ranched west of Butte, their home overlooking the Deer Lodge Valley. Mac had expected to live on his father's pioneer outfit until the end of his days, grow the herd, and wrap his life around his wife Carrie, the Mountain Woman intuitive healer. When his cows ran into toxic mine runoff in the creeks, he'd had to reassess his ranching and attempt to alleviate the problem for himself and ranchers downstream.

That didn't happen after the assassination of Kent Berrigan. Mac Tarynton became a broken man. He drove his stock over the Continental Divide to set up ranching in Beaverhead Valley. Antonio broke off on his own, but Jackson stayed on with Mac. Similarly, Patrick found he could not turn his back on his strong connection with his mentor. He shoved his hat back on his head, as if clearing the residue of insights.

Thinking too much is like fellin' corral poles with Jackson, Patrick grinned. *There's dead trees layin' every which way before I can see the direction I'm headin'.*

The stiff wind in his face and talking to himself like a wrangler felt bracing for what was to come. The mare hastened her stride to join the other riders, anxious to get back to the barn, get the saddle off, and have a chance to feed for the night. Patrick's thoughts, conclusions and newly minted resolve remained private.

Jackson left at first light to return to the Beaverhead. He could not leave Nettie and their two-year-old for long, or his all-purpose wrangler jobs on Taryntons' sprawling ranch. Patrick finished his coffee while Danielle and Shelley cleaned up after breakfast.

"Have you met your neighbors down the valley? Or those folks in Milligan Canyon?" he asked.

Danielle nodded. "The men in Milligan Canyon come by borrowing sometimes, or looking for a lost horse or cow or dog. We do the same with them. They seem to be nice people, the one's we've seen. I've only met the women in the store in Willow Creek. Same with folks who live along the river, a fairly stiff English couple, and an Irish farmer with a temper."

Patrick swished the coffee dregs around in his cup, wondering what to ask, where to probe. Nothing came of it. There doesn't seem to be a suspicion of the Confederates, assuming they were Rebels, he concluded. Not finding leads, and not wanting to alarm Shelley, he let it go for the time being. She appeared to be adapting to their return to the Territory.

Instead of questions, he dropped a casual remark, "I'm thinking of going to see Lucas."

Shelley shot him a glance. "I wonder that you are so eager to go back to Butte. I would be happy to go back to our cabin, but we had to be rescued from unseen forces in Butte. You and I discussed other options before we moved back here."

"I wonder about that, too." Patrick did not want to admit he still lacked a clear plan, but he was going to do something, even if he had saddle sores.

He contrived excuses to tell Antonio and borrowed the bay mare for the two-day ride each way. He hoped to catch Lucas in his law offices, not traveling or such. It was a chance he'd have to take. The sense of being obsessed with the cold case he left two years ago overtook reservations he had about diving back into it. Shelley had no idea of the magnitude of his urgency, or sense of unfinished business. One that inflamed him over the best interests of his marriage. Or the promise he'd made to Shelley to "not take them back into the violence again." A wave of guilt momentarily plunged him into uncertainty.

I should not be doing this without telling her. But I did not lie to either her or Antonio. I just left out the part about finding that damn killer or killers.

The clamor in his brain almost blinded him to the landscape, to the Tobacco Root Mountains below a piercingly baby blue sky, to the ripening of summer bunch and rye grasses underfoot. He held to the river road to avoid climbing the rolling foothills that dipped to juniper-filled gulches. All too readily fears returned, fears from his furious ride two years ago to see Antonio about the shooting that occurred when Patrick was in Boston—the trash wagon, the rifle shots, the Rebel yell, "one for Jeff Davis," the only witness a street woman.

Patrick tried to outguess himself, the witness, the circumstances—what is different this time? I don't know why I would expect to find anything more. But I better check it out if I am going to settle in Montana Territory. He halted at Pipestone Pass stage stop to give his horse a good feed before pressing on toward Butte.

I left here under a threat—"give you folks a message—your presence ain't appreciated in these parts." I cannot let thugs rule our lives, not after I preached to Shelley about that. What is different this time is that I am not newly married nor as naive as I was then, and I have come back to the Territory for a reason. The threat is what I have to go on.

A new resolve settled in his bones, but the ride felt long, monotonous, and at times, purposeless. Yet his family had changed; that was different. Shelley had her own obsessions, women's causes and statehood, and a voracious appetite for literature. Neva's determination has made a world of changes for her, from invalid to trooper. The crippled leg no longer dictates her actions or her future. Her walk is almost normal. Bless the Mission school for embracing all kinds of lads and lassies, as well as all kinds of conditions. Turning Neva loose with other young'uns helped her become a healthy, happy child.

"I don't know that we would have let her be so free if we had stayed here." That line of reflection circled around to what he often said, marrying Shelley along with Neva was the best thing he ever did. They are every bit a part of me as Jackson is, actually more so.

The closer he came to Butte the more he questioned this ride to see Lucas because of concern for his family. His pulse quickened, knowing it was only another six or eight miles and he would be in town again. It was unlikely he would be recognized. He'd been away long enough to grow a beard, put on a few pounds and lose a lot of muscle. At the juncture of Blacktail and Silver Bow creeks, his first impression was that Butte mines and residences had bounded both up "The Hill" and overflowed down onto the valley floor. Zigzag streets gave it a sense of order otherwise lost among what appeared to the outsider to be a willy-nilly placement of claims. More tall slim smelter stacks cut the skyline through thick black smoke. A temperature inversion kept the smoke from heap leaching and steam-laden air low in the valley.

My father-in-law ought to be doing well for locating veins of copper, Patrick chuckled. He slowed the bay and followed the creek where clumps of willows and swamp grass tried to revive in old placer tailings. Murky oil topped with red and yellow scum skidded across small settling ponds created by the miners.

He wondered if anyone took up the banner for cleaning it up. If not, he knew pursuing it himself would sink him into the same dangerous situation he had fled two years earlier.

When he rode uptown the mare, a cow horse, skittered and snorted. Her nostrils had never inhaled such a concoction as Butte's air with its smells of Chinese cooking and stale beer from open doors of dozens of pubs and saloons. Winding among freighters with mule teams and an occasional hack, the bay shied and tried to buck. Imminent danger of being thrown and trampled under a screaming fire wagon got Patrick's attention. He stabled the horse and walked downtown to Lucas' new offices on Park Street near the Sheriff's office.

"Patrick, my good man, I expected you to come, but you probably shouldn't have. Marriage must agree with you, or was it burning the midnight oil at the Harvard Library?"

Patrick winced at the word library, which he would forever associate with Miss Violet Hamilton, but responded with a heartfelt bear hug. Lucas' sharp dress coat and vest covered scars he carried from the shoulder wound. His unusual gait would be a tell-tale souvenir of the hip wound.

"Lucas, you are on your feet and looking good."

"I have recovered but I depend on a cane for walking around town. Freighters drive up on the boardwalks forcing pedestrians to go around. If that isn't perilous enough, District women in flouncy skirts run a respectable man off into the gutter."

It was more than Patrick wanted to know, especially about women of ill repute, his sense of propriety newly cemented with Miss Meyer's relapse. He winced again. "Maybe I didn't leave anything here after all." But Lucas hustled him out the door toward the Continental Hotel for coffee.

"I bet you have not had a good breakfast in a day or two. That is some ride from Willow Creek."

"I have had a lot on my mind to think about."

The Hotel betrayed its age through two booms and busts, but now stood proud in its third reincarnation, flush with copper mining spoils. A deep blue flag of Montana Territory and one of United States of America flew from staffs above the street.

"Who knew Butte would become a pinnacle on an anthill? Miles of mine tunnels run back and forth beneath the town in a dizzying maze."

Patrick shuddered. "I had my fill of mining long before I left here, but it appears you all hit the Mother Lode in copper."

"You cannot even imagine what has developed recently, and as an Eastern attorney, I am not privy to the larger finds. Our office serves a number of the Johnny-come-latelys. Claims, contracts, miner grievances. The latter are routine. My father prefers that our firm accept small, relatively uncontroversial cases. That way he doesn't have to worry about me! But tell me, how was he when you left? What are things like in the office there? I have not been back to Boston since I set up this branch on your recommendation."

Lucas appeared robust, his natural urbanity in full force. Patrick could not help liking the Bosworths, both good stock who would give you their last dollar.

"He was generous to a fault. I would be the first to say I benefited from it and from his encouragement. Your father is a great man. If only more gentlemen would do as much. He does worry about you though. I have sworn to report back."

Lucas laughed. "I expected as much. It isn't enough that I keep the books in order. I am still tied to the apron strings. C'mon, tell me what brings you here."

"I—ah—you know how it feels to have an open wound. You have suffered greatly, both of us for the same reason—the Berrigan case. I cannot get it out of my mind."

Patrick remembered how Lucas took in information and sat with it, shuffled it, turned it over like a stack of hotcakes, and replied when and how you least expected it.

"Frankly, I can't either." He tapped the cane beside his chair. "I have not been in much shape to take it on, and I am not sure

I want to now." His eyes roved the restaurant in search of unwelcome eavesdroppers. "What exactly is your crusade?"

Patrick was brought up short. "I admit I have an obsession with this case, rightly a crusade if you call it that." He clenched his fist on the tabletop. "I thought a lot of Mr. Berrigan. He was good to me, like a father. Like your father. I feel I owe Mr. Berrigan something. Both Berrigan and your father have inspired and shaped my life."

The question of owing set off an endless round of conjectures for Patrick while Lucas chewed the idea over. At last he suggested honoring Kent may not mean solving his murder or taking up the toxic water cause.

"You are as wise as your father and sound an awful lot like him," Patrick chuckled. Beneath the words he felt chided for his single-mindedness and robbed of a burning desire. "There are some constraints on what I do," he admitted.

"I wonder if there is another means of public service for you since you earned a good portion of a law degree."

"Certainly attaining advanced studies is what Mr. Berrigan encouraged me to do all along." Patrick caught himself up short, sensing he ought to slip out before he said or did something he would be sorry for. Adopting all the casualness he could summon, he said, "I just wanted to check the whole business out with you. That's all."

The statement felt as though it cleared the air and gave him a way out. He shuffled his feet to leave.

"I hear the war whoops of Seceches and Federals coming from pubs all the time, especially late after too much liquor. We get Dixie flags coming out for parades and any kind of public event you can name. But we have not had any major uprisings. Some folks want statehood. Women and clergy promote temperance. The rest do not want more government at all. Territorial law, as you know, has an uneven hand. More so with the giants of industry gearing up for a showdown.

"I honestly don't think folks are looking back. Unfortunately, you may be the only one interested in the Kent Berrigan assassination." Lucas' tone lent a sense of finality.

"I will be off and let it stay a cold case— unless I get a hot lead and I have my doubts that will happen." A sense of relief sent his mood soaring, until Lucas dropped another remark.

"You might talk to Miss Irmgarde Meyer—"

"Gert—?"

"Miss Irmgarde Meyer. She's back. My father sponsored her attendance at the Women's Academy in Boston."

"I am well aware your father was her benefactor as well as mine."

Both men grinned at the irony, at the image of the stern, upright and righteous Boston aristocrat who funded a whore's higher education.

"A helluva leveling process in this democratic world, isn't it?" Lucas said. "It could feel like a comedown to a man, eh?"

Patrick shook Lucas' hand, and left with one lead. He would talk to Miss Meyer.

He hung around Parker's Mercantile until customers cleared out and Mr. Parker was available.

"Mr. Colter. Are you back from the Coast to stay? And Mrs. Colter?" H.S. Parker peered over Patrick's shoulder in search of her.

"We are both pleased to see old friends and family. I rode in to see Lucas Bosworth this morning."

"I trust you found the young man well." The Mercantile owner showed his age, hair thinning on top and a tremble in his hands, but the tricolor muttonchops were the same, as well as his nose for gossip.

"It will take more than a few shots in the dark to keep him down. May I ask if Miss Irmgarde Meyer came in?"

Mr. Parker did not bat an eye. "I get asked about the girls all the time by officials for one reason or another. She will be in around noon like she always does."

He went back to refilling candy bins beneath the counter, while pint-sized lads and lassies peered through the glass showcase, hoping for free handouts of broken candy canes and chocolate.

Patrick bought supplies for his family and Antonio and Danielle. His saddlebags were soon stuffed, and he tied extra bags on the front and back of the saddle. He left the stable just before noon. A nice looking woman dressed in plain street clothes came up the street. Her telltale hair, loose and free rather than severely tucked under a proper bonnet, suggested a street woman.

"Excuse me. I am Patrick Colter."

Gertie stopped as though she had hit a wall. Her bright eyes held a glimpse of humor, a laugh at the turn of fate. "I am Irmgarde Meyer. How is your wife?"

"Shelley is fine. She is with friends out of town."

"Since I studied in the East, I have had to reassess my ambition for higher learning, but I do work tirelessly for the rights of women. Your wife inspired me. I will not forget her."

Passersby paid no attention to the pair talking in front of the store. Butte's increasing hustle surrounded them on all sides, yet few looked twice at the encounter. The noon whistle from the mines pierced what few moments they had to hear each other.

"May I ask a question regarding the shooting of Mr. Bosworth?"

Gertie nodded. "I have been questioned repeatedly about the attempted murder."

Patrick felt thrown off balance with the candid remarks. Gertie was no fool. Strange but true, he felt he could trust her.

"I want to express my gratitude for all you did for Lucas. I worked in his office and for his father in Boston. I have not forgotten that the man who killed Commissioner Kent Berrigan and likely attempted to take Lucas' life is still at large. One man or several or a clan is unknown. Can you help me?"

"I only saw a man leap from the rear of the trash wagon and disappear. He was stooped or he stooped as he ran. It was dark and he was some distance down the block. But I have reason to believe he is still in Butte. Check the Southern saloons." Gertie turned to go into the store. "Do not expect Sheriff Ford to help. He is outnumbered by Rebels. Please give my regards to Shelley."

Patrick instinctively extended a hand to shake hers, but withdrew it. It was not done even anonymously in a crowd. And he was no stranger. Someone might recognize him from his years in Butte. He tipped his hat about the time his mother-in-law appeared at the Mercantile to work the afternoon shift as a file clerk.

"Mrs. Norton."

"Patrick, we have missed all of you terribly. John and I are so thankful you and the family arrived safely. We plan to drive out to see Shelley and Neva when John is free from his current contract."

"I'm sure Shelley sent you the message that we'll be staying with Jackson and Nettie on the Beaverhead for a week or so."

"Yes. We are so impatient to see Neva. Shelley wrote that we will be surprised."

"Mrs. Norton, I look forward to being there when you arrive. You certainly will be surprised!"

Grinning all the way, he walked across town to retrieve his horse from the stable. It does a man's heart good to have a chance to show off his family, he concluded. But sobering, he realized his family was the main reason why he should not risk snooping around the saloons, Northern or Southern. He passed the raucous Hound and Hare Pub, generally frequented by Irish and Cornish immigrants, who would not likely be embroiled in anything more serious than last night's street fight. Memories of shootings and violence in Butte lasted only a day or two, perhaps a week, and long forgotten after a year in the Territories. Two-year-old history, that was the definition of a cold case.

I have to quit this quest for vengeance, and leave the case for someone more shell-proof than me to solve. I cannot become a marked man. I cannot do that to Shelley and Neva. But damn, it seems I've made that decision time and again and I tend to keep chewing on it like dog on a bone.

He made the trip back to Antonio's at a leisurely pace, allowing his horse to rest occasionally, considering she carried a load of supplies in addition to his weight. The dry air tended to clear his mind. The ride and stiff westerly winds buffeted his city-worn body back into shape, and the obsession began to sink into the oblivion of associated fears.

An intuitive sense of self-preservation made the moral obligation easier: unseen forces threatened my family, dictating a difficult decision. Shelley may have envisioned it as simply one of my fleeting ideas—farming or horse breeding or becoming a politician. Yet deep down, we both accept that whichever we choose we will have to move away from Butte. Distance ourselves from Shelley and Neva's parents and the Lucas Bosworth firm.

Unfortunately, I will have to keep a distance from Jackson, Nettie and my nephew, too. Shelley and I both find we have to give something up. That is what love means to us.

18
PRICKLY PEAR CREEK

By the time Patrick rode back to Willow Creek, he found Shelley more than ready to settle back into their cabin on Bison Creek near Butte, their first home as a married couple.

"My yellow and blue curtains are probably faded by now," she said.

Patrick tried to explain they would first visit Jackson and his family and Mac and Carrie Tarynton. Shelley's mother and father planned to meet them there.

"I feel like extra baggage here," she whispered in the Delgado guest bedroom that night. "You forget that I spent months here on the ranch after the men rescued Neva and me from Butte. Antonio and Danielle's baby will soon be born. They need this room for a nursery."

Patrick seemed impervious to her pleas. She whispered louder. "I am embarrassed that I can't say to Danielle what our plans are."

"Hold on, I'm with you. It's just that I—I had to check out a few things. I had to figure out what I need to do."

"We need to get Neva a goat."

"Well, that solves all kinds of problems."

Shelley giggled. "Oh, it might create a few, but I am sure you can handle it, along with 'one hysterical mother,' as you called me."

"I am of a mind to move to Helena as I mentioned before we left Boston. Now that I've cleared up a few things it appears that a move to the capital would be prudent."

But a ready explanation was not forthcoming after his devious trip to Butte. His indefinite plans sounded lame. The truth was his trip had yielded no more than a passionate desire to work undercover until he ran a certain "stooped" man to hell and back. He could not disclose that to his wife.

"Patrick, you are speaking in riddles. I am of a mind to turn over and go to sleep. But I can't sleep not knowing if we will end up at our Bison Creek cabin or Prickly Pear Creek near Helena or Hogs Back Ridge near Jackson. Honestly, I don't know if you will be herding sheep in Warm Springs, or leaving me for a military campaign against the Sioux. You have never settled down."

Her tone reminded him of her first campaign speech—the one that threatened his position, his role in their relationship, indeed men's relationships and attitudes towards women in general because of the women's movement.

"I did not expect you to become a will o' the wisp when I married you."

Weary of the endless indecision, made acutely painful with Shelley's nagging, Patrick whispered back, "Prickly Pear Creek sounds like a good place for a goat," and gathered Shelley into the curve of his body.

Homecoming celebrations continued at the Taryntons' in the Beaverhead Valley. Mac and Carrie's well-known hospitality welcomed the clan, Patrick and family, Shelley's parents John and Winifred Norton, and Jackson and family. Mac and Carrie's new spread opened to wide vistas of grasslands with a backdrop of the glittering, snow-capped peaks of the Centennial Mountains. They seemed to have benefited from their unanticipated move from Butte City, as it was known then, though leaving Mac's father's pioneer homestead had been a bitter loss.

Patrick heaved more than one sigh knowing a reckoning was coming with his own family. They would not be pulling up stakes, other than leaving family, since they had no stakes set down anywhere. But the day soon came when they left the relatives waving goodbye at dawn.

Light glinted over the Beaverhead River with pale pinks before the sun was high enough to chase the chill that hung over the valley. Pronghorn antelope ranged over high, sparse bench land, their tawny backs glowing as they grazed in herds on both sides of the lightly traveled road. Herds of mule deer interspersed with cattle dotted the meadows below.

"We might as well have a covered wagon," Patrick joked. "We've accumulated so few worldly belongings in our itinerant years of marriage."

"We have moved so often I don't know where to hang curtains. They would just fade if I did make new ones." Shelley conveyed her sore feelings and surveyed the few trunks of clothing and treasures they had salvaged from the Colter cabin on Bison Creek.

"We could take them with us," Neva tried to be helpful from her warm nook behind the driver's seat.

"Yes. That is a good idea, sweetie." Shelley answered absently, still stricken that the cabin, her first home as a bride, was destined be torn down and replaced by another mine. In a burst of acquisitions, the Anaconda Company bought out properties from Butte to the East Ridge, a north-south range of the Continental Divide. Butte's smelter stacks, silhouetted against often dense, smoky atmosphere, became known around the world. "The Hill" was spoken of in reverent terms; the "Seven Stacks of the Neversweat" a destination of immigrants to the mushrooming copper city.

A mood of separation prevailed over the Colter family as they silently drove down the road, leaving behind the families they barely had time to visit. They had invited Shelley and Neva's parents to visit them in Helena when they were settled. And Jackson would be coming over when cattle were sent to market.

Stories were left untold of Shelley's passion for literature and innumerable causes not likely to fit in with the ranching crowd. Nor would Neva's intimate associations with immigrant children from all over the world, who gave her complete acceptance and led to maturity beyond her years. Shelley discovered they had returned remarkably changed from whom they were before they were heisted from Butte after an attempted murder. She made a mental note that only Patrick and Neva would fully appreciate those treasured months. She would keep their stories within her immediate family.

Their next stop would be at Antonio and Danielle's place prior to their taking the road to Helena. Shelley woke Neva for a second breakfast, the first having been chokecherry syrup over whole wheat hotcakes with Jackson and Nettie. Neva had been too excited to eat.

Again left with Danielle after breakfast while their husbands talked cows and ranching, Shelley had asked, "How will you manage when the baby comes? I'd like to help after all you have done for us if you alert me before the time comes."

Danielle beamed. "I'd love to have you. We will see. Nettie also offered. But I suspect they may be expecting a brother or sister for little Tucker."

Antonio overheard the conversation. His eyes had wandered from Patrick to Shelley and back to his wife. Shelley sensed she may have spoken out of turn. Clearly, the skilled ranch hand was now helpless as a newborn calf.

"You'll have yourself a nice family," Patrick encouraged, trying to smooth over the intimate women's talk.

"I suggest you send for Miss Adelaide Owens. Dr. Owens has had a Women's Clinic in Butte for years. I know her well. She attended Nettie." Shelley's spirits lifted. "It is some distance for her, but I am sure she would be delighted to come to Willow Creek for a friend of mine. Write to her immediately and find out. I would be so relieved if you did."

Antonio smiled and nodded. Danielle appeared to be counting weeks before the delivery.

"She could come quickly on the stagecoach if word were sent ahead." Shelley charged into brokering midwifery as if she had experienced multiple births. So far none had even hinted at occurring in the Patrick Colter family, however, arranging the lives of each other occurred like clockwork in the family.

"It's as good as done." Antonio's always tired, serious face lit up.

"Now my wife is making plans for your heirs. This tendency sure fits with twin talk."

The foursome around the kitchen table had laughed. They had lived some memorable overlapping events and survived. They could laugh. Shelley washed empty coffee cups, and they had soon headed outside to the loaded wagon for goodbyes.

Old Tornado made his last cross-country trip from Willow Creek to Helena on the toll road, roughly following the Missouri River from its headwaters at the fork of the Gallatin, Madison and Jefferson rivers. Patrick had teamed up the old horse with his spirited saddle horse who had yet to accept the harness and the steady pull that went with it. He often bolted into the brush, yanking the heavy wagon on an erratic course, in effect acting out resistance to the move that Shelley harbored.

"We need a better system of financing roads that are fit for travel," Patrick grumbled. "The Legislature contracted for toll roads. Hell, it's a piece-meal approach that statehood could tackle with more resources than the Territorial government."

Shelley gripped Neva to prevent her from bouncing off the wagon and let Patrick air his gripes and propositions. He seemed to be working toward taking a stand on certain issues dear to his heart and hers.

By the time the Colters reached the small port of Toston on the Missouri, the team had developed a common gait and pace, thanks to Old Tornado's wise and steady ability to anchor the saddle horse to the wagon. The flanks of both horses dripped with sweat. Lathers of white foam garnished their leather harnesses. At a small stream, Patrick unhitched and led the horses to water and a patch of grass.

Next stop was Radersburg. The team lagged behind a steady stream of wagon freighters, carriages, and a stagecoach on the way to Helena.

"May I drive, may I drive?" Neva needled Patrick for the remainder of the trip, bouncing on the front seat between Patrick and Shelley when she wasn't looping together a necklace chain from stems of horsetail grass that Shelley picked for her.

"I want to have Cookie. Aunt Danielle gave her to me. May I keep her, please, please?"

In a sentimental moment of leave taking, Danielle had indeed said Neva could have Cookie. Since then the story about having the goat had been rehearsed and reviewed numerous times. For a bright child, Neva was amazingly childish about her pet goat. Or maybe not. She had become accustomed to having her way as an invalid child. She was growing up with a mind of her own. Shelley had heard plenty from Patrick about his dismay over her request—his dream of a farm did not include a goat that would produce more goats. As proud as she was of Neva's achievements, the assertiveness of an eight-year-old grated on her nerves.

"You must be grownup about having a pet of your own, Neva. You have to be responsible if we allow Cookie to live with us."

"I will take care of her. And I can go to school, too."

"How will you be responsible for Cookie when you are in school?"

Neva slid back into her nook without another word. Shelley knew Neva would never willingly consent to being denied either the goat or attending school. The Mission school with its endless streams of penniless, possession-less children had deeply impressed her young mind. When her friends had stolen stubby pencils allocated to the students, Neva picked up a sense of their deprivation. When they stared at her awkwardly bent leg and hiccup-like gait, she accepted her own disability, a shortcoming she refused to indulge.

She had lived in that milieu for a year, her values keenly honed by experience. Wee lads and lassies with thumbs in their mouths, too shy to mingle, had gathered around Neva's skirt while she sat and read to them, words they did not speak nor interpret, but which Neva instinctively knew they understood.

""I wonder what she will want next," Shelley whispered to Patrick.

"First order of casework: never underestimate your opponent."

"I wouldn't want to deprive her," Shelley persisted.

"I guessed as much when I married the both of you. I just did not figure on having a goat."

Shelley blew him a kiss and tucked her arm into his. She appeared sunshine-fresh with her hair flowing in the breeze, her skin glowing and youthful, the way she looked when Patrick courted her. He relaxed, at last able to concentrate on what their future might hold.

Old Tornado flicked his ears back as if he had heard the conversation and he was satisfied with it. After all, he had overheard a few other marital discourses since the double wedding.

A week later, Patrick Colter had secured a parcel of land on a certain creek that a fortune teller might have foretold. Patrick unhitched Old Tornado and a thoroughly disgusted saddle horse from the wagon at a two-story home still bearing new paint on Prickly Pear Creek. Shelley and Neva helped unload household goods the family had hauled from the Colter cabin.

"The clerk in the Territorial Attorney General's office tipped me off that the home and property were available. The owner, a prominent legislator, has permanently returned to the East. The AG expects me to appear for an interview early tomorrow."

The interview and Patrick's plans, if he had more than hazy ideas, were left to chance as far as Shelley could see. An interview with the Attorney General sounded promising, but for what? For farming? Shelley almost laughed, yet she carried her husband's dress clothes into the house and left them in a prominent place for him to find by candle light the next morning.

A wildly ecstatic Neva located a shed and pen suitable for a goat that would one day occupy it, then set to writing a letter to her parents, John and Winnie Norton, in Butte.

Dear Da and Mum,

We live on a farm. I have a pen for my pet goat. Please bring Cookie from Uncle Antonio and Aunt Danielle's place. Come visit us soon.

Love,

Neva

P.S. I will go to school here.

Shelley sat on a chopping block outside the front door, spent from the turmoil of the last seven days. She shoved back her wide straw bonnet and let the breeze ruffle her hair, undone from a customary twist. The air felt different, warmer and substantially cleaner than Butte, flatter than that of sage-tinted air above the Jefferson River near Danielle's cabin, and it lacked entirely the moisture of her recent sojourn in Boston. A bowl-shaped valley stretched before her, surrounded on three sides by gentle mountains crowded by steeply rising foothills.

"It's comforting," she said to Patrick when he drew up a block of wood to sit beside her. He stretched out his long legs, kicking away wood chips and chicken droppings.

At last he caught her gaze. "What will you do when I'm in town, Shelley, when I'm interviewing or, hopefully, employed?"

She turned towards him. Without his coat and hat he looked like the young man she had married. He had unpacked a plaid wool shirt from a trunk and shaved, revealing fine lines that did not hide his youthful look.

Shelley smiled. He's still so handsome. Aloud she said, "I'll make curtains."

Patrick laughed, a long low chuckle that always amused her, not that he'd chuckled often since their marriage. "And we'll think about that set of fine bone china."

Shelley grimaced, remembering she had destroyed pieces of his mother's heirloom dinnerware.

Patrick leaned toward her and took her hand, his eyes full of concern. "I'm afraid you might feel left out here after your involvement in more circles than I can count in Boston."

"I will arrange for Neva to go to school, and volunteer at her school if necessary." She noticed herself distancing from the constant responsibility and care of the child that had shaped her life. "It seems as though Neva is my younger sister at last, rather than me being her parent in all but name. It feels nice, Patrick. I had not noticed until now."

Patrick squeezed her hand, his eyes earnest, hopeful as if looking for the woman he married.

"Shelley, you will be a wife rather than a wife and 'mother.'"

Unable to go down that path so soon, Shelley said, "We'll still have Neva with us most if not all of the time," and changed the subject to one of more immediate impact on her. "Do you think you will be accepted for the position in the Attorney General's office?"

Any romantic mood Patrick harbored about claiming his wife without a child in the next room shifted and he sighed. "Possibly as a legal assistant. I am more than qualified."

Gathering his thoughts, he rambled, "I expect to sound out the politics, especially pertaining to statehood. I became acquainted with the primary individuals involved when I worked for the Bosworth firm in Butte—William Clark, for one, who teamed up with Helena's Samuel Hauser and his co-investor, A.J. Davis to buy the Parrot mine. With the invention of electrical conductors and the process of making brass from copper and zinc alloys, these men have become extraordinarily wealthy. I understand they often seek undue influence through the Territorial Legislature.

"Their political manipulation appears to be one more reason why Territorial status has long ago run its course. They cannot be allowed to add the State of Montana to their coat tails. The citizens of Montana know they deserve a representative governing body. I'm interested in being part of that."

He paused, realizing he tended to present a case when a conversation with his wife would do. "There may be something new and welcome on our horizon, Shelley."

"Certainly the prospects for you are exciting." Shelley saw herself ironing white shirts for Patrick, which reminded her of Irmgarde's derogatory remarks about a woman's place. She suppressed one of her confoundedly, inappropriate giggles.

"I am happy for you, for us, and for Neva," she managed to say without disclosing images that would sour Patrick in an instant.

He stood and she came into his arms. "One more thing. Isn't Neva eight years old? We ought to get her a pony."

"Oh, Patrick!" She held him at arms' length. "Is that a scheme to keep Cookie from producing more goats? If so, I applaud it!"

"This property provides more than enough grass for Old Tornado and my saddle horse. A goat and pony would be natural additions to the farm."

"The farm" reminded her how shocked she was when he announced his plans earlier. Shelley shifted to rub the last of a worried crease from between his eyes. "You seem more settled than I have ever known you. Perhaps a farm is truly what you wanted all along."

Long shadows of the frame house crept over the couple and a chill wind gathered the scent of willows and junipers from along Prickly Pear Creek. Redwing blackbirds twittered in heavy marsh reeds. A dozen chickens left behind by the former owner clucked their unease about evening predators and scurried off to the henhouse for safety. The vast heavens west of Last Chance Gulch shone with a reddish blush until the sun dropped behind Mount Helena.

The Colter home, Prickly Pear Creek, and the valley faded into obscurity. Later that night Shelley sensed that she would be the one in charge of the poultry, the horses, the goat and a pony. She wondered if her aspirations were also doomed to fade into obscurity.

A Statehood Summit held late in 1879 in the Territorial capital of Helena, attracted proponents and an equal number of opponents of various causes who would give their eyeteeth to state their views. Fine buggies of wealthy delegates and flashy carriages belonging to dignitaries mingled within the narrow streets of Last Chance Gulch.

"It appears that Butte's oligarchy has transplanted itself to Helena this morning," Patrick groused.

"Surely Helena must have a stake in advancing the state. I would think citizens here would be supportive." Shelley pondered what the payback might be for proponents and those against statehood.

"Some are more visionary than others. Change can be difficult. We may hear rare, exceptional oratory regaling the benefits of joining the Union as a state. Governor Benjamin Potts finds the Territory is often discredited compared to the States. However, I understand he is out of town and not expected to attend. Speeches may be droll muddling about temperance and government meddling."

"Let's make the best of it, Patrick. You promised a fine day out while Neva is with my parents."

"I'm sorry. This is our day to see and be seen, Shelley. We will make the most of it."

"Neva walked into a stranger situation at the Mission school with more bravery than I feel about being seen here," she admitted. Neva so adaptable, so eager to learn and growing by day in self-confidence. The child they had over-protected was seldom viewed as being limited by family or new acquaintances. Her small face shone with happiness. John and Winnie had obligingly hauled a lonely goat in Patrick's old buggy with a borrowed horse when they came to visit. Patrick and Shelley had just as happily left Neva in her parents care while they attended the Summit.

Downtown Helena had flourished since its inception in mid-1864, when placer miners, including one hailing from Georgia, struck gold in a meager streambed. Either by luck or by the Georgian method of mining, the men staked their claims to the Gulch that produced millions of dollars' worth of gold over the next few years. The wealth inspired tall, brick edifices in Gothic architecture that replaced fire-prone frame buildings. When the easily accessed rich veins played out, investors plowed immense amounts of capital into hydraulic mining, that of hosing the overburden away with powerful bursts of water. The long, quiet stream beneath Mount Helena became the site of a muddy complex of claims, shacks, and opportunistic businesses typical of Montana Territory's gold camps.

Fifteen years later with a population of less than 3,500, Helena was hosting a Summit that would have been unimaginable in its early days. Supporters of statehood counted on the possibility of women getting the vote as they had in Wyoming and Utah. Opposing forces aimed to prevent or stall the process. Statehood was inevitably bound up with other considerations, economics being most influential.

"Were you saying that government meddling included citizens like us addressing the need for state funding of public schools? Neva really must attend Helena schools, including the high school. She benefited so greatly from the church sponsored elementary school back East."

Patrick appeared preoccupied, but Shelley read the answer in Old Tornado's plodding plainness. Compared to the fine buggy horses of other Summit goers, the Colters' graying horse and worn top-buggy lacked the prestige of carriages driven by affluent individuals, mine owners and politicians who were likely to speak and sway Summit-goers.

"Helena is young and times change. I lived in Nevada silver camps in their early days, and we both experienced Butte's rebirth in silver. We have the opportunity to grow up with this town, to influence it," Shelley argued, fearing her husband would have little clout in the prevailing atmosphere. Patrick did not contest her earnest pleas.

Unable to share anything meaningful with him, Shelley muttered, "I am not moving one more time." The braying of mules and curses of freighters bounced off steep walls of the Gulch, heralding for all to hear that Helena was just another upstart gold camp despite its pretenses.

The farm with its comforting hominess might save me from insanity after all, Shelley sighed. Katerina cautioned me to occupy my mind, carry the banner, and align with progressive thinking women. Did Boston give me airs and ambitions above my "place" in life while I was caught in the excitement of women campaigning for the vote? Shelley choked back objections and viewed Helena from the careening buggy that Patrick steered through the Gulch.

Sloping hillsides dotted with rabbit brush infiltrated backyards of small frame homes, a few with welcoming porches. Washing hung from clotheslines in yards along major streets. Sporadic boardwalks revealed the struggle for civility in the untamed city.

Shelley resigned herself to the role of spectator as Patrick drove past the three-story First National Bank of Helena, the first charter bank of Montana Territory. Cathedral Hill with its Catholic charities towered above Last Chance Gulch. The state capital occupied Courthouse Square downtown. Among nondescript frontier commercial enterprises of hotels, boarding houses and saloons, the stone building of Raleigh and Clarke's Dry Goods Store stood out with its stoutly designed corners and arches.

"I can always always find work in a general mercantile," Shelley mused. A prominent hardware store nearby was hardly impressive after touring enchanting boutiques in Cambridge. Patrick dropped Shelley off near the conference site and maneuvered the buggy into a line at a livery stable where Old Tornado would be cared for until the following day. The old horse perked up and pranced his large hooves at the smell of hay, providing a private show while onlookers smiled.

Within moments Shelley felt the sense of abandonment she had experienced after their double wedding, and again when Patrick left her in their honeymoon suite of the Continental Hotel for his first trip on legal business. She gazed at the passing crowd without recognizing a soul. However, her spirits soon rallied. She was in Helena, a capital city, and Montana statehood had long been a campaign issue for her. She straightened her worn straw hat firmly over her French braid.

I walked into worse in the Assembly at Harvard University when Miss Hammer was speaking.

Convened in an unremarkable building housing the Territorial capital, the Summit drew a notably scanty audience for the consideration of statehood. The movement appeared lost in the louder cause of temperance and unionizing for workers' rights, she noticed, though the latter attracted men in top hats and tails, along with a throng of representatives from labor. In addition, former champions of abolition now devoted themselves to a subsequent revolution, that of equal rights for one-half of society that suffered without equal representation—which included both black and white women who did not have the vote. Proponents differed on means to achieve this end. Factions held stations at tables on opposite sides of the hall under riotous banners.

Shelley wandered alone among the crowd, assessing the program for the day and the attendees as well, comparing them to her recent experiences in the East. She had been to women's parades on Beacon Hill, heard speakers at Faneuil Hall, and slipped into innumerable assemblies devoted to disputing a common belief in the inferiority of women due to "the delicacy of the female sex."

"That certainly does not hold true in Wyoming or Colorado Territories," she murmured to one of the women whose hands were sunburned and callused.

"They can't tell me women are incapable and incompetent," the woman laughed.

"My husband just bought a farm. I guess I'll get used to running it," Shelley said.

Elizabeth Stanton and Susan Anthony had learned very early to view the necessity for protesting the government as the oppressor, while other leaders took the campaign to the individual states. As a result, Shelley discovered that this Summit represented only a fraction of the energy that she had experienced in Boston. Notably, relatively few women showed up among the gentlemen who aspired to position themselves for higher office under statehood. The women's vote issue was like a distant echo here.

"Mrs. Colter. I heard by the grapevine that you had returned from Boston."

Startled, Shelley turned to find a woman of some prestige in Butte, who came striding the length of the hall to greet her. Miss Adelaide Owens, M.D. had come early for a good seat at the Summit.

"Oh, Miss Owens, I am so happy to see you. You cannot imagine how strange I felt wandering here by myself. My husband is tending to the horse. I should have known you would attend the Summit," Shelley ended breathlessly, holding Miss Owen's gloved hand.

"You have kept the faith with women in our movement, now with statehood, I see." Miss Owens rarely smiled, but she glowed with approval of Shelley Norton Colter.

"I was so grateful for your letters when we lived in Boston. You connected me to home in the Territory. It is because of your encouragement that I joined women's causes."

"My dear Charlotte, surely you are aware the reverse is true. Your presence at our meetings in my Clinic meant a great deal to those in the Women's Movement. And your sister's disability inspired me to see that women get a fair chance in life. How is the child?"

"A healthy eight year-old now. Her walk is greatly improved. You would hardly recognize her."

"I am pleased to hear of it. As you know, I am interested in her case as a physician, but also because your sister represents the spirit of modern women."

"You have no idea about her spirit, believe me. The scamp cajoled Patrick and me into letting her have a goat."

Adelaide laughed, a hearty guffaw betraying her strength, as well as evidence of the woman's leave no holds-barred approach.

"I mentioned in my letters to you that Neva attended a Mission school. That opportunity proved to assimilate both of us into immigrant cultures, surpassing that offered on the streets of Butte. She had been unable to attend a school before we left Butte because she is—was so crippled. In Boston, I served as a volunteer in the Mission school in order to assist her, however she soon outgrew my mothering." Shelley laughed in turn.

"Ideally, that is the goal. You have certainly succeeded in directing your sister on a wholesome course. That will permit her considerable independence in life." Adelaide's deep voice carried enough authority to shiver some men in their shoes. "We must regard each other in terms of what we aspire for young women growing up."

"Truthfully, only a moment ago, my aspirations died. I fell into viewing myself forever a pioneer housewife tending a goat!"

Miss Owens paused, momentarily nonplussed, then threw her head back and joined Shelley in mirth, until Adelaide sniffed and righted her straight-brimmed, black straw hat.

"'*We willing learners of all, teachers of all, and lovers of all.*' Walt Whitman," Shelley quoted, eager to show off her newly acquired literary acculturation.

Miss Owens raised an appreciative brow, and linked arms with Shelley. They found seats in a side room of the Summit hall where they could converse.

"We live on Prickly Pear Creek south of Helena now."

"And that is the goat farm?"

Shelley nodded, not convincingly enthusiastic. "My dreams were opening in a startlingly opposite direction, that of pursuing equal rights for women. The notion of living on a farm was as unnerving to me as it was to forward-looking students I met in Cambridge. They had little time and less patience for women retreating behind traditional roles. Suffragettes struggled harder to convert these women than to engage men in the cause."

"A few men were willing to adopt a liberal view. Elizabeth Stanton's husband was one of those, though the couple had eight children," Miss Owens said. "He worked to forward the cause, particularly by traveling and speaking on her behalf."

"If women gained the vote it would turn women's and men's world upside down." Shelley had to question her own investment in such a potentially outlandish reform. *Am I still holding my breath that Patrick will find direction in his life, other than relegating us to a dusty farm?* Shelley choked up recalling her long-held belief that "love means giving something up."

"I believe that Mrs. Stanton invites the possibility of overturning traditional roles. Despite her growing brood, she has not failed the movement."

It was Shelley's turn to raise eyebrows at the implicit suggestion.

At last Patrick appeared, and seeing Shelley with Miss Owens, he stopped briefly with a "Good Morning" to Miss Owens. "I couldn't help overhearing that my wife is facing interesting choices. Is it raising goats, or a brood of children, or raising the plight of multitudes by stomping for women's right to vote?"

Shelley and Adelaide were unable to respond quickly enough before Patrick added, "I am on the program, thanks to the Attorney General I interviewed with. I will wander over to stand with men who are also scheduled to speak."

Shelley dropped her voice. "Miss Owens, don't be surprised if you frequently see Patrick at the capital. I fear if I took a stand on any subject it might jeopardize my husband's chances in the Legislature. Patrick is drawn to politics, whether he admits it or not, though he has flatly stated that one politician in the family is enough."

She giggled a helpless yet cynical outburst that spoke of the very impasse women faced. Adelaide nodded. "Practically a generation has passed without women gaining equality. Why wouldn't red blooded women rise up!"

Shelley paled, comparing herself to Katerina and Gertie, women she considered more courageous than herself. Even Miss Hammer was a woman who went after what she wanted. "I—I have yet to become an activist such as those women who take to the streets. Or those who campaign by rail through the Territories which lack statehood."

"Perhaps you will find your voice here. Helena is certainly typical of the untamed frontier. I must leave you and join the others before the session begins. You may be surprised that I am speaking today."

Her ample, dark-clad figure moved toward the dais. Shelley was again left in an audience of strangers while the two people closest to her would present their "cases." With a sense of loss she recalled how she felt speaking her mind at the Mission school, and later in the Assembly Hall of Harvard University. Public speaking was a daunting experience at the time, but later one that felt natural, a means that gave her a voice for the cause. I should not be surprised that Miss Owens is in the vanguard of the movement, Shelley mused. I would expect Gertie to do the same—if she became respectable. How I do miss Gertie, really the closest person to me after my husband.

Shelley distantly heard the president, senator, or some dignitary making introductions.

"Mrs. Wilbur Fisk Sanders was an early proponent of statehood and opportunities for women to fully participate in affairs of the state." Many members of the audience stood and applauded Mrs. Sanders at length. Shelley whispered to the woman next to her, "Who is she?"

"A suffragette."

"Oh. From Helena?"

"I think so."

Helena instantly became more attractive to Shelley, the Summit more relevant, the East less essential if she could meet visionary women here. Shelley slid forward in her chair, riveting her attention on Mrs. Sanders, wife of Representative Sanders. A hazy image of herself as wife of a legislator occurred to her, depending on whether Patrick became involved in politics. Immediately rejecting a secondary role, she glanced around the Summit hall, observing that the presence of women changed the usual male profile of a conference. It appears that women have begun to emerge from ironing shirts long enough to make their voices heard. She realized she was smiling.

A succession of presenters argued for and against the effect of statehood on businesses, most of the discourse lost on Shelley, except the mention that many boarding houses in Helena were run by women, and "surely women as heads of businesses are the backbone of our cities and forth-coming state."

"Have you heard of Martha Edgerton Rolfe? Her husband is superintendent of public schools in Helena. She is outspoken for women's equality and rights for workers."

"I am delighted to hear of women in public affairs in Helena. I will certainly acquaint myself with the public schools on behalf of my younger sister," Shelley whispered back. To herself she mused, perhaps I will find like-minded women here after all. I am beginning to feel that I might become a part of women's circles again—and manage the farm.

Miss Adelaide Owens, M.D., representing herself, spoke at length in support of the establishment of public schools. Her trim, two-piece suit and crisp brimmed hat with a horizontal black feather were well known in Territorial offices, where she had continued to advocate for various pet causes.

A tall thin woman in front of Shelley whispered to a friend, "Speech-making is unseemly for women."

"I approach my husband with my opinions, then he speaks for me," another woman vouchsafed.

"But what if a woman is divorced? She cannot even speak up to keep her children or her property. He gains title to all of her property if they divorce."

"So, why would a woman divorce her husband? It is immoral."

"Excuse me. I want to hear the good doctor," Shelley said.

"The welfare of our families and children depends upon having an educated population," Miss Owens said. "In my medical practice, I witness the poor and ignorant who suffer inhumane conditions at home and at work. These conditions lead to disease, despair, alcoholism and criminal offenses. Often generation after generation has little hope for change. Elizabeth Cady Stanton, who has toured the West on behalf of women, admonishes us all that 'life's ills are the result of causes that we have power to control.'"

She repeated, "'Causes that we have power to control.' As a medical practitioner, I advocate preventative and curative measures for my patients. I believe that these same policies must be undertaken in civic affairs for the benefit of citizens who suffer life's ills."

A few vigorous handclaps erupted throughout the crowd, her supporters more men than women, though Shelley was unsure whether they applauded statehood, public education, or the outspoken visionary, Miss Owens.

Miss Owens hastened to conclude her remarks. Shelley was well aware that Miss Owens often found women respected a professional man more than a woman with similar qualifications, especially if the woman had an M.D. after her name. Miss Owens rarely garnered the respect enjoyed by male physicians.

Objections from the audience that were intended to be heard interrupted the speech. "It is blasphemous to allow women to be equal to men, according to our pastor."

"What will they think of next? Women in government? This idea of statehood opens a Pandora's box. The doctor's liberal leanings with the upstart Mrs. Stanton sheds doubt on all of her assertions."

Miss Owens stepped down from the dais without having uttered one word supporting women's right to vote or denying men the privileges and vices they currently enjoyed, insisting only that, "We have the power to control a good many ills of society, a prime one being lack of public education."

The following speaker acknowledged Dr. Owens as "a woman ahead of her times." The woman who had doubted females "speech-making" applauded along with the crowd. Adelaide nodded primly. Shelley saw the effort it took for Adelaide to withhold her comments about women's right to vote. She was too canny to sacrifice an immediate cause for another more remote.

Patrick Colter, clean shaven and alert, moved closer to the dais. A colleague of Wilbur Fisk Sanders introduced him as "a former resident of Madison County and Butte, who has recently returned from the East and law school at Harvard. He has broad experience in multiple fields of education, mining, and legal matters that behooves us to consider his qualifications for statehood leadership should we be so fortunate to achieve it.

"Mr. Colter," he said, and stepped aside, summoning Patrick to the podium.

"Many of us stand together on important issues, such as public education and protection of worker's rights, both of which will benefit families and children," he began. He glanced fondly at Shelley while enumerating timeworn causes relating to stewardship of the land and establishment of a separate, popularly-elected justice system. He was warming up to a plethora of issues when Shelley ducked her head.

"Get specific," she urged under her breath. We know all the tired old issues—bad roads, lack of bridges, minimal welfare, a desperate need for public education. We do not know how each and every cause affects individuals—such as us—Neva—or Irmgarde Meyer.

Shelley became increasingly anxious as Patrick's speech continued to consume his allotted time. At the last moment, in a vague mention of natural rights of citizens to have equal representation, he encouraged support for women's right to vote.

"Montana can set an example for the nation by adopting these principles in its initial Constitution."

Shelley gasped.

Patrick continued, his voice rising, his political inclinations finding sure footing. "It's not that we are working toward statehood or getting on the statehood wagon. We are readying ourselves to write the Constitution for the State into law today, in anticipation that statehood will follow. We know it will come in due time."

He dropped his voice to a low, cultured level. "I have lived in Montana Territory almost since its birth from Idaho Territory. I have seen it struggle and mature and gain population. I have been down in its mines and up on its mountaintops, and witnessed unbelievable wealth drawn from the land, the mountains and hills and plains that are envied around the world. My wife and I have crossed the continent where we experienced the vibrancy of Midwest states and the culture and establishments of Eastern states."

Shelley dared glance around. Members of the audience looked her way.

"Ladies and Gentlemen," he boomed, "We returned to Montana Territory for a reason. We returned to be a part of realizing its potential, of living its historic evolution as the Union's newest state, of writing into its Constitution those values we find unique to the West. Why delay? Failure to do will only drag out the efforts of worthy citizens who seek fundamental reforms. Why not secure the support of our Territorial legislators to further our goal of statehood?"

A hush settled over the audience when he stepped down. At last applause rose from all corners of the hall and became unexpectedly supportive of his remarks. Shelley began to breathe again, to recover from her stunned reaction to Patrick's declaration for women's right to vote. Patrick has been swayed if not persuaded, she realized, partly by her own staunch belief in the women's movement. The feeling of converting one traditional male left her limp; that is, when the male was her husband and occasional sparring partner. Shelley remained seated, listening to affirmative comments and attempting to reset her bearings. Patrick had joined a congratulatory group of men who surrounded him after his presentation.

At last Shelley slipped from the conference hall into the lobby and met up with Miss Owens. They barely had a chance to exchange words or discuss what just occurred when a woman sidled up to them with a brief, "Good day."

Shelley nodded and peered at the familiar features under a proper hat, then stared at the woman who smelled of saltwater taffy.

"Gertie!"

"Shhh. Miss Irmgarde Meyer."

Miss Owens' eyes crinkled and she too nodded.

"Shush yourself. I missed you."

"I came back to apply myself, if you can accept that, knowing I previously failed the opportunity to further my studies despite a generous sponsorship.

"Gert—Irmgarde—I thought you had abandoned us—betrayed the movement."

Gertie whispered behind a finely gloved hand. "I ran out of Montana gold. I did not want to become a kept woman on Mr. Bosworth's dime." The absurdity of her rationale struck all three women. Their laughs sounded wickedly conspiratorial. No one out of their circle need know Gertie's history.

"I heard—."

"I'm reformed, say no more. A Hail Mary for a second resurrection."

"You are here for—"

"To yank society from the barbarians, same as you. If enough women join forces behind Miss Owens and your husband we will have statehood and the vote permanently inscribed in the State Constitution."

Shelley's giggle edged into a laugh, but she had to doubt her eyes and ears. She recalled how deeply wounded she had felt when Gertie disappeared without saying goodbye, without acknowledging their friendship or the trust they had in each other, or the vision they had for women. Her downfall had felt like a betrayal. It still stung. Shelley walked a pace or two behind, caught in ecstatic joy for Patrick's speech that confirmed her own views and at last revealed his. And reuniting with Gertie tugged at her for attention, overflowing her heart with comfort and relief.

The sudden onslaught of feelings felt as if Old Tornado ran off with the buggy, twisting like his namesake, and she was inside rattling around like a creature lacking control of her fate.

Gertie. Shelley stared openly at her, transfixed with the well-dressed woman who formally presented herself at the Summit in a fitted, rust-colored suit over a ruffled ochre shirtwaist that complimented her hair. Not a glimpse of red stockings showed beneath her straight skirt that skimmed the tops of sensible leather shoes. Yet the old playfulness ran over her features; Gertie marched to a singularly unorthodox beat, self-proclaimed as not one to iron white shirts. Shelley wondered what the woman was up to.

"Immigrants from Europe, that includes Irish, Welsh, and Bretons, are pushing for statehood as soon as they arrive in the Territory," Gertie was saying to Miss Owens. "They are generally afraid of leaders appointed by the Federal government, and do not trust their taxes and fees going into the anonymous coffers of the United States of America. They have all seen revenues exploited in their homelands. Certainly I experienced that under the Kaiser."

"And their families are those who would especially benefit from education in American public schools." Adelaide Owens had to add another pitch. "We would need land grants for that to happen in the Territory. And yes, these immigrants are often our hardest workers. They deserve representation in Congress. We have to get statehood passed in order to move forward."

"Miss Owens, you have enough causes up your sleeve to qualify for keynote speaker."

"Believe me, Doc Gallagher would be the first to say I am a hardnosed lobbyist. He already thinks I am a propagandist of the most irritating sort." She clapped Shelley and Gertie on the back as if she were a practiced politician.

In a side room, Suffragettes attempted to get women's right to vote solidly in the forefront of the campaign for statehood, an uphill task for a host of reasons. Many citizens feared that men would not vote for the Constitution and statehood if women's vote were included. Statehood would be delayed, they argued, to which one woman archly defended her stance.

The painfully archaic processes of the entrenched Territorial government versus the statehood movement droned on throughout the day. Overwhelmed by sheer verbiage and the stamina required to sustain an onlooker, Gertie turned to Shelley.

"We need to sweep in a new breed. I guarantee few of these men now or to come will be interested in supporting women's causes. To tell you the truth, Shelley, I expected more citizens to rise up in support sooner. I am not one who is willing to put up with old ways or attitudes that downgrade us, you as well as me." Without belaboring the irony, she fished in her pocket for a handful of wrapped pieces of taffy and offered them to Shelley and Miss Owens.

Miss Owens waved away the treats but followed up on the thoughts. "The new breed will be educated women who have the opportunity to seek professions. The only way we'll get that is with public schools. A State of Montana could set the gold standard for education."

"Copper is the new standard," Shelley laughed. "My father might even herald in the new breed since the value of copper has risen. He is an educated man with a deep personal understanding of the poor. Our family struggled for many years with no relief in sight. We know how it feels with a child whose hopes for the future were as crippled as her body. Fortunately, she has had advantages and time to reverse that outcome."

Gertie shifted in her seat and groaned about "the old fossils deliberating with flowery rhetoric over no more substance than the clouds of cigar smoke obscuring the sunny windows of the Hall."

Shelley restlessly scanned the crowd for Patrick. Gertie rose to leave. "Men's talk without action is tedious. I am afraid it is terminally delaying both statehood and voter reform." She turned to Shelley, "Your husband said as much in his speech."

Gertie strode a few paces, then remembered to come back and whisper in Shelley's ear, "Tell your husband the man's name is Caleb Doughty."

———————

By late afternoon, Patrick wound through knots of men in the hallways rehashing the day's presentations, and rescued Shelley from the company of the indefatigable Miss Owens.

"Mrs. Colter, you seem to thrive on the elucidations of our backward Territorial citizenry," he teased, sensing that Shelley's glow had to do with someone or something special— long before she revealed that she had seen Gertie.

"Patrick, I was floored with your speech. You are a natural born politician." She tucked her arm in his and blew him a kiss for lack of privacy. "This is it for you, isn't it Patrick? It was not the farm. You have found what you want to pursue. What you feel is right for you and right for us."

"Shelley, my dear, we have a whole evening and tomorrow to ourselves on holiday since Neva is with your parents. We will have plenty of time to talk. It isn't often I can take my wife out to enjoy an evening in the city."

They strolled down Last Chance Gulch toward their hotel, marveling at the crisp air and attractive displays in shop windows, buoyed by the heady sense of an outing in their newly adopted city.

"At the podium I felt as if I ought to be there, Shelley. I had yearned for such an opportunity to see Montana Territory grow and mature. It was not only satisfying to me, but it felt like a fulfillment of my effort to honor Kent Berrigan. The spheres of politics and the justice system overlap with the intention to align for the public good."

His careful remarks avoided excluding Shelley from any ambitions she may have harbored in politics. He carefully dismissed his other equally burning desire—that of solving the case of the assassination of his friend and mentor.

Unable to contain her excitement any longer while they dressed for the evening banquet, Shelley admitted, "I saw Gertie today. She returned from Boston and resumed work in the women's movement under the guidance of Miss Owens."

"Shelley, you must distance yourself from this relationship with Miss Meyers. It isn't done —"

"Say it—it would jeopardize your position when you run for the Legislature."

"Shelley, let's not talk about this now."

"I think we will be seeing more of her, whether I maintain a friendship or not."

Shelley's smile hinted at disclosures that Patrick guessed he would find out soon enough. Shelley's unpredictability could be a major liability in one's political ambitions, he groused, and that street woman could mess up things for good. But he did not want to press the issue while they celebrated their night out.

String ensembles brightened festivities in the lobby and dining room, hinting at waltzes and reels to come at the evening's Summit Ball. The events served as coming out parties for wives, sweethearts and would-be socialites dressed in amazingly current Eastern fashions. The yards of burgundy silk and pink and blue satin twirling around tiny waists filled the immense rooms like living floral arrangements.

Patrick shepherded Shelley toward the Deer Lodge County contingent from Butte. Lucas was surrounded by attorneys, many representing the Anaconda Corporation. The assemblage kept a close eye on the opposition represented by William Clark in his usual dapper tweed suit. The clusters of Summit delegates were notably lacking in women. Patrick drifted aside until Lucas managed to free himself.

Lucas nodded appreciatively at Shelley. "I am pleased to see you, Mrs. Colter. Your gown is very becoming." Shelley's pale pink satin gown trimmed in rose velvet accented her tall, spare figure.

Shelley blushed. "My mother designed it for the Ball."

"Your husband distinguished himself this afternoon," Lucas added, obviously noticing Shelley's pride in her husband. "You two sparkle as if you were just married."

Aware that the men wanted to talk, Shelley said, "I must find Miss Owens in this crowd," and moved away from Lucas. Drawing Patrick aside a moment, she whispered, "I have a strange message for you. 'His name is Caleb Doughty.'"

"A message for me from—?" Patrick realized at once it was from Miss Irmgarde Meyer. His tall frame hunched, as if from force of a blow. Miss Meyer had identified Caleb Doughty. But why Caleb Doughty? Patrick turned toward Lucas, the color in his face fading, his hands trembling.

"Caleb Doughty. Then it was not about toxic water from mine runoff, or jealousy over a street woman, or a myriad motives we have ascribed to the case." His words came in short bursts. "'One for Jeff Davis,' yes. That would be Doughty."

"What is this? A message from the dead? You look as if you had seen a ghost, Patrick. Sit down and tell me what is going on."

Lucas led his former legal assistant to a round velvet settee. Patrick's knees let him collapse against the plush raised back in the center. He kneaded his fists together, at one time pounding them on the seat beside him. Seemingly unaware of Lucas' presence, he puzzled over the message, the message bearer, the name she revealed. Eventually, he found his voice, thick and raspy.

"Kent Berrigan was a Southerner through and through. Caleb Doughty came from the same region in Georgia that Kent Berrigan had." He paused, his thoughts flying in all directions trying to determine the connection.

Lucas stood over Patrick, clearly perplexed that the assassination case had come down to this, at this time. He frowned and stroked his chin. "I am not making sense of this babbling about Georgia and the war, but oughtn' we discuss this in the privacy of my office?"

Lost in reflections, in a scramble to make sense of the disclosure, Patrick did not respond. Deaf to the world, he braced himself, elbows on his knees. Background chatter from the crowd only sheltered his cocoon while his mind raced, searching incidents, memories of years passed. Lucas tried to penetrate the lapse of time between them.

"I will admit I did some investigating on my own despite swearing an oath to Father that I would leave it alone. I understand the culprit who assailed me yelled, 'One for Jeff Davis. I was considerably more circumspect about it after I was shot."

"You knew it was Doughty and you did not inform me?"

"No, my suspicions did not lead me to Doughty, nor did any evidence point to him, but I had heard of him around town. He is one of the outspoken Seceshes."

Summit goers passed by, avoiding the pair who appeared to be arguing.

Patrick's eyes refused to focus, their stare wandered unseeing around the room, while he combined and discarded conjectures in his mind. "We—I had considered a mining coalition or a Rebel clan of bootleggers, but it was one man."

"I am getting a sense of alarm right now, Patrick, about what you are telling me. A coalition or one man or a clan? You have stumbled onto a rattlesnake den. Give the case to the Territorial Attorney General. Brief him in private this evening then forget it. You and your family do not need to be involved. Remember what you have put them through."

Lucas' sharp admonition failed to have its intended effect—Patrick's obsession fired his entire being, a flare up he refused to let go of. He shrugged a shoulder at Lucas to stave him off, to get time to think. If Caleb also shot Lucas, it could mean only one thing.

"'One for Jeff Davis,' means that our investigation of the Kent Berrigan assassination was closing in on him."

"I am not following you, Patrick. You say it was not about

toxic water. Not by a clan—it was one man. You are like a dog ragging a dead rabbit."

"Caleb had struck down the man he thought was the Berrigan, a Yankee, of Woodland Hills, Georgia." Patrick's pained eyes lifted to Lucas.

Lucas' stare was blank. He shook his head negatively. "I do not understand where you are going with this."

"Caleb Doughty would not have known Kent was the younger of two Berrigan sons—that only one remained loyal to the South. He mistook Kent Berrigan, a Rebel like himself, for his brother Randolph, a Unionist—I can see it clearly, Lucas, as if both Berrigans were standing here before me. In his sinister way, Caleb stalked the wrong man."

Patrick's halting speech betrayed the turmoil boiling within him, the effort it took to work out the murder and attempted murder in his own mind. Lucas glanced around to ward off interruptions. Still standing, he shifted to his other leg, relieving pain from the old wound that was living evidence associated with Patrick's emerging hypothesis.

"Hell, Colter, this is getting too close for us to be talking about it in public. Leave it." Lucas conveyed the authority of his father, Reuben Bosworth, but Patrick was beyond reach.

"Kent and I spent many evenings one winter smoking his family's premium cigars. His older brother Randolph had sent them from the family estate in Georgia. Kent told me the story of how the war split their family loyalties. Randolph followed his father to the North. Kent remained with his mother in the South. After the war he fled to the West to avoid facing Rand, but they reconciled over time. Proof of that was the cigars! That was ten or eleven years ago."

Lucas sat down beside Patrick. Patrick's head sunk into his hands. Lucas waited. He had waited to hear Patrick out before. This time he would wait as long as it took.

At last Patrick exhaled from deep within. "Our investigation may have yielded results."

"I am not sure this case yet holds water. What else do you know?"

"That we will be making a case before Judge Kirschenbaum in the near future."

Lucas shook Patrick's shoulder, hard.

"Tell me what you know for certain. Your reputation and mine, indeed our futures, depend upon getting this right."

"Caleb shot a man he thought committed treason. But Randolph Berrigan, not Kent, fought for the Union. I know this for certain because Kent told me folks in his home state of Georgia considered his brother, Randolph, a traitor. Apparently Caleb Doughty was one of them.

Patrick raised his eyes, searching Lucas' face. "I'm sorry as hell. You were targeted by association with the case. The Rebel shot Kent Berrigan, mistaking him for Randolph. But it was Kent who stood with the Confederates, same as Caleb.

Historical Novels Set in Montana Territory
Trilogy by Jan Elpel

Berrigan's Ride is a love story that unfolds in the gold rush days of Sterling, Montana Territory, 1866 – 1868. Kent Berrigan heard the call to go West in the company of other Confederates seeking peace and a new identity after the Civil War. He pursues the one woman who captures his fancy, Marion Patton of Coloma, California, who has a vision of the future of the country if not her own destiny.

Berrigan's Ride is first in a trilogy exploring attitudes and relationships at a time of sweeping changes in the Territory and across the newly unified expanse of the United States.

Healers of Big Butte explores the clash of modern versus traditional medicine in Big Butte, Montana Territory in 1875 – 1877. Carrie Tarynton saves the life of a prized horse and confronts age-old superstitions and practices, as well as two "modern" physicians from the East. She enlists a Shoshone healer to heal her husband, Mac Tarynton, and her marriage. Mac seeks Kent Berrigan's help to defend his ranch against mining companies that spoil pristine streams, while rising conflicts lead up to the Nez Perce War.

Heirloom China is a murder mystery that pits Patrick Colter's obsession against unknown forces in the silver mining town of Butte, Montana Territory, 1877 – 1879. Patrick risks all for a chance to solve a cold case in revenge of his role model and mentor, a man who inspired him to attend Harvard and bring law and justice to the Territory. His wife, Shelley, becomes a rising star in the movement for women's equality and the vote, which threatens Patrick's sense of a man's place and position.

Heirloom China is the third novel in the trilogy and traces the early women's suffrage movement from East to West, 1877 – 1879, a sliver of time prior to the rise of copper kings of Butte.

Selected Bibliography

Baker, Jean. *Sisters, The Lives of America's Suffragettes*, 2005

Baumler, Ellen. *Historic Helena, Walking Tours*, 2014

Brothers, Beverly J. *Historical Butte*, 1977

Freeman, Harry C. *A Brief History of Butte, Montana, the World's Greatest Mining Camp*, 1900

Goldman, Marion S. *Gold Diggers and Silver Miners*, 1981

Griffith, Elizabeth. *In Her Own Right, a biography of Elizabeth Cady Stanton*, 1985

Helena Weekly Herald, Congress, June 11, 1874. Library of Congress

Joyce, James. *The Dubliners*, 1914, a collection of stories

Kearney, Pat. *Butte Voices, Mining, Neighborhoods, People*, 1998

Levine, Bruce. *The Fall of the House of Dixie*, 2013

MacLane, Mary. *Mary MacLane Herself*, 1902

Malone, Michael. *The Battle For Butte*, 1985

Malone, Michael, and Roeder, Richard. *Montana As It Was: 1876*, 1975

Montana Women's History. *Martha Edgerton Rolfe Plassmann: A Montana Renaissance Woman*, 2014

Stevens, Doris, Ed., O'Hara, Carol. *Jailed for Freedom, American Women Win the Vote*, 1955

Taylor, Patrick. *An Irish Country Girl*, 2009

Ward, Geoffrey. *Not for Ourselves Alone*, 1999

Wheeler, Marjorie Spruill, Ed. *One Woman, One Vote*, 1995

Whitman, Walt. *"On Journeys Through the States," Leaves of Grass*, 1950 Ed.

Wollin, Muriel A. *Montana Pay Dirt*, 1937

Writers Project of Montana. *Copper Camp*, orig. pub. 1943

About the Author

Jan Elpel, Psy. D., is the author of **Berrigan's Ride** and **Healers of Big Butte**, a series of historical novels preceding **Heirloom China**. The stories arose from the author's life and times growing up near the Headwaters of the Missouri in Southwest Montana. She had the opportunity to participate in Lewis and Clark pageants, explore backcountry of Madison and Gallatin counties with Back Country Horsemen, and ride the Nez Perce Trail in Idaho and Monument Valley in Arizona with horse clubs. She has written freelance news and features over the years while her six children were growing up, each creative in their own way. Elpel attained a Doctor of Psychology degree in Family and Child Counseling, a background underlying her narratives.

Reviews of Series

"In **Berrigan's Ride**, *Southerner Kent Berrigan heads West, settling in Hot Spring District of Montana Territory. In the evenings, from the door of his shabby miner's shack, he could hear a herd of wild horses tramping about the hills, neighing to one another. "Like the wild horses, another life formed as he ran from his past—or towards a future, he wasn't certain."*

Working a mining claim is arduous and Berrigan distracts himself from his past anguish with hard labor, but even the love and companionship of a beautiful woman cannot alleviate his demons. It will take a mining tragedy to shake Berrigan from his mindset and confront an unresolved relationship, torn apart by the war."

—Judy Shafter,
State of the Arts,
Montana Arts Council

"**Healers of Big Butte**, *Jan Elpel's second novel, is centered on Carrie Tarynton, an intuitive healer who plies her trade in Butte during the 1870s, a sliver of time between gold and copper mining and just before the Nez Perce War. The conflict between natural healers and western medicine provides an analogy to that of mining interests and ranchers, settlers and Indians. Through the trials of her characters, she weaves a story of the early effects of mining on the land and the people—issues we are still dealing with today. I was moved by her observation that the book's healers are part of 'the larger universe of women yearning for peace and healing for all.'"*

—LK Willis,
State of the Arts,
Montana Arts Council

Women campaigned for 72 years before the United State Constitution granted women the right to vote in 1920. Montana achieved statehood in 1889 yet denied women's suffrage for another 28 years until 1914.